A PASSIONATE INTERLUDE

Mesmerized and unable to control his heartbeat, the earl tried looking the other way, only to have his gaze return to rest on Ruanna.

"This is outside of enough," he at last exclaimed. He would go to her and shake her.

And he did go to her, with great swiftness, but he did not shake her. Instead, he imprisoned her against his hard frame, as his mouth claimed hers, and an exhilarating ecstasy washed over him, obliterating all caution.

For a long, heavenly moment, Lady Ruanna Moreton floated on a cloud, transcending all things real. The earl's hot breath caressed her cheeks when he kissed her eyes, the tip of her nose, her chin. And when his lips again claimed her mouth, spinning her senses, it seemed natural for her to surrender to his kiss. . . .

THE BEST OF REGENCY ROMANCES

AN IMPROPER COMPANION   (2691, $3.95)
by Karla Hocker
At the closing of Miss Venable's Seminary for Young Ladies school, mistress Kate Elliott welcomed the invitation to be Liza Ashcroft's chaperone for the Season at Bath. Little did she know that Miss Ashcroft's father, the handsome widower Damien Ashcroft would also enter her life. And not as a passive bystander or dutiful dad.

WAGER ON LOVE   (2693, $2.95)
by Prudence Martin
Only a rogue like Nicholas Ruxart would choose a bride on the basis of a careless wager. And only a rakehell like Nicholas would then fall in love with his betrothed's grey-eyed sister! The cynical viscount had always thought one blushing miss would suit as well as another, but the unattainable Jane Sommers soon proved him wrong.

LOVE AND FOLLY   (2715, $3.95)
by Sheila Simonson
To the dismay of her more sensible twin Margaret, Lady Jean proceeded to fall hopelessly in love with the silver-tongued, seditious poet, Owen Davies—and catapult her entire family into social ruin . . . Margaret was used to gentlemen falling in love with vivacious Jean rather than with her—even the handsome Johnny Dyott whom she secretly adored. And when Jean's foolishness led her into the arms of the notorious Owen Davies, Margaret knew she could count on Dyott to avert scandal. What she didn't know, however was that her sweet sensibility was exerting a charm all its own.

Available wherever paperbacks are sold, or order direct from the Publisher. Send cover price plus 50¢ per copy for mailing and handling to Zebra Books, Dept. 3519, 475 Park Avenue South, New York, N.Y. 10016. Residents of New York, New Jersey and Pennsylvania must include sales tax. DO NOT SEND CASH.

A Mischievous Miss

Irene Loyd Black

ZEBRA BOOKS
KENSINGTON PUBLISHING CORP.

The Mischievous Miss
*is dedicated to
the late Audrey Wheeler,
who introduced me to the Regency period,
and to the dearest of all mothers,
the late Laney Talley Loyd.*

ZEBRA BOOKS

are published by

Kensington Publishing Corp.
475 Park Avenue South
New York, NY 10016

First printing: September, 1991

Printed in the United States of America

Prologue

The East India sun sliced across the splendid book room and glinted off the red hair that tumbled in disarray between the girl's narrow shoulders. It was late. Through the window, she could see mauve and violet swirls move against the red-streaked sky. Tears clouded her eyes, and her chin quivered until she could hardly speak. "I don't get your meaning, Papa."

The words came as if they were dragged by rack and screw from Lady Ruanna Moreton's throat. Holding herself perfectly still, she waited for a response, but only stony silence met her words. Finally, she said, "You can't have spent it all. You can't have gambled away even our home."

Charles Moreton, a small man whose dark hair was flecked with gray, pulled himself back and squared his shoulders. His eyes were brilliant in the shadowy book room. "I am afraid so, my pet," he said. "Our wealth is gone, and I am in debt. We have not a feather to fly with. So when Archibald Bennet offered for you, I accepted. In exchange, my debts will be forgiven."

He turned then and stood looking out the narrow window, as if, Ruanna thought, he were intrigued by what he saw, as if something or somebody was much more important to him than the way she felt. More than anything she wanted to fling herself into his arms and ask

5

where her dear Papa had gone. Pain beyond bearing ripped through her. This man was a stranger who had been struck with the sickness of the gaming tables. She searched for words, and when they finally came, she struck out vehemently. "Archibald Ben . . . Bennet! That fat pig! You would barter your own flesh and blood to pay your debts! What would Mama say?"

Without answering, Charles Moreton took a bottle from the sideboard and, tilting his head back, drank deeply from it. Which bottle, Ruanna could not see. Probably the one holding hard liquor, another habit he had acquired of late, and now she knew why. She thrust her small chin out. Encompassing anger, her only mechanism to keep from crumbling into a pile on the floor, flamed. "I will not be your sacrificial lamb."

"Stop the tomfoolery," Charles Moreton demanded. "You will marry Bennet! The arrangements have been made for tomorrow noon."

"Tomorrow! Papa, this is 1816. Marriages aren't arranged—"

"Of course a father arranges his daughter's marriage, if he so chooses. And I've chosen to do so. You are to marry Bennet on the morrow. As you know, his father owns most of the gambling clubs in India."

"Yes, I know *who* Archibald Bennet is, and I vow that I will not marry him. I will go to England."

No sooner had the words left Ruanna's lips than she regretted having said them. She knew well the bitterness that festered in Charles Moreton's heart against their homeland. She flinched when he whirled about, at last looking at her. His words were an angry shout. "Go back to the world of snobbery from which I escaped for your mother's sake . . . to keep them from tearing her heart out with the *ton's* ridiculous strictures." He mimicked bitterly, "She married a man of the trades."

And then he added, "They turned their back on her." His voice softened, Ruanna noticed, and she thought for the flight of a second that fright showed in his eyes when

he said, "You will be better off married to Bennet. . .
And I am afraid if you should be so foolish as to refuse
him, he will hunt you down . . . no matter where you are
Such action would cause him to lose face—"

She did not let him finish. She could not help what had
happened years ago. It would not change matters to
argue, and at the moment, she was too angry and hurt to
be afraid of Bennet hunting her down. Let him, but she
would not marry him. She would die first. She turned and
slammed out of the house, and through the arched gate
Her long skirt whipped about her ankles as she ran as fast
as her legs would take her, until they felt paralyzed. It
was only her strong will that moved one foot in front of
the other until at last she came to the tiny graveyard on
the back of their property. Sobbing uncontrollably, she
fell across her mother's grave and pounded the mound of
earth with her small fists until she was spent. Resting her
cheek against the coolness of the green grass, she watered
its roots with her tears. "Oh, Mama," she said, "I'm so
sorry; I have no flowers."

Often in the past seven years, since she was ten years
old, Ruanna had come to place fresh flowers on her
mother's grave, but never in this distraught state. Today,
her sobs mingled with eerie silence, broken only by a bird
trilling into the wind, and by the rustling leaves on the
tree under which she lay.

"Mama, I'd rather die than marry Archibald Bennet,"
she sobbed into the silence. The wind took her words and
scattered them. She thought about her threat to go to
England and wondered how she would get there, and how
she would live should she manage the journey. She knew
no one in London. Her grandmother had died long ago.

Shivering, though she did not feel cold, Ruanna
pushed herself up and sat for a long time leaning against
the tree trunk. The rough bark bit into her back. Her
thoughts whirled about. Dusk came, then the night, and
she was lost in its darkness.

Then, from nowhere—perhaps from out of the stillness, she rationalized—the answer came. She was an accomplished musician, a harpist. She would go to England and support herself by giving harp lessons.

Enormous relief swept over her. She lifted her eyes to peruse a canopy of star-studded blackness. There's always a moon in India, she thought, but tonight it was blessedly absent. "I must needs hurry," she said as she jumped up and again started running. When she regained the house, she entered stealthily and went to a closet, where she pulled out a gray drugget cloak that had belonged to her mother. She fashioned a knapsack from the cloak, then stuffed it with the bare essentials she would need, except for one fine thing: her beaded reticule. Her mother had given it to her. Before adding it to her essentials, she clasped it to her breast lovingly. Just then she heard footsteps and her father calling her name. Quickly she scooted, belly down, under the bed, holding her reticule with one hand, dragging her knapsack with the other.

As she lay motionless, Ruanna felt her heart pounding; she held her breath as long as possible, then sucked in and expelled only shallow breaths. Several times he called her name, his voice sharp. She waited, then sighed with thanksgiving when she heard a door slam, and only moments later the sound of carriage wheels rolling down the graveled drive.

Still, Ruanna waited for her father to return, as if he knew she was hiding. But he did not return. So after awhile, she crawled from under the bed and hurried to the gardener's cottage. There, she donned a dun-brown coat, knee breeches, a boy's cap, and buckled shoes, all of which were three sizes too large for her. The clothes had belonged to a young Indian boy who had been their gardener when they still had servants.

Regarding herself in the looking glass, she was pleased that with her hair stuffed under the cap she looked remarkably like a boy. She pulled the cap low on her forehead, almost covering her eyes.

8

Ruanna knew that she could not leave without touching her beloved harp one last time. She removed to the parlor and knelt beside it, resting her head against the rosewood frame, while plucking at the strings, letting the music say good-bye. How would she manage without it, she wondered. As long as she could remember, music had been a great part of her life, as it had been her mother's.

At last Ruanna rose to her feet and quit the house that had been her home since Charles Moreton and Lady Mary Moreton had brought her to India when she was but a baby of three months. By using the darkness as a shield, and by traveling the back alleys, she safely reached the docks. A glance at her watch told her that only an hour had passed since she left the house, but she knew that time was of the essence.

How fortunate, she thought, having visited the ships with her father many times, she knew the way they were built, and the proper procedure to board one. She strolled around the docks, listening, and right away she heard that a ship was scheduled to depart for London—that very night.

"'Tis thet one thar," a sailor said, pointing his finger in the direction of a ship bustling with activity, cargo being loaded, men going aboard.

So, with her knapsack slung over her shoulder, Lady Moreton walked haughtily up to the sailor guarding the gangplank, looked him straight in the eye, and asked, "Aye, sirrah, ye be going to England, would ye not?"

When the sailor answered in the affirmative, hardly giving the boy in the too-large coat a glance, Ruanna skittered past him. "This be the right ship, I reckon. I be reporting to 'ork," she said, going quickly and finding a place to hide.

In no time at all, so it seemed to Ruanna, the ship sailed out of port and onto the vast ocean. Relief swept over her, and for the first time since hearing her father pronounce her fate, she took a long, easy breath. From her obscure spot, she peered over the ship's railing at water stretched endlessly, a glowing black, like velvet. She listened to the water sloshing against the side of the ship; fog settled downward, inexorably, and as India faded to a tiny speck on the horizon, she whispered softly into the night, "Good-bye, dear Papa."

Then, knowing she could not stay where she was hiding, Ruanna stole out onto the deck for one last look. Her chin set in an implacable line, she held onto the rail to steady herself against the ship's pitch. The strong wind whipped at her coat, but she stayed thus, while the ship moved out into deeper water, settled, and rocked gently.

Her pain softened by the feeling of unreality, Ruanna turned and picked up her knapsack. Swinging it over her shoulder to rest on her back, she said aloud, "One must do what one must do, and I must needs find a place to hide."

Silently, as she stole below deck, she calculated the time. Within two months she would be in her Mama's London—if the captain did not pitch her overboard, as captains had been known to do when stowaways were discovered on their ships.

Chapter One

Long strides took Lord Julian Aynsworth, the fifth earl of Wendsleydale, along the hall and down the stairs to the second floor of Grosvenor House. He was frowning. An early riser, he had gone for a morning gallop in Hyde Park, and was about to change his clothes when a servant brought the message that his old cousin was in an agitated state and begged to speak with him—at once. An emergency, the servant said.

As the earl neared the withdrawing room on the second floor where his cousin was waiting, his concern grew. He only hoped she did not wish to continue their discussion of last evening. Surely they had laid that to rest.

"What's the emergency, Isadora?" he asked when he entered the room.

"Julian . . . ," she started to explain; but His Lordship, upon noting a servant present raised a hand to silence her, and turned to address the servant. "Fustian, Robert, finish and have done with it."

"Yes, m'lord," answered the servant, not hurrying a whit, the earl noticed. Methodically, the servant parted the heavily fringed, red velvet draperies and tied them back with a gold rope. Morning light spilled through the windows, warming the room in its brilliance and casting shadows on the old but exquisite furnishings.

The sunlight also caught the dust on the earl's black

11

top boots. This displeased him, for he was a fastidious man and a fashionable dresser. This day, his riding coat of impeccable tailoring was of blue superfine, and his riding breeches of soft moleskin hugged his muscular thighs like a second skin.

Perfection could have been used in describing the fifth earl of Wendsleydale's handsomeness, but had someone dared pass such a compliment in his presence, a sardonic laugh would have no doubt been forthcoming. But handsome he was—imposingly tall, with broad shoulders, a trim waist, and hair as black as a raven's wing. Side-whiskers as black as his hair covered his square jaw.

But it was the earl's eyes that one noticed first. They were a cold, piercing blue, like the sea at rest after an angry storm.

As the servant languidly went about his chores, the earl's impatience grew by leaps and bounds. The summons from Lady Throckmorton disturbed him immensely, for he never knew what to expect of his cousin. Not only was she a champion for the underdog, she was also one of the Beau Monde's greatest eccentrics. He loved her dearly, and for good reason, he reminded himself.

He lowered himself into a high-back, red leather chair and looked across the room at the old woman. He looked into her blue eyes, faded with age. A spare woman with sunken cheeks, her hair was streaked with gray, and her age was known only to herself. He had one and thirty years. He could not remember when she had not been in the household.

While the servant padded about the room, the earl cocked his head curiously and studied his cousin. It seemed that this day she looked hauntingly sad, and as if she might cry, which was something he had never seen her do. But she was definitely in a pucker, he concluded, the way she was sitting, ramrod straight, tapping her cane on the floor.

"The devil take me, Robert," the earl exploded to the

12

servant. "Pray hurry."

"Yes, m'lord," the servant answered as he struck a flint and bent to light the fire he had set ready in the hearth. The wood caught quickly, and the servant smiled. He then removed to the door and turned, bowing first to Lord Julian and then to Lady Throckmorton. "Anything else, m'lord, m'lady?"

"No, thank you, Robert, that will be all," the earl replied curtly.

After the door closed behind the servant, the earl waited for his cousin to speak, but she sat as silent as yesterday's song. He took a pinch of snuff and sniffed it into first one nostril and then the other. The cane tapping stopped. He closed the cloisonné snuffbox with a flourish, returned it to his pocket, then repeated his earlier question. "What's the emergency, Isadora?"

"Pertaining to what I spoke of yesterday—"

His Lordship bristled. "The answer is still no! I thought we came to an understanding on that. It don't bear thinking of. As I told you, Cousin Isadora, and I thought you understood, I cannot oblige you. What an unlikely idea, to ask me to take into my home one of your pet charities. I bound enough is enough!" This time, he would not give in, he resolved.

"Julian," the old woman said, "you do not attend what I say. I own that in the past I have asked a lot of you for the downtrodden, but this young lady is not one of my pet charities. Indeed not! She is a cousin, although a bit removed. A member of the Aynsworth family. I knew her grandmother well; she was a relative of mine, and of yours, but that had nothing to do with our friendship."

Lady Throckmorton's voice broke. She pulled herself up straight in the chair and gave the earl a loving smile, which caused him to chuckle. He knew her intent and tried to imagine what she had been like when she was younger and had wanted her way. "Go on, Cousin," he insisted with a tinge of cynicism. "Tell me about this stray cousin you have found, and whom I have no

13

intention of allowing into my household."

"My dear Julian," Lady Throckmorton entreated. "Surely you have *some* family feeling. We simply cannot allow it—a young female relative of the Aynsworths, living in wretched poverty, near the docks, and going about unchaperoned to teach hourly lessons on the harp. It is intolerable."

The earl made a vain effort to hide the smile that quivered around his mouth. He leaned back in his chair and fixed his eyes on his old cousin. "Oh, I agree with you that it's intolerable, Isadora. Just imagine the agony of listening daily and hourly to platter-faced chits murdering Beethoven and Mozart on the harp."

"Lord Julian! This is no time for levity. Lady Moreton is starving. She is alone in this big wicked city, with no one to turn to for succor. Have you no compassion? Surely your heart is not completely of stone."

"Compassion, Cousin? Lord, I have compassion, great compassion, but it's for Beethoven and Mozart, not for a bacon-brained female who is teaching little brats to butcher beautiful music."

"But, m'lord, how can you assume that Miss Moreton is a poor musician? It's unfair of you, most unfair. And you pride yourself on your justice."

The cane tapping started again.

"Demme," the earl swore inaudibly. "Lady Throckmorton, this time you go too far! In the past, I have overlooked your eccentricities and winked at your Whiggish bent. I've even contributed to your charities—the rescue mission for climbing boys; the home for orphans of the veterans of the Napoleonic Wars. I've supported a school for the rehabilitation of young pickpockets, though I doubt it was a very successful venture. But I will not, I repeat, I will not welcome into my household a person whom we know nothing about, this antidote, this . . ."

The earl rose from his chair and went to stand by the window. He raised his quizzing glass and looked down on

Grosvenor Square, one of the most fashionable areas of London. A high-perched coach-and-four passed; he could hear the rhythmic clopping of the horses's hooves beating against the cobbled street. Reluctantly, his mind came back to the business at hand. He had no interest in this stray cousin. The estate books needed his attention.

But so did his cousin, he reminded himself, and he could not turn his back on her. Having come to the Aynsworth household soon after his birth, she had made his unbearable childhood bearable. He turned back to face the old woman. "How did you find this stranger? This antidote? And how do you know so much about her accomplishments?"

"I have it on good authority . . ."

The earl groaned and shook his head.

Lady Throckmorton pursed her thin lips. "You may call her whatever you wish, m'lord, but Lady Moreton hardly can be called an antidote. She has not yet reached her eighteenth year, and she is an accomplished musician. And Jenny might well benefit from having her here. I've noticed that our little darling has a penchant for the harp."

Jenny Aynsworth, the earl's nine-year-old niece, had lived in the Aynsworth household since her parents had died with the fever. His Lordship adored the child, and he knew Lady Throckmorton was not beyond using that adoration for leverage to win her argument.

"All the more reason we should not bring a young girl of questionable character into our home," he countered. "Jenny will be returning from her stay with her grandparents within a very few weeks, and I demand she be exposed only to ladies of quality. Faith! Isadora, do you not realize where this Miss Moreton has been living? Why, it is one of the very worst spots in London, where beggars, pickpockets, and light-skirts abound. She might even be an escapee from one of the prison ships launched offshore, might she not?"

"She has been on a ship, but not a prison ship," Lady

15

Throckmorton said primly.

"She what?" The earl's gruff voice boomed across the room. This had gone too far!

The old woman sprang from her chair and commenced pacing. The plush carpet muffled the sound of her green kid Roman boots hitting the floor. "Stop that pacing," the earl demanded.

Lady Throckmorton thrust her sharp chin upward and returned to her chair. She took up her cane, but did not tap. "She was a stowaway on a ship from India. She's lived in that foreign country since her mother took her from here as a child."

The earl cocked a quizzical brow. "Go on, Isadora. Obviously you know more about this . . . this Miss Moreton than you have relayed to me thus far."

Lady Throckmorton pulled in a deep breath. "As I told you, Ruanna Moreton's grandmother, the Countess Elizabeth Waite and I were bosom-bows. I say were, because she is now dead. We were closer than sisters, and I suffered with her when Lady Mary, Ruanna's mother, married a man of the trades and removed to India." The old woman paused before continuing, as if she were fighting for composure. "Even though Ruanna's mother was the daughter of a countess, after the marriage, she . . . they . . . were cut by the ton, so much so that Charles Moreton could not bear it. He took his family to India and severed all ties to their life here in London. Only occasionally did a missive come, and then in great secrecy." Lady Throckmorton dabbed at her eyes with a delicate, lacy-edged handkerchief.

The earl waited. The story was becoming more intriguing by the moment. "And?"

"After Ruanna Moreton's grandmother, the dowager countess, died, though it broke my heart, I lost all track of her daughter, and of her granddaughter, Ruanna. For indeed how could I keep in touch when Lady Mary's husband, this Charles Moreton, had forbidden her even to mention her homeland? Then one day, a week or so ago, I received a missive from Captain Tidesdale who masters a ship that sails between India and London. He said he felt compelled to tell me about this young girl, even though he promised Ruanna Moreton to keep her secret."

Again, Lady Throckmorton dabbed at her eyes with her handkerchief, for it seemed that she could not stop the flow of tears. The earl was taken aback. His cousin was usually so stoic that she appeared hardened to life.

"Well, it seems he had found her," the old woman continued, "dressed as a boy and stowed away on his ship. He took an instant liking to the brave girl and, instead of casting her overboard as was his policy with stowaways, he watched over her, and when they landed in London at the East India Dock on Blackwell Reach, he helped her find a place to live. She still lives there, not too far from the Thames. It *is* a mean, lowering area, Lord Julian, I concede to that, but it is the best the poor child can do, and that is all the more reason why we shall have to rescue her."

"But why—"

Lady Throckmorton raised her hand. "Pray, do let me finish, m'lord. Last evening when we talked, I did not impart to you what Captain Tidesdale had told me in his missive. I hardly slept. I finally concluded that if I wished to receive help from you, I must needs tell you all that I know. Well, since the child had little money and only a knapsack with a precious few of her belongings stuffed into it, the captain had to find her a place that would cost no more than a few shillings per week. She assured him, so the captain's missive related to me, that she was capable of earning her own living by teaching harp lessons. And that is what I learned when I checked."

Lady Throckmoreton did not tell the earl that Captain Tidesdale suspected the girl was of a stubborn, independent nature. Best that Lord Julian think she is adept at embroidery, and of a sweet nature, which she isn't, according to the captain, Lady Throckmorton thought.

17

The earl's concern grew. "The devil take me! You haven't been to *that* area of London?"

"I have, and I have seen the child from a distance. She is quite small; I could see that. I have made inquiries. And I had a footman deliver a basket of fruit— anonymously, of course—to the chandler's shop over which she is living. I requested that it be given to her."

"Don't you know that a crested carriage carrying members of the nobility is set upon in that area of town, that the occupants are sometimes killed? After they are robbed, of course."

Not only was His Lordship concerned for his cousin, but for any other member of the household who might be assisting her in this caper. What would she do next? "How could you even think of doing such an addlepated thing?" he asked.

"Oh, Julian, I went incognito. I hired a hackney, and I dressed accordingly." A wry smile spread across Lady Throckmorton's long, thin face. "And I took Suthe with me, dressed as a farmer."

Lord Julian grew silent, and for a long moment he just sat there, thinking. Then he threw his dark head back and burst out laughing. The image of Lady Throckmorton dressed in clothes of the lower orders, and Suthe, the burly, two hundred and fifty pound footman dressed as a farmer, was ludicrous.

But the humorous images quickly faded. His thoughts returned to the more serious problem of admitting this chit his cousin had discovered to his household. It was beyond bearing. Ruanna Moreton could even be an imposter.

Perhaps she was not Countess Waite's granddaughter, and the ship's captain could be a crook, expecting monetary gain in some way. One could never be too careful.

"Did this young lady not know about relatives that she might have in London?" he asked. "Otherwise, why would she come? Or do they not know in India of the poverty and crime that haunts certain parts of London? That it is especially dangerous for young women who have no means of support?"

Lady Throckmorton started to speak, but the earl silenced her with a lifted hand and continued talking without thought of the impropriety of the subject. "I am surprised that she hasn't been forced into an unfavorable profession as so many girls have. Or maybe she has? And how did the kind Captain learn about Ruanna Moreton's connection with you, and why, upon learning about it, did he not go to her and urge her to come to us immediately? This sounds extremely suspicious to me, Cousin. It could be a conspiracy between this captain and the chit, a hoax of some kind."

Lady Throckmorton tapped her cane sharply against the floor. "Let me answer, m'lord. First, let me tell you that she *is* a lady of propriety. As I told you, Suthe and I have investigated. And furthermore, according to this most generous Captain Tidesdale, Lady Moreton knew nothing about relatives in London. And he also opined, had she known, she would not have come to us anyway, that she was too prideful to ask for help."

Just like her mother, the old woman thought.

"And the captain," she continued, "feels she is fearful for her life. Scared to death, he said, and he could not fathom why. She wants no one to know of her whereabouts. He is certain that if he had gone to her, telling her he had learned of a distant cousin, she would not have come to us. So he concluded it best to apprise me of the situation." The old woman sighed and tapped her cane lightly. "Keep in mind, m'lord, he knew nothing about us when the child first arrived here. It was later, after he had inquired in London, that he learned of my long-ago friendship with Ruanna's grandmother." Lady Throckmorton crossed herself. "Only the good Lord in the heavens knows how he could have learned anything in India, even if he had tried, since Ruanna's mother was not allowed to mention her past to anyone."

"The girl's mother, what happened to her?" asked the earl, grimacing when Lady Throckmorton's lower lip trembled until she clamped her teeth over it. He sensed her struggle to speak and thought he heard a muffled sob.

"Dead. Since the child was ten. She has no one, Julian. It is incumbent upon you to play fair, m'lord." The aging woman lowered her eyes.

The earl threw up his hands, then heaved himself up from his chair, "Enough, Isadora, enough!" He went to her and bowed over her hand, pressing it to his lips. Next time, I will not give in, he thought, knowing that he would. "Little Jenny has been such a pleasure to have with us. Perhaps another child, though this Miss Moreton is a little older, will not be such a bother. But I warn you, Cousin, someday you are going to push me too far. This *distant* cousin may have an audience tomorrow in the afternoon. I shall make myself available at four, in the book room. But remember, I said only that I would sit for the chit. And, Cousin Isadora, don't build your hopes. There's the possibility this stray cousin may not want to be rescued."

Lady Throckmorton's relief was evident in her smile, and in her faded eyes. She jumped to her feet and clapped her hands with glee. "Thank you, m'lord. I shall send her an intelligence today."

The earl chuckled and took from his pocket a huge, round watch. Glancing down at it, he swore, though not aloud. It was well past midmorning, and since he had planned to have lunch at White's, it was too late for work. He would barely get started. Besides, he told himself, after losing the argument to his cousin, he needed relaxation, and he knew of no better place to acquire that than with the beautiful Katrina Medcalf, his mistress of the past three years. He would visit her after going to White's. Feeling the anticipation, he bade his cousin good day, then turned on his booted heel and left.

Lady Throckmorton watched His Lordship's retreating back as his purposeful strides took him across the room and out the door. Such broad shoulders, she thought, and so incredibly handsome was this man she had reared as her own son, and so cold . . . so cruel . . . and so soft.

She listened to his jaunty steps taking the stairs, then to the sound of the huge entrance doors closing behind him. The house seemed empty when he was gone. She moved to stand by the fireplace and placed a blue-veined hand on the mantel. The fire had burned itself out, leaving only gray coals in its wake. She stared unseeing at the coals, her mind still on Lord Julian. "He does have a kind heart," she murmured, and her mind painfully winged back to recall how, as a child, he had been mistreated by a cruel father who blamed him for his mother's death. The old earl's wife had died giving birth to Julian.

The father's hatred for Julian had been shared by his two older brothers. And they, too, had let him know. When he was but a small lad, he had been sent off to Eton—just to get him out of their sight. After that, it was Oxford, and then into His Majesty's service.

Even so, she thought, her Julian, though jaded and hard crusted, had made a fine man and was now an exemplary peer of the realm. She recalled how one woman after the other, all ladies of quality, had tried to capture his heart. One by one he had pushed them away. All except Lady Charlotte. Charlie, Julian had called her, Lady Throckmorton thought, grimacing.

"Only the redheaded she-devil succeeded in bringing him to his knees," she mused aloud. "The more's the pity. Let the devil take her."

She felt anger roiling up inside of her as she stood alone in the room, listening to her own words spill out into the quietness. Shaking her head, she turned away from the dying fire to retrieve her cane. Swiftly then, she repaired to her bedchamber, where at once she took from a writing desk a quill and paper and started writing. Her big heart lurched inside her chest as leaves of memories rustled in the recesses of her mind. Vividly they marched

21

before her mind's eye, but this time they were her own secret memories.

"How I wish I could tell Lord Julian the whole of it about Ruanna Moreton," she murmured.

As her hand sped across the page, a terrible fear gripped her. What would she do if the young girl did not respond favorably to her invitation? The thought was unbearable, and her hand shook until she was forced to stop writing.

Copious, unbidden tears came then, and the old woman was helpless to stop them.

Chapter Two

Lady Ruanna Moreton, her red curls framing her face and falling onto her shoulders, sat at the side of her pupil and watched the child's fingering. The same mistake again! And this was the third time through the passage.

"Betsy, if you would hold your thumbs high, you wouldn't strike the wrong strings. Now, be careful about your timing and run through it again. And count. One . . . and two . . . and three . . . and . . ." The child was so small, the harp so large in comparison.

Caring deeply about her student's progress, Ruanna waited, holding her breath as the young girl tried again, and again. When at last Betsy hit the B string, Ruanna smiled. She had been there for over an hour, which was her alloted time for each student.

"Thank you, Betsy. That was very good. This is a pretty little minuet, and if you will practice a little more, perhaps an hour a day, you should have it in acceptable form by the time I return for your next lesson. Run through your scales each day, and always count."

"I promise." The little girl turned a demure smile on Ruanna. After thanking her graciously for her time, she gathered together her music and prepared to leave the room.

"You're most welcome, Betsy," Ruanna answered, watching the girl go. Left alone, she felt an overwhelming sense of loneliness creep into her being. Only when she was involved with her music could she escape the lonely, unfamiliar world about her, a world which, since she had left India six months ago, consisted of a lonely room in a mean section of London.

It was not where her dear Mama had lived, nor was it the London she had described so gloriously, and longed for so painfully. Lady Mary Moreton's London was the West End, where members of the ton lived, the upper orders, who had turned their backs on her when she married a man of the trades, though her husband was as wealthy as many of them.

Until he lost it all.

"One never marries for love," they had said. "One marries for position, a proper place in society."

Ruanna wished she could stop thinking of her mother. She must needs look to the future, not the past, she told herself. More important than her mother's West End, was that Archibald Bennet would not look for her in the mean part of the city where she lived. He would never dream that she, Charles Moreton's daughter, would live over a chandler's shop.

Were it not for my music, where would I be? Ruanna asked herself. The sound of her voice in the silent room startled her, and then she heard Besty's mother: "Miss Moreton."

Ruanna turned and smiled. She hadn't heard the woman enter the room. "Please have Betsy practice more," she said as she rose and took the few shillings the woman owed.

Ruanna shrugged into her cloak and buttoned it high around her neck. Mindful of the wind, she tied the ribbons of her bonnet tightly under her chin and pushed at the loose curls so they would not show. A losing battle, she thought, as she glanced into a looking glass that hung on the wall. Despite her efforts, recalcitrant red wisps framed her face.

When she walked out onto the stoop of the tenement

24

building, cold air that smelled of rain hit her in the face and whipped her drugget cloak about her legs. She looked up at the canopy of water-laden clouds and prayed it would not rain until she was through for the day.

Only one more hour, she thought as she hurried toward the street where Jeremy Fielding, her next and favorite student, lived. She always saved his lesson for the last, for sometimes she stayed longer than an hour. The young boy showed great promise, and she had hopes that eventually he could study under the tutelage of the great harpist Bochsa.

At the end of the street she rounded the corner and headed south, her head bent to the cold wind. Clutched to her bosom was her beaded reticule, which held enough shillings to purchase a fresh loaf of bread. She smiled in anticipation of the delicious smells that would greet her when she walked through the bakery door, for she had not eaten since early morning and pangs of hunger were sharp inside her stomach. Soon Ruanna was on the street where Jeremy lived, and when his building came into sight, she began running. Bounding up the steps, she called to him, "Jeremy, Jeremy, are you here?"

"I'm here, Miss Moreton." The little boy, already sitting by his harp, fingering its strings, answered. He gave a big smile, and they were immediately down to serious work.

As Jeremy's hands caressed the strings, beautiful music filled the room, and Ruanna's soul. In India, her own instructor when she was Jeremy's age had called her a child prodigy, but she had never made music so encompassing of one's spirit. The notes that rose beneath Jeremy's small hands were like rushing water, and sighing winds in a dark forest. He only had trouble with the notes when he played works of others, but never with his own creations, those that came from within him. Today, the notes were his own.

Ruanna felt her heart race; tears misted her eyes. Music heals one's soul and fills the heart, she thought.

When the little boy stilled his fingers and looked at her with his big velvet-brown eyes brimming with pride, she could not resist hugging him fiercely.

Oh, she knew the staid English were standoffish and any display of affection was frowned upon, even considered common by some, but she did not care. She ran her fingers through the little boy's mop of brown curls and spoke enthusiastically of his splendid progress.

"With only a few more guineas, I'll be able to purchase Bochsa's new book of études, and we'll work from that. I saw the book advertised in the *Times*," she told him, becoming puzzled at the look of unhappiness that had spread across his face. She asked, "What is it, Jeremy?"

His little chin quivered as he spoke. "Mum says she can't afford any more lessons. Her protector left her high and dry."

"Can't afford . . . but Jeremy, we can't stop now." Forcing a smile, Ruanna knelt down beside the little boy. "Don't worry, Jeremy. I shall be here next week at this very same time. You just be here waiting for me."

"But Mum said . . ."

"I don't need the money," the redhead lied, and the smile that lit Jeremy's face made the lie worthwhile. She hugged him again and left. She would walk the few miles home and save the shillings it would take to rent a hackney, even though it was late. Because of the hovering clouds, it was darker than usual, and she walked as fast as she could, she slipped her hand into the pocket of her round skirt and wrapped her fingers around the small stick that had a steel ball the size of an egg securely affixed to its end. On two different occasions the homemade weapon had been the only thing that had saved her from losing her day's earnings, or worse yet, from being soiled by a man, and perhaps killed. With a flip of her wrist the weapon could render an assailant senseless, until she could make her escape.

"Blister it," she exclaimed, her green eyes darting from side to side. The street noises were exceptionally loud today—the Charlies in their boxes, calling out the time and the weather. They were supposed to watch the crowd, but she had seen them more than once turn their heads to avoid a confrontation.

The calling out of the time and weather was, in Ruanna's opinion, a strange custom. Why indeed would the city pay men to call out the time and the weather to the sleeping populace until they were so accustomed to the cries that they slept on, not caring what was said?

When a ballad seller called out the news of a murder, Ruanna recoiled. Then another gave the dying confession of a wrongdoer who was to die at Newgate, the infamous prison where hangings took place outside its walls—for the masses to watch. She stepped aside to let a raucous, pie-eyed, totally foxed sailor and his splotched-faced light-skirt pass. The girl poked a finger in Ruanna's direction, and she could hear them laughing as she pressed onward, not looking back. Finally, her steps quickened into a run until she darted into the bakery to purchase the loaf of bread. As expected, the delicious smells wafted up to meet her, and she felt her mouth salivate and her stomach churn. So that she would not be tempted to spend more than the amount she had alloted to a loaf of bread, she made her purchase quickly and left. Only a little way more, and she would be home. She would make hot tea, then sit and drink it while eating her bread.

Home to Ruanna was a room, three stories up. Narrow, rickety stairs climbed up the outside wall, and Ruanna had just started up when a shrill voice calling her name gained her attention. She looked up to the barely coherent voice and saw standing on the landing before the door to her, Ruanna's, room, plump Miss Sherrill, the proprietress of the chandler's shop.

"Yes?" Ruanna answered.

"Miss Ruanna, Miss Ruanna, I wuz jest up to yer room, knocking on the door. I have a missive fer yer. It wuz delivered jest a few minutes ago by a footman

27

wearing grand livery. Guess since there wern't no nobility riding in the coach they felt safe in coming to these parts. The elegant coach, with its fine, 'uge driver, who was all proper like, waited in the street. The coach being all shiny and black . . . and it 'ad a coat of arms on its panels. It did! Belonging to the earl of Wendsleydale. Ain't that some stuff?"

The words spilled from the woman's mouth so fast, and with such a broad cant, it was impossible for Ruanna to understand all that she said, and she was selfishly glad for the momentary reprieve the shortness of the woman's breath brought.

"Yer as white as ash," Miss Sherrill exclaimed when she was standing a step or so above Ruanna. She thrust the letter out. "I'll hush natterin' and let yer read it."

The big grin on the woman's face told Ruanna she expected her to open the intelligence and read it aloud, but Ruanna murmured only a short "Thank you," and pushed past her, running fast up the stairs.

"Well, I never . . ." A crude expletive spilled from the proprietor's mouth. And then, "Totty-headed snob."

Ruanna did not care what the woman called her. Her hand shook so she could hardly insert the key into the lock. But her determination paid off and, once inside the room, she closed the door and leaned against it, fearful her trembling knees were going to give way under her.

Waiting for her heart to still, Ruanna stayed that way for a long while. "How can this be?" she asked aloud. "No one . . . no one knows of my whereabouts."

But someone did, she realized. On the outside of the envelope, which had been impressively sealed with the earl of Wendsleydale's crest, was her name: Lady Ruanna Moreton.

After lighting a candle, Ruanna, without thought for the elegant paper she was ripping apart, tore into the envelope, jerked out the exquisitely handwritten message, and read:

Dear Lady Ruanna Moreton:

I have been informed that you are returned from India. I am a cousin of your grandmother's. Please call on me at Forty-Three Grosvenor Place in Grosvenor Square for tea tomorrow at three o'clock. A carriage will be sent for you.

Affectionately,
Lady Isadora Throckmorton

A trap, Ruanna's mind screamed at her. She had no cousin! Panic floated around her, an amorphous swirling haze. She prayed that she would not swoon, something she had never done in her life. But she had never been this frightened, she reminded herself. Crumpling the letter into a ball, she closed her small fist tightly around it. Throwing it across the room, her only thought was of escape. She must needs hide again. Had she a distant cousin in London, her mother would have told her. And then Ruanna's thoughts turned in another direction.

Grosvenor Square! That is the West End, Mama's part of London. And I, Ruanna Moreton, have been invited there.

She should be happy, she told herself. In the cold room, furnished with a narrow bed pressed against the wall, a table, and one straight-backed chair, she had never felt more utterly alone in her life, or more frightened. Even the smell of the loaf of freshly baked bread, now lying on the table, failed to cheer her, and they were desultory steps that took her to the open hearth to build a fire and make tea.

"The fire and hot tea will warm me," she said aloud, and she tried to smile at the sound of her own words echoing around the tiny room. She was extremely cold, but the chill, she knew, was caused by fear that Archibald Bennet had come for her . . . from India, by way of an invitation to tea.

The fire caught quickly, but before the water was hot enough to make the tea, a low, rumbling noise caused

29

Ruanna to jump. She tilted her head and listened, and just then a big boom of thunder seemed to explode beside her. She went to the window and looked out. The storm that had been threatening all day had reached fruition and was striking with vengeance.

The wind roared through the slashing rain, torrents of it, sluicing downward. The building trembled, eaves hummed, and lightning shot down to chase rumbles of thunder across the dark angry sky. The sound was everywhere, above and below.

Ruanna closed the window with a bang, then listened as wave after wave of rain pounded the roof. "As if God is hell-bent on cleansing De Quincey's town," she said.

Though frightening, the storm could not long hold her thoughts. Her mind was on the morrow. Where could she find to hide that she would not be found? Turning back into the room, she retrieved from the floor the crumpled-up missive and, with trembling hands, pressed out the wrinkles. In the circle of yellow light afforded by the lone tallow candle, she read again:

"Please call on me at Forty-Three Grosvenor Place in Grosvenor Square for tea tomorrow at three o'clock. A carriage will be sent. . . ."

Chapter Three

After the storm had blown itself out, Ruanna slept, but fitfully. The next morning she awoke with a start. Through the window faint signs of morning light were manifesting themselves in an early dawn. The room was strangely quiet, and quickly she was assailed by the thoughts of the invitation to tea that might be a trap, the storm that had kept her from leaving her room from over the chandler's shop and finding a place to hide. She wanted to pull the dingy sheet over her head and forget her fright. Instead, she sprang out of bed, ran to the window, threw it open, and leaned out.

Above, the sun shone from a cloudless sky covered by a blue mist, making whorls of gray fog. She pulled in deep breaths of the rain-cleared air. On the street below, people moved about aimlessly, men pushed market carts, and then there were the children on their way to present themselves to be hired out for the day. Women carried buckets of water, while, over the din, Charlies shrieked out the time and weather. She closed the window and turned to start a fire, warming water to wash herself, saving only enough for tea. That left the bucket empty, and, to her chagrin, she was afraid to go to the well at the back of the house to fetch more. Her father's words— "Archibald Bennet will find you . . . he doesn't take kindly to rejection"—resounded inside her head.

31

Ruanna felt shivers dance up and down her spine. Tossing her head of red curls to one side, she exclaimed, "Balderdash! I don't credit being afraid."

She thought about her dear Papa and grief lay like a weight around her heart as she determinedly descended the stairs and went to the well, where she drew up enough water to fill her bucket. Later, she sat at the table, drinking the tea and fortifying herself with chunks of the bread she had brought home last evening, this time adding sugar and cinnamon. Somehow, suddenly she knew that she would go to Grosvenor Square, that she had probably known all along.

Now that the decision had moved from her unconscious to her conscious mind, Ruanna found herself filled with ineffable joy. I'm going to Mama's Mayfair, she thought. Her heart raced, but she knew that it was not so much that she was going to Mayfair as it was that she needed a friend. Since coming to London, she had been so terribly lonely.

The hope that Lady Throckmorton would become her friend turned to a prayer in Ruanna's heart. Tears found their way to her eyes, and a slow throb of pain beat inside her as, although she willed them not to, thoughts of her father returned. Vividly she remembered the fleeting moment of fright in his eyes when he spoke of Archibald Bennet.

She asked herself why she was thinking of her Papa today, but she already knew the answer. One could not wash away years of one's life because of a single wrong. She pulled close the image of the Charles Moreton of happier days, savoring the feeling for a short moment. "Stuff," she finally said, and jumped up from the table to dress for the important journey ahead; and she dressed with such speed that long before the specified time for the carriage to arrive, she stood by the window and anxiously watched. For once, she was glad she did not have a lesson scheduled for that day.

Time dragged interminably. She forced herself to

breathe normally. More than once her gaze turned to the small clock that told her it was not yet time.

But at last the sleek black carriage, pulled by four handsome grays, arrived, the emblazoned Wendsleydale crest on its panel. "'Tis here," she shouted, and went flying down the stairs and out to the carriage, where she almost landed in the arms of the liveried footman who waited to hand her up. She smiled, and thanked him graciously.

When the footman gave her an icy stare, she gave him another smile, trying to coax one from him. Now that she had made up her mind to go to the West End, nothing would deter her, and she primly arranged herself on the forward-facing banquette and leaned back into the plush red velvet squabs.

When the footman's eyes focused on her clothes, Ruanna bristled. She looked down at her gray drugget cloak spread against the red velvet. Her hand reached to straighten the cloak in perfect folds, and she stubbornly thrust her chin upward.

"I'm wearing the best clothes I own," she told the footman, who turned away with a shrug.

Ruanna's dress was the blue sarcenet she had stuffed in her knapsack when she fled India, and the gray cloak had served as her knapsack, those long months ago. Atop her head was a gray bonnet, under which her red curls were crammed out of sight.

"I have one fine thing," she reminded herself, holding her beaded reticule to her chest. With a handkerchief she took from the small bag, she wiped at the tears that pushed at her eyes. "I bound this day I will not be bothered with worries," she resolved, and after that, she sat back and counted her greatest blessing: She had escaped marriage to Archibald Bennet, had she not? And, of course, she did not forget her ability to give harp lessons.

Ruanna's thoughts flew in every direction: Imagine having tea in a grand house in Grosvenor Square. It must

33

be grand—Mama's Mayfair!

And, she reasoned, an invitation to tea from Archibald Bennet simply did not signify. Afternoon tea was not his style.

After putting up the steps and closing the door with its golden crest, two lions rampant facing a spread eagle, the footman snorted disdainfully and jumped up onto the box beside the driver. The footman had not bothered to bow to the chit, and he certainly had not returned her smile, for, from the way she was dressed, her station in life was no higher than his own. He only bowed to his betters. Shaking his head loftily, he said to the coachman, "'Ods bodikins, what pray is m'lady thinking? To send a coach and 'our into sech a neighborhood, and for sech a mean-dressed chit yet?"

The carriage box shook under Suthe's laughter when he said, "Wonder m'lady didn't come 'erself."

Suthe had never shared with the other Aynsworth servants about his and his lady's visit to this part of town, but he wanted to tell, for it would certainly give him a place of importance in their minds. It was only that his lady had asked him to keep it to himself. Even now, he was about to burst from wanting to spit it right out. But no, he must needs not, he decided. Cutting his eyes around at the footman, he said authoritatively, "M'lady knows what she's doing, and we'd best not forget it."

When a resounding "Harrumph" came from the footman, the coachman smiled.

"These demme flies," the footman said, "the buzzing divils will fly right down yer throat." He covered his mouth with a handkerchief, through which he gave a muffled plea, "Git us out of here, lest the divils take us."

Suthe, laughing, cracked a whip above the horses' backs. The carriage lurched forward, then tooled carefully to miss the garbage strewn about on the street.

As the opulent carriage pulled away from the chandler's shop, Ruanna looked back, and up. Bodies with smiling faces, Miss Sherrill's included, leaned out the upper windows, their minds agog, Ruanna was sure, at the magnificent sight the coach-and-four made. They were probably even more agog that the aloof girl who lived on the top floor of *their* building rode in the carriage. When she waved to them, they waved back.

She had not meant to be aloof, Ruanna told herself. She was *not* a totty-headed snob, as Miss Sherrill had called her. Suddenly the loneliness of the past months engulfed her.

It was strange, she thought, that before the invitation to tea had come from Lady Isadora Throckmorton, she had been unaware of how much she craved company. Now, riding along in the fine carriage, going to tea at a fine house, visiting with a friend of her grandmother's, she felt like calling out to everyone she saw. She felt like Priny, the prince regent, riding in the royal coach and waving. Of course, she had only seen pictures of the prince regent riding in a fine carriage, but the comparison cheered her enormously. She smiled and waved to a young girl pushing a cart of fresh flowers, and she even took delight in the rough movement of the carriage as it bounced over the rutted streets. Reaching for a strap, she held on tightly.

When they rolled onto cobbles, Ruanna's eyes darted this way and that, from one window display to another. She knew when they neared Mayfair, for there the shop windows were filled with beautiful clothes, and the milliners' shops with fancy hats.

"Oh . . . oh," she said, smiling and not realizing she had uttered a sound.

When they passed the wide marble gates at Hyde Park, she turned her head, lest she see where the hangings of the criminals from Tyburn used to take place. A dozen or more at a time, her mother had told her. And people rushed to witness the macabre sight! How could anyone enjoy seeing another person suffer? She shook her head in disbelief.

Just then, the coach swung into another street, which,

so the sign said, was South Audley Street. They were nearing Grosvenor Square! She knew, because her Mama had spoken of South Audley Street, and Oxford Street, and Park Street. Her eyes widened. It was as if she'd seen it all before, and of course she had—through her mother's eyes. And there, on each side of her, were the stately homes of the West End.

Leaning far forward on the banquette, Ruanna unashamedly stared, and her mouth flew open when the coachman stopped the four prancing grays in front of a four-story edifice of red brick, with tall, narrow windows across the front.

"Well, I never!" she exclaimed.

Then, as if drawn by a magnet, Ruanna's gaze shot upward to a window on the second floor, where, through her lorgnette, an old woman peered down. She was smiling.

Ruanna returned the smile, then perused the townhouse, which was grander than any she had ever seen, and she wondered if Carlton House, where the prince regent lived, was any more grand. Her eyes were drawn to the front entrance, which looked like that of a palace. Hanging between white Ionic pilasters were two huge, intricately carved oaken doors.

The footman alighted, went to bang the knocker, and the door immediately swung open. A butler in high livery—black coat with tails, knee breeches over white silk stockings—stood in the gaping aperture.

Ruanna wondered how he kept the high collar points from digging into his dancing jowls. Not wanting to be caught staring, she smothered a giggle and jerked her gaze away to look at the minuscule yard, shut in by an iron fence.

But before she could look her fill, the footman returned to help her from the carriage and up the six brick steps. He announced with a formal air: "Miss Ruanna Moreton."

Not that the footman thought she deserved such an

honor, Ruanna decided after receiving another cold stare from him; but it was expected of him. Again, she thanked him nicely, then entered the imposing mansion.

"Oh, what a lovely house!" she exclaimed to the butler, from whom she received a look of total disdain.

Having been trained in the etiquette of the upper orders, Ruanna knew that rules of society forbade her speaking with familiarity to a servant. But stuff, she thought, servants are people, with the same feelings as anyone else. Her dear Mama taught her always to be kind to the servants. In India, she had even held the servant's babies when they were born and thought nothing of it.

"This way, ma'am, Her Ladyship is expecting you," the butler said as he turned his stiff back to Ruanna. He also had a long nose, she noticed, over which his gaze slid down when he spoke to her.

When Ruanna's feet sank soundlessly into Turkish carpet, she forgot about the uppity servant. He was not going to talk with her anyway. Before her was a cavernous hall, and hanging from the towering ceiling were huge chandeliers holding lighted candles, from which a mellow light bathed the dark-paneled walls and cast shadows on the bright carpet.

High-backed, gold velvet chairs were arranged along the walls, and great arched openings revealed on each side the most exquisite of rooms with fabulous furnishings.

Ruanna, covering her mouth to keep from exclaiming, walked behind the butler. She was not exactly walking, she realized, but almost running to keep up with him as his long strides took him the width of the hall. She continued to observe incredulously the magnificence of the house and its furnishings. Her home in India was fine, but nothing like this. She sucked in a breath. The place smelled of beeswax and fresh flowers.

In the center of the hall, a round marble table held a huge Wedgwood pot overflowing with flowers of varying colors.

Great curving stairs, made of beautiful dark wood,

swept upward to other floors. Ruanna looked up. The carved balustrades glistened with a highly polished shine, as did the wide steps of the same dark wood.

"Lady Throckmorton has a lovely home," she said to the butler's back.

"'Tis *not* Lady Throckmorton's house," was the terse reply flung over his shoulder. "It belongs to Lord Julian Philip Aynsworth, the fifth earl of Wendsleydale and lord of Wilderhope in Shropshire."

He has that down right well. He wants to make sure I know exactly whose house I am intruding upon, thought Ruanna.

Bemused, she stubbornly persisted with her quest for information. "Did you say this house does *not* belong to Lady Isadora Throckmorton?"

"Lady Throckmorton is the earl of Wendsleydale's cousin. She abides here with him."

"Oh!" she said, her curiosity now rapidly building about this fifth earl of Wendsleydale and lord of whatever. She wondered if possibly he could be as stuffy as the butler who worked for him. A shadow on the stairs caused her to look up.

Descending the stairs was the woman from the window. Again, Ruanna thought the woman looked quite old, but her steps did not appear so. If anything, there was an urgency about them. Nonetheless, even in a hurry, the lady descended the stairs like a queen. Standing on the bottom step, she stood ramrod straight, waiting, a black cane hooked over her right arm.

When the butler was yet six paces away, he stopped, stepped aside, and bowed. "Miss Ruanna Moreton, Your Ladyship."

"Thank you, Sutherland," a somber voice said after him as he turned on his heel and made to leave.

Ruanna sank into a deep curtsy, then straightened.

The old woman, tears dripping from her thin face, her shoulders quivering, lifted her lorgnette and looked piercingly at Ruanna, and Ruanna felt herself strangely drawn, as if by some overwhelming force, to this woman who had invited her to tea. Then, a peculiar charge raced through Ruanna. She felt, and she could not fathom why, that Lady Throckmorton was laboring to restrain herself from reaching out to draw her, Ruanna, to her flat chest.

Finally, the old woman smiled and a blue-veined hand reached out to take Ruanna's. "I am Isadora Throckmorton, Lady Moreton—"

When Ruanna took her hand, she felt the tremor in it. "I am most happy to meet you, Lady Throckmorton. Thank you for the invitation for tea."

"And I am ever so happy to meet you, my dear." Lady Throckmorton's smile broadened, making her seem suddenly younger. Elation seeped from her voice when she spoke. "And now that we have dispensed with the formalities, I promise to call you Ruanna if you should consider calling me Isadora."

"As you please, ma'am . . . Isadora."

A rather stout maid appeared then. She wore a dress of rustling black bombazine, over which was a white bibbed apron that covered the front of her. A white cap, reminding Ruanna of a pancake, sat atop the maid's head.

"Take Lady Moreton's cloak and bonnet, Marie," Lady Throckmorton said, and when the maid stared at Ruanna without moving, the old woman tapped the stairstep sharply with her cane. "Marie, did you attend what I said?"

"Yes, m'lady," Marie answered, taking the gray cloak and holding out her hand for the bonnet, which Ruanna removed, letting her red curls tumble onto her shoulders in total disarray.

"Ruanna, dear, let us remove to the yellow salon on the second floor. There will be a fire, and it will be much warmer. Besides, it is my favorite . . ."

Lady Throckmorton's words died in her throat, and she gasped loudly as her hands flew to her face.

Instantly old fears reached in to clench Ruanna's heart. What was wrong? Was she the person they were

39

looking for? And was this woman claiming to be Lady Isadora Throckmorton in shock from having found her?

Or was it the way she was dressed, Ruanna wondered, letting her gaze rake over Lady Throckmorton, who wore an elegant gown of green tobine stripes, with a divided skirt that looped back over a bustled underskirt.

"Is something wrong, Your Ladyship?" Ruanna asked, having already forgotten the old woman's request that she call her Isadora. "I apologize for my attire, m'lady, but these are the best clothes I have. Surely you knew...." Ruanna's chin went up. She would not be intimidated!

"Oh no, my dear! It is not that! It is just that your red hair shocked me. Come, my dear, it is of little importance. Come."

Together, the two women walked up the stairs. "Be careful," Lady Throckmorton cautioned, "these steps are slick. I tell the help not to keep them so highly polished." She stopped to chuckle. "I'm afraid my words carry very little clout. The earl prefers the steps mirror-bright."

"The entire house is magnificent," Ruanna said.

At the top of the stairs they entered a small salon decorated in bright canary yellow. A fire smoldered in the fireplace. Wrapped around two handsome Chippendale chairs were huge bay windows through which the sun sent slices of soft light.

"It is indeed a warm, lovely room," Ruanna said.

"Thank you, my dear." Lady Throckmorton went to the bell rope and gave it a hefty yank. Inclining her head toward the chairs, she said, "Let's sit over here," and when Sutherland appeared in answer to the summons, she ordered tea and biscuits. "And pile the biscuits high," she added.

They sat in the chairs, a pale light from the windows falling between them. While they waited, Ruanna felt Lady Throckmorton gaze on her pityingly, as if she knew how ravenously hungry she was.

40

Moments of embarrassed silence followed, and Ruanna was glad when Sutherland returned bearing an enormous silver tray laden with a silver teapot and two delicate china cups with matching saucers. A plate held a mound of biscuits, another, strawberry jam and clotted cream.

The butler quietly placed the tray on the table between the two women and gave a quick bow before retreating.

"Sutherland," Lady Throckmorton said when the butler had reached the door. "Please remind Lord Julian he is to receive Lady Moreton at five o'clock."

"Yes, m'lady." The door closed softly.

Lady Throckmorton poured two cups of tea, and, with her hands trembling until the cup clattered against the saucer, she held one out to Ruanna. As she sipped from her own cup, her eyes covertly studied Ruanna, regarding her well-scuffed half boots, her faded dress, and then, finally, her face.

Incredibly beautiful, even with a smattering of freckles across her small nose. She is but a child, with a smiling mouth . . . and a stubborn chin.

"And she's everything I could hope for," Lady Throckmorton said, sotto voce. Captain Tidesdale's words came to mind: "She appears to be rather stubborn and strong willed."

Oh, I hope not too much so! Julian will have my hide.

"My dear," she said, addressing Ruanna, "your grandmother was married to the seventh earl of Mellville. *His* grandfather was His Grace, duke of Manchester, a direct descendant of King Charles II. So your body is rife with noble, as well as royal, blood."

Because it had been the nobility, among others, who had treated her mother in such a shabby manner that her husband had taken her to live in India, Ruanna was not at all impressed with the noble blood to which Lady Throckmorton referred. Blood was red, noble or not. She mischievously leaned forward to ask, "Is noble blood red?"

"Of course, dear, why do you ask such a question?"

"Then my blood is the same as your stuffy butler's."

This brought hearty laughter from Lady Throckmorton. She clapped her hands in delight, then poured a second cup of tea for both of them, and Ruanna drank hers in big gulps.

"I'm so anxious to hear about my grandmother," Ruanna said. "Mama spoke of her when Papa wasn't around."

But she never spoke of Isadora Throckmorton.

Ruanna thought that quite odd, since this old lady and her grandmother were supposedly such good friends. After wondering about it for a moment, she dismissed it from her mind. She would think on it later.

Lady Throckmorton said, "And I am anxious to hear all about Lady Mary. . . ."

The ensuing conversation held Ruanna entranced, and time flew by on angels' wings as Lady Throckmorton spun remembrances of her childhood spent with Countess Waite, Ruanna's grandmother. Many of the things she imparted to Ruanna were the same as her mother had told her.

With this revelation, thoughts of a trap left Ruanna's mind. She let herself trust, and she found herself responding to the affection for the old woman that was already taking root deep in her heart.

Throughout the account, though, it seemed to Ruanna that Lady Throckmorton's mind occasionally wandered, and Ruanna could not rid herself of the notion that she was holding back some foreboding secret. The old woman spoke as if she had had no life of her own, as if she had lived vicariously through Countess Waite. Ruanna tried to imagine her young, vibrant, and in love, but could not.

Lady Throckmorton asked numerous questions about Ruanna's life in India and about her mother, which Ruanna answered truthfully, holding back nothing except the hurtful part of Charles Moreton bartering her to a notorious gambler. "Papa objected to my coming to

England, so I stowed away on a Captain Tidesdale's ship."

It was not all lie, and it was not all truth, Ruanna told herself, not meeting the old woman's eyes. "I am curious about something," she went on. "How did you know I was in London?" It was a question she had been dying to ask.

Lady Throckmorton chuckled. "Your Captain Tidesdale wrote to me."

She then told Ruanna about the captain's missive. She failed, however, to mention Captain Tidesdale's belief that Ruanna was frightened of something or someone. "Scared to death" were the words he had used. That could wait, the old woman decided, for at the moment there was something of greater importance about which she must needs decide: What was she to do with this child across from her?

Unaware of Lady Throckmorton's problem of what to do with her, Ruanna stayed busy by drinking two more cups of tea, more slowly now, and eating three biscuits, which she covered with jam and cream. Nothing had ever tasted more delicious.

Thinking how pleasant it felt to coze with another human being, Ruanna smiled often above the cup's rim as they prosed on and on.

Lady Throckmorton told Ruanna about little Jenny, the earl's niece, who was visiting her grandparents. Finally, the old woman glanced at the clock on the mantelpiece and said, "My dear, I am afraid it is time for your audience with the earl."

Ruanna gave the old woman a quizzical look. "You sound as if I am to have an audience with the pope. And why is His Lordship supposed to receive me? It seems that he should have joined us for tea if he wished to make my acquaintance." Embarrassed at her outburst, Ruanna stopped, then added in a conciliatory tone, "Does it not seem that way to you, Your Ladyship?"

43

Words came fast from Lady Throckmorton's mouth. "*He* wishes you to honor our household by coming to live here."

And then, without giving herself time to think, the old woman plunged on, knowing she was digging the hole deeper: "Because you are a relative, you will have a London Season; we shall sponsor your come-out into society. There will be parties, soirees, routs . . . and all the young bucks of the ton will clamor to marry you. . . ."

Oh, what a lie, Lady Throckmorton wailed inwardly, Lord Julian did not say any such thing.

But it was the right way, perhaps the only way, she reasoned, and her thoughts raced on: Surely Julian will not refuse this poor girl, not after I have asked her to come live with us, and made all these promises.

Or would he?

Her hand resting on the head of her black cane, the old woman pulled herself up in her chair and, looking straight into Ruanna's eyes, said in a clear voice, "My dear, do not let the earl frighten you. He may try, but at the core of his hard-crusted being, he has a very soft heart."

Ruanna instantly conjured up imagery of a doddering old earl who no doubt was as lonely as this woman who stood before her. Why else would the two of them ask a stranger to share their home? And more than that, promise a come-out into society. Could it be that they were lonely and wanted someone younger than they to ramble around in this big mansion with them? Silently Ruanna scolded the niece for staying away so long when she was needed here. And it certainly would not hurt if occasionally the servants smiled.

But had all that been so, Lady Throckmorton might not have sent for her, she thought, hardly able to contain the happiness that washed over her. It was strange how fate sometimes stepped in and changed things. The worst part of her life since coming to London had been trying to

44

keep herself hidden as best she could. Now it was going to gloriously change.

Ruanna jumped up and went to hug the old woman. "Oh, I'm certain your old cousin must be positively wonderful to be so generous as to offer me shelter in this beautiful house. And to be near you, Isadora. If Mama could only know how things have turned out."

Lady Throckmorton smiled and rang for the butler, and only a few minutes later Ruanna bade her good-bye, curtsying deep into her sarcenet dress.

The old woman took her hand and lifted her up. "Remember, we will not do that." She leaned toward Ruanna and whispered, "I'm almost as impressed with my noble blood as you are, my dear."

The old woman's laughter tinkled like bells, filling the room with musical gaiety. Ruanna hated to leave, and she had no desire to meet the old earl.

Lady Throckmorton watched Ruanna follow Sutherland from the room. After the door closed behind them, she returned to sit in her chair and take up her cane. The yellow salon was suddenly quiet, and so lonely. She started to cry, but clenched her jaws instead, for she could not bear a simpering woman. She thought about Ruanna, about Lord Julian . . . and about what His Lordship would do when he saw yet another redhead in his household. Had she not many times heard him say that he would burn Grosvenor House down before he would allow another woman with red hair to abide under its roof?

What a bumble-broth she had made of things in asking Ruanna Moreton to come here and live. And she had rashly promised her a London Season!

"It don't bear thinking on," she mumbled under her breath as she crossed herself and reverently turned it over to a higher power. She commenced tapping, and thinking.

After a long while, the old woman said into the stillness that spoke loudly in the room, "'Tis true. Julian does have a soft core—if one can find it—and he also has a ferocious temper when he is reminded of the she-devil who betrayed him by marrying his brother."

Lady Throckmorton wanted to put an ear to the book room door, as a servant would do. The thought startled her, for never before in her life had she had such a desire. And, of course, she would do no such thing. Swallowing the lump in her throat, she began to pray—very, very hard.

Chapter Four

There not being an Aynsworth heir was much on the fifth earl of Wendsleydale's mind as he sat in the master book room waiting for his solicitor to answer his billet. What a turn his life had taken. If the fever had not taken the old earl, and then, within a week, his oldest son, who was next in line for the title, and if the second son, Geoffery, had not been killed in an unfortunate duel, Lord Julian would not be there with his mind clogged with thoughts of producing an heir.

His Lordship shifted about in his chair and tried to focus his eyes on the estate books in front of him, but failed. Instead, the years he had fought with Wellington came back to him. And the days before that, when he'd been a rakehell of the first order.

At first, while fighting with Wellington, his courage against enemy troops had been the result of the pain that bit into his brain like acid. But later, after many battles, he had matured and fought because he believed in what he was fighting for. Duty must needs come first, he had learned, and he was still of the same notion. Heaving a heavy sigh, he raked a hand through his thick, black hair. It was up to him to produce the heir to inherit the earldom and the entailed estates. There was not even a distant male cousin to whom the title and estates could pass.

Blister it, I have no desire to get leg-shackled to some chit.
The earl pulled his watch from his waistcoat pocket and glared at it. "Where in the devil is the man?" After worrying the problem of an heir at length by himself, he had decided to speak with George, who was his solicitor, and his confidant as well.

Leaning back in his chair, the earl closed his eyes. Reluctantly he let his mind wing back. He had not always abhorred the thought of marriage. Only a few years past he had wanted nothing more than to marry Lady Charlotte Loyd-Dobbs, and she had taught him a lesson he would never forget. He smiled sardonically.

Lady Charlotte had been his youthful obsession. Her image had been before him, day and night, like a low-hanging cloud, and even though he was the impoverished third son, he had ridiculously allowed himself to dream of the time when they would marry. They had promised to love each other always.

"Youth!" he spat out. Then, at the risk of becoming melancholy, His Lordship let his mind dwell on the painful truth: Lady Charlotte had married his brother Geoffery when Geoffery was the fouth earl . . . for his title, for the Aynsworth wealth, for the Aynsworth jewels.

"Demme, demme, demme," he swore as unpleasant, unbidden memories danced before his mind's eye. He tried to push them away, but they came, with all the intensity, with all the pain he had felt four years ago when he had learned of his love's betrayal.

Nostalgia engulfed His Lordship. He rose from the chair and went to stand by a window overlooking a walled garden. He was helpless against the memories that tortured him beyond endurance, and stagnant anger boiled up inside him. As if it had happened yesterday, as if it had happened to someone else and he was privy to the play, he could see a red-coated soldier and a beautiful woman with red hair standing in the garden, her gown the same shimmering green as her bewitching eyes.

She was a witch. Again, a smile curled the earl's lips, but he felt no mirth. Lady Throckmorton called her the she-devil.

That day, four years ago, green ribbons had trailed from under Lady Charlotte's bosom to touch her small feet; creamy flesh swelled invitingly above the low-cut bodice. How he had wanted her, and, even now, as he thought back, desire rushed through his veins, as deliciously painful as it had been then.

Her red hair, lit by the sunshine, had glowed like a halo of gold-tipped curls, and shadows danced off her exquisite, heart-shaped face. Her bright pink lips parted . . . seductively.

"Julian, my darling," she had said, "my marriage to your brother doesn't mean a thing."

She laughed, and the sound of it was like bell chimes swinging gently in the wind. "Now I can be your mistress," she said. "That will be much better. Your brother's masculinity doesn't compare to yours. God's truth, he doesn't appeal to me at all in that sense. I went to him pure, which, sweetkins, as you know is required of ladies of quality, but now I am free to take a lover. I could never love Lord Geoffery as I love you." She lifted a small hand and, with a curved finger, raked the side of the soldier's face, and then let it caress his chin, touching the corner of his lips with the tip of a slim finger.

"Then why did you marry him?" the soldier asked, his eyes coming to rest on the Aynsworth jewels roped around her neck.

"Do you not know, Julian?" she purred, smiling, as if what she had done was all right, as if the man before her, the man she had promised to marry, should understand that the Aynsworth jewels, the Aynsworth wealth, and his brother's title were of more importance than the soldier's love. Two delicate arms came up to twine around his neck.

But the soldier flung her from him with such force that she fell to the ground. "Yes, I know, you greedy strumpet . . . Countess Charlotte Aynsworth." Her new title rolled off the soldier's tongue as if he were spitting bitter bile. Then, without so much as a glance over his shoulder, he strode from the garden, and he did not look back at his brother's wife, who crouched on the ground, called his name again and again, "Julian . . . Julian . . ."

Even now, the sound reverberated through the earl's head. Determinedly, he stopped his thoughts, and, for a long while stood and looked out, at nothing, at no one. He banished the images, the voice, from his mind. The roiling in his loins disappeared, leaving excruciating emptiness.

After leaving the garden that day, he had returned to his regiment, where he had fought fiercely and without fear, until he had been summoned home by a message saying he had become the fifth earl of Wendsleydale. The fourth earl, Countess Charlotte's husband, had been killed fighting an illegal duel over his wayward wife.

The earl let a half smile play around his mouth as he recalled that, upon inheriting the title, he had banished the dowager countess from his sight. The Aynsworth jewels remained with the entailed estate.

Why today? His Lordship asked himself. Why was he thinking of *her* today? The question was meaningless, he thought. It was this business about needing an heir.

"The pain was damnable real, but a long time ago," he mumbled as he turned from the window. Itchy with boredom, he paced the floor. Get married indeed! Since Charlotte, he had done his share of unrestrained wenching, but the affairs had been interim indulgences, impermanent and insignificant. Finally it had become quite a bore, so he had come to depend entirely upon Miss Medcalf to take care of the physical side of his life. But soon that must needs change.

With his desperate need for an heir, His Lordship had settled on Lady Elise Westerhouse to wed. She would make him the perfect mate, he reasoned. And she was willing. Without subtlety or shame, the lady had made it known she was anxious for his addresses.

Departing from his feelings toward forward women, the earl had not found Lady Elise's blatant forwardness objectionable. In truth, he welcomed it, for he certainly had no desire to pursue a wife.

Lady Elise was well trained as a lady of quality and knew how to go on in society, he further reasoned. And she was not beautiful, which was a prerequisite for any woman he should choose to wed.

"Demme his soul! Why does George not come?" the earl scolded. Again he looked at his watch. He hated to admit it, but this day he was having difficulty not thinking of the redhead who had wreaked havoc on his life.

"Codswallop! It was nothing! And the experience taught me an invaluable lesson," he informed the empty room.

So engrossed in his thoughts was the earl that he failed to hear the door open. When he did look round, he found his solicitor standing there smiling at him, as if he were not an hour late. The earl gave the small, nattily dressed man a quick perusal. Impeccably dressed as always, George reminded him somewhat of a London dandy.

"What say, m'lord? Why the urgent summons?" the solicitor asked.

"I've been waiting for you on tenterhooks, but now that you are finally here, pray, have a seat."

The solicitor sat in a chair facing the earl's desk.

The earl reached behind him and tugged on a bell rope. When a servant materialized in the doorway, His Lordship asked that ratafia and glasses be brought, and then he plunged headlong into the business at hand. "George, I am thinking of taking a wife. I need an heir to whom the title can pass, and to secure the Aynsworth holdings. If little Jenny had been a boy . . ."

Unfortunately, a year after the oldest Aynsworth heir had died, his wife, mother of Jenny Aynsworth, had followed him to the great beyond. Jenny had lived in the Aynsworth household since.

51

A chuckle accompanied the smile that curled the solicitor's lips. "But she did not oblige. And from what I've seen of your niece, though she is only nine, she is well on her way to becoming a femme fatale." The solicitor paused for a long moment before going on. "So whom have you chosen for the great honor of becoming your wife and producing this male heir."

Wishing to dispense with the subject as quickly as possible, the earl answered with alacrity, "Lady Elise Westerhouse."

"Julian!" The solicitor looked at him, then averted his gaze, knowing for sure that this time His Lordship had gone queer in the attic. George had always envied His Lordship's height and his handsomeness, as well as his other attributes, especially his awesome effect on the opposite sex.

With his wealth and the earldom, His Lordship can have any woman of his wont, and he picks Lady Elise Westerhouse!

When George didn't speak, the earl cocked an eyebrow and urged a reply: "You were saying?"

"Gad, m'lord, she is not a whit beautiful. I don't credit a word of this."

Slightly embarrassed, the earl replied, "That's why she's my choice. I would never take a beautiful woman to wife. They are too fickle, too full of themselves. Besides, one makes love in the dark, and I only want one issue, a son. After that is accomplished, we will have a ton marriage. A marriage of convenience, as the French would say."

Silence filled the room as the servant entered and set a tray with the requested ratafia on a table between the two men, after which he gave an obligatory bow and retreated quietly.

The earl poured a glass of the almond-flavored cordial and passed it to George, then poured one for himself. He lifted his glass. "Here's to any Aynsworth heir."

George, ignoring the toast, downed his drink in one

gulp. His eyes narrowed on his friend. "You're a cold jackanapes, Your Lordship. She's not worth it. You should throw down the willow."

Between the two men it was understood that *she* meant the Dowager Countess Charlotte Loyd-Dobbs Aynsworth.

Jumping to his feet, the earl exploded in the grandest of fashion: "You know perfectly well that does not signify. I am over her."

"Oddso? Then why . . . ?"

A diffident scratching on the book room's huge oak door interrupted the conversation.

"Come in," the earl said, practically in a shout. He brought his glass down hard onto the table, and his eyes cut sharply to George. "I do not recall an appointment."

"Should I leave, m'lord?" the solicitor asked.

"No! I'll dispense with the intruder in short order. I do not take to unexpected interruptions when I am conducting business! The servants know this."

"Perhaps it's the future mother of the Aynsworth heir," George said, trying for a little levity, but seeing none in the earl's stormy eyes.

"Come in," His Lordship said again, even louder this time.

Beyond the closed door, hearing the angry words spill from His Lordship's lips, Sutherland stood quaking in his boots. He had forgotten to remind Lord Julian of his audience with Miss Moreton . . . Lady Moreton, so Lady Throckmorton had called her, though in the butler's mind the curtsy title was questionable. The way she was dressed was not that of a lady of quality. Tremulously, the butler pushed the door open and gave a quick bow. "So sorry, m'lord."

When the servant bowed, he gave Ruanna a good view of the doddering peer of the realm. She gasped. He was not old! And he was scalding her with a blue-white gaze. The hair on the back of her neck prickled.

"Who might you be?" the earl queried as he looked over the butler's shoulder at a frail girl, who was

53

scornfully regarding him down the length of a pert little nose, and who had an exquisite face framed by red curls.

"Lady Ruanna Moreton, m'lord," announced Sutherland in a strangled voice. He turned and ran along the balcony, the tails of his coat flapping against his short legs.

Standing in the door, Ruanna watched the butler disappear out of sight, then turned to offer a deep, cold mockery of a curtsy to Lady Throckmorton's cousin. She, too, had heard his unkind remarks.

The earl came to bow over Ruanna's hand. "I wish I could say it is a pleasure to meet you, Lady Moreton."

Her eyes are too large for her thin face.

What was he thinking of; what was his cousin thinking of? He hated redheads, and he would see Grosvenor House go up in smoke before another one lived there. Lady Throckmorton knew that all too well.

Then another thought entered the earl's mind. Had Miss Moreton come for the Aynsworth jewels? Even though he knew he was making a cake of himself, the earl plowed doggedly on in a sarcastic manner. "What may I do for you?"

Ruanna took a deep breath, "Please, sir, disabuse yourself of the notion that I want anything from you. You are the earl of which Lady Isadora Throckmorton spoke so glowingly, are you not? Well, if I can locate her in this ostentatious mausoleum you call a home, I shall inform her of how wrong she was, then I shall leave. And that will be that."

Ruanna took a quick glance around the handsome room. *Oh, why did I say that? This room, the whole house, is beautiful.*

For a moment, all the bottled-up loneliness of the past months exploded inside Ruanna, and she bit into her lower lip to stop its trembling. Not waiting for the earl's reply, she whirled round and made to quit the room.

The earl grabbed her arm. "Oh, no! You're not—"

"Pray, m'lord, unhand me," Ruanna demanded.

His Lordship released her arm abruptly. He felt his senses reel. *I'll kill Isadora Throckmorton. This is no child!*

Contrary to his desire, which was to draw Ruanna into his arms and kiss each soft eyelid—for a start—the earl inclined his head toward a chair and ordered nastily, "Sit down. This shouldn't take long. You brought your *knapsack* along, did you not? Ready to move in?" He fixed her with a steady gaze. "Do you have relatives in England, other than Lady Throckmorton?"

Ruanna clamped her mouth shut.

The earl felt her anger. He went to sit in the chair he had shortly left.

Across from His Lordship, George sat with a look of incredulity on his countenance.

Meeting silence from Ruanna, the earl went on in a silky soft voice, "I understand you are a distant cousin. I've known only one Aynsworth with red hair, and she married my brother."

Ruanna's delayed answer was a scold. "You needn't sound so contemptuous, m'lord. Where are your manners?" Filled with barely restrained fury, she tried to focus her thoughts on the portraits of His Lordship's ugly ancestors, suspended by gold ropes on the paneled walls. When she felt herself sway, she determinedly straightened. "I have no relatives in England. And not that I know of, am I your cousin. Your Lady Throckmorton claims we are related in a distant way, but God's truth, I had never heard of either of you until late yesterday when I received this beautifully written missive, asking that I come for tea."

"And you did. Now would you sit down! I dislike anyone standing in my door. And no gentleman sits while a *lady* stands."

"I prefer to stand," Ruanna answered.

"Be that as it may," the earl snapped, returning to his own seat. "We can talk while you stand." He drew in a sigh and paused long enough to take a pinch of snuff. "Knowing I distrust women with red hair, and knowing

55

that when I saw you I would put a kink in her proposal that you join this household, let me guess what my dear cousin has said to you." He eyed her speculatively. "Thinking I would not have the heart to refuse, Lady Throckmorton probably extended to you the invitation to come live with us."

"How bright you are, m'lord, but you don't have to guess, and you don't have to rip up on me in such an unkind manner. I shall be happy to inform you of your cousin's and my conversation. She extended to me a gracious invitation to share this magnificent household with her and her most kind and generous cousin, the earl of something or other. I suppose she spoke of you, though I find her description quite deceiving. No man can be kind and generous and so arrogantly rude at the same time, and I would like someone to explain why my red hair seems to turn everyone about. When I removed my bonnet in the presence of Lady Throckmorton and she saw my red hair, she seemed to near swoon. Have not you Londoners ever seen red hair before?"

"Well—"

Ruanna cut short his answer. "I'm not through, Your Honor . . . sir . . . Your Lordship. I want to tell you this and then have done with you. I suspect your cousin is bored living here with you and is looking for someone to launch into society so she can go to the socials, and routs, and . . ."

Ruanna suddenly ran out of words. With a decided toss of her head, she turned away from the earl and hoped the gesture would say the rest of what she wanted to say.

"And you jumped at the chance!" the earl said. "What exactly did you tell Cousin Isadora?"

"At that time, when we were having such a pleasant coze over tea, I thought coming here to live a wonderful idea, feeling Her Ladyship's loneliness the way I did. But since meeting you, m'lord, I have changed my mind, and I am not interested one whit in your cousin's invitation."

The earl found himself smothering a smile. He had

never seen such fire. He cast another glance at his solicitor, who was holding his sides, no doubt thinking the conversation too delicious for words.

The earl turned back to Ruanna. He spoke bitterly. "Just what are you interested in, *Cousin*? Finding a fine home? And then a rich husband? Maybe one who owns the family jewels?"

Ruanna's answer was quick. "I care not for jewels, yours or anyone else's; moreover, I am not looking for a husband! Marriage would interfere with my music, which holds all my interest. It is my wont to continue teaching harp lessons to my students, and someday I shall buy a fine harp to replace the one I left in India."

"A lady of quality does not teach music lessons to the lower orders, nor does she hire hackneys and drive off without an abigail, as I understand from my cousin you do. Now, our little Jenny could possibly benefit—"

"Faith! Balderdash!" Ruanna cut in. "I can ill afford a hackney. I walk mostly. Well, no matter. I have no desire to be one of your useless, simpering ladies of quality, parading around looking for a husband while my music dies, along with my soul. So I shall take my leave now— without looking for Lady Throckmorton."

She bobbed another mocking curtsy, while she glared straight into the earl's blue eyes. "Will you convey to Her Ladyship that, after meeting her *kind and generous* cousin, I have changed my mind about living here. It is no longer my wont, and please also tell her I think you have no heart, and she should sleep with one eye open, lest you cut her heart from her."

Ruanna had no idea where such words came from. Never had she spoken in such an unladylike manner to anyone, and most especially not to one of the noble class. But for His . . . His . . . His Lordship to imply she had brought her knapsack with her because she planned, or schemed, to stay, when it had been his cousin's gracious missive that had brought her here . . . well, it was just too much to bear.

The earl smiled.

Ruanna turned and made to leave. Seeing from the corner of her eye the earl's swift leap in her direction, she ran with great speed along the balcony to the head of the staircase, bumping into a servant on her way.

"Lady Moreton!" It was Sutherland.

Ruanna grabbed blindly for a banister and missed. Then she was tumbling head over heels, until she lay in a heap at the bottom of the stairs, darkness swallowing her up.

How long she lay there, she did not know. Shadows and colors shifted in her mind, and then she became acutely aware of two muscular arms holding her against a warm body, her face nestled in the crook of a big neck. The beating of a heart drummed in her ear, and hot breath fluttered across her cheek.

Footsteps struck sharply against bare wood; someone was carrying her up the stairs, the same stairs she had fallen down. Consciousness flickered. She struggled to see a face and couldn't. A voice roared, "Sutherland, call Dr. Barnard, and be quick about it."

Even in her semiconscious state, Ruanna felt a sharp, tingling sensation knife through her. Later, she heard a door open, and gently she was put on a huge bed that held mounds of white pillows. She felt as though she were scudding about on a soft, white cloud. Time and place held no meaning.

Then she heard an unfamiliar voice saying, "It seems the fall did very little damage. Oh, perhaps a bruise or two, and it may take her a while to come around, but pray, do not fret about it. I expect the young lady swooned before she fell, thus making it an easy tumble."

That must be Dr. Barnard. Ruanna slitted an eye and saw a man wearing a black coat with a wide cowl collar. He had a pigtail, and his shirt was white, with very high collar points. In a way he reminded her of the stuffy butler. Then the man with a pigtail bent over her, peering at her through a quizzing glass.

'Why in the devil would she swoon?'' someone asked. *The earl's voice.*

The physician straightened and moved to stand at the foot of the bed. He gave the earl a sharp look. ''This child is starving, m'lord, and she has probably been working very hard.''

''She is no child!''

The earl's blustery voice ripped at Ruanna's eardrums. She half-opened her other eye to steal a better look at his harsh face. How she hated him!

''Feed the girl and have done with her,'' His Lordship ordered. ''I don't take to beggars coming to Grosvenor House.''

Ruanna gasped. *A beggar! Well, he's the lord and master of this household, so I shall go. No one calls me a beggar.*

''Feed her and get her out of here,'' the earl said again.

Just then, like a battleship under full sail, Lady Throckmorton charged into the room. ''What goes on here? Get *who* out of here?'' Holding her lorgnette to her eyes, she peered down at Ruanna and wailed, ''Oh, my dear child.''

''Stop calling her a child!''

That was the earl's mean voice again. Ruanna lay quieter still. It was best they not know she had regained consciousness. Not yet.

''That is what she is, m'lord. A child!'' retorted the old woman. ''Pray, Dr. Barnard, tell me what is going on! I asked the child to share this house, her being so frail and needful.''

''She swooned and fell down the stairs,'' Dr. Barnard explained, but Ruanna doubted that anyone heard him.

''Well, get the vinaigrette,'' the old woman ordered as she bent over Ruanna again.

''That should not be necessary,'' the physician said. ''Let her rest. It is best that she wake up on her own.''

The earl spoke. ''I know about your magnanimous invitation, Cousin Isadora, and it was a mistake. As I said, feed *the chit* and have done with her.''

That's three times he has said that.

Ruanna managed a covert look by squirming about and flinging an arm across her forehead, half covering her eyes. She gave a low moan. She had never seen anyone unconscious, and she could only imagine how one would act. Peeking from underneath her arm, she smiled when Lady Throckmorton pulled her tall, thin body up and glowered ferociously at the earl. The old woman then took the cane looped over her arm, unabashedly pointed it at the earl, and said, "That is unconscionable, Julian Philip Aynsworth! I say she stays! I raised you, m'lord, and I must have failed somewhere, for you to be so hard and jaded, and so unkind."

Lady Throckmorton's voice broke, and her lips trembled as she continued to stare at the earl. "Now, this child . . . Lady Moreton . . . stays here with me or I bound I shall take her to Scotland where I have property."

The earl gave a quiet chuckle. Never in his life had he seen his prodigiously proper cousin act in such a way, and never had she pointed her cane at him, not even when he was younger and had misbehaved atrociously. And he had not seen this monstrous old townhouse so full of life since he'd become master over it. Smoothing his face into seriousness, he ordered, "Fatten her up, and have her come-out, Isadora, if that is your wont. And marry her off as soon as possible. And for gad's sake, Cousin, take her to a modiste. I shall make sure we never again have to endure the sight of her in that dreadful dress she wore when she came in."

Only Ruanna's determination forced her to lie still. She watched as Lord Julian swung round and strode across the room. He had something—she could not discern what—tucked under his arm.

"Good day, Doctor," the earl said. Then, while holding on to the doorknob, he turned to Lady Throckmorton. "No point in making more of a hobble of this than it is. A husband should be easily found."

Ruanna gave a quick cough to expel some of her fury. She was not looking for a husband! When the door closed behind the earl, she was ever so glad he was gone. Now if Lady Throckmorton and the good physician would leave . . .

"She'll mend nicely," the black-coated man said to Lady Throckmorton. "A few days in bed. Food. I would not awaken her. She desperately needs rest." With that, he retrieved his high-crowned beaver and left.

But Ruanna was not listening to the physician's parting words, nor to Lady Throckmorton's motherly clucking. Her eyes perused the room, looking for her dress. Under the coverlet, she wore only her chemise and pantalets. And her feet were naked. Even her stockings and garters were gone.

"I suppose the devil earl saw me in my underclothes," she murmured to herself, becoming silent when Lady Throckmorton asked what she had said.

Ruanna wanted the old woman to leave, so she could leave. If need be, if she could not find her dress, she would have the maid bring her cloak to wear over her pantalets.

Lady Throckmorton reached for the bell rope and signaled a maid. "Bring the vinaigrette," she ordered when the maid appeared. "Then fetch a tray of food, please, Marie. I don't take the good doctor's meaning. *I* think Lady Moreton needs the sustenance of food more than she needs rest."

"Yes, m'lady," Marie said, bobbing, then leaving in a swirl of rustling black bombazine.

Lady Throckmorton called after her, "Also, Marie, have water brought for a bath, and bring one of Countess Charlotte's night rails from the wardrobe in the yellow-and-green bedchamber."

"Yes, m'lady," the maid called back.

Hovering solicitously over Ruanna, the old woman

clucked and patted her hand, while talking to herself. "After we awaken her, and after she has eaten, she must needs have a long, luxurious bath. I bound that plenty of food, a hot bath, and a soft night rail will enable the poor darling to sleep straight through the night. A few days rest is all she needs."

With great effort, Ruanna stifled a groan.

Chapter Five

She would think of a way to leave the hateful earl's house this night, Ruanna resolved, and that was that. She would not be called a beggar, and the last thing she wanted was to have vinaigrette waved under her nose. The mention of food made her salivate, so the best thing for her to do, she decided, was to wake up. Then, when Lady Throckmorton left . . .

Laconically, Ruanna sat up in bed, rubbed her eyes, and asked, "What happened?"

Lady Throckmorton, now sitting in a chair beside the bed, leaned forward. "You had a nasty fall, my dear. Dr. Barnard came and ordered food and rest. I've ordered supper for you."

Ruanna had to admit that the mention of food had been an incentive for her sudden recovery. She was near starving. "Thank you. I am a little hungry," she responded.

Shortly thereafter a maid brought a silver tray laden with roasted gammon and sweetbreads, and a bottle of wine. When Ruanna started to get out of bed, she was stilled by the old woman's hand.

"Stay in bed, dear. Rest, that is what the good physician ordered. The food will give you strength."

"I can't eat lying down."

Ruanna pulled herself up against the curved headboard, and immediately Lady Throckmorton was on her feet, plumping fat pillows behind Ruanna's back. Then, she pushed Ruanna's red curls back from her forehead, smiling at her.

Ruanna wished the old woman would not be so kind. It would only make it harder for her to leave.

Lady Throckmorton turned to the maid. "Marie, put the food in front of her. Can't you see she is starving?"

The smell of the food wafted up to claim Ruanna's attention. She ate ravenously of the roasted gammon and sweetbreads, washed down by a glass of wine. When she was finished, she tried to will the old woman to leave, but it was obvious that Lady Throckmorton did not feel disposed to do so. She chattered away, insisting that Ruanna, poor darling child, stay in bed until her bathwater was brought.

If I could only turn back the clock, the old woman thought; but as tears clouded her vision, she knew that should she be able to relive her life, nothing would be different than what it was. She was just fortunate to at last have Ruanna with her.

"Did you enjoy the food?" she asked, to negate the embarrassing silence that had filled the room.

"Wonderful!" Ruanna exclaimed. "Thank you for your kindness, Isadora."

The use of her name made Lady Throckmorton smile. She shook her head and insisted that more food would be brought if Ruanna was still hungry.

Touching her mouth with a white serviette, Ruanna returned the smile. She felt sorry for Isadora Throckmorton for having to live with the odious earl. Being tenderhearted herself, Ruanna did not tell Lady Throckmorton that her cousin had fooled her completely, that he was not at all the nice person she thought him to be.

"I can't tell you how sorry I am about Lord Julian's behavior, dear Ruanna, but tomorrow he will be sorry," Lady Throckmorton said in an aggrieved way. "He does have a soft core."

Good! He should be sorry, Ruanna thought. She said aloud, "Nonetheless, I will not stay here."

Until Lady Throckmorton moved closer to the bed, Ruanna hardly realized she had actually uttered the words. "What did you say, dear?" the old woman asked.

"I was just mumbling to myself." Ruanna gave a wan smile, then chuckled. "With me talking to myself, mayhaps you will think that my fall down the stairs was more serious than the good doctor diagnosed."

"I should hope not," Lady Throckmorton said, "for, as Lord Julian instructed, tomorrow we shall go to the modiste. I am greatly looking forward to it."

Ruanna looked away. She would not lie and say she would go to the modiste. She only lied when it was of the utmost necessity.

Lady Throckmorton reached for a silver bell on the table near her chair, then shook it heartily. Instantly, Sutherland bowed himself into the room.

Ruanna suppressed a giggle. *That old gossiper; he was listening at the door.*

"You rang, m'lady?"

"Yes, I did, Sutherland. Please assign someone to Lady Moreton. She will be living at Grosvenor House."

"But, m'lady," Sutherland said, "Lord Julian has already requested Katie, saying she is a trained lady's maid."

"Then send Katie here."

The butler bowed again and retreated, and within seconds the maid was in the room, a pale green, silk night rail with green ribbons draped over her arm.

Wondering if she could count on the maid for help in her escape, Ruanna cautiously gauged Katie, who wore a starched black dress, a white apron, and a white cap that tied under the chin. Beneath the cap, a youthful face registered her years as being no more than Ruanna's. So Ruanna's plan for escape formed in her mind.

"Lady Moreton, this is Katie. She will be your maid," Lady Throckmorton said by way of introduction.

The maid curtsied to Lady Throckmorton, then turned her brown eyes on Ruanna.

Ruanna acknowledged the introduction with a trace of a smile and a slight nod of her head.

"I will tend 'er," Katie said, bobbing another quick curtsy. "Marie sent this nightdress. Said yer requested it, m'lady."

"Yes, I did, and that is a pretty one." Lady Throckmorton bent and planted a kiss on Ruanna's forehead. Taking up her cane, she walked to the door, then turned back. "Pray, get a good night's sleep. I have such wonderful plans for you."

"Good night, Isadora," Ruanna said, "and thank you for your kindness."

"Good night, dear."

When the door closed behind the old woman, Ruanna's first thought was to bound out of bed, but before she could do so, she heard a knock on the door, and three liveried footmen came in, each carrying a brass-bound tankard of steaming hot water. The young men marched single file through the bedchamber and into the adjoining dressing room. Ruanna heard the water being poured into the tub.

In only moments, the footmen marched back across her bedchamber and, without a word, out the door.

Ruanna smiled. She had never seen so many servants, or such solemn ones.

Katie reached to remove the coverlet that Ruanna clutched under her chin. "The butler said yer was to 'ave a bath, m'lady."

"The butler? Sutherland?"

"Yes. His Lordship told Sutherland," Katie answered. "Here, let me help yer get undressed."

Ruanna clearly recalled hearing Lady Throckmorton order water for a hot bath, so what did the earl have to do with it? She raised an eyebrow. "Are you sure the earl ordered a bath for *me?*"

"Yes, m'lady. 'Twas the earl who told Sutherland.

He said so when he came to fetch me. The butler told me of my new duties, that of being a lady's maid to yer."

No point in arguing, Ruanna thought. Best that I make friends with Katie if I am to expect her help in getting out of this mausoleum. She hugged her knees to her chest. "Katie, are you as stuffy as the butler?"

The maid gave Ruanna a startled look. "Who?"

Ruanna giggled. "You heard me. You know— Sutherland, the man with the flapping tails and a long nose that obscures his vision when he is looking at someone. Most especially me."

Ruanna smiled at her own levity and was pleased to see a smile parting Katie's thin lips and her brown eyes catching a sparkle of life.

"Why do yer ask if I'm stiff like Sutherland?" the maid asked.

"Because I do not like stuffy people, and that includes butlers and maids." Ruanna, laughing, hopped down off the bed. "Let's get the bath the earl ordered over with."

Without waiting for assistance from the maid, Ruanna went into the dressing room and stripped off her pantalets, then climbed into the tub of hot water, cautiously lowering herself until delicious suds covered her naked body. A cloud of lilac steam rose to assault her nostrils. She lifted her chin toward the ceiling and breathed deeply of the scent.

But soon Ruanna's mind left the smell of the suds. She had to get out of the earl's house! Looking at the maid, she asked, "Do you know where they put my dress, Katie?"

When Ruanna had queried Lady Throckmorton of its whereabouts, the old woman had reminded Ruanna a new wardrobe would be furnished on the morrow. "The night rail the maid brought is all you will need this night," she had said.

"I think they burned it, my'lady," Katie answered. "So Sutherland said. He did it 'imself. On the earl's orders."

"Burned it! The earl—"

Though furious, Ruanna stopped quickly. She had better give this latest turn some thought. If the dress indeed had been burned, there would be no getting it back. She sank deeper into the hot sudsy water, her first decent bath since leaving India. In her room over the chandler's shop, she had had to be satisfied with a good washing from a pan of water heated over the fireplace, and when she washed her hair, she used the trough beside the well.

Using a bar of Joppa soap, Ruanna lathered her hair, and Katie poured warm water from a tankard to rinse the red curls.

"Katie," she said, "I am sure they didn't burn the cloak and bonnet I wore to Grosvenor House. While I finish my toilette, would you be so kind as to fetch them for me? And my reticule. Marie met us below stairs and took my cloak and bonnet, and my reticule. I'm sure you know where she deposited them."

"But I'd be scared."

"Oh stuff! Do not be so. No one will see you if you will do it surreptitiously."

"What?"

Ruanna laughed. "I mean if you steal down the stairs and find the cloak and bonnet, and my reticule, of course, then steal back up again without anyone seeing you."

Noting the fright in Katie's eyes, Ruanna inveigled, "No one will ever know. I shall never tell, and I know I will feel so much better. It should help me sleep, I am sure, just having some of my own things close by. This being my first night here, I feel a little lost."

"All right, m'lady. I can see no 'arm." Katie bobbed a curtsy and left.

Ruanna smiled triumphantly as she took the wet cloth the maid had left for her and scrubbed her skin until it tingled. Then she got out of the tub and rubbed herself down with a big towel that had the Wendsleydale crest stitched in the corner.

68

After shaking the water from her hair, she slipped the silk night rail over her head and shivered when the luxurious fabric touched her skin. For a moment she thought she was back in India, before they became so poor. Looking down, she blushed; her bosom was practically naked. She had never had a gown quite this revealing.

Katie returned with the gray cloak and bonnet draped over her arm, covered with one of her own black uniforms. Also hidden was Ruanna's reticule, which Katie carried in her hand. "I met Sutherland, but I don't think he suspected anything, seeing that I was carrying my own uniform."

"You are very wise," Ruanna told her. She took the cloak and bonnet and placed them on the bed near the pillow where her head would rest. Her beaded reticule went *under* the pillow. Then, because Katie insisted, Ruanna let her brush her hair until it was dry.

"Like fire," the maid said after several strokes. "And the green night rail is the color of yer eyes. It belonged to Countess Charlotte."

Now, who was Countess Charlotte? Ruanna wondered. She thanked the maid and climbed up onto the high bed, settling herself against the bank of down-filled pillows.

Resting thus, she looked around the room, noting the understated elegance of her surroundings.

Despite the rose-colored silk trappings hanging suspended from the carved wood frame and gathered back at the corners with gold ropes, the room had a masculine feel. The same silk framed the row of mullioned windows to her right.

"Whose room is this?" Ruanna asked.

"No one's now. His Lordship used to sleep 'ere. He took larger chambers when he returned from fighting with Wellington, when he come to be earl."

All the more reason to leave. Imagine staying in his room, Ruanna mused. she turned to stare out the window, beyond which a fuzzy haze fought with the moon for dominance. "Please close the curtains, Katie," Ruanna said, and the maid did, robbing the room of the light from the moon's glow. The clock on the mantel struck nine time. Ruanna counted, then finished her appraisal of the room. At its far end, a fainting couch and a group of high-backed chairs, covered with white and rose brocade, circled the fireplace.

Ruanna's gaze moved to the Adam mantel, above which a large painting or portrait *had* hung, faded wallpaper marking the place. Had someone fallen in disfavor, she wondered, so much so that his or her portrait had been removed?

Feeling a little chilled, she pulled the white coverlet over her and asked Katie to strike a flint to the wood already laid in the hearth. After Katie had done as she was asked, she lit a candle beside Ruanna's bed, then crossed the room and held the flint to the wick of an oil lamp on a table near the fire. The lamp glowed and cast a circle of yellow light onto the rug, which was splattered with colors of pink and green. A pleasant odor emanated from the candle, unlike the candles she burned in her room over the chandler's shop.

"Thank you, Katie," Ruanna said, her lids made heavy by the large meal she had consumed.

Katie hummed as she worked, as if she had done the same chores a million times before.

"Have you worked for the earl long?" Ruanna asked.

"My mum worked 'ere. She had me 'ere."

"Then you have known His Lordship a long time."

Ruanna wondered if Katie found the man in question as insufferable as she had found him.

The maid's answer surprised Ruanna. "Oh yes. I know lots about 'em. He's a grand bloke."

Ruanna's mouth flew open. "Why was he so terribly rude and ugly to me if he is *so* grand? He was most unendurable." She almost added that he had called her a beggar.

70

Katie answered without looking at Ruanna. "We think 'tis yer 'air, miss."

"My hair! We? You mean all the servants?"

"Yes, m'lady. *She* 'ad red hair."

Katie still didn't look at Ruanna, and it was obvious that she was inventing things to do to keep from leaving. She talked in a monotone as she swayed around the room. "Sutherland says 'is Lordship is on a tear the likes we've never seen, 'less it was the time when he ordered Countess Charlotte from the 'ouse."

Vexation showed in Ruanna's tone of voice when she finally spoke. "Who had red hair? And who is Countess Charlotte?"

"Countess Charlotte was the fourth earl's wife, the one I was just speaking of. Her 'air was like flaming fire, and 'er face was *sooo* beautiful. Just like yers, m'lady . . . without the freckles. This earl loved 'er so much . . . until she married 'is brother."

"That is utterly ridiculous! What does all that have to do with me? Where is this Countess Charlotte? Does His Lordship think I am his precious Charlotte, that I've come back to haunt him?"

"Might be," answered Katie. "All I know is after she married 'is brother, Lord Julian couldn't abide 'er, and when he was the next earl, he 'ad her picture took from this room. And jest like I told you, he ordered Countess Charlotte from the 'ousehold, not even waiting for his brother to be buried." Katie stopped to catch her breath. "Now, Earl Geoffery, the one before this earl, he was a terrible man."

And so is this one, Ruanna thought. But she realized that she must be the only one around who thought so. Even his poor cousin kept speaking of his soft core.

Suddenly the earl's words came back to Ruanna: "Fatten her up, give her a come-out if you wish, and marry her off as quickly as possible." She fumed inwardly.

71

As far as anyone fattening her up and getting her ready for market, it would be a cold day where Satan dwelled before that would happen to her.

"I think I'd like to go to sleep now, Katie. You may go, but first, in case of fire, is there a back staircase by which I might leave the house?"

"Oh, yes, m'lady," Katie answered with alacrity. Then she gave directions by flailing her arm. "Outside the door, turn right and go to the end of the 'all, to the servants' stairs. They'll take yer to the kitchen, then yer can go right out the back door."

Ruanna thanked her and said again, "You may go now, Katie. I'm terribly sleepy."

"I'll fetch a cap."

"Oh no, thank you. I never sleep with anything on my head," Ruanna lied. She wanted to be left alone. It would only take a moment to get dressed. Since she did not have a dress to wear, she would wear her cloak over her pantalets. Her bonnet would cover her cursed red hair.

"Please blow out the light in the lamp, Katie, but leave the candle burning. I'll extinguish it later. The glow from the candle and the fire will be light aplenty. I shall be asleep in no time."

"Yes, m'lady," Katie said as she gave a quick bob. "I will tend yer in the morning. Good night, m'lady."

"Good night, Katie. And thank you for being so helpful."

When the door had closed behind the maid, Ruanna sighed. So much had happened, she needed to think. She asked herself why she had not told Lady Throckmorton she would not be staying in the earl's household and had done with it.

Because the pitifully lonely woman would have resisted and an argument would have ensued between her and the earl.

"By leaving like this, I am a peacemaker, and, tomorrow, I'll pretend I was never asked to come here and live. I shall forget the fifth earl of Wendsleydale, but

72

I must needs be kinder to Lady Throckmorton and leave her a missive."

Ruanna sank deeper into the bed, and she found that she could hardly keep her eyes open as she watched the red flames in the fireplace shoot up the chimney in a dazzling display. Her hand reached to touch her cloak and bonnet, and for some inexplicable reason, she slipped the garments under the coverlet, out of sight. Then, a fatigue so great as to overcome her carefully laid plan of escape took hold of her, and soon she was asleep, and the dream began.

The earl held her in his arms. He was looking down at her, his eyes boring into her face, her soul, squeezing her heart. She heard his voice, deep resonant.

The earl opened the door and stood with his palm pressed to the door frame. His gaze fell on the red hair splayed onto the pillow. Light from the candle danced on the red curls, shadowing them with gold. Sooty lashes made crescents on her cheeks, and her pale lips were parted just slightly, invitingly. Creamy white breasts showed above the low-cut nightdress.

Memories flooded His Lordship's being, and the devil that had ridden his shoulder since the day he met Charlotte Loyd-Dobbs made its presence known.

He turned to leave, then swung back, drawn like a magnet to the side of her bed. "You wench, you beautiful redheaded witch, spawn of the devil," he murmured as he brushed a curl back from her forehead.

Ruanna heard the words as clearly as if she were awake. Then, warm lips brushed her cheeks and claimed her mouth cruelly, biting into her lips. Arms, like iron grips, held her against a broad, heaving chest. Then, he was parting her lips with his tongue, kissing her in a way she had never before been kissed. He cupped her breast with his big hand, kneading it until she felt bittersweet pain. She heard herself moan. "Charlie," a deep voice whispered close to her ear.

Charlie!

When the earl's dark countenance floated into focus with wrenching clarity, his raven black hair, his hard-set chin, Ruanna jerked free of his arms. "I'm not Charlie!" she clearly announced, and she watched as the earl shook his dark head, as if to clear it.

Quickly, the earl rose from the side of the bed, while his eyes locked with Ruanna's. "I did not mean to wake you . . . I . . . uh . . . it was not my intent to kiss you at all. I came here thinking I should apologize for my rudeness today. But when I saw you there, your red hair haloed around your head, the soft light on your beautiful face. I lost my head." The earl smiled wanly.

Ruanna spat out, "That you lost your head was obvious. And you are in danger of losing it literally if you dare to stay in this room. I suggest you quit it . . . leave me be . . . immediately."

Ruanna was amazed at her own temerity. A storm roiled her insides, and she prayed His Lordship had not been cognizant of how she felt when he kissed her. She was acutely aware that she had kissed him back. *Stuff! He had not been kissing her! He had thought her someone else.*

"You liked the kiss," the earl accused. He lifted a brow quizzically.

Ruanna felt herself blushing. Then she was even more annoyed with herself for acting like a schoolgirl. "I was dreaming about my lover in India," she lied. "You cannot blame me if I responded slightly to an amorous kiss from the man *I love,* can you?"

"Has he offered for you?"

"No . . . but . . ." *Oh, that was the way things went. One lie led to another.*

"Then you should not have been kissing him with such fervor."

Ruanna looked up at the earl, who was standing there so terribly tall, arrogant, domineering, scalding her with his cold eyes and being judgmental. Shadows played on his black side-whiskers. His white cravat was impeccably tied, and he was smiling.

74

She summoned her anger against the smile and gave the coverlet a yank to cover her exposed bosom, which seemed to have His Lordship mesmerized.

Ruanna said accusingly, "And you should not have been kissing me, thinking I was someone else. And speaking of fervor! Who taught you to kiss like that? Have you offered for someone who permits such liberties? or is it good ton for the gander to do what the goose does not dare?"

The earl snapped, "Ladies of quality do not—"

"Balderdash, I do not give a fig for your lofty rules, putting ladies of quality on pedestals, while men run off to their mistresses."

The earl inquired of himself: Why had he let Lady Throckmorton convince him that this was a child in need? She was every inch a woman. He looked at the upturned face and found himself trembling with the need to stop her words with a kiss. Impulsively, he sat back down on the side of the bed and reached to gather her into his arms.

Ruanna pushed him away and slapped him, hard, the slap stinging her palm. She hissed, "If I were a man, I would call you out."

"And if you were a man, I would not be kissing you," the earl retorted, his ardor now sufficiently cooled by the slap. He stood beside the bed. Obvious mockery lit his eyes when he said, "I suppose it would have been all right if I had been your lover in India. Do you lead him on? Kiss him back the way you did me?"

Ruanna did not answer. Why should she?

"Do you?" the earl asked again, moving away from the bed.

Ruanna tossed her head to one side. "Do I what?"

"Lead men on."

"I most certainly was not leading you on. Cannot a woman respond to an innocent kiss without a man acting like a rutting sheep? Trying to expose one's bosom."

"Most of which was already exposed," the earl glibly

75

replied. He paused, then sighed audibly. "The language you use to express yourself is quite vulgar, Miss Moreton, and that was no innocent kiss. If you are that uniformed about seduction of the male, then I suggest you confer with Lady Throckmorton on the subject. Ladies of quality . . ."

The earl laughed then. A terrible laugh, Ruanna thought. The look in his blue eyes sent a chill up and down her spine. And she had been afraid of Archibald Bennet! This grand lord had probably seduced more women than King Henry VIII.

"How many times do I have to tell you that I have no craving to be one of your snooty ladies of the ton. And I was not trying to seduce you, and you were a long way from seducing me."

The earl walked over to lean against the mantel. When he turned to face the bed, a perfectly aimed pillow hit him in his chest. Without a word, he picked the weapon up and tossed it back onto the bed. Then, feeling that he owed the chit an explanation—and an apology—he said, "I was lacking in propriety, and I am sorry about coming to your bedchamber and kissing you. It will not happen again, I assure you."

He went on to explain: "Being unable to sleep, I had gone for a night walk in the park, to cogitate on what to do about you. I came here to check on you, thinking that if you should be awake, I would explain to you about Lady Throckmorton's absolute refusal to let you leave this household, and to ask you to stay for her sake. I had no notion to kiss you . . . until I saw you."

Lord Julian refrained from telling her that she brought painful yearnings back to haunt him, passionate yearnings he thought were dead, that from the moment he had first cast eyes upon her he had wanted to kiss her and run his hands through her hair, that he had wanted to make love with her.

Ruanna felt a captive under his blue gaze. It would be easy to tell him she would stay. It would also be easy to yield to the devil. "So you came to check on me and decided to take advantage of me while I was asleep. Did I not hear Lady Throckmorton refer to you as an honorable man?"

Ignoring the angry remark, the earl retorted, "I have already apologized. I do not beg."

The hardness was back in his voice. Above his piercing blue eyes, dark brows snapped together in a ferocious frown. Ruanna allowed herself a quick glance at the rest of him; his breeches hugged his thighs like gloves, exposing muscles that rippled when he moved. His coat tapered from broad shoulders to a trim waist. His . . .

Appalled at the way her heart was pounding, Ruanna stopped her perusal. She felt blood suffuse her face and knew she was blushing. "And neither do I beg, Your Lordship," she said haughtily. "I am *not* a beggar. I do not need your charity. I shall leave your household tomorrow."

The earl rejoiced at the pronouncement. If she left after he had apologized for his behavior, and after he had asked her to stay—for Lady Throckmorton's sake—then it would rid him of all guilt, and Lady Throckmorton would just have to understand.

Good riddance and Godspeed, he thought as he moved across the room, his steps long and fluid, a whisper in a room filled with quivering silence.

At the door, he stopped, thinking that perhaps he should say something else so that he would not feel guilty when Lady Throckmorton had a spell of the vapors, which she was sure to do tomorrow when the girl left. Lifting a brow, he asked, "Will you not reconsider, Miss Moreton?"

"No."

"Lady Throckmorton and I will train you in such a manner that a suitable husband can be found for you—unless you still hold to your lover in India. She will see that you are properly cared for. You are too young to fend for yourself in the part of London in which you live."

77

The earl wanted to add that with her looks, she was sure to be soiled by force.

"I don't need . . . I have my music."

"I know. And, as you've told me before, you're capable of taking care of yourself. Quite frankly, I don't agree."

He turned to leave. He would go this time, he resolved, but he didn't. He returned to Ruanna's bedside and, with his hand lowered, lifted her hand to his lips for a lingering kiss. After placing the small hand back on the bed, he swung around and walked toward the door, which, this time, he resolutely closed behind him. And as he did so, he prayed that Ruanna Moreton would indeed leave on the morrow. He had done his duty for Lady Throckmorton.

"Of all the odious . . . damn you . . . you jackanapes." Turning to a priceless Ming dynasty vase reposing on the table near the bed, Ruanna's mind toyed with the idea of throwing it, but she reconsidered. Instead, she threw the pillow, this time at the closed door.

She listened until she heard belowstairs a door slam. No doubt His Lordship was going to his mistress, she thought, just where he should go in his state.

Quickly, she gathered up her cloak, bonnet, and reticule from under the coverlet; then she climbed off the high bed and, with great speed, went to the adjoining dressing room, in search of her pantalets and scuffed half boots.

Chapter Six

The missive Ruanna had written to Lady Throckmorton rested on the mantel beside a French gilt clock
ticking away the tedium of time. With the door open only
a portion, Ruanna, wrapped in her gray drugget cloak and
matching bonnet, listened intently for the earl's return,
her hands clapsed around her beaded reticule which
rested in her lap.

After dressing hurriedly, she had realized that if she
left before His Lordship was asleep she might meet him
face to face, and, no doubt, he would throw her over his
shoulder and pitch her back into bed, or, worse yet,
awaken the household, and then she would have dear
Lady Throckmorton's supplications to contend with. *I
cannot bear that.*

As it grew later and later, Ruanna realized that if by
near morning she had not heard the front door open and
close, and His Lordship's footsteps on the stairs, she
would take a chance on his seeing her and leave anyway.
Perhaps she could outrun him, she thought, knowing
better. Not with his long legs.

And then another fear assailed Ruanna. What if Lady
Throckmorton came to the bedchamber and found her
sitting there with her white pantalets showing below her
gray cloak? With great speed, Ruanna jumped up and
went to stuff pillows under the white coverlet. If the dear

79

old woman carried a candle, the outline of the pillows in the dim light would fool her. If she came in and lit the oil lamp . . .

Ruanna blew out the candle and sank into a chair, back in the darkest corner of the room. Katie had drawn the curtains against the moonlight; the fire in the fireplace was as dead as last Christmas and furnished no light at all.

Waiting impatiently, Ruanna refused to think upon the what-ifs. Everything in life was a chance, she told herself. All one could do was take precaution. She had crammed her red hair under the bonnet for protection from Archibald Bennet's men, should one be about when she reached the street.

In the quietness, Ruanna, against her will, nodded off, woke with a start, then nodded off again. The clock struck twelve, then one . . . then two . . . three times. Why did the jackanapes earl not come?

If His Lordship had not called me a beggar . . . There was so much she did not know about men. She did remember her dear Mama telling her that a man could make love to a woman while loving another, except Lady Mary had not called it making love; she'd called it rutting.

Most likely, that was what the earl was doing with his mistress, Ruanna thought. A hot flush started at the nape of her neck and moved up to cover her face. How could she have returned the earl's kiss? Her face grew even warmer. In truth, her face grew hot with embarrassment, she conceded. She had not just returned his kiss; she had savored it, letting him pour all of himself into her.

Another new feeling entered Ruanna's being, the feeling of jealousy. Suddenly she was jealous of Lady Charlotte, of the earl's mistress, and she had no right.

"Stuff! What did one kiss mean?" she mumbled into the darkness. She did not know the answer, but she knew that it was imperative she leave—tonight. What if he should return and kiss her again?

She heard the clock strike four times, into the eerie

stillness, and she told herself that the time was *now*.

Clutching her reticle to her bosom, she crossed the room with great speed, then eased outside the bed-chamber door, where she waited, listening for the slightest sound. Enveloped by darkness, she crept in the direction Katie had said the servant's stairs would be, carefully measuring each step. She stopped abruptly, for she heard a door open and close, footsteps on the stairs: *the earl's.*

Sucking in a breath, she tried to open the door, but found it locked. Running with light steps, she gained the corner where the hall ended. With little hope, she turned the knob and pushed. When the door opened easily, she darted inside and flattened herself against the wall. Through uncovered windows, moonlight danced shimmeringly across the room.

Ruanna listened for steps to come closer; instead, she heard a door open and close, then a deepening silence. Knowing she could not wait until His Lordship fell asleep, she decided to leave quickly the room she had escaped into, and would have, had not something caught her eye.

The door of a chiffonier had been left open, exposing beautiful gowns hanging from a rack. Knowing instantly that the gowns had belonged to the other redhead, Ruanna could not resist walking closer and examining each exquisite garment. Such splendid clothes, she thought, fingering the delicate fabrics. She opened a drawer and found silk night rails, and chemises, all trimmed with French lace. In another drawer, there were silk, lace-trimmed drawers, not pantalets like she wore.

Katie had said Lord Julian had banished the countess from Grosvenor House. Without her clothes, I suppose, Ruanna mused. She shook her head when she remembered how hard-set his countenance could be. Remembering also that she was trying to escape that hard countenance, she turned to leave, but again the glimpse of something stopped her—almost hidden by a chair, a framed portrait leaned against the wall.

Ruanna moved closer, bent and stared, and found herself mesmerized. The beauty of the gorgeous gowns did not compare to the beauty she beheld, even in the shadowed moonlight. Little wonder the earl had lost his heart . . . and his head . . . and his good senses, she thought. She moved the chair and brought the portrait into the stream of light. Wide-set green eyes met hers.

As Ruanna studied those eyes, iridescent with light and glittering catlike in the darkness, she felt the cunning nature hidden in them, for they seemed to peer right through her. They were bottomless pits of jade green water in which a man could drown.

Goose bumps rose on Ruanna's arms, and she felt chilled, even with her cloak held tightly around her. Her eyes moved to the beauty's other attributes; high cheekbones and skin like fresh, warm milk. Her nose was small; her smile enticing, flirtatious.

Framing these enormously beautiful features were red curls that tumbled down to rest on bare shoulders. And it seemed that a laugh gurgled up out of the slender throat.

"But our resemblance stops with the red hair," Ruanna said aloud. "I am not beautiful, not in the way she is beautiful, and I do not have cat eyes."

By now, the room had taken on a sinister feeling for Ruanna and she wanted to escape from it as much as she wanted to escape from the earl. Again she started to leave, but found that she could not, though she did not know why. She stopped to explore the room further. At one end, there was a huge white bed, with carved posts.

Yellow curtains, tied with bright green tassels, draped the bed's corners. Ruanna wondered if the earl had slept in the bed with Countess Charlotte. Mayhaps he had come while she slept and had stolen a kiss.

Another thought invaded Ruanna's mind. She went back to the chiffonier and searched for nightcaps, finding none. She smiled. Had she worn the nightcap Katie offered to get for her, the earl would not have kissed her.

Well, from now on she would wear a nightcap.

A little voice inside her head asked: You silly goose, you are leaving Grosvenor House never to return, so what difference does it make whether or not you wear a nightcap?

She eased the door open, listened for a long moment, then darted out. With the quickness she had learned since coming to London, she came to the stairs Katie had told her about and descended to the next floor.

There, she found herself in a large open space that was not the kitchen at all; yet, it was enclosed by walls. She looked up. Through ribbons of mist, a white moon floated in an ebony sky sprinkled with stars.

It must be a dividing room between the kitchen and the rest of the house, Ruanna thought. There was a walkway shelter for the servants to walk under if it were raining. The purpose for the open roof, Ruanna guessed, was to let fresh air circulate and take away the smells of the kitchen.

And circulate it did. The wind eddied around her, whipped her cloak unmercifully, then wrapped it around her mummy fashion. While struggling to straighten the cloak, she looked for and found the door going into the kitchen, which was unlocked. Inside, smells of hot meat accosted her nostrils. Turning on a spit in front of the roasting range was a large haunch of beef. The fire cast ample light, and Ruanna's curiosity drew her closer.

"Thank heavens dogs are no longer used to turn the spits," she whispered. A barking dog most certainly would alert the household. She had read that some ingenious ironmaster had devised a system of gears to operate a weight to turn the spit, and that the new version needed to be wound like a grandfather clock. She bent to examine the contraption.

Somebody had wound it up tightly enough, for it was turning, and she had never smelled anything quite so tempting as the meat from which fat dripped into a long trough.

83

Without thinking, the redhead grabbed a fork and ripped off a chunk the size of both her small fists, and then she took from the warming oven a pigeon and several biscuits. Might as well be hanged for a big crime as a little one, she told herself. Not that she was hungry after the huge supper Lady Throckmorton had fed her, but soon enough she would be ravenous. She wrapped the food in a newspaper she found on a table, placed the package under her cloak, along with her reticule, and then stepped out into the night, finding herself in an herb garden enclosed by high brick walls.

"Demme," she said, sprinting across the garden to the iron gate. Finding it locked, she stood for a moment, wanting to shake it to alleviate her anger at such bad luck. Knowing that she would not do that, lest she wake someone, she looked for another means of escape and, at first, thought she could crawl under the gate. But the gate was dog-proof. A sheet of iron measured at least two feet up from the ground. Her gaze then fell on a wooden box filled with dirt, with nothing growing in it.

After placing the food and her reticule in a patch of growing herbs, she tugged at the box until it was near enough to the gate that she could stand atop it and reach the first iron bar. After retrieving the food and reticule, and stuffing them in the pocket of the cloak, she stepped up on the box, smiling when her foot touched the first bar, and then, gingerly, the second one. It would not be easy, but there was no other way to escape the enclosure. Unless one was a lizard and could slither up a brick wall.

Hand over hand, she climbed to the top, then catapulted over. Fright that someone might have heard the fall kept her from feeling the pain, and she prayed that she would not look up and see the earl's cold blue eyes staring down at her, accusingly. This time, instead of calling her a beggar, he would call her a thief.

Ruanna quickly looked about, but found no one in evidence, although something worse had happened. Her beaded reticule and the package of meat had fallen from her pocket. The food, she could reach, but her reticule was far inside the garden.

Ruanna, thinking she would climb back over the gate, jumped up. She could not leave her precious reticule. But there was no box to stand on; besides, she cautioned herself, I must needs not tarry that long. She looked for a stick she could use to fish the reticule up to her and, failing to find one, swore at the meticulous servants who kept the place barren of refuse.

She asked herself why had she not just pitched the small purse and package of food over the gate and then followed?

"Because stray dogs would have grabbed them up," she said.

Ruanna denied the tears that pushed sharply behind her eyes, and knowing she had no choice other than to leave the purse, she stared longingly at it for a moment. Then, with great agility, she was up and on her way toward the mews, running as fast as her legs would take her, back to the slums, back to loneliness.

"'Tis the earl's fault," she said when she slowed to get her breath, but she knew that that was not entirely true. The fault lay in her cursed red hair! She poked at her curls, pushing them deeper under her bonnet.

At Grosvenor House, if the earl thought Ruanna Moreton had enlivened the household yesterday with her sharp tongue and less than graceful fall down the stairs, it was nothing compared to the commotion that her slipping away in the middle of the night caused. It was barely light the next morning when his valet awakened him by shaking his shoulder in a desperate way while saying, "Wake up, m'lord, Her Ladyship is in a swoon."

But it was not a swoon Her Ladyship was in, the earl discovered when he reached the sitting room that adjoined Lady Throckmorton's bedchamber. She was prostrate on a fainting bench, and she was in a fit of rage directed at him. She did not address him as m'lord, nor did she call him Lord Julian. Without preamble, she asked, "Julian Aynsworth, what did you do to that child? What did you say to her?" Her faded blue eyes were brilliant and fierce in their sockets as she glared the earl down, her chin quivering.

The earl had only seen his cousin this angry once before in his life, and the memory washed over him now. When he was nine, his father threatened to hide him for some small offense, as the old earl often did. In his anger, he had shouted that Julian had killed his mother. "She died to bring a worthless son into this world," he had harangued.

As if the hateful words were being spoken just this minute, pain shot through the earl like a sword aimed straight at his heart. He found himself trembling with the memory.

Then, as now, Lady Throckmorton had stood her ground. "Don't you dare attack my charge, you evil old man," she had shouted back at the old earl, her hands on her hips, her chin jutted out. "It was you," she accused, "spilling your seed into the frail woman that killed her. 'Tis a shame the dear woman could not have lived. She would have been proud of her son . . . as I am."

Lady Throckmorton had held him—her Julian, she had called him—to her flat bosom while he sobbed out his pain, and his gratitude, and his anger.

How he had fought the memory all these many years. Doing the same now, he pushed it from his mind. Let the immutable past stay buried, he prayed.

The earl watched as Lady Throckmorton's maid hovered over her with a damp cloth in one hand, a bottle of vinaigrette in the other.

"You may go now, Marie," Lord Julian said.

The maid curtsied. "Yes, m'lord." At the door, she looked anxiously back over her shoulder, as if she, too, were angry with the earl and did not trust him to take care of her mistress.

"I shall take care of her," the earl assured her, his voice kind. He went to the door and closed it.

"Calm down, Isadora," he scolded gently when they were alone. "Do you desire all the servants to hear? What are you talking about?"

"Lady Moreton is gone. She left in the night, leaving this missive addressed to me. When Katie went to attend her, she found it and right away delivered it here to my apartment."

The earl took the piece of crumpled paper and read the message, noting the flowing script. His brow shot up. No wonder Isadora was in such a state. The blasted chit had said she could not bear staying under the same roof as the haughty, presumptuous, and insolent earl. How dare she? He had not been *that* unkind. Sudden anger attacked him, and he felt his face flush hot from it. "I do not attend, Isadora. Last evening when I went to her bedchamber . . ."

The old woman sat bolt upright. The look emanating from her eyes was formidable. "You went to her bedchamber! No wonder the poor darling left in the middle of the night. You probably frightened her to death." She stopped to heave a big sob, and then she said, referring to his mistress, "Julian, you have Miss Medcalf."

The earl managed a smile. His cousin did not mince words. "It was not like that at all. I went there to apologize for my rude behavior when we met, and to ask her to live here because it meant so much to you."

If I should tell her that Ruanna Moreton stirred me in much the same carnal way as Countess Charlotte, and that I kissed Ruanna Moreton, and that "her child" kissed me back because, in her sleep-drugged state, she thought I was her lover in India . . .

Nor would he tell her that he was happy Ruanna Moreton had gone—that is, he could be happy if only his cousin were not so upset. He took a deep breath before saying, "My dear cousin, I warned you that Miss

Moreton might not desire to be rescued from the slums of London. That seems to be the case here."

The words did not console Lady Throckmorton one whit, and it was immediately obvious to the earl that they did quite the opposite. She burst into another fit of tears. Hunching her shoulders, she buried her face in her hands and swayed from side to side, sobbing uncontrollably.

The soft core of the earl wanted to go to her, hold her as she had held him so long ago, but that just was not done. God's truth, it was not done back then, he thought. Among the upper orders, it was thought vulgar to show emotions.

But Lady Throckmorton had never adhered to the measures of the upper orders. She was of noble birth, but there was no denying that she was not at all in the accepted mode, and neither was this stray cousin she wanted to take under their roof. The earl grimaced.

"For God's sake, Isadora, stop it! Your sobs sound like a stuck hog gurgling up its last breath. Why is this so important? Are you so terribly lonely? Little Jenny will be returning soon."

The earl moved across the room to sit in a chair. He felt helpless and empty, and, for a moment, the thought to shake his cousin to bring her to rationality lingered in his head. But, fearing another outburst, he refrained from doing so and decided to wait her out.

With his long legs stretched out in front of him, he studied the room. Early sunshine streamed through the windows and shadows danced on the rug, and on the walls that were covered in a soft shade of Chinese silk.

Thinking a sniff of snuff would ease his agitation, he searched in his pocket for his snuffbox, only to become acutely aware that he still wore his robe, and that his feet were bare. He could not remember ever before leaving his rooms in such a state of undress. But the valet's words had frightened him. His old cousin simply did not swoon.

"Blister it," he said sotto voce.

After a while, when Lady Throckmorton's sobs had

sufficiently subsided, the earl reached for the silver teapot on a table near the chair. "May I pour hot tea, Isadora?" When he did not receive an answer, he filled the cup anyway, added the lump of sugar he knew she desired, then handed it out to her.

"Thank you, Julian," she said, taking it with trembling hands and placing it on the tray. With a delicate white handkerchief, she wiped tears from her red-rimmed eyes.

The earl's words were gently spoken: "Now tell me, Isadora, why are you so surprised that this Ruanna Moreton did not want to accept the hospitality of the Aynsworth household? There was no reason for her to leave. God's truth, I went to her and apologized." Without giving Lady Throckmorton time to respond to his question, he went on to repeat a question he had asked earlier: "Pray, why is this so important to you? Until a few weeks ago, you did not even know the girl lived in London."

"I cannot tell you, m'lord, I cannot tell you," Lady Throckmorton said, her voice quavering. Her flat chest rose and fell with each breath, and it was obvious to the earl that she saw nothing that was in the path of her gaze. He waited patiently.

Lady Throckmorton reached for the cup of hot tea, lifted it to her lips, and looked at the earl over its rim. "Pray, Julian, do not ask me to tell you."

The muffled sobs started again, and they ripped at the earl. He smiled at her, trying to coax a smile in return. To no avail. Leaning forward, he pleaded, "Please forget Miss Moreton, Cousin—"

Lady Throckmorton jumped to her feet. The cup and saucer clattered back onto the tray. "No! I shall go after her, and I shall take her to Scotland."

His patience pushed to the limit, the earl exploded. "You cannot live in that drafty old castle with its crumbling walls!"

When the earl was quite young, she had taken him to her castle in Scotland. He was no stranger to the place.

"There is a small cottage that will hold us. I've saved over the years. Your father was many things, but he was generous with his allowance to me, as was your brother, and you after him."

"I will not allow it, Cousin Isadora. It would be your death. If you are determined to carry through with this folly, I shall accompany you to that terrible place were Miss Moreton lives, and I shall do everything within my power to reason with her." He wanted to argue that it was useless, but he saw the determination on his cousin's face and knew it would not be wise. Instead, he swore under his breath.

"Would you, m'lord? I told her you had a soft core."

Lady Throckmorton smiled through her tears, but when a servant knocked on the door to deliver up Ruanna's small beaded reticule to her, saying Cook had found it in the herb garden, the old woman burst into another fit of tears.

The earl rolled his eyes upward in a beseeching manner, then said, "We shall leave just as soon as you have had sustenance, which I am sure you need."

He made a bow, took her hand, and kissed it, after which he strode hurriedly out of the room. His voice roared down the hall. "Sutherland!"

"Yes, m'lord," was the almost instant reply.

The earl snapped, "Bring a breakfast tray to my bedchamber, and order the carriage brought round front. And have Suthe on the box."

The butler bowed. "Yes, m'lord."

Then, for some reason the earl did not understand, Ruanna's sweet, impertinent face danced before his vision, her gorgeous red hair spilling over her shoulders in a lush, wanton mass, while her mouth curved into a smile and her eyes laughed.

And only a moment later, they were glistening in murderous anger, he remembered.

Why did she have to have red hair?

After Lady Charlotte married his brother, he had

90

studiously concluded that any woman so unfortunate as to be born with red hair was nothing more than a *femme d'esprit,* one who would betray everybody in turn, if it should suit her purpose.

Now, because of my cousin, I'm cursed with another red-head.

Nonetheless, upon gaining his quarters, His Lordship told his valet to lay out his best morning coat and breeches.

In front of Ruanna was the chandler's shop, light showing through the small windows. The smells were there, the garbage, the Charlies in their boxes, calling out the time and weather. She had stopped only to eat her food, and to rest, for tiredness finally overcame her and she could not put one foot in front of the other.

While sitting in the shade of a church, she watched acrobats performing for the coins that were occasionally pitched to them. She regretted not having a shilling to give, and shared her food instead. Later, in a park, she managed a few winks of sleep.

Now that she was near home, she realized her feet had been sorely used. Even so, she ran until she reached the foot of the outside stairs, where she stopped abruptly—her key was in her reticule.

"Miss Sherrill will faint dead away when she sees me dressed like this," Ruanna murmured as she opened the door to the chandler's shop.

A chandler's shop was a place where the poor could buy supplies for the day, and have a cup of tea if they liked. Tonight, Ruanna thought when she stepped inside, it could be some fabulous club, perhaps White's. Tables were about on the sawdust and oyster shells that covered the floor, and everyone was talking at once. Over the din, Miss Sherrill's shrill voice grew louder when she turned and saw Ruanna.

If she noticed Ruanna's white pantalets protruding

below her cloak, she gave no sign as she talked in her broad cant. "There ye'are, my dear, and 'tis about time. Yer dear friends 'ave been here . . . twice. They came early, then left to go search for yer, and then they returned. Sitting right over there, they had a cup of tea, they did, while waitin' for yer." She stopped a moment for breath. "And that grand coachman, wearing a three-cornered 'at and dressed to the first stare, waited atop the big black coach. 'Andsome he was. I could not bear not to offer him a cup of tea."

Obviously, Ruanna thought, the entire neighborhood had been alerted that nobility had visited the shop, and now they had come to listen to Miss Sherrill's grand tale.

"I am sorry I missed them," Ruanna said, though she was not sorry at all. She would have hated for her day's walk to have been in vain.

"The 'andsome earl asked many questions, Miss Ruanna, and 'er Ladyship left this for yer." Miss Sherrill handed the beaded reticule to Ruanna. "She stuffed some pound notes in it and threatened me with thievery charges if I opened it up, saying she would most certainly learn if I did. Of course I charged her a guinea for my trouble. Being in business like I am, I can't work for nothin'. It seems that she left a basket of fruit for yer and someone took it before I could deliver it to yer."

Ruanna grabbed the precious reticule and clasped it to her bosom. She knew all too well what had happened to the basket of fruit. "Did you say Lady Throckmorton was accompanied by the earl of Wendsleydale?"

"Oh my, yes! The one with those beautiful side-whiskers and a clean chin, and such deep blue eyes. 'Andsome, he was. Not many men wears side-whiskers now days. That shows he's his own boss, and as tall as he stood, he looked as if he could be boss over many things." The fat woman winked at Ruanna to further explain her meaning.

"Is he married? If not, I will take 'im on," a woman with frizzed hair joked as she sidled up to stand near

Ruanna. Another woman, grinning over the first woman's shoulder, added her bit, "I dan't care if he 'as three wives." Raucous laughter followed her words.

Ruanna addressed the first one who had spoken. "No, he is not married, and I am sure that we have seen the last of His Lordship."

"Oh, no, Miss Ruanna," Miss Sherrill said. "They will be back tomorrow fer sure. They said so. And there was another gentleman 'ere making an inquiry about you. For heaven's sake, I said to somebody, I ain't never seen anyone grow so popular all at once as that higher than the Lord redhead."

"Another gentleman? What did he look like?" Ruanna could barely force the words from her throat. She felt her body tremble, and she felt as if she had suddenly been struck with a fever.

"Oh, he wuz nothing like yer quality friends, he wern't. He looked more like a river rat, with at least a week's stubble on his face. Dirty, too, and he 'ad a tooth missin' right in front." The squat woman opened her mouth and pointed to a row of yellowed teeth.

But Ruanna did not need such a graphic description. How many people with a front tooth missing would be looking for her? And for what purpose? It had to be one of Archibald Bennet's hired henchmen. She asked, "What was the gist of his inquiry, Miss Sherrill?"

"How long yer been 'ere, things liken to that. If yer had red hair. And when I told 'im you did so have red hair, he said you were from India. Is'at right?"

Ruanna did not answer. She felt as if the death knell had just rung over her head.

The proprietress took Ruanna's arm. "Miss Moreton, can I get yer a cup of tea? Yer look perfectly gooseish. Sit down, I'll get the tea. 'Tis only a shilling. 'Ere, take this chair."

"Thank you," Ruanna murmured, and sat down in the proffered chair. From her reticule she produced the required shilling.

93

"Stepping out of 'er class, that one is. Always means trouble," the woman with the frizzed hair said as she moved to regain her seat at the table she had left.

"That's bad. Yer 'ave to know yer place," her companion answered, following.

Ruanna heard the words, but they held no meaning. Her world had collapsed around her, and there was nothing she could do. The tea tasted bitter in her mouth. She sat for a moment longer, but only for a moment, for she knew what she must needs do. Jumping to her feet, she bade Miss Sherrill good night, thankful that with the return of her reticule, she did not have to ask for the use of her key.

Charging into her room, Ruanna grabbed the scissors and sent them slicing through her red hair, and when the last curl lay on the floor, she gathered them up into the newspaper that had held the food and crammed them into her knapsack, to be disposed of later. She then pulled the boy's cap she'd worn from India down to rest just above her eyes, taking care that not a red hair showed. From her reticule, she took three shillings and laid them on the table, her rent until the end of the month. Then, without thinking where she would go, she picked up the knapsack, slung it over her shoulder, and descended the rickety stairway. She wore a dun-colored coat and boy's baggy breeches, the same clothes she had worn six months ago when she stole aboard Captain Tidesdale's ship.

Ruanna remembered how her heart had pounded then, and it was doing no less now. After glancing in all directions, she darted into the alley, to become lost in the milling crowd. She kept her head down, lest the man with the missing tooth was waiting for her.

Chapter Seven

In the Bedford, a coffeehouse in the theater district most often frequented by actors, two men sat at a corner table far removed from the flickering candles which lighted the place. One had a missing front tooth, was dirty and unkempt, while the other was impeccably dressed in skintight breeches, a flawless coat of deep blue superfine, and a snow white cravat creased with immaculate folds. His hair was midnight black, above small eyes just as black. His dark complexion laid claim to Indian origin, but his clothes were decidedly British.

Only one glass was on the table. This was deliberate. The dark man had no notion of drinking with the dregs of London's East End.

Leaning back in his chair, he curled his lips into a smile, lifted the glass of blue ruin, and, though he tried to keep the intonation from his words, spoke condescendingly to the man across from him. "So you found her, Rocco. That is good. Very, very good. Who would have thought Charles Moreton's daughter lived near the docks? Pretty ingenious of the chit. I've been looking in the wrong section of London. Did you not say she teaches harp lessons?"

"Aye," the man with the missing tooth answered, "if yer want a job done, just call Rocco. Now if I ken 'ave my promised pay—"

"Not so fast, Rocco, my dear boy. Not so bloody fast. Tomorrow, you will help me grab the lass." He arched his brow and allowed his smile to expand to the corners of his lips, curling them upward in a meaningful manner. "There might be more in this than the guinea I promised. Archibald Bennet did not say *when* I should be turning his delectable morsel over to him."

Rocco jumped from his chair and leaned across the table toward the dark man. "Guinea! Yer promised me two pounds if I'd find the Moreton girl."

"Two pounds it is if you should help me grab the miss." He paused to fix Rocco with a cold stare. In a voice heavy with threatening menace, he hissed, "And if you should choose another route . . . that is, refuse to cooperate . . . then the fish shall feast on your body."

Even in the shadowed dimness, Rocco's blanch was visible. This did not escape the dark man's notice. He loved men when they were scared.

"What did ye say yer name was?" Rocco asked.

The stranger took another gulp of blue ruin, licked his lips with his tongue, pushed his chair back, and stood. "I didn't. Meet me here tomorrow morning."

Chapter Eight

The earl took his high-crown beaver from the butler and, without the aid of a looking glass, adjusted it on his head of thick black hair. As he reached for his gloves, he said, "You know, Danby, I don't recall ever having spent a more enjoyable three weeks than these last I've spent at Wilderhope. Your service, and that of the other servants, has been superb."

The butler bowed from the waist. "'Tis always a pleasure to have you here, m'lord. And if I should say so myself, the fresh air and sunshine has done you well. You are even more brown than when you came."

"Well, I do enjoy the out-of-doors, and when I settle in with a wife, Danby, my home will be Wilderhope, not London."

The earl smiled; his plan was simple: First he would pay his addresses to Lady Elise. . . .

Suddenly a head of red hair and flashing green eyes danced before his mind's eye, a small nose with a smattering of freckles, an implacable chin.

Can I not stop thinking of her?

It had been three weeks since he and Lady Throckmorton returned to the disreputable lower East End of London where Miss Moreton resided, only to find she had disappeared without a trace.

"She's gone fer good," Miss Sherrill had said. And

they found that to be so. He had begged Lady Throckmorton to forget the chit, but she had became distraught, almost losing all sense of reason. So, to appease her, he had looked for Ruanna Moreton for three days, failing to find even a hint of where she had gone. Finally, over his cousin's protest, he had given up, and he had been genuinely glad when the missive came saying he was needed at Wilderhope. The steward who managed the estate had become ill, and there was a drainage problem. This year, the spring rains had started early.

The time in the county had been a great respite for the earl, and he was sorry to see it end. "Find a footman and have the carriage brought round, Danby. Regretfully, this day I shall return to London. I trust you can handle the household here, with the help of Lizzie and Cook."

The tall, thin butler's smile spread to his eyes, which were already twinkling. "Of course, m'lord, as long as Lizzie knows her place."

The earl chuckled. A struggle for who was in charge, the housekeeper or the butler, had been going on for years at Wilderhope, and Cook often was forced to mediate between the two.

The butler left, and in no time at all, so it seemed to His Lordship, the carriage and four waited out front, a liveried coachman on the box, the tiger on the lead horse.

Dressed in black coat and black trousers, more in the fashion of a country squire than the formal clothes he wore in town, the earl was handed up into the crested carriage by a footman, who gave the driver office to be off.

As they drove off, the earl thanked the footman and settled back to enjoy the wild profusion of wildflowers and heather marching up and down the rolling hills, and the flowering spikes of horse chestnuts standing proudly against a pale sky. In the shallow valley, sun-kissed mist rose up from the earth.

His Lordship sucked in the air's freshness, for he knew

that soon he would be in London, where the air would be thick with smoke from the chimneys, and where the early morning fog hovered until almost midday. He found himself frowning, for he was not looking forward to returning to town. The social whirl of the Season was not to his liking. And although he had some time ago decided to pay his addresses to Lady Elise, and eventually propose marriage, something had held him back, something he had not been able to put his finger on.

A weary sigh escaped the earl's throat. At Wilderhope, having had time to think long on it, he had decided his dallying had lasted long enough. As soon as he arrived home he would go straightaway to call on Lady Elise. There was this need for an heir.

Worry bore down upon the earl with such intensity that the beauty of the countryside passed unnoticed. The horses' hooves throbbed against the hard road, and he hardly heard that. Alone in the carriage, he felt lonely, and he called to the driver to make haste. Against his will, he was thinking of Lady Moreton again, and the shameful stirring that was all too familiar came to keep him company.

This time I will be stronger, he resolved, and summoned his buried anger at Countess Charlotte to bolster the resolve. Lady Moreton, with her rash tongue and lack of decorum, is definitely not the sort of woman I will choose for the mother of the Aynsworth dynastic heir.

He shifted his weight and crossed his long legs. He shook snuff on his wrist and sniffed it, seeking comfort, but finding none. He muttered oaths. Why did the girl persist in disturbing his sleep? At Wilderhope, he had stayed busy in the day, but at night, when he could not forget her soft lips under his, his passionate nature flared, and he had risen from his bed and walked out into the meadows, wading in the lush grass. And there were nights when he rode his stallion at breakneck speed to get her out of his mind . . . and to alleviate the desire that surged through his veins, like a raging river out of control.

"'Tis insane," he said aloud, "especially so since she has a lover in India." The earl recalled that she had unabashedly admitted that she was not pure. "And that's a definite requirement for any woman I would marry."

And Ruanna Moreton, he reasoned, instead of casting her eyes down demurely, as a young girl who is not yet out should do, stares one straight in the face.

"And one is quite put out by it," he said to the empty carriage, scowling when he realized that he had spoken aloud. He could not remember ever before having a conversation with an inanimate object. His mind went to the first redhead.

Of course, in the end, there had been nothing demure and fragile about Countess Charlotte, he reminded himself, and although she had done all the things pleasing to the ton, she had hidden her deviousness behind a facade of gentleness and infallible manners.

Unwillingly, the earl envisioned Ruanna Moreton sitting on the banquette across from him, or better yet, beside him, touching him where he throbbed. He scolded himself for his thoughts, but could not stop them. Like a serpent rearing its head, the thoughts and feelings, it seemed, would be with him for the duration of the journey. He decided that the best course of action was to relax and enjoy his unwanted fantasies.

At least he felt alive, he told himself. For so long, he had felt dead inside. He went to Miss Medcalf for release of his physical need, but he never thought about her; she never made him feel ten feet tall.

Having made the decision not to fight what stubbornly occupied his thoughts, the earl found the time passing quite swiftly. Even so, he was pleased when a posting inn came into view, and, after telling the groom to cool the horses with a walk, and to rub them down afterward, he went to his room on the second floor of the inn and ordered his supper sent up. Although he had been alone all day, he did not crave company. Through the window he could see clouds banked in the west, obscuring the sun as it settled inexorably downward. He hoped it would not rain. It would only delay his journey.

After eating ravenously, he went quickly to bed, and the next morning he rose before dawn to get an early start, with fresh horses. He did not rent his beasts, but kept a stable at the inn between Wilderhope and London.

As the carriage pulled away from the inn, the earl's thoughts again tumbled forward anxiously, and when they were at the edge of town, he glanced about, looking for narrow shoulders holding a mass of red curls.

But the mill of people produced no one with red hair.

Hope, however, died hard in the earl, and when the driver pulled the coach-and-four to an abrupt stop in front of Grosvenor House, he looked anxiously up to see if her small round face was framed by one of the narrow windows. Mayhaps his cousin had found the girl, or mayhaps she had returned of her own volition. He castigated himself vehemently.

Had Miss Moreton wanted to reside in the Aynsworth household, she would not have left the place in the middle of the night, crawling over an iron gate in a fashion that was unheard of for a lady.

"Best I get my mind on Lady Elise and keep it there," he said, and then, "Speaking of the devil . . ."

Coming out of the huge oak doors of Grosvenor House were Lady Elise and her companion, Miss Warren, a woman whom he had met on different occasions and had thought rather unpleasant.

Even before His Lordship could alight, both women curtsied, with a big flourish.

He bounded down onto the ground, bowed over Lady Elise's hand, and brushed it with his lips, after which he honored her companion in the same fashion. "Lady Elise. Miss Warren."

101

"Oh, Lord Julian," Lady Elise tittered, "we called on Lady Throckmorton, but she isn't receiving. It seems that she is ill."

The earl felt Lady Elise's sharp eyes encompass his informal dress, and thought, though he was not sure, that her gaze bespoke disapproval, and he found himself bristling. Quickly, he said, "Please forgive my attire. I have been in the country, at Wilderhope."

"Oh, do not think of apologizing, m'lord. I love the country just as you do. There's a certain smell there that makes me rapturous, and I much prefer the openness the country affords one. Such a sense of freedom!"

The earl's brow shot up quizzically. It had never occurred to him that Lady Elise would favor life in the country over that of fashionable London with all the routs and soirees, the morning calls. It was a pleasant turn.

"I am pleased to hear that," he said. He nodded in the ladies' direction. "I beg your forgiveness, but I must needs inquire of my cousin. With her health being poorly, it is possible that she needs me."

"Oh, m'lord, you are so kind and considerate. Just this morning, I said as much to Miss Warren." She inclined her head toward the woman beside her. "I even went so far as to say that never have I known a kinder man. Did I not, Miss Warren?"

Miss Warren bobbed her head up and down.

The earl's gaze moved approvingly over Lady Elise's dress of thin muslin with tiny blue flowers embroidered on the sleeves and bodice; ribbons of the same color fell from the high waist to the hem, and her fashionable hat held two feathers, which curved around her cheek.

M'lady knows fashion, and she knows the rules of comportment and propriety. She would never leave home without the required companion, and heaven forbid that she should ever run around the streets of London giving music lessons to the lower orders.

When Lady Elise's opulent carriage arrived, a footman

let down the steps and turned to hand the ladies up, all the while mouthing that the visit had not lasted long enough for the carriage to have been taken round back.

The earl chuckled at the footman's barely audible remarks, bade the ladies a gracious good-bye, then turned back to the house. Before he could bang the brass knocker, the doors opened in front of him and Southerland stood in the great central hall.

The butler, after giving a stately bow, reached for the earl's beaver and gloves. "Welcome home, m'lord."

Just then a voice intruded, and the earl turned to it.

"Lord Julian, Lord Julian," Lady Elise called as her carriage started to roll, her head jutted out its window. "You will be at Almack's tonight, will you not? I shall save the first dance for you."

"Perhaps," His Lordship said. His next words were wrought from determination more than from desire. "Yes, yes, I shall be there."

In Lady Elise's carriage, she craned her neck to look back at the earl until the huge doors closed behind him. For a long moment, silence ensued, and then, when they had rounded the corner, Miss Warren set Lady Elise with a scold. "Lady Elise, you are a pattern card of duplicity." She clucked her tongue against the roof of mouth. "Downright scandalous is what you are. You know you hate the country, and I could not help but notice that your lip curled upward when you looked at the earl's country attire. Do you want the man to marry you and stick you in the country?"

Falling back against the squabs, Lady Elise brought her fan up to cover her face as she laughed gleefully. "Oh, Miss Warren, you are a card! Of course I hate the country, you peagoose, and I deplore the earl in those ruffian clothes. But what woman lets a man know exactly how she feels before she is married to him? That is, unless she is stupid."

She laughed some more, and when she could calm herself, she added, "Lord Julian knows all he needs to know *before* we are married."

And there is plenty for him to learn, she thought. As she let her laughter die to a smile, she envisioned His Lordship's countenance when he learned—after they were maried, of course—that she could not give him a precious heir to inherit the earldom, and the Aynsworth wealth. A physician in Paris had taken care of that a few years back, when she had been so unfortunate to become in the family way without benefit of marriage. Since then, the thought of performing what were referred to as wifely duties repelled Lady Elise, and she readily admitted as much to herself. But she wanted to be married. She wanted to be the earl's countess, wear the Aynsworth jewels, and she saw nothing wrong in a little deceitfulness to attain those desires.

His Lordship deserves what he will get from me, she reasoned, as she set her chin in a hard line. I'm no fool; I know why he plans to offer for me—if he ever gets around to it.

And then she wondered with even more disdain if Lady Throckmorton really was indisposed. Or had she just not wanted to receive her and Miss Warren?

After chatting for a moment with Sutherland, the earl, taking the steps two at a time, ascended the stairs to the second floor. He instantly regretted telling Lady Elise he would go this night to Almack's. If Lady Throckmorton were ill, it would be impossible. He would not leave her.

His Lordship managed a smile, for he suspected there was nothing wrong with his cousin, other than not wishing to receive Lady Elise and her companion.

Meeting a footman on the steps, he inquired of Lady Throckmorton's whereabouts.

"She's in 'er bedchambers, in a fit of the vapors," the footman said.

The earl's brows snapped together. This did not bode well, he thought, and hurried down the long hall. At his cousin's door, he banged the brass knocker, then entered before he heard a reply. "Are you ill?" he asked anxiously.

Silence met his inquiry. There was just the rustling of her dress when she moved. From her writing desk she took a folded parchment, which she thrust toward him.

"'Tis another missive from Captain Tidesdale. It seems that on his last voyage from India he had as a passenger a Mr. Witherspoon who very mysteriously kept hinting that he was coming to London to look for a certain redhead. Captain Tidesdale thinks that, taking the man's innuendos into consideration, this Witherspoon is in the employ of Mr. Archibald Bennet, a notorious figure from India, a man whom our Ruanna had been contracted by her father to marry."

A whistle escaped the earl's lips. He wanted to remind his cousin that the young girl was *her* Ruanna, not his. But, seeing the distress in her faded eyes, he thought better of making such a remark and replied as kindly as he knew how, "Did you not say that Captain Tidesdale had thought Miss Moreton was terribly frightened of something or someone when she stowed away on his ship?"

"Yes, that is what he said in his first missive, but Ruanna made no reference to a problem of that nature when we were having tea."

"Nor when she was with me," the earl said.

And she did not appear as if old Lucifer himself could frighten her, he thought.

The earl studied his cousin, who had gone to sit in a rocking chair near the hearth, her cane resting against the chair's arm. Though the room was chilly, there was no fire in the grate. Finally, he said, "I do not mean to scold, Cousin Isadora, but you should have sent to Wilderhope for me right away. When did this come?" He tapped the missive against his open palm.

"Two days after you left. Julian, you were in such a state when you left for Wilderhope, telling me to forget the ungrateful girl, and saying that with her running off the way she had that she was not deserving of a home here."

Lady Throckmorton shook her head worriedly. "Since you had made it plain that you felt that way, I could see no reason to send for you. Suthe and I looked until we gave up."

The earl straightened. "You what? You did not go . . . you know it ain't proper."

"Yes, we did." Lady Throckmorton lifted her sharp chin. "After Lady Moreton disappeared from that odious place of Miss Sherrill's, she never returned, and I am convinced that she never will. I am so thankful that I left the extra pounds in her reticule. At least the poor child will not starve."

"Would you stop calling her a child!" the earl demanded. Pushing at the lock of hair that had fallen onto his forehead, he walked pensively across the room, then back again. He could feel his cousin's eyes on him, blaming him, and he was sure that any moment now she would point her cane at him and accuse: "If you had not been so unkind to the girl . . ."

"Did this Miss Sherrill say anything else about Miss Moreton's leaving?" he asked. "Why she would have left so suddenly, without a word to anyone?"

"Yes, she did. She told me that the very day you and I were there waiting for our Ruanna, the day she left Grosvenor House, there was a man at the chandler's shop inquiring about a certain redhead by the name of Ruanna Moreton. He had a front tooth missing." The old woman's voice broke. "It seems that when Miss Sherrill told the chi . . . girl about the man looking for her that she had to be helped to a chair."

The earl felt his face flush with anger. "Why did Miss Sherrill not apprise us of this the day we returned to the chandler's shop?"

"Because we failed to offer her a monetary reward for any information she would give up. That is what I did when Suthe and I went back there—"

"I forbid you to go there again, Cousin Isadora. Surely you know how unsafe it is. It does not matter that Suthe is with you."

"Then, pray, find her yourself, Julian," the aging woman pleaded, and the earl answered sotto voce, "I will find her, dear cousin. I *will* find her, and when I do, I shall joyfully strangle her."

For his cousin, he managed a smile. Bending over her, he kissed her sunken cheek and gave her thin shoulder an affectionate squeeze. "I will look for her," he promised.

Without going to his chambers to change from his country attire, His Lordship hurried belowstairs, and on to the stables, where, instead of waiting for a carriage to be brought, he went to get one himself, for he wanted the equipage and horses that could travel the swiftest. He helped the stableboy harness two of his best bays. They hitched them to a two-wheeled chaise known for its easy maneuverability. No crest this time.

After discarding his beaver and borrowing a coachman's three-corner, the earl bounded up and took the reins. He thanked the stableboy, then cracked the whip over the horse's back.

The chaise lurched forward and at Mount and South Audley streets feathered the corner on one wheel. Having decided to ask for his solicitor's help, the earl then guided the horse in the direction of Charles Street.

"George is going to adore doing this," the earl mused, and, despite the gravity of the situation, he gave a wry grin.

George, after having been summoned by his butler, stood at his door peering through his quizzing glass at his visitor, who had just stated his business. Not believing his ears, the solicitor blurted out, "M'lord . . . Julian,

107

have you gone queer in the attic?"

"'Tis for Lady Throckmorton. Now, come along. I shall pay you well for your time, and if we are lucky we will find the girl in short shrift."

The earl laughed when George, with obvious reluctance, invited him to wait in the foyer while he went for his hat. "Short shrift. Are you sure?" the solicitor asked as they climbed into the chaise.

But the earl did not promise a second time. As it turned out, he was glad that he didn't, for they were well into their fifth day when, at Holles Street at Oxford, they sat in the chaise and stared at a gel who stood in a wash of sunshine, her face pressed against Boosey and Hawks' glass storefront. Beyond the glass was a magnificent seven-pedal harp, which had caught the earl's eye in the first place.

The earl and his solicitor had been arguing. Finally, George said with a goodly amount of agitation, "That gel does not resemble your Miss Moreton in any way, Lord Julian." Then he further accused, "I believe you've taken leave of your senses."

"Oddso. But you'll have to admit that she's the first gel I've been in the least inclined to identify as our runaway. For the life of me, I cannot explain it, but there's something vaguely familiar . . ."

"You've only seen her back. There's not a red hair showing—"

"She's wearing a bonnet," the earl snapped.

"And the bright dress . . . with patches. When I saw your Miss Moreton in the library at Grosvenor House, she was dressed in a much more drab manner."

"I burned that one."

The solicitor gave the earl an incredulous glance and said, "Little wonder she ran away."

After that, a long silence ensued. George could be right, the earl thought. Perhaps the girl standing there was an apparition; perhaps the harp did not exist except in his imagination. They had been searching too long, and in such awful places.

By day, they had combed the streets, starting near the docks and working their way toward the center of town. At night, they had searched for the man with the missing tooth, in coffeehouses, in disreputable gaming places, and they had gone to cockfights, and to see pugilists batter each other senseless.

Last night, over George's strong protests, they had descended into the Coal Hole, and then into the notorious Cyder Cellars in Maiden Lane, to carouse with the lowest dregs of the underworld.

"With your legal brain, George," the earl had said, "when we find the man with the missing tooth, you should be able to worm out of him where Ruanna Moreton is living."

Now, as they watched the girl staring at the harp, the earl sensed the solicitor's impatience, and the solicitor made it abundantly clear when he said, "By damn, Julian, you ask too much of a man. Let the chit go. No offense, m'lord, but our clothes are beginning to smell."

Once, George had suggested they purchase fresh clothing to wear, but the earl thought they fit better into the environment in which they were searching in clothes that were dirty and smelly.

"Let's go back to the sane world," George suggested, and when his words were answered with a resounding no he added a little more forcefully, "Damn you, Julian, this is outside of enough." Again, he said, "Let the chit go, I say."

The earl's succinct answer came quickly. "I can't. Besides, you are being well compensated for your time, are you not?"

"Of course I'm being well paid, to say nothing of the expensive wines and delectable food you've afforded me, the best these cheap places have to offer."

The solicitor cocked a quizzical eyebrow, eyed the earl steadily for a moment, then asked, "Codswallop, why can't you let her go?"

Lord Julian pulled in a deep breath. "I cannot say why, George, because I don't know. Other than our finding Miss Moreton means a great deal to Lady Throckmorton. Almost life and death it appears. Her attachment to the chit seems a bit abnormal, but who am I to say? Mayhaps the old woman is just so terribly lonely in Grosvenor House."

George knew about Lady Throckmorton's raising the earl, and he understood why His Lordship felt deeply indebted to his old cousin. He shook his head.

"I owe her," Lord Julian said. "Now that she's old I cannot do less for her than what she did for me. 'Twould not be honorable."

The earl did not mention that, while at Wilderhope, visions of the green-eyed temptress haunted his sleep so much that he could not sleep, that, against his will, he had wanted to hold her . . . and make love to her. He was ashamed of his thoughts, but they were there anyway.

Passion does not signify, he thought, wishing the desire was not so strong. Passion dies; but passion is not love.

"Your loyalty to Lady Throckmorton is commendable," George said, and then he laughed. "I used to think your heart was made of flint. But aside from wanting to please your cousin, are you sure you don't have an ache in your loins for the redhead? I seem to remember another redhead. . . ."

The earl felt his face flush with guilt he was not going to admit. Instead, he did quite the opposite: "George, if it were left to me, I would turn this chaise around and beat it back to Grosvenor House, or to Wilderhope. I have no desire to have my life disrupted as it was once, and you know to what I allude. Miss Moreton is unwelcome trouble, but I've decided that there's a way out of this bumble broth."

"Odso! And what is that?"

"I have just recently learned that Lady Elise prefers living in the country. After we are wed, we will reside at

110

Wilderhope and leave Grosvenor House to my cousin and her new charge, this Ruanna Moreton. She can be the chit's chaperone, launch her into society . . . that is, if I can find her before Archibald Bennet's henchmen cart her off to India. I'm beginning to wonder—"

George's head snapped up. "Julian, the girl staring into the window is taking her leave. Do you still think—"

"Who else would be staring at a harp?" In a flash, like a leopard springing from its perch, the earl sprang down onto the street, and he swiftly closed the distance between him and the girl, taking her by the arm. "Miss Moreton, Miss Moreton."

The arm was jerked from his grasp, fiercely. The gel turned; fright leapt from her eyes. For a moment, the earl stared into a delicate, finely sculpted face, framed by a hideous bonnet and tiny wisps of red hair. Then, something akin to a ball peen hammer hit him squarely between the eyes.

The three-corner was knocked from his head, he felt his big frame buckle and start to slide, and then darkness, like a great spiraling wave, swallowed him up. The last thing he remembered was swearing loudly.

Stunned and momentarily unable to move, George watched the gel who had brought His Lordship down disappear into a dark alley with the speed of a scared deer. Shaking himself, he climbed down out of the chaise and went to bend over the earl. Letting loose Lord Julian's collar, he told the gathering crowd, "Stand back, give His Lordship air."

A woman wearing a bright red dress and carrying a bucket of water pushed through the crowd. With perfect aim she sloshed the water into the earl's face. "Faugh! The upper orders!" She turned and left, and George lost sight of her as quickly as he had gained it.

The earl spat, sputtered, coughed, and opened his eyes. Water dripped from his hair onto his face, and from his side-whiskers onto the shoulders of his black coat, soaking through and chilling him. Languorously, he struggled to his feet and, by holding to George's shoulder, stood erect, all six foot, two inches. When the crowd cheered, he attempted a bow, but swayed precariously.

A little boy picked up his hat and handed it to him. The earl managed a wan smile, took the hat, and put it back on his head, while George fumbled in his breeches pocket for a coin to place in the boy's outstretched palm.

"Thank you," the earl said to the little boy, and thanked his solicitor as well. Then his hand went to his forehead, which throbbed with great intensity, and when he felt a knot the size of a goose egg between his eyes, uncontrollable rage engulfed him. So, turning to George, the fifth earl of Wendsleydale exploded in grand fashion: "The devil take her, George. Let's go home. I hope I never see the rag-mannered wench again."

Knowing no permanent damage had been done to His Lordship, the solicitor smiled and helped the earl to the waiting chaise.

Chapter Nine

The tangled sheet gave evidence of Ruanna's restless night. Although she had been so frightened that she had not seen the face of the man who had grabbed her am— she only knew he looked unkempt and that stubble grew on his face—she was sure it was the same man who had been at the chandler's shop asking Miss Sherrill about her. She wished that he had smiled so she could have seen if a tooth was missing.

A chill played hopscotch up and down Ruanna's spine; she wanted to pull the sheet over herself, to hide from the man who was trying to kidnap her. Second thoughts ran through her mind about the wisdom of her flight from Grosvenor House, where a footman stood at every corner and a mountainous coachman rode on the box of the earl's crested carriage.

So what if Mr. High-and-Mighty did call me a beggar? she asked herself. Archibald Bennet's man, or men, would surely hesitate to search her out if she shared the household of a titled man of the earl's eminence.

Ruanna pushed herself up and leaned against the iron rungs that constituted the head of the bed. Pulling her legs up to her chest and wrapping her arms around them, she rested her head on her knees. Sitting thus, she stared out into the room, which, in her new dwelling in Cheapside, was more than a narrow cot shoved against the wall. Here she had two windows, a full bed, a dresser with a looking glass that was not cracked, a small round table, two chairs, and a chipped porcelain chamber pot.

Noticing the time, Ruanna slipped out of bed and went quickly to strike a lucifer and hold it to the chips of wood, which flamed quickly. In a short time, steam spilled out of the spout of the teakettle that hung over the fire.

Determinedly, Ruanna hummed a happy tune as she heated a chunk of buttered bread in a skillet. Pungent smells filled the room, and she sucked them deep into her lungs as she ate heartily and drank the tea she had made.

But worrisome thoughts persistently invaded her mind, and savage pains of loss moved through her in endless waves when she thought of her home in India. She longed to return to the warm cocoon of familial love she once knew, where she was not afraid, where she had felt loved. But she could not go back. Her Mama was not there, and her Papa had changed. Archibald Bennet was there.

Ruanna turned her thoughts to little Jeremy, for thinking of his big brown eyes under a thick mop of dark hair, his little round face that seldom smiled, and his extraordinary talent manifested into the one happy thing in her life. She could envision his performance at King's Theatre, the audience awed into silence as beneath his small hands notes dipped and rose, hovering at last into silence. It was a dream, of course, but did not dreams come before things happened?

Since her windfall from Lady Throckmorton, she had bought Bochsa's method and other masterful arrangements, but she knew that Jeremy's talent was far too great to be limited to her teaching. She must needs bring him to the great harp master's attention.

As Ruanna washed herself and dressed in the dun brown coat and baggy trousers—in case Archibald Bennet's man was lurking about outside, looking for a girl in a dress with patches—she pondered long on her incredible dream, and then an ingenious thought came to her. Just recently she had read that Bochsa had been obliged to leave Paris, where he had been court harpist for Napoleon. He had fled to London to avoid arrest for forgery, the paper had said, and was now professor of harp at the newly founded Royal Academy of Music.

Ruanna felt her heart quicken. She would wear her new dress and go call on him, and perhaps she would purchase a new bonnet.

"See there, everything starts with a dream," she told the silent room. Filled with renewed hope, Ruanna considered sending Bochsa a missive, then thought better of it. Any day she might have to move, and if he should answer, she would not receive the message. "No, 'tis best I go in person and speak with him."

Ruluctantly, she donned the boy's shoes with wide buckles, and the boy's cap. She looked longingly at her new dress with patches that hung on a nail, but warned herself not to let vanity push her into being stupid.

How lovely it would be to live with Lady Throckmorton and visit the modistes, and the milliners, as the old lady had planned. If it were not for the hateful earl . . .

"A pox on the mighty earl of Wendsleydale," she said as she pushed his brooding countenance from her mind and closed the door behind her. As quickly as possible she melded into the crowd. As always, morning, noon, or night, the streets were jammed with people. The morning fog hovered close to the ground, holding the smoke from the chimneys with it. The acrid smell assailed her nostrils, and already the ballad singers were hawking their sad news. Carts filled with merchandise, most often pushed by children, maneuvered past her, and the Charlies were calling out the time.

With plenty of time before her first lesson, Ruanna decided to take an alternate route. A longer walk would be pleasant, she concluded, and started out, whistling, while her eyes darted about for a man with a missing front tooth. In her pocket was her weapon, the leather strap secured about her right wrist.

Before she had gone far, Ruanna saw in front of her a crowd so large that a hackney that was trying to pass could not do so. In the middle of the street was a newly constructed platform, which she immediately recognized as a hustings, on which local elections were held. She stared with interest at the three splendidly dressed men in long-tailed coats, long, leg-hugging trousers, and high-crown beavers who stood on the platform.

Filled with curiosity, Ruanna drew nearer and watched as a well-dressed man—a property owner of course, else he would not be voting—climbed the steps of the platform to write something into what she presumed to be the election book, then retreated down the steps.

One of the gentlemen on the platform, the one who Ruanna thought was the election judge, placed his quizzing glass to his eyes and bent over the book, after which he called out the voter's name, also the name of the candidate for whom he had voted. A roar went up from the crowd, one roar angry, the other happy, and louder. Arms waved the air.

No doubt paid supporters, Ruanna surmised, and it did not take long for her to discern that each candidate had his supporters on *his* side of the platform. She moved closer and instantly regretted it, for she found herself pressed into the crowd without an avenue of escape. Now, the deafening roars lasted as long as five minutes.

Things, however, went on in orderly fashion, if not quietly, until one candidate outdistanced the other in the number of votes, and then grumbling started.

Wanting nothing more than to escape, Ruanna called out, "Pray, let me through."

When her plea was ignored, she, like the others, shouted, until a big hand clamped over her mouth, smothering her as well as silencing her. Above her head, a man's gruff voice swore terrible words. She bit into his hand, then sputtered and spat, swiping where the dirty hand had been.

The swear words grew louder, but died to a groan as the man edged away from her.

116

"That should teach you not to attack a lady," she called to him, but the man did not turn to look back. She did hear a snort and the word "lady" uttered in a disparaging tone.

Another man cast his vote and started back down the steps, and when he reached the bottom, he was set upon by the opposing faction. Amid shouts, curses, and exchanged blows, Ruanna again made another futile effort to escape, only to get knocked to the ground and trampled under booted feet. She screamed for someone to help, but no one did. There was no air, and she felt that she would die. Her Papa's face floated before her eyes, and she felt guilt for having left him. She thought about her mother. In her mind's eye, she saw her beautiful face. Ruanna even wished for the earl. With all his gruffness, he was large and powerful; he could save her.

Then, a hand reached down to yank at the collar of Ruanna's coat. She thought she was dreaming when she heard a small voice saying, "Yer dirty bastards, let the girl up."

The hand gave another yank, and Ruanna was miraculously on her feet. She felt the small hand slip over hers, holding tightly, and when a Charlie commanded that the crowd move, without a word, he pulled her along.

"Move yer arses along now. Move along, 'tis off to Newgate fer the likes of yer," the Charlie said.

At the moment, being arrested seemed better to Ruanna than being trampled to death, but later, in a cold, below-ground cell, she thought that to have been trampled to death might have been better. The cell was so small that everyone had to stand, and the air was stupefying, the stench of unwashed bodies offensive. They shoved each other, and quarreled.

Ruanna and the little boy clung to each other, and soon the others began to leave, as their names were called. Fines had been paid, the little boy told her, by the politician for whom they had been hired to cheer and to fight.

117

When the cell was empty, with the exception of the ragamuffin and herself, Ruanna inquired as to his name and was told that it was Jim.

"Jim what?"

"Jest Jim," he answered testily.

"Are you the one who pulled me to my feet?" she asked, knowing that it was.

"And what if 'twas me?"

Ruanna smiled at him, for he looked as if he would rather die than to admit he would do a kind thing like that. But he did not deny it, and she could not stop the tears that brimmed her eyes. He was so small, and so frail. And so silent. She watched as he hunkered down on a straw pallet in the corner and pulled a dirty quilt over his slight frame. She went to sit beside him and pulled him close to lend warmth from her body. From down the narrow hall outside the cell came sounds of wailing and crying, and people cursing.

Amid all this, Ruanna worried about her students. What would they think when she did not come to teach them, especially little Jeremy?

Three days passed, with the speed of a snail climbing a mountain, and it became clear to Ruanna that she and the boy had been forgotten. Gaol fever would be next, or the gallows. Londoners loved to see people hanged.

She asked Jim, "Should they not take us before a judge, so we can tell His Honor that we aren't guilty, that we were just innocent bystanders?"

The boy's derisive look said more than words. "Leddy, are you stupid? A wanwit, here-and-thereian? There ain't no innocents in Newgate, less you got money. How'd you think them others got out? Paid out, that's 'ow, by the jackanapes they be fightin' for. How much blunt you got on you?"

"I had thought of that, but with us being innocent bystanders . . ."

Ruanna stopped. What would it avail to proclaim their innocence? As Jim had so adequately informed her—

there ain't no innocents in Newgate.

She was wearing a hand-sewn sack containing a few shillings strapped around her waist. Now, opening her coat, she reached under her skirt, removed the sack, and counted, "One guinea and six pence." She looked at Jim.

The little boy laughed. Obviously he knows more about what it takes to buy freedom that I do, Ruanna thought, and she noted the bitterness, the hardness, and the sad oldness in the little pickpocket's laughter. His brown eyes, too big for his little face, were void of tears, and she wondered if he had ever cried in the whole of his life.

"Is'at all?" he asked. He pulled a money pouch out of the top of a ragged, dirty-white stocking. His other stocking was black, with just as many holes, and his legs below his knee breeches were so thin they looked like matchsticks. His shoes, worn to shreds, were tied to his feet with twine.

"Where did you get that?" she exclaimed.

"Why do you think I was in that crowd, leddy? Not fer me health. It's just that I got caught in the crunch the same as yer." He counted his coins. "More'n yer."

Reaching out, Jim offered the coins to Ruanna. "Here, yer take'em. I don't mind stayin' here so bad. They'll let me out when they tired ah feedin' me. It'll be a rest against thet out there."

The boy inclined his little head toward a windowless wall, but Ruanna knew he meant out there where he had to steal to survive. "Jimmy! Are you aware they hang people for stealing? You stole this, didn't you?"

"Leddy, don't look a gift horse in the mouth. Call a guard. And stop callin' me Jimmy. Me name's Jim!"

Ruanna's cellmate returned to the straw pallet, again pulling the quilt over his frail body. This time, he turned his face to the wall.

As Ruanna fought back the tears, a plan took shape in her mind, a plan formed from desperation. "Guard!" she called loudly and when no one came, she rattled the iron

119

bars on the cell and screamed at the top of her lungs.

At last a guard appeared. "What's yer wont?" he demanded, and not kindly. He added in a threatening tone, "Ye'd best be quiet."

With more bravado than she felt, Ruanna looked the stocky, broad-chested guard straight in the eye, thinking he looked like a pugilist, though she had never seen one. But he looked like pictures she had seen. "My cousin is the fifth earl of Wendsleydale and Lord of Wilderhope in Shropshire. If he only knew my brother and I got caught up in that terrible mess, which we had nothing to do with, and if he knew we were in Newgate, he would be most happy to pay any fine for me and my brother."

She stopped to give him another long look. "If he just knew we were here," she repeated. "And he would be most generous with you, for there is no limit to his enormous wealth. Would you be so kind as to—"

Ruanna's words were drowned out by raucous laughter. She felt the guard looking her up and down, his gaze blatantly raking over her boy's attire, the cap drooping over her eyes, her baggy breeches.

"If yer wants me to believe thet, stand on yer head. If yer cousin's a earl, saints help us!"

"But 'tis true," Ruanna implored. "Give me a piece of paper and a quill, and I shall prove it to you. He resides in Grosvenor House in Grosvenor Square and, as I said, he will reward you something beautifully, perhaps even give you a place in his employ if you act favorably toward me and my brother here."

Ruanna nodded her head toward the little pickpocket. "His last name is Moreton, the same as mine, Jim Moreton. The earl of Wendsleydale is very fond of all his relatives, and we are dear cousins of his."

She crossed her fingers behind her back for the lie and smiled demurely when the guard took the folded piece of paper . . . and the coins she pressed to his palm.

"His Lordship will be pleased," she said when the guard, without a word, turned to leave. The sound of his footsteps on the stone floor echoed ominously against the cold, damp walls. Ruanna watched after him and, dropping her haughtiness, whispered a prayer that she had not seen the last of him.

But straightaway, he returned and handed through the bars a piece of paper and a quill. He held the inkwell in his hand.

Ruanna reached through the bars and dipped the quill into the ink. She tried to still her shaking hand as she scribbled a plea to the earl's kind mercy. Lady Throckmorton did say he had a soft core, she thought prayerfully.

When she was through, she folded the missive and pressed it into the guard's hand, along with another coin. "Remember, His Lordship will reward you greatly for your kindness," she called after him. "The earl will be ever so glad to right the horrendous mistake that was made when we were wrongly arrested."

Two hours later, Ruanna was saying to the fifth earl of Wendsleydale, whose swollen forehead was a goosish blue, "I will not go without him." Ruanna inclined her head toward Jim. She wondered if he had slept through all her efforts to get them set free.

"And who is the him you speak of?" the earl asked.

"Jim. He's a pickpocket."

Fury showed in the earl's scalding gaze. "Now listen here, Miss Moreton, don't flummer me. You're in no position to bargain. It is only due to my love for Lady Throckmorton that I am here. Who, besides myself, would come to this dreadful place to save you after being laid low by a steel ball between my eyes, placed there so tenderly by no one but you?"

Ruanna shuddered, but hid her fear behind a most serious look of apology. "I told you I was sorry about that! I was so intent on looking at the beautiful harp that when you took my arm, I thought you were one of

Archibald Bennet's men, whose intent is to take me back to India. If only I had taken time to look you in the face before hitting you."

When the earl first stomped into Newgate, Ruanna had explained to him why she had left India, and that someone planned to kidnap her and take her back there to marry Archibald Bennet. "I should have told you right off when I first came to Grosvenor House," she said.

The earl did not tell her that Captain Tidesdale had already warned Lady Throckmorton that what Ruanna had just told him might be so. He would leave the telling to his cousin.

Now, in a voice asking for understanding, she told him, "Archibald Bennet is dreadful man."

And she said again, "I'm ever so sorry I hit you. If only I had not stopped to admire the harp . . . if only I had looked at you and recognized your kind face, m'lord. But there was stubble growing all over your face, not like you are now, your side-whiskers neatly trimmed and pomaded. And why were you wearing a three-corner?" And then she added, "Little wonder I didn't recognize you," now satisfied with her argument.

"I looked unkempt because I'd been looking for you," the earl retorted. He shook his dark head. He would *not* take a pickpocket into his household.

But do I dare return to Lady Throckmorton without Ruanna Moreton? "What a coil," he said aloud.

As His Lordship paced, turning round and round in the small cell, he argued, which was entirely beneath his dignity, "There has to be another way."

"Then leave us both," Ruann said.

"Mayhaps, if you are returned to India, your lover can save you from Bennet."

The earl watched closely for Ruanna's reaction. In truth, he reluctantly admitted to himself, he wanted her to deny she had a lover. No lady of quality would admit to having a lover. But when did Ruanna Moreton lay claim to being a lady of quality?

122

"Mayhaps," Ruanna said, becoming silent after that.

The earl continued his agitated pacing. "And what is this nonsense you mentioned in your intelligence about wanting to work if you return to Grosvenor House? And Jimmy as well?"

"Jim" said the boy on the pallet, his face still to the wall.

"Jim," the earl corrected, and snorted. How was it that he was in a prison cell being manipulated by a hoyden from the slums of London? he asked himself. Then he stopped pacing long enough to stare incredulously at his attacker. Her small chin was set in an absurd, implacable line, and her eyes were on some inanimate object across the cell. He had an almost uncontrollable desire to shake her, or better yet, to beat her. Why had he responded to her summons? She should rot in Newgate. He started to speak. "I—"

"If I go, Jim goes," Ruanna said. And then she added in a soft tone, "He saved my life."

The earl glared at her for a considerable length of time before saying, "I'll be back shortly." Then, he called to the guard.

Before the guard came, Ruanna, out of the corner of her eye, stole a glance into His Lordship's strong, tanned face, seeing an angry frown above dark-lashed, fathomless blue eyes. She took a deep breath before telling him, "I said I would be happy to return to your household if you would assign chores for me to do, so I could earn my keep. I am *not* a beggar."

The earl did not answer. He had no choice but to agree to her terms, but only on the surface, and he would take the boy until he could think of some way to get rid of him, or, better yet, until such time as the little pickpocket would run away. "All right, we will take the boy," he said laconically.

Jim at last turned over and looked at the earl. "Don't bother doing favors for me."

"Be quiet," the earl ordered.

"Thank you, m'lord," Ruanna said in a dulcet tone. Then, cringing, she made her final request: "The . . . the guard, the kind man who brought the missive to you . . . I promised him a place in your employ. Could you—"

"No!" the earl exploded, then roared even louder, "Where is that guard?"

To Ruanna, His Lordship sounded like a ferocious lion . . . and she had not yet told him that, along with the chores at Grosvenor House, she planned to continue giving harp lessons to the lower orders.

Much later, after making the rounds to explain to Ruanna's students why she had missed their lessons, the Wendsleydale carriage, drawn by four glossy, high-stepping horses draped in trappings of black and gold, bounced along cobbled streets toward Grosvenor Square. On the box sat Suthe and, beside him, the guard from Newgate.

Inside the carriage, the earl, his eyes focused straight ahead, sat in brooding silence, his rigid back pressed against red velvet squabs, his chin lowered to touch his high collar points.

Sitting beside the earl was Ruanna, holding her knapsack, which they had gone by her place in Cheapside to fetch.

The earl glanced down at her and wondered where she had acquired that dreadful cap. With her face half-hidden, it was difficult to discern whether she was a boy or a girl. And those awful clothes!

The pickpocket, his eyes wide, sat on the other banquette. He stared openly at the gaslights, the store windows, the fine homes of the West End. "Sweet Jesus," he exclaimed.

A motley bunch, the earl concluded, wishing, as they neared Grosvenor Square, the ground would open and swallow them up. He looked at his watch and groaned. It was nearing five o'clock, the fashionable time when members of high society made their rendezvous in the park—to see and be seen.

Men mounted on magnificent horses raced by, and opulent carriages, all bearing fashionably dressed beauties of the ton, were entering the park through the marble arches. And there were the dressed-to-the-nines demireps, the women who offered their services for the monetary benefit they could derive from having favored a lord. Or if they were lucky, an earl, or a duke.

Meeting the Wendsleydale carriage was a high-wheeled stanhope, carrying the duchesses of Rutland, Argyll, and Gordon.

Hoping to pass unnoticed, the earl tipped his hat and nodded, then cringed as the duchesses craned their necks to look inside his carriage. For them to see Ruanna in such a state of dress was unthinkable. Later, when and *if* she could be made presentable, she would join the squeeze to ride in her own carriage. Having little else to do, the ladies of the ton thrived on gossip, and Ruanna's reputation would be in shambles if she should be seen wearing breeches and a boy's cap.

And heaven forbid should they learn she had been in Newgate.

The stanhope passed on, and the earl prayed that the duchesses' eyesight was bad, and just as he started to breathe a sigh of relief, a superbly appointed carriage, attended by a powdered footman wearing plush knee breeches and a gold-laced coat and by a bewigged coachman wearing a three-cornered hat and French gloves, pulled alongside his carriage.

Lady Elise, with her head protruding from the window, waved a white handkerchief and smiled into the earl's face. Miss Warren, her companion, sat beside Lady Elise. She, too, was smiling.

The earl reluctantly called to Suthe to stop the carriage, then tipped his beaver. "M'ladies."

"M'lord, where have you been?" asked Lady Elise.

125

"You naughty boy! You promised to come to Almack's, and you failed to appear. After I had saved *all* my dances for you."

"I'm sorry, Lady Elise," the earl said. "Please forgive me. I was as disappointed with the turn of events, but I assure you that it could not be helped." The earl looked at Ruanna, the culprit who had been the source of both his and the Lady Elise's disappointment. If he hadn't been out searching for the chit, he would have been at Almack's as he'd promised the woman for whom he planned to offer.

That he had not wanted to go to Almack's had completely escaped his memory.

Miss Warren, as the duchesses had done, craned her neck to look into the earl's carriage. "Who are the young boys you have with you, m'lord, chimney climbers Lady Throckmorton wishes to save? Or new gardeners? Stableboys? Surely a footman could have fetched them."

Ruanna felt fire spark her green eyes. She resented being called a boy, and she especially resented being referred to as a chimney climber, or a gardener, or a stable boy. She was an accomplished musician! Besides, she had never seen such outrageous flirting on the part of women who were supposed to be ladies of quality. Reaching up, she removed her cap and let fly her short-cropped red curls before saying, "I'm Lady Ruanna Moreton, and this is Jim, he's a—"

The earl let out an audible groan. "Good day, ladies," he said quickly.

Gasping, Lady Elise covered her mouth, and her eyes widened.

"Cry off, leddy," Jim said.

"Watch your tongue," the earl ordered. He glared at Jim and, in a loud voice, gave the coachman office to start the horses. "Lud, Suthe, don't drive as if we are going to a funeral. Pray, put them to their bits."

The carriage lurched forward, but not before the earl caught the look of disapproval and disgust that had so

126

quickly spread across both ladies' faces.

"Blister it," he said, sotto voce, and when they reached Grosvenor House, he unceremoniously jerked the coach door open and alighted without the aid of a footman.

Leaving Ruanna to be helped by the footman, the earl bounded up the steps and banged loudly on the massive doors with the brass knocker, and when the startled butler appeared, His Lordship stepped back to reveal Ruanna and Jim.

"Take them to Lady Throckmorton, Sutherland. Ask her to find decent clothes for Miss Moreton, and send the boy to the stables. And have both of them scrubbed and deloused. And, pray, see that Miss Moreton's bedchamber is locked tonight. If she leaves again, I will not look for her."

"Yes, m'lord," the butler said, bowing, his small eyes looking down his nose at Ruanna and the ragamuffin by her side.

Ruanna moved closer to the little boy, just waiting for the butler to make a disparaging remark. But when the staid butler looked away, acting as if they weren't there, she turned her attention to the earl.

"M'lord . . ." She wanted to tell him Jim was too young to work in the stables, but had she done so, she would have been talking to his back. Already he had turned and was headed back to the carriage. She called after him, "M'lord, you must listen. Jim is too young for the stables. He might be misused in some vulgar fashion. . . ."

Whirling around, the earl came back to stare into Ruanna's upturned face. Her lashes dropped to cover her eyes, and he wondered if she were flirting with him, or if she had something in her eyes.

What in tarnation has she done to her hair?

In truth, Ruanna was scared to death.

"Where'd you learn about such things?" the earl demanded. He took Ruanna by the shoulders to shake

127

her, then stopped abruptly, letting his hands fall. His gaze fell on her softly curved lips. "Where?" he barked.

Ruanna lifted her chin. "Is it because I am a *mere woman* that I should not know about such goings-on in the world, Your Lordship?"

"You demme sure ain't no child," the earl retorted, again turning toward the waiting carriage.

"Can Jim stay with me?" Ruanna called after him.

"As you like! As you like!" His Lordship roared as he flung himself up into the carriage. "By the stables, Suthe, to leave the man on the box. I assign him to you. then take me to Miss Medcalf's. At least there, *I* will be in charge."

A chortle drifted back from the big coachman.

Chapter Ten

Katrina Medcalf was the perfect courtesan. She was of good humor, never made undue demands upon him, and was eager to please.

These things the fifth earl of Wendsleydale told himself as the carriage bounced along on the way to her house. Although she was not embraced by the ton, she afforded him the companioship he felt the need for; lovely dinners in her home, card parties to which she invited many of his friends, and of course he was always welcome to visit her boudoir.

And that is all I need.

His Lordship smiled in anticipation as the carriage swayed rhythmically; the horses' hooves pounded against the cobbles in a high-stepping manner. The pleasant sound did much to soothe his tattered nerves, and he wished that he did not have to think of Ruanna Moreton, now ensconced, probably forever, in Grosvenor House. He could visualize his cousin clucking over the young girl, who was so independent in nature she would turn any man off. Women were *supposed* to be subservient to a man; *he* was in charge.

Thoughts of the little pickpocket Ruanna had adopted as her brother made the earl cringe.

Then thoughts of Lady Elsie invaded the earl's already troubled mind, which was in a whirl.

"Gad, she is beautiful," he said aloud, meaning Katrina, not Lady Elise.

Always, in preparation for his visit to Katrina, he let his mind dwell upon her beauty, her skin the color of warmest honey, dark brown hair that swirled around delicate narrow shoulders, eyes huge and dark and laced with shades of gold, giving them a soft, demure look.

Demure! Immediately, without conscious provocation, Ruanna Moreton returned to the earl's mind. The girl did not know the meaning of the word. Fuming, he crossed his legs and scooted around in his seat. What a spectacle she had made of herself when they met Lady Elise near Hyde Park.

The earl felt his face burn from the mortification of the encounter; yet, he found himself smiling. A flush of warmth suffused his body.

This sudden yearning embarrassed His Lordship, and he was sure that the answer was a simple one. She had awakened in him that youthful passion he'd felt for Countess Charlotte. He remembered all too well that passionate time, his infatuation with the she-devil, and the pain. . . . It did not bear thinking of. He had not succumbed to such weakness since. Nor would he, he resolved, as errant thoughts chased through his mind. His Lordship felt the dark, chilly emptiness he had endured upon learning of the first redhead's deceit seep inward. Swallowing the angry words that lay silent in his being, the earl forced his thoughts back to his mistress.

Katrina had the most incredibly thick lashes, black as night, which fluttered coyly when she looked at him. And there was her sweet little welcoming smile. . . .

Usually the earl felt his need rising when he thought in such a vein, but today, it was not working, and he laid it to the trouble caused by Ruanna Moreton.

Pulling in a deep breath and letting it out in the form of a sigh, His Lordship sank deeper into the soft squabs of the carriage. "Demme," he said, frowning.

Ruanna Moreton would have to be made presentable to

the ton—for Lady Throckmorton's sake. But he did not delude himself. The task would be formidable, undoing years of the wrong training.

How could the granddaughter of a countess be reared as such an infernal gudgeon? And why did he get stuck with her?

With all Lady Throckmorton's fussing about the plight of the less fortunate, never had he seen her actually shed tears and go into such a state of the mopes as she had over this girl. As His Lordship mulled it over, he concluded that surely Lady Throckmorton, in her dotage, desired the excitement of launching a young girl into society. Had not Ruanna Moreton suggested that might be the case?

When His Lordship recalled the infinitely sad look on his cousin's countenance when Ruanna had run away, and the same look again when she'd received the missive from Captain Tidesdale saying that Miss Moreton might be in danger from a man who had sailed on his ship, he vowed, "Well, on the life of the prince regent himself, I will see that the young girl does not disappoint my cousin."

Quite a formidable task, he thought, and he wondered how he would accomplish it. He said aloud, "By Gad, the defiant redhead will learn the rules of comportment and propriety if I have to teach them to her myself."

As far as the little pickpocket was concerned, the earl decided not to think about him. However, he would offer up a prayer of supplication, asking that the ragamuffin run away.

The carriage made a quick corner, shaking the earl from his reverie. He caught the rope to steady himself, and, for the first time, noticed that pink light and gray shadows danced across the deep blue of the carriage's upholstery and the dark breeches he wore, and that the pale sky had taken on a rosy patina. He took notice of how far they had come and was pleased to see they were nearing the street where Katrina lived, in a house which

131

he had purchased for her some three years ago.

The tall, slender houses were pleasant to look upon, and the location top-notch; near, but not in, Mayfair. Though much smaller than Grosvenor House, his mistress's house was an elegant dwelling, and Katrina herself had added much of her expertise to its decor. He took a goodly amount of pride in the residence, as well as in Katrina, and he was glad that society did not frown upon a man having a mistress.

He thought about how many times other members of the peerage, well-financed and with deep pockets, made such remarks as to let him know he was the envy of every virile male within miles of London. Yet, those same gentlemen were not willing to pay the price for a top-notch mistress. They often placed their "ladies" in mean dwellings with hardly the necessities of life, much less any of the nicer amenities.

When the carriage lurched to a stop in front of Katrina Medcalf's house, the earl alighted sprightly, taking long steps to the front door.

As fit as a fiddle, an onlooker might say when looking upon the earl, but His Lordship knew that his appearance was deceiving, for he did not feel as he looked. A turbulence raged within him. At the door, he rapped loudly.

Immediately the door swung open, and a liveried butler bowed, addressed the earl as m'lord, then announced: "The earl of Wendsleydale, ma'am." After which he disappeared as quickly as he had appeared.

Katrina has well-trained servants, as she herself is well trained in her trade.

Like a silver bell, her voice trilled across the room, and he smiled as she took quick little steps to cannon herself into his arms.

"M'lord, I have missed you sooo much," she said. Without a word of reproach for his long absence, she lifted her face to his.

For all her effort, the earl could not offer more than a perfunctory kiss. He gently put her aside and strode to

132

the sideboard, where he poured himself a hefty drink from one of the fine crystal decanters filled with his favorite spirits.

"May I fix you a drink, Katrina?" he asked, turning back to look at her. He did not miss the pained look in her eyes, but she smiled sweetly.

"Thank you, no, Lord Julian. I think I shall concentrate on you this day."

Miss Medcalf's dulcet voice made the earl cringe. Why? he asked himself. Codswallop, always before, he had thought her subservient manner toward him appealing.

"You are very kind, Katrina," he said, and then he forcibly focused his attention on her seductive gown of pink silver-shot India gauze, no doubt a creation from Madame Dumosse's shop.

When he had met Katrina, a dancer in the theater, she had not had a feather to fly with. Perhaps that was why she was so appreciative of him, he thought. He had never limited her spending.

"Tell me about yourself, m'lord. What has the wonderful earl of Wendsleydale been up to of late?" she asked.

The earl moved to stand by a long, narrow window, letting his gaze linger on the garden below. While sipping from his drink, he told her about Ruanna Moreton, alluding to her as Lady Throckmorton's latest altruistic goal of saving a child from the slums of London. Chuckling, he made the part about paying Ruanna and Jim out of Newgate as humorous as possible, and Katrina joined him when he laughed. He felt no compunction about confiding in her about the Newgate incident. Katrina never talked to others about what he told her. That was one of her finest attributes.

"But darling boy, you must have a bath after being in that dreadful place." She rang for a maid and ordered a tub prepared. "And make the water unbearably hot, Delfy."

Something must needs warm His Lordship's blood, she

133

thought as she studied him and wondered what had transpired in his life since she had seen him last. Something dreadful had happened; she could feel it.

Pray, what is wrong? her mind queried, but she did not ask him. Her training would not allow it. Mayhaps he would tell her—when he was in a better mood, after he had made love to her.

Had she, at that moment, asked Lord Julian why he was seemingly reluctant to make love to her, he could not have told her, for he did not know.

"The tub is ready, ma'am," the maid announced from the door, then left quickly.

"Are you ready, m'lord?" asked Katrina, teasingly, flirting with her eyes, her smile, the way she moved.

"Yes, my lovely Katrina, I am ready."

Together they climbed the stairs to the second-story bedchamber, where she undressed him, slowly, methodically, rubbing her hands over his muscled body, nipping at his neck with her tiny teeth.

Naked, the earl climbed into the tub.

Knowing the loveliness of her body when it was in the state of undress, Katrina undressed herself, and, when she bent over the tub, two round, pink-tipped mounds, like two ripe peaches hanging from a tree, moved seductively before the earl's vision. Painstakingly, she scrubbed his skin vigorously, making it glow in the circle of soft candlelight that was the only light in the room. The heavy draperies were closed.

The earl reached for the enticing fruit. Taking a breast in each hand, he rolled the hardening nipples between his thumbs and forefingers, increasing the pressure until he heard her moan with pleasure.

Then, and only then, did he feel a warmth begin to uncoil deep within his body, the natural feeling of manly desire. He stepped out of the tub and took her to hold as water ran in rivulets through the coarse black hair that covered his chest, down his long legs until it puddled on the floor at his feet.

Catching his breath in a gasp, he took her lips in a wildly demanding kiss and pressed the soft curves of her body against the hard angles of his own. His labored breathing made the only sound in the silent room.

"What are you thinking?" asked Katrina, breaking the silence. Again, she tilted her head back to smile up at him, glorying in her success.

The earl chuckled. "That you are delightful in bed."

"I can't wait," she answered, and she rubbed her upthrusting bosom against his hard chest. She had never known a man so virile, or so mysterious. Which, no doubt, added to his charm.

As if she were as light as a feather, the earl swung her up into his arms and carried her to the awaiting bed, where he made love to her, expertly, with wild abandon, pushing everything else from his mind.

Afterward, rising to leave while Katrina slept, His Lordship dressed quickly. On a table near the bed he left an expected surprise, a velvet-lined box that bore the name of one of the finest jewelers in London, Rundle and Bridge. He was no fool. A woman wanted two things from a man—her passion assuaged, and the monetary rewards—and he bitterly believed the latter of more importance. Had not Charlotte Loyd-Dobbs proved that to be so by marrying his brother for his title and his wealth?

At least women know what they want.

What do I want from life? he asked himself. He looked at the beautiful woman still asleep on the bed, the answer to any sane man's wont.

Obviously, I am not sane.

Shaking his head and moving stealthily to the door, the earl admitted that he honestly did not know what he wanted, what would fulfill him. He only knew that it was not this, for he felt as empty now as when he had stood at the front door, waiting for the butler to announce him in.

Chapter Eleven

Upon arriving at Grosvenor House, the earl rushed to his chambers and asked Adam, his valet, to order hot water for a bath. He had not intended to be this late. A quick wash was all he had time for, which he did himself, while the valet laid out his clothes.

When His Lordship was only partly dressed, he turned this way and that in front of the looking glass.

The valet, a tall man, but not as tall as the earl, admonished his master to stand still so he could place a ruby stickpin in his cravat. "Be still, m'lord, or I shall be in danger of sticking this in your throat."

The earl complied, then complained, "A dandy, indeed, Adam."

Adam clasped his hands together, sighed dramatically, and said, "Not so, m'lord. Understated. All the crack, the beau himself. Fine as a fivepence. You look superb, m'lord, and that is what you told me you wished when you rushed in here saying you needed my help to dress for supper. So unlike you to dress in such finery to dine at home, and to ask for help in dressing. Since your time in His Majesty's service, you've been too independent about asking for my help."

The earl laughed. "In the heat of battle, Adam, a man learns quickly that he can do for himself quite well." He cocked a brow. "An embroidered waistcoat!"

The valet giggled and held his waistcoat up.

"I don't understand," the earl mused aloud as he slipped the waistcoat on.

"You don't understand what, m'lord?"

"My solicitor. Every time I mention Miss Moreton's name in his presence the most asinine smile appears on his face."

The earl started to tell his valet, but then thought better of it, that on his way home from Miss Medcalf's he had dashed by to tell George about finding Ruanna in Newgate, and before he could get the whole of it out of his mouth, the solicitor had doubled up with laughter. Servants were such gossips, he thought, and he was certain that the lot of them were wondering where the little ragamuffin had come from.

When the valet stood there, grinning, the earl sputtered, "You're grinning just like George."

"I hear *she* is quite beautiful, m'lord, and that she has red hair."

The earl exploded, "I thought you above gossip, Adam. Besides, what does Miss Moreton's red hair have to do with my desire to help my cousin—the earl had not accepted Lady Throckmorton's curtsy title of lady for Ruanna Moreton.

When the valet remained silent, obviously smothering another giggle, His Lordship went doggedly on. "I was thinking of Lady Throckmorton. No lady of quality should have to deal with two dirty . . ." He heaved a heartfelt sigh. "That is why I rushed back here tonight— to help Lady Throckmorton with that chore."

In the quarters assigned to Ruanna, the same as she stayed in before she ran away, and where the portrait was missing from over the mantel, Lady Throckmorton was in a quandary as to what to do about clothing when Ruanna got out of the tub. Lord Julian had said to find something for her to wear, and one did not just go purchase clothing for a young girl without proper fittings.

Lady Throckmorton looked at the clock. There was not much time, and her instinct told her that His Lordship would be present for dinner, although he had not said as much, and he usually informed her if he planned to dine at home.

She tapped the floor with her cane, playing a tune, while she searched for the answer on what to do. She had sent a footman to purchase clothing for the little boy, but that was impossible for Lady Moreton. Tomorrow they would go to the modiste. . . .

Discounting the worry about clothes, the aging woman found herself downright giddy. Her happiness surpassed any she had ever known.

"One does what one has to do," she finally said, and, with the black cane looped over her arm, she rose and walked swiftly to the yellow-and-green room, the hem of her gown flapping against her boots. When she pulled from the chiffonier one of Countess Charlotte's gowns, her mind winged back to the untimely death of the fourth earl; to Julian's return from the wars and his becoming the new earl; and to Countess Charlotte, who had departed in such a hurry that some of her things had been left behind. Rumor was that Lord Julian had ordered her gone, never to return, but Lady Throckmorton had not heard the words with her own ears.

With hardly a glance at the gown, or at the silk chemise and underdrawers she had chosen for Ruanna to wear, Lady Throckmorton hurried back to Ruanna's chambers and called through the door, "Ruanna, I brought these for you to wear tonight."

When the door to the dressing room opened, she handed the chemise and drawers to Katie, but kept the dress. "These were Countess Charlotte's, but I promise that after tomorrow, you will not have to wear her castoffs. Except that she was taller, you are near her size. We're fortunate there; otherwise, you would have to wear something of mine."

Lady Throckmorton laughed at her own levity, for she was as thin as a broomstick, and as flat-chested as a pancake. It would be impossible to fit Ruanna, with her budding curves, into one of her dresses.

In the dressing room, Ruanna slipped the articles of clothing on. They smelled of lilac water still. Coming out in the bedchamber, she smiled at the old woman, and a great gush of love filled her heart. She was so lucky to be here with Isadora Throckmorton, and she was sure that it was her good Mama watching over things that had made them turn out this way.

Now if she will just handle the obstinate earl.

Ruanna slipped the dress on and heard two audible gasps, and when she turned to the old woman, she became acutely aware that there were tears in her faded eyes. Again, as she had so often done before, Ruanna wondered why Lady Throckmorton cared so much about her.

"You are the loveliest creature living, my dear Ruanna," Lady Throckmorton said.

"Thank you," Ruanna said, her words spoken in a low tone, as she twisted and turned in front of the looking glass. Never had she seen a dress as lovely. Never had she looked more grown up. It seemed that she had matured into a woman. And she soon would be, she told herself. Her eighteenth birthday was only weeks away. She smoothed the green silk over her flat stomach, and over her slender hips. The skirt opened to reveal a panel of lighter green fabric embroidered with garlands; a low décolletage showed the creamy white tops of her bosom.

The gown was too elaborate for dining at home, Ruanna thought, but, for fear of hurting the old woman's feelings, she did not say so. She turned to look quizzically at the maid.

Katie rolled her eyes upward. "But he won't like it, ma'am."

"Are you speaking of the earl, Katie?" Ruanna knew

full well she was. "Why should His Lordship take a dislike to this beautiful gown?"

"Because it wus 'ers. She wore it the day he learned she had married his brother. I saw them in the garden when he flung her from 'im and she fell on the ground, and he—"

Lady Throckmorton cut in sharply. "That will be enough, Katie."

Ruanna stood pensively for a long moment, then said, "I wager he will not even remember. Men pay so little attention to clothes women take such pains with. At least that is what Mama always said. But never mind the dress. The earl has made it painfully plain that he does not want me at Grosvenor House, so I don't think he cares a fig about what I wear."

Impulsively, Ruanna hugged the old woman. "You are so kind, Isadora."

"The earl has a—"

"I know. He has a soft core . . . if one can find it." Whirling around, Ruanna looked again into the gilt-framed looking glass. The gown was too long, but she could lift it when she walked. Bouncing onto her toes, she strained to make herself look taller than her five-feet, three inches. The earl was so enormously tall. Her heart began to pound when a vision of his hard countenance flashed before her eyes. Even when he was angry, he was imposingly handsome, and he seemed to be angry most of the time, especially with her.

Lady Throckmorton gave Ruanna a fond smile. "Even your short-cropped hair does not diminish your beauty."

Ruanna laughed. "Isadora! You will turn my head." Then, to change the subject from herself, she asked, "How is little Jim faring? Will he be dining with us?"

"I sent a footman after clothes for him, and another is giving him a good scrubbing, though that may take all night. He was in such a dreadfully neglected state."

"Poor little boy. I see so much hurt in his little eyes, and he tries so hard to pretend that he is cock of the walk and not afraid of anything or anyone. It near breaks my heart."

Reluctantly, Ruanna turned away from the mirror. Why was she suddenly so vain? She could not stop wondering if the earl would like the way she looked. Well, she might not be beautiful, but she was certainly prettier than Lady Elise. It would take a fool not to see that, and the earl was not a fool. Then, remembering that he had called her a beggar, she turned to Katie and asked, "Where did you put my clothes?"

"Why ever do you want to know that, my dear?" Lady Throckmorton asked, her eyes widening. "Surely you are not thinking of dressing like a boy again. There will be no need—"

Ruanna's eyes perused the room. "I should not want His Lordship burning my breeches and cap, as he did my dress. One never knows what one will need."

"I put them in here, ma'am," Katie said. She lifted the lid of a dome-topped, leather-strapped brass trunk that sat near the wardrobe.

"Is there a key?" Ruanna asked.

"Yes . . . but . . ."

"Since my clothes are in there, may I have it?"

Ruanna took the key which Katie handed out to her. She then locked the trunk and dropped the key down the front of her bosom. Turning to Lady Throckmorton, she smiled and said, "Well, I guess I am as ready as I shall ever be to face the earl's ire. It seems that every time I see him, he has something else to be angry with me about. Honestly, Isadora, I do not know how you stand the man."

"When you get to know him, you will feel differently."

"I certainly hope so," Ruanna commented as she looped her arm through Lady Throckmorton's. The two women then quit the room, going out in the long hall and turning to the left at its end.

"We are dining in the smaller dining room at the back of the house," Lady Throckmorton said. "It overlooks a lovely garden and is smaller and more intimate than the dining room on the first floor." She stopped to chuckle. "And it is not far from the kitchen, which makes it more convenient for the servants. I think you will find, dear, that our help is quite spoiled. Neither the earl nor I are extremely hard on them."

"I am glad to hear that. When I asked the earl's help to get Jim and me out of Newgate, I offered to do chores for my keep."

Lady Throckmorton's mouth flew open, and she looked at Ruanna incredulously. "He did not agree! I cannot conceive of such a thing!"

Before Ruanna could respond to the old woman's protests, she looked up and saw the earl descending the stairs from the next floor up. He was decked out in fawn breeches, a velvet evening coat, and a waistcoat embroidered in a design of flowers and hummingbirds.

Ruanna had to contain herself to keep from gasping. His raven black hair and neatly trimmed side-whiskers glistened in the candlelight. As he moved with the grace of a sleek leopard, an animal magnetism emanated from him. She remembered his sensual lips on hers, stirring her in a strange, delicious way.

Ruanna was brought back to the present by a squeal, followed by a string of swear words. Dashing by was Jim, naked as a picked bird, a footman in fast pursuit.

Ruanna watched in horrified amazement, and somewhat bemused, as each time the servant came close to touching his prey, the fleeing boy ducked behind a piece of furniture, escaping with the deftness of a slippery eel.

"What is going on here?" the earl demanded angrily, his voice booming in the manner Ruanna had come to know.

"The little scallywag warn't wear the clothes 'er Ladyship bought for 'im," the servant answered, now chasing Jim in a zigzag circle around the room, once barely missing an urn of flowers perched atop a round marble table.

The chase ended when the footman came close and Jim, his movements as quick as lightning, swung round behind the earl, knocking His Lordship's legs from under him. His legs flew toward the ceiling, and he hit the floor with a thud.

To Ruanna, it seemed an incredibly long time that the earl's booted feet flailed the air, before coming down to imprison naked Jim, who was now on all fours. The earl burned the air with invectives.

"I'll get ye," Jim said to the footman, raising his head to glare up at him.

Ruanna's hands flew to her face, and she burst out laughing; then she was joined by Lady Throckmorton.

The earl glared at them. "Do something with *your brother*," he shouted at Ruanna.

But then he smiled up at her, and she could not help but notice that the smile removed a decade from his countenance. There was a definite twinkle in his blue eyes when he raised his head to look at his captive. "We have you now, Jim," the earl said.

Jim, with daggers shooting from his eyes, glared at the footman.

Ruanna reached out to touch the little boy on the shoulder, but he shrank from her.

"The little—" the footman started.

Straightening, Ruanna said with alacrity, "Don't you dare call him a dirty name." She then hunkered down beside Jim and looked into his face. His long, wet hair hid his eyes. Knowing he would knock her hand away, she resisted raking the hair back. "What's wrong, Jim?" she asked.

Fie on him, I ain't wearin' them damn clothes. I ain't no pointy-beaked bird."

"But you simply cannot eat in your birthday suit, now can you. There's a delicious dinner waiting for us, and just look at me. I am wearing a dress that I really would prefer not to be wearing. But as hungry as I am, and as I know you are, we can't be too choosy about what we wear. Go get dressed and come to the dining room. . . ."

Refusing the proffered hand of the footman, the earl scrambled to his feet. His eyes were on Jim, his thoughts on the tender way Ruanna spoke to the boy. He felt a lump come up to lodge in his throat. Even so, he spoke gruffly. "Jim, get dressed."

Turning, the earl offered an arm to both Lady Throckmorton and Ruanna, and the footman led Jim off.

When the earl and his ladies reached the dining room, he seated Lady Throckmorton at one end of the long table and Ruanna on the side, near the middle, before taking his place at the head of the table.

It was a beautiful room, Ruanna noted. The fire that smoldered in the high grate of the black marble fireplace furnished the intimate atmosphere of which Lady Throckmorton had spoken. The table was laid with heavy, ornate silver, sparkling crystal, and fine bone-china plates, all engraved with the earl of Wendsleydale's crest.

Silver candelabra held tall tapers that spun circles of light on the table, and fresh flowers spilled from silver epergnes.

Though appreciative of the room's beauty and the elegant table setting, Ruanna did not feel out of place amid the finery. She had grown up with such amenities, always served by a liveried butler—until the servants left when their salaries were no longer paid. She pushed the thought from her mind, and just then a footman bowed Jim into the room and seated him across from Ruanna. She smothered the smile. He did look like a penguin! And his eyes looked like two chunks of coal about to erupt and send sparks in every direction.

But his clothes were exquisite, a black coat, an immaculately folded white cravat, and gray, full pantaloons, above silk stockings and low-cut shoes. One would think the footman who had picked the clothes was used to dressing little boys, she thought appreciatively.

She gave the footman a smile and thanked him

graciously, after which he gave a quick bow, then left.

Ruanna brought her attention back to the little pickpocket. "You look perfectly handsome, Jimmy."

"Don't lie, miss. And ain't I tole yer not to call me Jimmy?"

The earl laughed, but tears, which he hoped no one could see, clouded his vision as he teased, "He certainly did, Miss Moreton. I distinctly remember his telling you that his name was Jim. Can't you remember anything?"

The earl's words brought a smile from Jim, the first Ruanna had seen since she had met him. She remembered that most of the time in that horrible cell at Newgate, the little boy had kept his face turned to the wall.

"I am sorry, Jim," she said. "I'll try to remember not to call you Jimmy."

"You may serve now," the earl announced to the servant standing by the sideboard laden with food.

When the footman placed plates of stewed kidneys, roast beef, and a variety of colorful vegetables before them, Jim, without preamble, bent his head over his plate and scooped the food into his mouth.

Excruciating memories rushed through the earl's mind, and when Jim had scraped the last morsel from his plate and carried it to the silver-laden sideboard to fill it again, the lump grew larger in His Lordship's throat.

"May I serve you?" the stiffly formal footman asked. He reached for Jim's plate, only to have it jerked from his reach.

"I ken wait on m'self," Jim said, and he dug his spoon deeply into each silver dish, while the footman held the cover aloft.

Tremulously, Ruanna waited for the earl to scold, but, strangely, she thought, he didn't. Across the length of the long table, Ruanna caught the look that passed between the earl and his cousin and wondered about it. Then the earl looked at Jim and smiled.

And just today, he called Jim a pickpocket, Ruanna thought.

"Leave the boy," Lady Throckmorton told the footman.

"Miss Moreton," the earl said, then stopped.

"Yes, Lord Julian?"

"Would you honor me with a stroll in the park after dinner? 'Tis a lovely evening."

When a scolding look appeared on Lady Throckmorton's face, the earl explained, "At Newgate, I signed papers to the effect that Miss Moreton is my ward, so there will be no need for a chaperone."

Ruanna's heart thrummed uncontrollably and pounded in her temples. "Your kind offer is accepted, m'lord. A walk would be pleasant."

Ruanna's answer came too quickly, she was to learn only seconds later, when the earl continued, "Since delivering you and Jim here this afternoon, I have had considerable time to think and plan for your future, and I have a workable plan in mind. If I may, I shall tell you what is expected of you, and then what I am willing to do in turn."

Ruanna found herself fuming; the thrumming in her heart ceased. She should have known that behind the earl's sudden pleasant demeanor, there was a plan to take charge of her life . . . and maybe little Jim's. She had been misled by the earl's smile. A leopard doesn't change its spots, she told herself.

Shooting the earl a scalding look, she said, with a note of defiance, "I shall be glad to discuss my future with you, m'lord."

Another set down from the mighty earl of Wendsleydale and lord of whatever.

The earl did not answer, which did not surprise Ruanna. She was now sure that he was only biding his time until they were alone to chide her for wearing the countess's dress.

147

A short, awkward silence fell over the room, but then the meal was finished with a discussion of the excellent weather now upon them, and how the crops on the estates must be thriving.

Lady Throckmorton questioned Ruanna about her life in India, and the earl directed several forthright queries to Jim, getting nothing more informative than his name was Jim.

His Lordship said little to Ruanna, though from time to time she felt his eyes on her.

After the dessert was elegantly served by the footman, and had been devoured and exclaimed upon by those around the table, the earl, pushing himself back from the table and standing, suggested they have a sherry in the small salon adjoining the dining room.

"You may be excused," he said to Jim.

His words were not unkind, and Ruanna knew they were not meant to be. She supposed the upper orders spoke to children in such an aloof manner. At least that was what her Mama had told her. "In England, children are to be occasionally seen and hardly ever heard," Lady Mary had said.

Ruanna also knew that it was quite unusual for a boy of seven to be allowed to dine with adults, as Jim had been tonight, and she was most appreciative. Rising from the table, she smiled sweetly. "I shall join you in the salon later, after I have seen Jim ensconced in a soft bed."

After complimenting Lady Throckmorton on the lovely dinner, Ruanna graciously thanked the footman for his wonderful service. He bowed to her, smiling broadly.

When Ruanna nodded to the earl, she felt his blue eyes strangely studying her. Without taking time to think on it, she took Jim by the hand and they quit the room.

Still holding hands, they walked up the stairs and down the hall to the bedchamber that had been assigned to Jim. Lady Throckmorton had pointed it out to Ruanna earlier, and now, she noticed, it had his nameplate attached to it.

Jim, it read, nothing more. Remembering that the little boy had positively refused to reveal more of himself, Ruanna smiled.

When they entered the room, Jim's brown eyes glared in open astonishment. "Ye mean I'm to sleep 'ere." He jerked his hand from Ruanna's and ran to press down on the feather mattress. As he rubbed his stomach in a circular motion, he added, "Gemini! Thet was some whopping meal."

Ruanna gave a soft laugh. "And there will be lots of good food as long as we stay here."

She cupped his small chin in her hand, lifted his face, and looked into his brown eyes. She spoke to him as an adult, the way her mother had spoken to her when she was a child.

"A child can understand more than we think," Lady Mary had said.

"Jim," Ruanna said, "there is a reason why I cannot go back to live in that other part of London. I ran away from a man in India, a very dangerous man, and they have found me once. As long as I am here, as a ward of the earl, I will be safe. But I should not want to stay without you. I need you here with me. Just in case something goes wrong, you can protect me . . . as you did when I was near being trampled to death in that awful riot."

Jim, squaring his small shoulders, stuck his bony chest out, and his big eyes glistened. "Aye, Lady Moreton, at yer service."

Gone was some of the hurt in his eyes that Ruanna had been so cognizant of, and had worried so much about. She raked her fingers through his long, corn silk hair, pushing it back from his face, which, at the moment, was as innocent as a babe in swaddling cloth.

But Ruanna knew better.

Jim swept his hands over his new clothes. "I ain't wearin' these thing agin'. And I'd not be wearin' em now, if it weren't fer yer. I like me own clothes to sleep in. 'Tis safer, and quicker, if it's my wont to leave."

149

"Make sure that it is not your wont to leave tonight," Ruanna said kindly. "Tomorrow, with the money Lady Throckmorton stuffed in my reticule, I shall purchase clothing more to your liking; though, in the earl's household, you will be expected to dress differently than you have been."

Ruanna rang for a footman to help Jim undress—heaven forbid should she try—and when the footman came, she hugged the little thief and told him good night. At the door, she turned. "Promise me, Jim, that you will not run away."

When she did not receive an answer, she coaxed, "Even you will have to admit that life among the quality beats stealing, and being cold, and hungry." She paused before saying, "Jim, I want your promise."

"Aye, I promise," Jim said, and Ruanna believed him, though she did not know why. She went back and hugged him again, then kissed him on both cheeks. He seemed shy, but did not pull away.

What a life he must have had up until now, she thought, and when the door closed behind her, she prayed silently to her maker that He not let the little boy run away.

And she prayed even harder that the higher power not let Jim steal the household into poverty.

On her way back to the salon where the earl and Lady Throckmorton were waiting, Ruanna's mind moved to think upon the earl and their stroll. Instead of feeling giddy with happiness—for she had found herself terribly attracted to His Lordship—she felt that soon she would meet her executioner. As if she were in a hurry to get it over with, her steps gained in rapidity. She said aloud, "No matter. Whatever the earl says, I am going to be pleasant. I am *not* going to lose my temper."

A little voice at the back of her mind chided, You peagoose, 'tis your heart that you are in danger of losing.

Knowing that only trouble could come from such an unthinkable turn of events, Ruanna shuddered.

"I know whereof I speak, Miss Moreton," the earl was loftily saying.

They were sitting on a bench near a copse of trees, having walked there under a full moon. While walking, their conversation had been amiable enough, even mixed with laughter at times, and Ruanna had found herself quite gay. She thought mayhaps she had been foolish to have been so worried.

Now, catching a glance at the earl's stern features and listening to his authoritative words, Ruanna had an overwhelming desire to spit.

"You must guard your reputation," the earl said. "Never, never tell anyone you had a lover in India. To obtain a proper marriage, a woman must be pure. Since your indiscretion occurred in another country, and since I am the only one who has been apprised of your misconduct, so I hope, we shall hold it our secret, and I shall do everything in my power to get you on in society. As my ward, you will have my protection. Lady Throckmorton will chaperone you when I am not available.

"By escorting you to the balls and soirees, I can point out to you how the ladies of the upper orders act. I have observed that you are a quick study."

His Lordship paused to offer a slight smile. "Why, even this evening, your manners were impeccable, just from the short time you have been in our household. You should learn fast . . . if you try. But I must have your cooperation. No more escapades such as the one you pulled this afternoon with Lady Elise."

Ruanna had bitten her tongue as long as she could bear it. She was sure that any moment blood would ooze down onto the countess's beautiful gown, which, so far, the

151

earl had failed to notice. "Balderdash!" she exclaimed.

"Miss Moreton! Pray, refrain from such language. A proper husband will never be found for you."

"I believe I told you once that I do not give a fig about your marriage mart. I think it is absolutely abhorrent, and your rules are positively too strict. One can do this, one can do that," she mimicked, looking straight out in front of her. "Mama thought so, too. And I did not used to have a lover in India—I *now* have a lover in India."

Ruanna was lying. She flung her head of red curls sideways to look up into the earl's abashed countenance. Now, unlike the way she had felt earlier, when she had thought him so handsome, he reminded her of Satan: his thick black hair and heavy brows above such piercing blue eyes.

And to think I wanted him to kiss me, she thought. He deserved the lie she had just told him. One had to do something to preserve one's dignity.

Even though they were not touching, she felt the earl bristle, and she definitely heard a disgruntled snort. She smiled. He should have someone get the better of him occasionally.

"Do not mention that lover again," the earl said sternly. "As I said, I shall teach you the nicer amenities of proper society."

Ruanna studied him, and shook her head in dismay. Why was it so difficult to get His Lordship to understand? He certainly was not a quick study where women were concerned. She knew how to act in proper society!

"You are queer in the attic," she told him. Bringing her knees up, she hooked the heels of her shoes on the edge of the bench, then cupped her chin in her hands. And even though her legs were adequately covered, she knew that it was a very unladylike posture.

She heard the earl's groan, and she took great pleasure in that, too.

After the groan, which was unintentional, the earl

The Publishers of Zebra Books Make This Special Offer to Zebra Romance Readers...

AFTER YOU HAVE READ THIS BOOK WE'D LIKE TO SEND YOU 4 MORE FOR *FREE* AN $18.00 VALUE

No Obligation!

MORE PASSION AND ADVENTURE AWAIT... YOUR TRIP TO A BIG ADVENTUROUS WORLD BEGINS WHEN YOU ACCEPT YOUR FIRST 4 NOVELS ABSOLUTELY *FREE* (AN $18.00 VALUE)

Accept your Free gift and start to experience more of the passion and adventure you like in a historical romance novel. Each Zebra novel is filled with proud men, spirited women and tempestuous love that you'll remember long after you turn the last page.

Zebra Historical Romances are the finest novels of their kind. They are written by authors who really know how to weave tales of romance and adventure in the historical settings you love. You'll feel like you've actually gone back in time with the thrilling stories that each Zebra novel offers.

GET YOUR FREE GIFT WITH THE START OF YOUR HOME SUBSCRIPTION

Our readers tell us that these books sell out very fast in book stores and often they miss the newest titles. So Zebra has made arrangements for you to receive the four newest novels published each month.

You'll be guaranteed that you'll never miss a title, and home delivery is so convenient. And to show you just how easy it is to get Zebra Historical Romances, we'll send you your first 4 books absolutely FREE! Our gift to you just for trying our home subscription service.

BIG SAVINGS AND FREE HOME DELIVERY

Each month, you'll receive the four newest titles as soon as they are published. You'll probably receive them even before the bookstores do. What's more, you may preview these exciting novels free for 10 days. If you like them as much as we think you will, just pay the low preferred subscriber's price of just $3.75 each. *You'll save $3.00 each month off the publisher's price.* AND, your savings are even greater because there are never any shipping, handling or other hidden charges—FREE Home Delivery. Of course you can return any shipment within 10 days for full credit, no questions asked. There is no minimum number of books you must buy.

4 FREE BOOKS

TO GET YOUR 4 FREE BOOKS WORTH $18.00 — MAIL IN THE FREE BOOK CERTIFICATE T O D A Y

Fill in the Free Book Certificate below, and we'll send your FREE BOOKS to you as soon as we receive it.

If the certificate is missing below, write to: Zebra Home Subscription Service, Inc., P.O. Box 5214, 120 Brighton Road, Clifton, New Jersey 07015-5214.

FREE BOOK CERTIFICATE

4 FREE BOOKS

ZEBRA HOME SUBSCRIPTION SERVICE, INC.

YES! Please start my subscription to Zebra Historical Romances and send me my first 4 books absolutely FREE. I understand that each month I may preview four new Zebra Historical Romances free for 10 days. If I'm not satisfied with them, I may return the four books within 10 days and owe nothing. Otherwise, I will pay the low preferred subscriber's price of just $3.75 each; a total of $15.00, *a savings off the publisher's price of $3.00.* I may return any shipment and I may cancel this subscription at any time. There is no obligation to buy any shipment and there are no shipping, handling or other hidden charges. Regardless of what I decide, the four free books are mine to keep.

NAME

ADDRESS _____ APT _____

CITY _____ STATE _____ ZIP _____

( )
TELEPHONE

SIGNATURE _____ (if under 18, parent or guardian must sign)

Terms, offer and prices subject to change without notice. Subscription subject to acceptance by Zebra Books. Zebra Books reserves the right to reject any order or cancel any subscription.

039102

sighed, also unintentionally. He jerked his gaze away from the redhead and kept it straight ahead, so he could keep his mind on the plan he had come upon this afternoon on his way home from Miss Medcalf's. Uncommonly at a loss for words, he waited a long moment before trying another approach, one that he hoped would work.

After observing Ruanna's concern for Jim, he was sure she had a kind heart, so he said, "Lady Throckmorton and I talked of your come-out into society while you were with the boy. She desires it very much, and I cannot conceive of your disappointing her, any more than I myself can hurt her. With your being so kind, I think it would haunt you for the rest of your life should you cause her worry." He put strong emphasis on the part about causing his cousin worry.

When Ruanna sat staring out into the park, her face shrouded in stubbornness, the earl cajoled, "If you will obey the rules required of you, I shall see that *your brother* is sent to the best schools, and I shall purchase a harp for you. When my niece, Jenny, returns, you may give her lessons in exchange for your keep, since that is one of your requirements."

What more can I offer? the earl wondered. He sighed deeply when silence met his words. Never had he encountered anyone so stubborn.

Ruanna was tired to death of the conversation. Why should there be so many rules? And all for her! Turning her face from His Lordship, she noted the surroundings.

Trees with silvery, shimmering leaves surrounded the park bench on which they sat. The moon cast slivers of light down through the long boughs, through which a soft wind whispered; dappled shadows danced on the ground.

Ruanna stared at the shadows, studied them, silently swore at them. She wanted the earl to kiss her in that delicious way that made her feel so strangely warm. "M'lord—"

153

The earl raised a hand to silence her. "Since we are going to be spending considerable time together, I prefer that you dispense with the formality of calling me m'lord. I came upon my present standing quite late in life. Until three years ago I was just plain Julian, and I would very much like to be just Julian to you."

When Ruanna quizzically raised an eyebrow, he added, "I have told all my close associates this, even though all of them do not comply."

This was not all true. The earl had never requested that Miss Medcalf or Lady Elise dispense with his title. He had, however, from time to time, chided Lady Throckmorton for using it, and she continued only from her own desire.

Ruanna started again. "Julian, now that you have the road into my future so perfectly orchestrated, what are *your* plans? Other than making a *lady* out of me?" She tried for levity. "Have you not heard that old adage that one simply does not make a silk purse out of a sow's ear?"

The earl visibly blanched. "It is only fair that you ask. Soon, I will offer for Lady Elise. There is a need for an heir in the family, and I shall produce one through her. Why, just today I learned that she prefers living in the county, as I do."

"Balderdash! You are going to make a brood mare of her! How you can think of lying with a woman you do not love is beyond me. Just to have an heir! Poor little child! To be born to parents who only come together to couple for the sole purpose of producing an heir. And I suppose you will keep the beautiful paramour you already have."

Ruanna was only guessing about that part.

"Of course. You do not understand. That is the way things are with the ton. Mistresses are perfectly acceptable. And you will come to accept it."

"Not with me are mistresses acceptable. I plan to marry a man with whom I am in love, and I shall make sure he never, never, never goes to a strumpet's bed."

"Miss Moreton!"

"Ruanna," she requested.

"All right! Ruanna, if you desire. You must refrain from using such vulgar sayings."

The earl felt beads of perspiration on his upper lip, and his heart was beating exceptionally fast. Looking at Ruanna, he shook his head despairingly. She was a willful, terrible, and improvident girl, and at that moment he wanted to enfold her in his arms and press her body against his more than he wanted to draw his next breath.

"'Tis the dress," the earl said sotto voce. "And the red hair, and the green eyes."

Almost instantly, he felt the long-ago stirring, the devil passion that had ridden his shoulder when he was but a youngster, and wanting Charlotte in such a desperate way. He no longer thought that he had been in love with the she-devil, but he could not deny that he had desired her with a burning, uncontrollable passion.

Only this afternoon, His Lordship had wondered if he had done something terrible to displease his heavenly master. At times, his desire for this hoyden his cousin had brought into his household was beyond bearing. As he watched her, he felt the ache start, and he swore under his breath, turning his head to stare out into the park.

Deciding that she would force the earl to mention Countess Charlotte's dress whether or no, Ruanna sprang to her feet and began to dance with the shadows. The dress swirled, hugged her legs, then swirled again. As a child she had been quite proficient in the ballet, and she had been trained in carrying the tune to song.

Ruanna then ran like a sprite through the trees, humming lightly. She stopped once to call to Lord Julian that he was much too serious for such a lovely night, after which she broke into song, a lovely Indian ballad.

It had been a long time since Ruanna had felt so young, so happy: only because she had willed it to be so, she told herself. This night, she would not worry about the earl's rules, and she savored the moments as she raised her

155

voice in song, letting the notes float on the soft wind.

The earl watched as Ruanna moved from tree to tree, ethereal, like a fairy dancing in the moonlight, pirouetting, swirling. Silver rays of moonlight caught the loveliness of the green dress, and the stars, leaving the heavens, came to nest in her glinting red hair.

She is torturing me on purpose. She is a witch.

The beads of sweat on His Lordship's upper lip increased. He took a white linen handkerchief from his pocket and wiped at them, and at his brow. Mesmerized and unable to control his heartbeat, he tried looking the other way, only to have his gaze return to rest on her.

"This is outside of enough," he at last exclaimed. "She is so flighty that she does not want to talk of anything of a serious nature. No doubt this is the way she lost her virginity in India."

A man could only withstand so much, the earl decided. He would go to her and shake her.

And he did go to her, with great swiftness, but he did not shake her. Instead, he imprisoned her with his long arms and pulled her to him, pressing her against his hard frame.

The earl was leaning against the tree trunk, and the rough bark bit into his back, but he did not feel the pain. A guttural groan escaped his lips as he grabbed a handful of unruly red hair and pulled her head back.

His mouth claimed hers, cruelly, brutally, deliciously, while an exhilarating ecstasy washed over him, obliterating all caution. "You witch," he whispered against her mouth, "you wicked, wicked witch."

He lifted his head to look into her green eyes, and she smiled at him.

"Don't smile at me like that," he said, and when he heard a gurgle of laughter, he released her, pulled himself erect, then stood like a statue against the onslaught of feelings ravaging his body, his being, his soul.

Ruanna did not want the earl to stop kissing her. She pushed herself up on her toes, slid her hands up along his hard chest, and twined her arms around his neck. And when the earl yanked her back to him, she felt tremors vibrate through his bulging muscles. She heard his labored breathing.

Ruanna's inexperience with men left her totally unaware of anything more than the thrill that passed through her own body when the earl kissed her. She knew nothing of a man's passion; her mother had died when she was twelve.

So, for a long, heavenly moment, Lady Ruanna Moreton floated on a cloud, transcending all things real. The earl's hot breath caressed her cheeks when he kissed her eyes, the tip of her nose, her chin. And when his lips claimed her mouth again, spinning her senses, it seemed natural for her to open her mouth to his probing tongue and give herself to his kiss. She heard her own involuntary whimper . . . and she heard an owl hoot in the distance.

Which obviously the earl heard, also.

As if awaking from a laudanum sleep, he said, "You should not kiss a man in such a manner . . . not until you are married. Did your mother not teach you anything?"

Before Ruanna could think of an appropriate retort, the mighty earl took her by the arm and started walking, taking long strides and pulling her alongside him as he would a recalcitrant child.

"Come on, peagoose, I shall take you home," he said, his voice thick and guttural. Then he sighed perceptibly. "It is imperative that we find a husband for you, right away . . . as soon as possible."

"You arrogant, domineering jackanapes, I'll thank you not to call me a peagoose," Ruanna sputtered as she stumbled and almost fell over the hem of Countess Charlotte's dress. Her eyes shot upward, toward the night sky. Where was that damn owl? She would kill it.

Then, looking into the earl's inscrutable countenance, she asked, "M'lord, what is wrong with an intensely pleasureable, perfectly innocent kiss?"

157

At the door of Ruanna's bedchamber, which they had gained without slowing their steps, the earl turned Ruanna to face him, as if to start another lecture. She jerked her arm free from his grasp and glared at him as she said, "Good night, m'lord."

The earl's next words were sharp. "I shall wait until you remove *that* dress. Have your maid hand it to me . . . without delay."

Chapter Twelve

The next morning, Ruanna awoke with a start. She yawned and stretched, then threw her legs off the side of the bed. All at once, and strangely, it was of the utmost importance that she check on Jim. Her night had been filled with dreams and half-wakefulness, nightmares about the earl, about Archibald Bennet's man with a front tooth missing. She did not think she could bear Jim's being gone.

Hearing a diffident knock on the door, she knew that it must be Katie, for, had it been the earl, the rap would be an authoritative one. His anger of the night before came to her in sudden clarity, sending a shudder across her shoulders.

"Enter," Ruanna said to the person outside her door, and when Katie did as she was bade, Ruanna greeted her with forced levity.

The maid curtsied into rustling black bombazine. "Good morning, m'lady." She went directly to draw the curtains.

Bars of hazy sunlight streamed through the windows, and shadows danced on the colorful Turkish rug and across the white bed:

"It appears we will have another beautiful day," offered Ruanna.

"It does at that, ma'am. Lady Throckmorton—"

"Jim," Ruanna interrupted, "is he all right? He is still here, is he not?"

Last night, after the earl had delivered her to her chambers, then left with the countess's dress, Ruanna had gone to Jim's room and had found him sleeping. But that had been early in the evening.

"He's still here, m'lady."

Ruanna whispered a prayer of thanksgiving. "I am sorry I interrupted you, Katie. What were you saying about Lady Throckmorton?"

"It was early when 'er Ladyship sent fer the little feller, and I found out from Marie, 'er Ladyship's maid, that they was in Her Ladyship's chambers talking and laughing and eatin' like nothin' she'd ever seen. Marie said the little waif could eat more than any two men. Where did you find him, m'lady?"

Ruanna laughed. "You would not believe me should I tell you." She stopped there, for she did not want to be accused by the arrogant earl of gossiping with the servants. It was his intent to make a lady out of her, and ladies of quality did not speak with familiarity with household help, Ruanna thought disdainfully; and then she exclaimed with considerable feeling, "Balderdash!"

When Katie shot her a quizzical look, Ruanna said, "I often talk to myself." Going about washing herself and getting dressed, she waved the maid's offered help aside and pulled her dress with patches out of the chiffonnier. She wished she had worn it last evening instead of Countess Charlotte's green gown, though beautiful it was. Slanting a look at Katie, Ruanna asked, "What did the earl do with the gown I wore last night?"

Katie's eyes rolled back in her head, showing more white then brown. "He was in a red-hot rage, m'lady, he was. He went to the wardrobe where all the countess's dresses hung, and he took them out all wadded up in his arms."

"And?"

"He hauled them down to the burning pit and burned

ever last one of 'em, he did. Seeing the direction he was headed, I followed, though I were scared to death he would see me." Katie paused to get her breath. "M'lady, I ain't seen 'is Lordship like that since the day he found out that redheaded she-divil 'ad married 'is brother. Lady Throckmorton even come down, and she scolded 'im plenty fer burning perfectly good gowns when there's so many poor people in the world who could use them."

"And what did Mr. High-and-Mighty say to that?"

"He told her to mind her own business, he did, and he said that poor people would not know what to do with dresses such as the countess wore, and she told 'im that the poor could sell them." Katie sighed. "My, my, it was a farrago, it was."

"I guess no man has ever loved a woman more than Lord Julian loves his Charlie," Ruanna said wistfully. She remembered too vividly that the first time he kissed her he had called her "Charlie."

"Oh, no, m'lady. No man ever hated a woman more than His Lordship hates thet woman."

Only a thread separates hate and love, thought Ruanna.

"Oh, I most forgot, m'lady," Katie said. "'er Ladyship wants yer to meet 'er in the garden after yer've finished yer toilette. Here, let me help."

Ruanna laughed. "I suppose I shall have to get used to someone helping me."

"Lady Throckmorton said that while yer having breakfast that yer can have a nice coze, that she has something of extreme importance to discuss with yer."

An involuntary frown creased Ruanna's brow. What could the old woman want? She had said they would go to the modiste today. Thoughts tumbled through Ruanna's mind. Under the earl's orders, had the old woman agreed to send her and Jim away?

"Then bring my tray to the garden, please, Katie," Ruanna said as she hurried to quit the room. As fast as possible, she descended the stairs and went directly to the

161

garden they had viewed last evening from the dining room. There, Lady Throckmorton sat beside a lawn table, under the shade of a sprawling oak. The old woman wore a dress of yellow cambric, with bright yellow boots protruding from under the skirt.

Glancing around, Ruanna thought that she had never seen a prettier or a better-kept garden, minuscule though it was. Flower beds overflowed onto small patches of grass clipped to perfection. The early morning sun glistened against drops of dew on pink and white blossoms, and on honeysuckle that exuded a delicious aroma.

Ruanna took a deep breath, smelling the sweetness. She smiled at Lady Throckmorton. "Good morning, Isadora."

Lady Throckmorton rose from her chair and came to take Ruanna's hand. "Good morning, my dear." She bent to kiss her on the forehead. "Come sit with me," she said, and led Ruanna to the table, which was draped with a white linen cloth.

Sensing the worry behind Lady Throckmorton's smile, Ruanna did not hesitate to speak. "Katie said you had something of importance to discuss with me. Is it about Lord Julian? Last night he was terribly angry."

"No, it's not about the earl," Lady Throckmorton said. "Not directly. However, he *was* in a state last night. I never should have brought that dress out for you. But I did so want you to look lovely at supper. And you did, dear." The old woman smiled wryly. "At that we did not fall short."

The two women sat down at the table, and almost immediately Katie appeared with Ruanna's breakfast on a silver tray. After filling a cup of tea, she turned to Lady Throckmorton and bobbed a curtsy. "I brought a cup fer yer, m'lady. Shall I pour?"

"Pray, do, Katie. I know I drink too much tea, but I do so enjoy a good cup."

Katie poured the extra cup, then left when Lady

Throckmorton told her that would be all. As soon as the maid was out of earshot, Lady Throckmorton leaned toward Ruanna and said in a low voice, "Last evening when you and the earl were walking in the park, George came to call on him, and he brought some frightening news, which, upon finding Julian absent, he relayed to me. That is why I was looking for Julian when I found him burning the countess's dresses."

Ruanna felt the blood drain from her face. "What sort of news?"

"It seems that one evening when George went to the Vauxhall Gardens, the pleasure gardens across the river, he arrived just as the lights were fired and was immediately set upon by a dapper-looking man with a rather dark complexion. He ventured into conversation with this man and, from the stranger's accent, the solicitor surmised he was from India. The man denied it, saying only that he was working for the government of India. However, George did not believe him. Nor do I. And last night, after the earl calmed down and I was able to talk with him about what George had told me, His Lordship and I concluded that he is the same person Captain Tidesdale spoke about in his missive, the man who was a passenger on his ship his last time out."

Lady Throckmorton stopped for breath, and to sip tea. She then told Ruanna about the missive from the good captain, in which he described the man he had brought over from India, saying he was suspicious of him.

Ruanna noticed that the old woman's hand shook as she lifted the cup to her lips, and Ruanna was forced to wait a long time before Isadora could go on, which she eventually did. "In the conversation with the man in the Gardens, George was asked if he knew a Ruanna Moreton, a girl with red hair who had just recently come to London. It was his job, the man said, to find the girl, that she had committed a hanging offense in India."

Ruanna quailed. "You do not believe that, do you?"

"Of course I do not believe it, child. And neither does

the earl. We talked at length about the precautions that must be taken to protect you."

Relief swept over Ruanna. "And what were those precautions?"

"Lord Julian says that you are to go nowhere without proper escort, either he himself, or a groom of his choosing. He plans to talk with the Bow Street Runners and apprise them of the situation, and he will tell them, so he said, that if you are accosted by this man who doubtlessly intends to bring you harm, he will kill him, and he expects no questions asked."

"I am most appreciative of the earl's concern," Ruanna said, "but after last evening, when he was so angry, I felt that mayhaps he would gladly turn me over to anyone, just to get me out of his sight."

Lady Throckmorton, shaking her head, said, "As I have told you, Ruanna, the earl has a soft core. But pain of one's heart is more difficult to heal than pain of one's body, and Lord Julian's pain goes much deeper than what happened between him and the she-devil, the Countess Charlotte."

Ruanna did not know what to say. She had not known pain when growing up, except when her mother died, and when her father had changed so drastically. Other than that, she had had a happy and privileged life. Of course, she discounted the time she had lived in the East End, where she had often gone hungry.

Lady Throckmorton asked, "Did you not take note of the kind way Julian regarded little Jim last night at supper when the boy went back to load his plate the second time?"

"I saw the look that passed between the two of you, and I saw the earl's eyes follow the boy."

"Well," Lady Throckmorton said, "no doubt His Lordship was remembering when he was as hungry, and it had been I who had slipped him food to keep him from starving."

"Starving?" Ruanna exclaimed. "Why in the world

would a man of such wealth ever be hungry."

"It was the old earl, who was the cruelest man I have ever known. He hated his third son, and so did the older brothers. Julian's mother died giving birth to him. Had I not come when I did, there's no doubt that the little boy would have perished. He was locked in his room for days at a time, often without food, and lashed when he escaped. Finally, he was sent away to school, just to get him out of the old earl's sight."

Ruanna was crying. She could not help herself. As her gaze rested on Lady Throckmorton, she understood perfectly the close bond between the earl and his cousin.

"Once," Lady Throckmorton continued, "when the old earl was blasting little Julian—he was only a little older than Jim—and the old earl was telling him that he had killed his mother, and Julian was sobbing his heart out, I faced the old man down and told him that it was he who had spilled his seed into the frail woman, that *he* had killed her, not the boy." The old woman emitted a little laugh. "I thought he would strike me dead, but I didn't care. I gathered Julian up and took him to Scotland, where I have property. Then, not because he wanted Julian, but because there was no one else to run the household, the old earl came for me. But it was only after he promised that no more unkind deeds would be dealt Julian that we returned to Grosvenor House, and soon after that Julian was sent to Eton."

Ruanna, her breakfast now cold on the tray, listened with her heart, and she was glad that the earl had taken to Jim. But why did His Lordship hate her so? Did he not know that every woman was not deceitful like Countess Charlotte?

Another problem surfaced in Ruanna's mind. What would she do about her students? With this latest turn of events in Vauxhall Gardens, the earl would surely demand that she not return to the East End.

But the children depend on me. I must needs find a way.

Ruanna knew that she did not presently have time to

165

think on the situation and decided that she would approach the earl when he was in a good humor—if that should ever be.

Silent communication ensued between Ruanna and the old woman who had brought her out of the East End. Ruanna felt their hearts reaching out, each for the other. If nothing else, there was a bond between them because the old woman had brought her here to share Grosvenor House and all its privileges. But Ruanna felt that it was more than that, and finally, she broke the silence by asking, "Isadora, when you received the first missive from Captain Tidesdale, why did you go to such lengths to find me? Why did you risk your relationship with the earl to bring to his household someone he obviously detested?"

She almost added, "And still does."

When Lady Throckmorton did not answer, but looked out over the garden, Ruanna blurted out the most burning question of all: "Did you bring me here to marry the earl? Did you think that because I was your good friend's granddaughter, I could heal his hurts?"

Lady Throckmorton whipped her head around to stare into Ruanna's face. "Oh, no, child! It was not that at all. The earl is far too calloused and hard for a sweet girl like you. He would crush you. He will make a marriage of convenience, a ton marriage, to produce an heir, and that is the way it should be."

Then she will not be shocked to learn His Lordship plans to offer for Lady Elise.

"Why then did you search me out?" Ruanna asked succinctly, her eyes intent on the old woman's long, thin face.

Above, a bird chirped, flapped its wings, and flew to another tree. A soft wind moved the huge boughs and rustled the leaves.

At last, the old woman spoke, her voice soft and guarded. "I promise that someday I will tell you, but not now. When the time is right, I will know, and then I shall come to you. . . ."

Wishing that she had not asked, Ruanna reached to touch the old woman's blue-veined hand. "I did not mean to pry. I'm sorry—"

Just then the earl appeared with Jim. He held the little boy's hand. Jim's clothes had been washed and patched, but, to Ruanna, he still looked like a ragamuffin. His blond hair, which, now that it was clean, was more yellow than blond, had been cut straight across his forehead, and it fell straight on the sides to cover his ears and frame his little face.

Ruanna looked at the earl, dressed all the crack in morning attire. Above those piercing eyes, his black hair caught the sunlight; a recalcitrant lock fell down upon his sun-bronzed forehead. For a moment, her heart raced, until she remembered his anger of last evening.

Why was she so attracted to him, she queried her being, while castigating herself. Then, reluctantly, she answered her own question. It was quite simple . . . and stupid; she was in love with the jackanapes. There, she had admitted it, she thought, and their eyes locked, until the earl tore his gaze away and looked out over the garden.

"Jim, I like your haircut," Ruanna said.

"Cut bait, leedy. I look like a sissy."

The earl threw his head back and laughed. "We near had to tie him in the chair. He kept demanding that we come for you, Miss Moreton."

"I think you are absolutely handsome, Jim," Lady Throckmorton said. With a long, bony finger, she reached to touch his cheek. The little boy did not shrink from the touch, and Ruanna was glad. Mayhaps he was not as scared as he had been when first they met; mayhaps he was growing used to affection.

"Jim and I had a wonderful breakfast together," Lady Throckmorton said. "He entertained me with tales of his years as a pickpocket."

"Did he tell you where he came from? Or his last

167

name?" the earl asked.

Jim's dark eyes shot up to scold the earl. "Demmet, I tole yer it don't matter, so don't ask no more."

The earl chuckled. "You are right, little man. It does not matter where you came from, and I shall refrain from asking again."

The earl turned his attention to Ruanna and Lady Throckmorton. "If you ladies will permit us, Jim and I will accompany you on your shopping spree. When you have finished, we will make a few purchases of our own before we escort you home. By the days's end, Jim will be sporting a new wardrobe, and you, Ruanna, will have lovely gowns of your own."

Ruanna knew that he did not care a whit whether or not she had lovely gowns of her own. He was only striving to please Lady Throckmorton. And he was going shopping with them to protect her from Archibald Bennet's rogues—to please his cousin. "I vow that none of my new gowns will be of green silk," she said.

Then, as if the earl had not heard Ruanna speak; as if, she thought, he could read her thoughts concerning her students, he said authoritatively, "I am certain that Lady Throckmorton has told you what my solicitor learned in Vauxhall Gardens, Miss Moreton. Under the circumstances, there must needs be no thoughts of your leaving Mayfair and going into the less desirable sections of town to give music lesson to the lower orders. . . ."

Chapter Thirteen

When three days had passed and Ruanna had not had a chance to discuss her students with the earl, her worry became an obsession. What would the children think of her? It did not bear thinking upon. She had been sure that she could convince the earl she must needs go to them, but she had hardly seen him since he and Jim had accompanied her and Lady Throckmorton on their shopping spree. And it seemed that she was a prisoner in Grosvenor House.

Then something happened that momentarily drew Ruanna's thoughts away from her problem. Her new clothes arrived. She counted the stunning gowns, twelve in all, with more ordered. They were spread out on the bed; morning dresses, walking dresses, and two beautiful gowns to wear in the evening, all whipped up quickly because Lady Throckmorton had insisted. Of course, the gown for her come-out would take more time, and many fittings, the modiste had said.

Even though she had seen the wonderful articles of clothing before they were bought, Ruanna's eyes nearly popped out of her head when she opened the boxes that held French gloves, bonnets, shawls, and lastly, an exquisite green satin palatine to wear when the evenings were exceptionally cold and damp, as many London nights were.

She had vowed not to buy a green garment, but the cape was so striking, and Lady Throckmorton had been so taken with it, that she had relented and bought it.

While shopping, Ruanna had wondered aloud how she would repay the earl for all the wonderful garments.

"Lord Julian is not paying for your wardrobe," Lady Throckmorton had said, "I would not allow it."

And when Ruanna had protested even more strenuously about that, the old lady said, with a catch in her voice, "Pray, do not deny me." And Ruanna had not had the heart to do so.

Hanging the last garment in the chiffonnier, Ruanna moved to sit by the fireplace. Staring at the cold ashes, her mind drifted away from her new clothes to think about the earl, and thoughts of little Jeremy were again much on her mind.

If only I could speak with the earl about Jeremy's talent; if only I could speak with Bochsa.

Why is the earl avoiding me as if I have the pox? Ruanna wondered. She felt sure that if she asked for an audience, he would refuse her. "Stuff," she said, and got up and began pacing the floor. While she was doing so, another thought came to her, a temporary solution.

Without further reasoning, lest she change her mind, Ruanna fished the key to the trunk from the vase in which she had hidden it and hurriedly opened the trunk. Quickly she took out the boy's breeches and put them on. The scuffed boots, chambray shirt, and dun-brown coat followed. Then she pulled the boy's cap down over her red curls.

Without even a glance in the looking glass, she bounded out the door, down the back stairs, and through the courtyard, heading toward the stables. She would ask Guard to take her to her students. He was experienced with handling prisoners and would let no harm come to her.

As Ruanna ran, she planned. At least she could leave her students short missives. They would at least know

170

that she had not deserted them, and that she would be back to teach them as soon as something could be worked out. But before she could reach the mews, a loud, blustery voice stopped her in her tracks.

"Miss Moreton, where do you think you are going?"

Ruanna knew that voice well. She stiffened, pulled her shoulders back, and looked round to see the earl coming toward her, his strides long and quick. She guessed that he had been for a morning gallop, for he wore riding clothes and his black hair was wind-tossed. Dust dulled his long black boots and streaked his buckskin breeches.

When the earl stopped in front of her, Ruanna forced herself to be calm and, in a dulcet voice, said, "I am going to see my students, m'lord, and set up a new schedule for their lessons. I have neglected them far too long, and, as you know, when someone depends on you, it is not honorable to let the person down."

The earl's frown turned to a ferocious scowl. "Do you not recall that I forbade you to go to the East End?"

"I most certainly do recall your saying that, m'lord, and I have wanted to speak with you about it, but I have not had the chance. You are never about in the daytime, and I know for a fact that you gain your bed in the first faint flush of dawn. I think someone should worry about *your* health."

"Never mind my health." The earl took Ruanna's arm and started walking back toward the house, in much the same manner he had dragged her from the park. After he had kissed me, she thought. Now, it appeared he was more apt to turn her over his knee and beat her.

"It is my duty to see that nothing happens to you, for, should you disappear again, I do not believe my old cousin would survive." He slid her a sideways glance. "Is that your plan? To let Archibald Bennet kidnap you and take you back to India so you can see your lover again? Do you miss him that much?"

Ruanna jerked her arm free of the earl's grasp. "I'll thank you not to drag me."

171

Without slowing his stride, the earl swooped her up into his arms. "Then, I shall carry you."

This time, Ruanna did not pretend unconsciousness, nor did she let her head rest on his big chest, listening to his heart beat; instead, she kicked and fought and swore.

This only caused the earl to tighten his hold and mumble something about making a lady out of her if it killed him. Once inside the house, he set her down and demanded that she go to her room and remove those odious clothes. "When you are presentable, meet me in the withdrawing room on the second floor," he said.

His voice would scare the devil himself. . . .

Ruanna thought about skittering up the stairs to her room and locking the door behind her, but she knew that His Lordship, with his long legs, would overtake her before she gained the first step. He grasped her arm again, his fingers biting into her flesh. While holding onto her with one hand, he rang for Katie with the other.

The maid came within seconds, it seemed to Ruanna. The earl said, "Help her dress, then bring her to the yellow salon. I shall hold you responsible if she escapes," he told the maid.

Katie bobbed a curtsy. "Yes, m'lord," she said, making Ruanna want to spit.

"Yes, m'lord, yes, m'lord," Ruanna mimicked as soon as they were out of earshot of the earl. "Why does everyone bow to him as if he were some sort of god?"

"Because 'is Lordship is our master," Katie said. She gave Ruanna a big smile. "Where was yer going anyway?"

Realizing how badly she had failed in what she had intended to do, Ruanna felt tears brim her eyes. She brushed them away, then thought that maybe she had not failed after all. She had the earl's attention, and when they met in the withdrawing room, she would tell him in no uncertain terms that she did not intend to let her students down. She could not live without her music, and if she did not go to Jeremy, his wonderful talent would go unnoticed. Someway, she must bring him to Bochsa's attention. And how could she do that if she had to live as a prisoner in Grosvenor House?

When they were in Ruanna's dressing room, Katie pulled from the chiffonnier a blue morning dress. "'Tis so beautiful," Katie said.

"Put it back," Ruanna said shortly. "I'll wear my dress with patches." Nor did she change from her scuffed boots. She did, however, relent and let Katie brush her hair. Sitting in front of her dressing table, she could see the maid's reflection. "Why are you smiling?" Ruanna asked.

"Outside of Lady Throckmorton, yer the only one who 'as ever defied 'is Lordship since he became the earl, and she only does it when she means business. Like when she wanted yer to come 'ere and live."

"Well, I mean business when I say I will not stop giving music lessons to my students. They depend on me. Especially little Jeremy. He will think I stopped coming because he didn't have the money to pay."

And that is what she told the earl when she went to the yellow salon. Even though he had changed from his dusty riding clothes to impeccable morning dress, and was so handsome it made her heart hurt to look at him, she stated her case before he could open his mouth.

Lady Throckmorton was there, sitting in her usual chair, holding her cane as usual, and smiling much as Katie had.

Ruanna wished she could find something to smile about. She talked so fast her breath ran short, but she did not stop, not until she had explained fully her feelings, coming as quickly as possible to the part about Jeremy.

"He will think I've forsaken him, and I cannot bear that," she said. Then she remembered she had not curtsied to His Lordship. If she wanted to get anywhere with her plea, she must needs be nice. The earl had risen from his chair when she entered.

In deliberate, obvious supplication, Ruanna sank into

173

a deep curtsy. For her students, she was not above begging.

Smiling, the earl took her hand and lifted her up. "I told you that you need not bob to me."

"I was not bobbing. I gave a courtly curtsy."

"Nor is that necessary. Please sit. In the park, I spoke with you of my intentions, but, as yet, I have not told Lady Throckmorton. That is the purpose of this meeting, to inform her of my future plans."

At the moment, Ruanna did not care a fig about his intentions. She supposed His Lordship thought his marrying Lady Elise and producing an heir to inherit the Aynsworth title and the sinfully enormous wealth was more important than her students, but she begged to differ with him. "What about my students?" she asked, as she made to take the chair opposite Lady Throckmorton.

The earl strode about the room in a restless manner while he talked. "You will not go into *that* part of town! It is far too dangerous—"

"But I was going to ask Suthe and Guard to accompany me. Surely they would scare Archibald Bennet's men away—"

"No! I forbid it. Now, let's not speak of it again. I called this meeting to tell Lady Throckmorton that I shall soon marry Lady Elise. I have not proposed yet, but she has given every indication she will accept."

The earl paused for a moment and took a deep breath, as if he were reluctant to finish what he had started. "The reason for my delay in paying my addresses to Lady Elise is that she would no doubt object to my plan to train you, Ruanna, to go on in society. We must needs find a proper husband for you; but first, your rough edges must be taken off so that a gentleman of the upper orders will find you acceptable as a wife. You simply must stop swearing."

His Lordship took another turn around the room, while Ruanna fumed. She looked at Lady Throckmorton, who, if looks could tell, agreed with everything the earl was saying. Ruanna ground her teeth together.

Finally, the old woman spoke. "I think Lady Elise is a fine choice for a ton marriage, but the Aynsworth heir, I pray that he will take his looks from you, Lord Julian . . . and I do hope that I do not have to live under the same roof with the lady in question."

"Albeit, Lady Elise is not a raving beauty, but I do not wish to marry a raving beauty. And no, Isadora, you will not have to live under the same roof with Lady Elise. Once we are wed, Lady Elise and I will live at Wilderhope, leaving Grosvenor House to you and Miss Moreton, and, of course, to the husband we will find for her. He will most likely want to live here." The earl's countenance brightened. "That is a capital idea. I will make his living here a requirement, and I will provide an adequate dowry, but not so much that it will attract fortune hunters. My plan is very simple . . . and necessary. An heir necessitates marriage, else I would not marry at all. I like my life as it is."

Ruanna stood. "Well, I am most happy that you have settled on a plan for your life, and a plan for mine as well. When shall we start this training?"

Ruanna knew how to go on in society. She didn't even swear except when she was angry with the earl, which was most of the time, it seemed.

How can I be so stupid as to fall in love with a man who plans to marry someone else?

"Now, come with me," the earl said, looking at Ruanna. Meekly, she followed him from the room, down the long hall, until they came to the music room, where he threw open the door and stepped back.

Ruanna's breath caught in her throat. By the row of windows bright with refracted sunlight stood the harp she had admired in Boosey and Hawks' store window. She could not help herself; she threw her arms around the earl and kissed him on the cheek. "Oh, thank you, m'lord. In some ways, you are quite wonderful."

175

The earl pulled her arms from around his neck and pushed her back, holding her at arm's length. His frame rigid, his countenance set in an implacable line, he said, "I have written to little Jenny's maternal grandparents, asking that she return to Grosvenor House right away. When she arrives, you may start her lessons, thus earning your keep as I promised."

From behind them, Lady Throckmorton's voice scolded, "Lord Julian! Lady Moreton does not have to earn her keep."

The earl ignored the old woman's protest and continued, "I have noted that you are well read. You may spend a part of each morning teaching Jim his letters and numbers. Eventually, I will hire a fine tutor for him, but he seems so fond of you, I think mayhaps he will take to learning faster with you than with a tutor. After you have civilized him a bit, other arrangements will be made. For now, though, for gad's sake, stop his swearing."

"Whose? The tutor's?"

Silence met Ruanna's jest. Nonetheless, she felt a flush of happiness. Even if things were in a horrible mess for her, little Jim would have a chance in life.

"Teaching Jim his words and figures still does not take care of my students," Ruanna argued.

The earl looked thoughtful. "I have thought about that—"

Ruanna's words were slightly sarcastic. "I was sure you had a plan."

"I will take their names and addresses, and I shall personally make arrangement for another instructor to teach them."

"Not just any instructor can teach Jeremy! He has far surpassed all that I can teach him. I was going to Bochsa—"

"That will be no problem. I have met Napoleon's harpist, and I am sure arrangements can be made for him to teach Jeremy—if the young man is as talented as you claim."

176

And then, before Ruanna could express her gratitude, the earl said in a conciliatory tone, "Miss Moreton, it seems that you do not realize how dangerous it would be for you to return to that part of town. I do not wish to be unkind, or to appear too—"

"Domineering," Ruanna finished for him.

"Whatever," the earl said stridently. His frown increased. "I will not allow you to put yourself in danger and worry Isadora."

It seemed to Ruanna that she would have to compromise. And she admitted that, in truth, His Lordship was right. With his plan, at least her students would not be left without a teacher. She would write each of them a note and explain. Surely His Lordship would allow that.

And Ruanna knew exactly what she would do about the earl. She would be a very difficult student. It might take him forever to teach her how to go on in society. The redhead found herself smiling.

Within the day, Ruanna had written the missives to her students, and the earl had delivered them. When he returned, he reported that all was taken care of, and that Bochsa had agreed to tutor Jeremy. Twice a week, Suthe would deliver the boy to the conservatory.

At last, she could let go of her concern for Jeremy and concentrate on her little pickpocket. "'Tis remarkable how the earl has taken to Jim," she mused aloud.

I could use a little kindness from His Lordship, too.

One morning, a day or so later, after Ruanna had finished with Jim's lessons, the earl announced that he would be taking the boy to see the pugilist, Gentleman Jim, do a bout of boxing. When Ruanna asked to go along, Lord Julian laughed at her, and when she objected to his taking her little brother to a den of depravity, he told her to cry off.

"All men enjoy a fine bout," the earl said, "but it is

no place for a lady of quality."

"But I am not a lady of quality yet," Ruanna argued, but it did little good, for off they went, laughing and talking, riding in a high-sprung carriage like royalty itself.

Ruanna almost wished she did like to sew, a pastime which the earl had hinted was appropriate for her. Earlier in the day, she had played the new harp until her fingers were sore. And she had even suggested that she teach Jim. "Na," he had said, "I ain't no sissy."

Ruanna and Lady Throckmorton shared lunch together, eating in the garden, as had become their custom. Then, the old woman went to her room to write letters of invitation to Ruanna's come-out ball, which was to be held on the first floor of Grosvenor House, in the huge ballroom that opened into the center hall. At Ruanna's insistence, the date decided upon was a month away.

"To give time for the earl to train me properly," Ruanna told the old woman, who offered a smile, and Ruanna wondered if she knew of her plan.

Left alone, Ruanna became very lonely. In desperation, she went to the kitchen, where she found the cook preparing a fine pastry for the sideboard. "I would like to help," she offered, and the cook laughed at her, his big belly shaking like a jar of jelly that had not quite set.

"And what could you do to help me?" he asked.

"I can cook. I cooked at my home in India. The cook there was nice and—"

"Non, non, the ladies of Lord Aynsworth's household do not cook. *That* is my job. Your job is to eat. Here, take this and off with you. Have done."

He handed Ruanna a delicately browned fried pie, then waved his big hand toward the door. "Out! Out! Out!"

At the door, Ruanna stopped and looked back. She took a bite of the pie, chewed, and swallowed. "This is excellent, Whittier," she told him, and when a big grin broke across his fat face, she knew she had made a friend.

He tipped his white-hatted head, and said, "Thank you, m'lady."

Feeling utterly useless, Ruanna climbed the stairs to the second floor, where she pushed the big oak doors of the master library open and went in. A soft, honey-colored shimmer of sunlight flooded the room, dancing on the rich patina of the paneled walls, on the floor-to-ceiling bookshelves, and on the leather-bound books that filled the shelves. Right away, her gaze was drawn to a set of books on a huge desk piled high with papers, all in a state of disarray.

"Men!" she exclaimed, and she decided that the least she could do for the earl was to straighten the papers and put them in chronological order. After seating herself behind the desk, in a chair with a back that reached high above the top of her head, she went to work, deftly piling the vouchers to be paid in one pile, those that were marked paid in another. The receipts for the income from the estates went into their own pile. Then, she set about making entries in the books.

She added each column of figures, checked her answer for accuracy, then carried the amount forward to the next page.

The earl should appreciate this, she thought, and time passed swiftly. Not since she left India had she looked at a row of figures. So far, she and Jim were working on adding two and two, and on getting him to say "can" instead of "ken."

All went well with the redhead until a large sum and the name Countess Charlotte Loyd-Dobbs Aynsworth jumped off the page and landed right between her eyes. Her heart hammered against her rib cage, and when she checked back through the books and found that the same amount was mailed monthly to 131 Faubourg Saint-Germain in Paris, to Countess Charlotte, Ruanna's breath began coming in short spurts. And, as if that was not enough, Ruanna thought, another shock was soon added to her dismay.

It seemed that the fifth earl of Wendsleydale also made payments to a certain Katrina Medcalf, as well as paying servants at the dwelling where the strumpet lived. Of course, she did not know that the woman was a strumpet, but it seemed obvious what was taking place. Beside Miss Medcalf's name were large sums, which had been paid to jewelers.

The woman must be dripping with expensive baubles.

Ruanna's nostrils flared. Knowing that men did this sort of thing soothed her not at all. The earl was not just any man. He was the man she loved.

"What a despot!" she exclaimed. "What a degenerate, what an odious—"

"Are you speaking of me, Miss Moreton?"

Ruanna looked up. The deep, resonant, and angry voice had come for the doorway, where the tall earl stood, almost filling the aperture.

Before Ruanna could answer, the earl said in a clipped voice, "Miss Moreton, just once I would like to return home and find you with your sewing basket, wool knitting thread spilling onto your lap. Or perhaps find you embroidering a piece of cloth."

When Ruanna's eyes met the earl's, their gaze held like links of chain forged together. Caught in the intensity of his gaze, she felt his unleashed fury flung in her direction.

She waited for him to go on, but he just stood there, an awesome, predatory power lurking beneath his hard-chiseled exterior.

The skin on the back of Ruanna's neck prickled. She felt a warmth spread over her. Even when he was angry, the earl was an exciting man, and she wondered if he had that same effect on other women, knowing with certainty that he did. The books did not lie.

Breaking the gaze with the toss of her head, she rose to her feet, lifted her chin defiantly, and braced herself for another set-down from the mighty earl. But when he started to speak, she told him, "In truth, I was speaking of you. I think I shall tell Lady Elise what a sorry prospect for a husband you are. You are a keeper of women—"

"One woman," the earl snarled, then added, "First, I will have a good laugh about that, and then I will allow myself to be very angry with you." He paused. "Not that that would be anything new. What were you doing snooping in my books?"

"I was not snooping," Ruanna said. "I was working, bringing them to balance, while you were off teaching my little brother your degenerative way of life."

"I think mayhaps your *little brother* could teach me a thing or two about a degenerative life, and I am coming to believe that you could be a teacher of deception. What do you know about estate books?"

Ruanna stared at him, her mouth set in an firm line, and the earl looked back at her, quizzically, as he walked closer to the desk. "Miss Moreton, how is that no matter what happens, you have the ability to turn it to your advantage, making you the innocent? Like now, pretending to work on books when you know nothing of estate business?"

Then he accused, "'Tis obvious that you wanted to learn about my affairs."

"I *am* innocent," Ruanna proclaimed. "I was only trying to earn my keep, which you promised that I should be permitted to do. And I do know about estate figures. I worked on Papa's books in India."

"I do not believe you," the earl said. "Women do not know of such things. There's no need. Men are in charge of family affairs."

He moved to stand before the desk, leaning forward, his face dangerously close to Ruanna's. "If you are so demme determined to be useful, I suggest you go about doing women's work. Lady Throckmorton insists that we give up this idea of your earning your keep, and I agree with her. It is not at all necessary." His Lordship's voice became more stern. "You are here because my old cousin

181

wants you here, not because we need extra help. Balancing my book indeed! Snooping is more like it," he accused again.

As the earl talked, his gaze dropped to look at the books. Even upside down, he could see the amounts had been neatly entered, the totals figured. His countenance fell.

"Are you not ashamed of yourself for being so unkind?" Ruanna asked. "Shall I have Whittier make a crow pie for your consumption?"

The earl did not answer.

"And what do you have to say about these astronomical bills for your kept women? Do you not feel that they are a drain on the estates? And I wonder how Lady Elise, your intended, would like it if she knew. I think it is utterly deplorable. Being in love with Countess Charlotte as you obviously are, and keeping a certain Katrina Medcalf, while you plan to offer for Lady Elise. What a tangled life you lead, m'lord."

Ruanna remembered that Katie had said the earl hated Countess Charlotte, but for the moment she chose to ignore the maid's remark. She wished so much for the earl himself to tell her that he no longer cared for his brother's dowager countess.

But the earl did no such thing. Instead, he offered a sardonic smile. Straightening, he hooked his thumbs in the pockets of his waistcoat. "I believe you have alluded to my way of life before, Miss Moreton. The night in the park comes to mind. But until you entered my life, my affairs were in perfect order, every thought orchestrated in the right direction."

He paused for a long moment, his eyes impaling Ruanna, and then he went on. "But I have noted that in a few short weeks you have succeeded in turning my whole existence into a mixture of confusion. There's no denying that you have succeeded in stirring emotions I experienced in my youth, and I'll mention that which I should not even breathe in a lady's presence . . . passion.

I believe that feeling was spawned by the devil, and I have no notion of losing control again. Now if you will kindly remove yourself from behind my desk and go change into something suitable, I shall take you for a ride in the park. It is near five o'clock, and it is time I get on with your training."

Ruanna removed from behind the desk and dropped into a deep curtsy. "You are so kind, my most gracious lord and master," she chided.

When she lifted her gaze, the earl fixed her with a stare, and she felt a shiver along her spine, while her heart throbbed in her throat. She waited for him to lift her up, to touch her.

Knowing that if he touched her, he would unwillingly take her into his arms, the earl wheeled round and quit the room, slamming the door behind him so hard it quivered on its hinges. As he strode down the hall, he swore, "The devil take me."

His Lordship added three demmes, and after that, he asked himself why it was that Ruanna Moreton could, without fail, make him forget his well-orchestrated manners.

Chapter Fourteen

Ruanna chose an afternoon dress of blue sprigged muslin to wear to the park, and a fine bonnet with plumes to match. Katie helped her dress, while Lady Throckmorton looked on and clucked. "Your hair is growing so fast, Ruanna," the old woman said, "and the bonnet frames your face beautifully."

Ruanna, having grown used to Lady Throckmorton's compliments, smiled and thanked her.

When the maid and Lady Throckmorton were satisfied with the fit of the dress, Katie took a piece of coal and darkened Ruanna's eyebrows. Ruanna then left to go to the master book room, where a footman had said the earl waited.

As she drew near, she heard voices and did not immediately go in. Standing unobtrusively outside the door, she could see the earl and Jim, who was dressed much like the earl, all the crack. Each wore a dark coat, white cravat, and light-colored breeches over white stockings.

Ruanna found herself smiling as she watched the big earl and the little boy. If it were not for Jim's blond hair and his round face, she would not have recognized him as the little ragamuffin with mismatched stockings who had saved her from being trampled to death. He sat in the oversized chair and, of all things, was smoking a brown cheroot. But so was the earl. Ruanna smiled when she heard Jim say, "I take your meaning, m'lord. I can see that I must mend me ways."

The earl drew on his cheroot and blew out a puff of smoke. "Just because a boy starts out under unfortunate circumstances does not mean he must needs let that ruin the rest of his life," the earl said.

He paused for a moment, as if, Ruanna thought, he was thinking back, remembering, and pondering on what to say. His handsome face was dark and harsh in the shimmering light that sliced the room in half. A dimness dulled his eyes. Finally he spoke again. "My childhood, though much different from yours, was not a happy one. But I feel I have overcome those adversities, and now, since I have inherited the earldom, I strive to be an exemplary representative of the Crown. I enjoy my days in the House of Lords. I would like to see laws on the books that protect children such as you; the government should stop child labor. The little chimney sweeps are a disgrace, and the school for pickpockets such as you went to should be outlawed. And I would like public schools, paid for by the government, provided for poor children."

"I prefer Lady Moreton's teaching," Jim said quickly, as he squirmed in his seat and sucked deeply on the long, brown cheroot. Tilting his head back, he let the smoke curl up in front of his face. When he coughed, Ruanna, feeling laughter bubble up inside her, put her hand over her mouth to smother the sound.

Sitting on a sofa opposite Jim, the earl took a huge puff of his cheroot, blowing his own cloud. "That is well and good for the present, but soon I will locate a male tutor, and then later, after you are prepared, you will go to Eton."

"Eton! Odd zookers! A pickpocket goin' to Eton?"

The earl leaned forward. His voice was slightly stern when he said, "Stop using such slang words, and, pray, stop referring to yourself as a pickpocket. Those days are behind you."

"Yer right, me lord. I forgot. I ain't no pickpocket no more."

Ruanna saw the earl grimace, but he kept quiet. She well understood that she had a long way to go in teaching Jim proper grammar, and she would chastise the earl for teaching the boy to smoke. When she stepped inside the room the stench of the burning cheroots wafted up to assault her nostrils.

"Lord Julian, Jim, I am ready for the ride in the park," Ruanna said, and felt two pairs of eyes turn in her direction.

Jim whistled through his teeth, and the earl's eyes raked over her, approval registering in his gaze. His Lordship rose to his feet, and Jim followed his example. Except he did not merely rise; he jumped out of his chair. His legs being so short, when his feet hit the floor, the thud was quite loud.

The earl ground out his cheroot in a silver container near the sofa; Jim did the same.

"I hope that I am appropriately dressed," Ruanna said.

The earl cleared his throat. For a moment he could not speak. As he looked into Ruanna's enormous green eyes, he felt desire pulsing through his body, unwelcome, but there nonetheless. "You are appropriately dressed, Miss Moreton. . . ."

"Why don't yer call her Lady Moreton like the old woman calls her?" Jim asked.

"Jim! The old woman is Lady Throckmorton," Ruanna scolded.

The earl looked down at the little boy. "You are right, Jim. I should address Miss Moreton by her curtsy title. By rights of succession, she is entitled to the same title as her mother, who was Lady Mary Moreton."

The earl, half-smiling, gave Ruanna a leg, called her Lady Moreton, then took her hand and lifted it to his lips, holding it an inordinately long time.

Laughing, Ruanna said, "I believe we settled on your calling me Ruanna."

Because she was becoming flustered, and because that familiar yearning began to spread through her body, Ruanna withdrew her hand and held it out to Jim, who giggled and kissed it with aplomb. She asked, "Are you going to the park with us, Jim?"

"I think he should come along," the earl interjected. "He needs training of how the upper orders act as much as you do, Miss . . . Lady Moreton. But both of you must needs remember that the top of the ton will be there, and good behavior is required." He turned his clear blue eyes onto Ruanna. "No cork-brained antics this time. We will not have a repeat of what happened when we encountered Lady Elise and her companion on our way from Newgate."

Why can he not forget that? Ruanna thought. A portent swept over her. Why do I have the feeling that this ride is going to end in disaster?

Aloud she said, "I shall strive not to embarrass you in front of your intended."

"Perhaps we are safe there. I doubt that Her Ladyship will be in the park today. I hear she is ailing. But Lady Jersey often holds court in the park, and if you make a good impression, perhaps I can obtain a voucher for you to attend the subscription dances at Almack's."

He paused. As if embarrassed, Ruanna thought.

"I'm sorry Ruanna, but with your mother having married a man of the trades, it might prove to be a little difficult."

Ruanna knew that with the earl's influence he could obtain a voucher to Almack's for the devil himself, but she let the remark pass. It was clear to her that the earl's training to make her a lady would take place when Lady Elise was not present. Looking His Lordship straight in the eyes, she asked, "Do you not think it a little deceitful to do things behind Lady Elise's back?"

"I prefer not to expose you overmuch to Lady Elise at this time. There's a chance she would misunderstand my intentions, and since Lady Throckmorton is determined to keep you with her, and since I am to wed Lady Elise, the relationship between the two of you will be a long-lasting one. I prefer it to be amicable."

A part of Ruanna wanted to spit, the other part wanted to cry. That the earl would soon offer for Lady Elise was, with each passing day, becoming a reality. And the pain was more intense because Lady Throckmorton seemed pleased with the news. Ruanna had no one on her side, no one with whom she could speak of her feelings. If she told Katie, the whole household would know.

Tears brimmed Ruanna's eyes, and that made her even more angry. But the thought of the earl being married to *any* woman other than herself was more than she could bear, and the thought of his having a child by Lady Elise did not bear thinking upon.

Produce an heir; mind the strictures of the ton; it is acceptable for a man to have a mistress, she mimicked inside her head as she remembered that long ago her mother and father had loved each other. "And that is how it should be when two people wed," she said, sotto voce.

But pride held the redhead in good stead. Grinding her teeth together, she set her chin in an obdurate line as she followed the earl and Jim from the room, feeling more like she was going to her own inquisition than to a pleasant ride in the park.

As they descended the stairs to the great center hall, walked across it, then down the front steps to where the crested coach waited, the earl held Jim's hand. And instead of letting a footman hand Jim up, he handed him up himself, leaving the footman to help Ruanna.

She sat on the seat opposite the little boy and was surprised when the earl lithely sprang up into the coach and sat beside her, and not in the corner as one would expect, but close enough that his thigh touched hers.

From the corner of her eye, Ruanna caught the earl looking at her. But there was no smile. In truth, he was as cold and stiff as a fish fresh out of the North Ocean.

Clearly he was doing his duty by exposing her to the pink of the ton, now that she was dressed properly.

In a pleasant enough voice the earl gave Suthe office to go, and then they were off. The sleek, black horses' hooves clopped loudly against the cobbled street, while, inside the carriage, silence hovered like a waiting cloud.

After the carriage turned left into Park Lane, they were soon at Stanhope Gate and entered the park there.

Men dressed in fine riding clothes rode excellent horses, the likes of which Ruanna had never seen, and the women were dressed to the nines. Ruanna could not help leaning forward to look, and felt thoroughly chastised when the earl put his hand on her shoulder and pulled her back against the squab. "One does not gawk—"

From narrowed eyes, Jim gave the earl a piercing look. "I don't know why not. How's she to see if yer don't let her look."

"She can see enough, Jim, by sitting erect in the carriage."

The earl did not move his hand from Ruanna's shoulder. As the carriage jolted along, his thigh rubbed against hers, and desire ripped through his body, until the need to touch her, to hold her, to make love to her, became the roar of a lion wanting to mate.

He could smell her freshness, her cleanliness. A huge constricting knot tightened his throat, and heat filled his loins, until he forced anger to replace the roaring passion. How dare she tempt him so? he silently asked, jerking his hand from her shoulder.

Sitting perfectly straight, the earl smiled at Jim, whom he had no compunction about loving.

The carriage tooled around the outer rim of the park, and when they reached the center, Ruanna saw off to the right a smart black vis-à-vis, a lady sitting in it.

Ruanna immediately knew it was Lady Jersey, and when men on horses vied for a place to be near her, and carriages stopped so that women could pay their respects,

Ruanna supposed that Lady Jersey was holding court, as the earl had called it.

"I'm pleased Lady Jersey is here," His Lordship said to Ruanna. "When the crowd around her has dispersed somewhat, I shall introduce you to her. I'm sure you will make a good impression." He paused for a long moment before going on. "You are beautiful today. The dress becomes you."

"Thank you," Ruanna said.

Feeling her face grow warm, Ruanna looked away, and when she did, she saw another carriage just as popular as Lady Jersey's. Except with this one, there were no women clamoring around, just handsomely attired men. Some had even left their horses and were walking alongside the carriage.

"Harriette Wilson," the earl explained.

"And who is Harriette Wilson?" Ruanna asked. That was one thing her mother had not told her.

"The most famous of the fashionable impures. You will find that the cyprians come to the park and ride along with the Upper Orders. Most of them want to be seen in the finery their protectors have provided, and often one is shopping for someone new, having grown tired of the gentleman who has been keeping her."

Ruanna's mouth was agape. "Gentlemen! The women are—"

"Whores," Jim said quickly, as if he did not want Ruanna to soil her mouth by using the word.

The earl gave him a fierce look. "Your mouth should be washed out with soap, Jim. It is acceptable—"

"I know, I know," Ruanna interjected, "It is acceptable for a man to keep a mistress. You have said that before, m'lord, and a ton marriage is acceptable, even expected . . . to produce an heir," she added sarcastically. But she could not keep the pain from her words.

Then, something captured the earl's attention. Ruanna followed his gaze and saw drawing up beside the Wendsleydale carriage an elegant carriage with a

191

beautiful woman leaning demurely against red velvet squabs. When the woman straightened, ropes of pearls tumbled down to touch her near-naked, pink bosom. The arm she lifted to wave to the earl held glittering bracelets, and a diamond pen sparkled from her dark hair.

Miss Medcalf! The jewels alone told Ruanna that much. Here was the strumpet on whom the earl squandered his money. And it must be even more than the books showed, Ruanna thought. Miss Medcalf's coachman wore a three-cornered hat, a highly liveried footman rode on the back of her carriage, and her horses were sleek and tasseled. *And she's dressed like Madame de Pompadour.*

Before Ruanna could utter a word—she had decided she would not show her anger—the earl called to Suthe to stop the carriage, and with a slight smile playing around his mouth, said to Ruanna and Jim, "I shall return shortly." He then bounded down onto the ground and made his way to Miss Medcalf's equipage, which had also stopped.

They were too far away for Ruanna to hear what they were saying, but she saw the earl's smile come full-blown as he let the steps down and reached up to help Miss Medcalf alight.

Ruanna prayed: Dear Lord, do not let him bring her to talk with me.

And the earl didn't. Together, he and his mistress walked alongside her carriage, which moved slowly, as did the earl's own crested carriage. Obviously, Suthe knew what was expected of him, Ruanna thought.

"Is that his ladybird?" Jim asked.

"She's his mistress, and, as you know, that is acceptable—"

"His Lordship is a cabbage-head."

"Why do you say that, Jim? He has really taken to you. I believe you have reached that soft core Lady Throckmorton is always talking about."

"Only a cabbage-head would be out there walking with

192

her when he could be riding by yer, yer being in love with him the way yer are."

Denial sprang to Ruanna's lips, and she said, "That is not true." Ruanna knew, however, that she could not lie to the street-smart kid. "Well, he does not know I am in love with him, and it is stupid of me, and. . . ."

Before Ruanna could finish, Jim was out of the carriage, and almost immediately out of sight. She had never seen anyone or anything move so quickly.

"Jim, come back here," she called to the empty space around the carriage, which had picked up its pace and was now ahead of the earl and his paramour.

She started to call to Suthe to stop and let her out so she could find Jim, but she knew that her search would be futile. If Jim did not want to be found, he would not be found, such was his training.

A wave of aching loneliness washed over Ruanna. What if Jim was gone for good? It would be beyond her power to endure. The brightest spot in her day was when she helped him with his lessons, and when he sat and listened to her play the harp.

If Jim is gone; if the earl marries Lady Elise . . .

Ruanna's worry about Jim being gone for good was short-lived. She heard a squeal, much like a stuck pig, and then she saw him running into the crowd gathered round Lady Jersey's vis-à-vis, the earl in strong pursuit.

Calling Suthe to stop the carriage, Ruanna was quickly on the ground.

Sure that the squeal had come from Miss Medcalf, Ruanna went to see what damage had been done.

The lady in question was not hard to spot. A crowd had gathered, and even before Ruanna closed the distance between them, she heard her hysterical sobbing. "The little thief took my bracelet. How, I don't know. I hope Lord Julian beats him within an inch of his life . . . and it was my most expensive bracelet . . . gift from His Lordship. Look! My arm is bleeding."

Ruanna knew *how* Jim had taken the bracelet. More

than once she had seen him slip a sharp shiv under the top of his stocking. When she questioned him about it, he had merely said it was for his protection . . . if someone attacked him. But he had also told her it would cut delicate metal, if held at the right angle.

More worried about Jim than she was about Miss Medcalf's sliced arm, Ruanna turned in time to see Jim dart under the bellies of the two rearing horses hitched to Lady Jersey's vis-à-vis. Her Ladyship was pulling back on the leathers, while screaming at the top of her lungs.

When the earl grabbed at Jim, the little boy was long out of his reach. So His Lordship landed flat on the ground, and Ruanna could only imagine the invectives spilling from his mouth as he scrambled to his feet and gave chase again.

Not knowing what else to do, Ruanna returned to the Wendsleydale carriage. Suthe guided the horses out of the stream of traffic, and soon the squeeze was on again, as if nothing untoward had happened.

Men galloped by on their beautiful stallions, vying for position, and the demireps looked demurely at the men who approached their carriages.

Ruanna looked around for Miss Medcalf's carriage, only to find that it had disappeared. She could only guess that she had gone to have her arm taken care of, although Ruanna doubted that the cut was more than a scratch. She had confidence in Jim's expertise.

Ruanna, impatient, wanted to try to find Jim, but, knowing it would be a futile search, decided not to try. She wondered if the earl was still chasing the little boy, and, if he had caught him, what he was saying to him. Knowing the earl's temper, she shuddered, and then panic swept over her. What if the earl retrieved the bracelet and sent Jim on his way, away from Grosvenor House? The thought started her heart pounding again, and the wait grew interminable.

Finally, with relief, she heard Suthe say, "Here they come."

Leaning out, Ruanna saw the tall, dusty earl practically dragging Jim by the scruff of his neck. There was no way Jim's short legs could keep up with His Lordship's long strides. "Stop dragging my brother," she called.

By now, the two were near enough to the carriage for the earl to practically pitch the boy onto the seat beside Ruanna, after which he flung himself up onto the opposite seat. "Your *little brother* has just ruined your chances for a voucher to Almack's. I'm sure Lady Jersey does not take kindly to being scared out of her wits. 'Tis a wonder her horses did not bolt. . . . 'Tis all singularly embarrassing." He said again, "I fear a voucher is out of the question."

"*That* does not signify," Ruanna countered. "The horses did not bolt, and Jim is all right."

Jim held out the bracelet to her. "Yer deserves this more'n the whore."

His head tilted back and pushing against the squabs, the earl groaned. He closed his eyes, as if, Ruanna thought, the whole happening had been a nightmare and he wished to shut it out. "Give the bracelet to Lord Julian," Ruanna said.

Smiling at the little thief, she reached to give his bony knee a loving pat, while a lump the size of an egg formed in her throat. She had a friend, after all.

Chapter Fifteen

The incident in the park was soon forgotten, or, if not forgotten, it was not talked about. The earl seemingly had forgiven Jim, and the household returned to normal. Each morning Ruanna sat across from the little boy, teaching him his letters and numbers, while the earl stayed she did not know where.

Ruanna had heard from Katie, who had heard from the head housekeeper, that His Lordship was often at White's, gambling excessively. One morning he escorted Ruanna and Lady Throckmorton to Bond Street, where they purchased more fabric, then took it to the dressmaker.

Ruanna wondered *when* her training would resume . . . or if she was doomed to live like a prisoner for the rest of her life. That the earl was angry with her, there was no doubt. When she asked about dear Miss Medcalf's cut arm, he had told her to mind her own business.

On rare occasions, Ruanna and Lady Throckmorton made morning calls, which Ruanna hated. But, according to the earl, the calls would teach her correct comportment, and His Lordship tagged along, watching over her as if she were a two-year-old.

This was not the kind of training Ruanna had in mind when she decided to pretend she did not know how to go on in society. She wanted to go to parties, to routs, and to the opera—with the earl. Even if Jim had ruined her chances of going to Almack's, the earl *could,* if he wished, take her to the other social events that Katie told her about.

There was, however, one bright spot in Ruanna's life. One day a messenger brought a beautifully scrawled missive from Bochsa, in which he expressed his appreciation for her having sent little Jeremy to him. She was glad that she had persevered on Jeremy's behalf, and when she sent Guard and Suthe with inquiries of her other students, the reports were equally satisfying. The earl had retained excellent instructors, so it seemed.

Then, a week after the park incident, His Lordship came to the yellow salon where Ruanna and Lady Throckmorton were having a nice coze. Without preamble, he announced, "Lady Moreton, tonight, we will go to Almack's, where I shall instruct you in the proper way to dance with a gentleman."

He paused for a moment, as if he were embarrassed at what he was about to say. He did not look directly at Ruanna when he finally spoke. "Using a fair amount of subterfuge regarding your background, and, by apologizing profusely for Jim's behavior in the park, I have obtained a voucher from the patronesses for you to attend the subscription balls on Wednesday evenings."

He turned and looked out the window, through which the late evening sun poured the day's last light. Turning back to give Ruanna a studied look, he added, "I pray that you will extend the courtesy of not embarrassing me."

The redhead jumped to her feet. "I will do my utmost, m'lord, and I cannot say how sorry I am about what happened in the park. I am pleased that you have decided to give me another chance. I had no idea Jim—"

The earl interrupted. "After a long talk, he promised to try harder to give up his stealing. The bracelet has been repaired and returned to Miss Medcalf; the cut on her arm was a mere scratch, and now, may we consider *that* subject closed?"

The earl knew that he must needs explain everything, or the inquisitive hoyden would keep asking.

Of course she does not know that in proper society one does not pry into another's business, he reasoned.

Her lips pressed together, Ruanna waited. She knew by the look on the earl's face there was more.

"About Almack's," the earl said, "until you have proven yourself, you will not participate in the waltz. Because it is considered a sensuous dance, you must have special permission."

When Ruanna smiled, the earl wanted to shake her. "Do you understand?" he blustered.

"You are so kind," she said as she curtsied low and long. When he fixed her with a stare, then turned and abruptly left the room, a shiver traversed Ruanna's spine, and her heart throbbed in her throat. Why did he speak so condescendingly to her? And why was he so damnably handsome?

But it was difficult for Ruanna to be angry when she was to be escorted to Almack's by the fifth earl of Wendsleydale, lord of Wilderhope in Shropshire, she thought, and she practically skipped her way to her rooms, where she found herself surrounded by three chattering women, all wanting to decide which gown she should wear.

There was Katie, of course; Lady Throckmorton's maid, Marie; and Her Ladyship herself, who had followed when Ruanna left the yellow salon.

Even Sutherland, dressed in his long-tailed coat, his white collar points pricking his chin, which was in that perpetual upward tilt, found an excuse to knock on the door. "May I be of assistance?" he asked.

Knowing the butler was only seeking a morsel of gossip to report to the other servants, Ruanna asked his opinion on which lovely garment she should wear. He gave Ruanna a rare smile and assured her that the dress she was wearing was lovely enough to wear to the fanciest of balls.

"Oh, but I must look my loveliest, Sutherland."

Lady Throckmorton's mouth flew open at this familiarity, but then she smiled, thinking that only Ruanna could get such a response from the staid butler. The servants, one and all, had come to love her dear Ruanna. How they had hated the *other* redhead!

Using his quizzing glass, the butler peered at one gown after another as Ruanna held them up to herself and whirled lithely about the room.

Lady Throckmorton clucked, and the maids squealed with delight.

The butler pointed to a blue satin, shot with platinum thread. "I think that one, m'lady."

It was the very dress Ruanna herself had secretly chosen. She told him, "You are so astute, Sutherland. This gown it shall be."

Beaming, the butler bowed and left, and when Ruanna was dressed, the delightful ahs from her three helpers echoed off the walls of the room. "Do you think the prince regent will be there?" Katie asked, giggling, her hand over her mouth.

"I certainly hope so," Lady Throckmorton said. "It would be a shame if His Majesty missed such an exquisite picture of perfection."

"All of you, do not go on so much," Ruanna said. "I am sure there will be many women at Almack's dressed more beautifully than I."

Ruanna turned to look in the gilt-framed looking glass that hung on her dressing room wall, and was pleased with the reflection that looked back at her. A low neckline exposed a creamy-white neck; the empire bodice molded her upthrust bosom; the sleeves were tiny puffs at the shoulders.

Her red hair, which she had so assiduously cropped, had grown to a more becoming length, almost touching her shoulders, and little wisps curled against her cheeks.

Katie pulled long red strands up and worked them into a becoming French twist on the back of Ruanna's head, letting tendrils fall on her neck, and then she added a blue comb with tiny flowers.

Ruanna smiled her approval, but when she turned to see Lady Throckmorton's thinking, the old woman was gone. "Where did Her Ladyship go?"

Marie answered, "Didn't say a word. She jest left."

But it was only moments before the tall, straight woman reappeared, a velvet box in her hand. With shaking hands, she opened and took from it a necklace of sparkling diamonds and glittering emeralds. Matching eardrops reposed on the black velvet lining. Her voice trembled noticeably when she said, "These were given to me years ago. I want you to have them." She held the necklace out to Ruanna.

"Oh, but I can't, Isadora. They were given to you," Ruanna protested.

The old woman's voice broke completely, and she waited a moment before going on. "I want very much for you to have them. Pray, wear them in good health."

As she fastened the necklace around Ruanna's neck, and the earbobs to her ears, silence pervaded the room. Not even an ah went up, and Ruanna felt three sets of eyes on her. What could she do but accept?

She could not hurt the old woman, Ruanna thought, but she wondered, just as she had wondered about a lot of things since meeting Isadora Throckmorton, *why* the old woman would give her such an expensive gift.

"The emeralds match your green eyes," Lady Throckmorton said. "And the earbobs twinkle when you move."

"Thank you. Thank you so much." Ruanna had trouble pushing the words out. She swallowed, but the lump remained in her throat. She put her arms around Lady Throckmorton's thin shoulders and kissed her on both cheeks. "You have the kindest heart of anyone I have ever known, Your Ladyship, unless it was my dear Mama."

Turning to the two hovering maids, Lady Throckmorton asked them to leave. "I want to speak to Lady

Moreton alone," she said. After they were gone, she turned to Ruanna. "If only Lord Julian were not so jaded, and if you were not so tender, I would wish that he could return your love. But I am afraid he would abuse your sensibilities, crush you like a flower."

Ruanna's mouth opened to protest. *What's the use; she knows.*

The old woman paused for a moment and stood pensively, looking at the floor, and then she said, "It isn't his fault that his heart was turned to stone, but that does not change the fact that an uncaring woman like Lady Elise would be more suitable for him. I've given it much thought."

Ruanna was glad that Lady Throckmorton had explained her feelings to her. She did not, however, want the old woman to know the pain she felt. Giving a slight shrug of her shoulders, she said, "The earl hates me. His devotion to you is his reason for taking me to Almack's. He has made that plain enough."

"Lord Julian hates all women with red hair . . . it was the she-devil. . . ."

The old woman looked as if she were going to say more, but then the solemn, faraway look returned to her eyes, and she remained silent.

Not wanting anything to ruin the night, Ruanna thought it was just as well that Lady Throckmorton did not say more. She took her beaded reticule in hand and lifted her skirt. Her eyes misted when she looked at the old woman. "Thank you, Isadora," she whispered, and then she left.

The earl, dressed in elegant evening attire; black, tight-fitting knee breeches, burgundy evening coat with tails, a black cape, and his chapeau bras tucked under his arm, awaited Ruanna at the bottom of the stairs—the same stairs which, earlier on, she had fallen down. From lack of nourishment, he thought, his heart hurting inside his big chest. When he saw her, he sucked in a breath.

Light from the chandeliers shimmered on Ruanna's red hair. He tried to harden his heart, but failed completely. Like a fire left to smolder, a surge of warmth rose up to engulf him. He swore inaudibly as she descended the stairs with her head held erect. When she stepped off the last polished step, she sank into a royal curtsy at his feet.

This time His Lordship lifted her up and kissed her hand, and Ruanna felt a flush of warmth fill her face, then move to her quivering depths. Fearing her feelings would show, she turned away. She would rather die than have the earl know the effect he had on her. She felt so vulnerable, and so inexperienced with men. Even if she wanted to change his mind about marrying Lady Elise to produce an heir, she would not know how to begin. Silently, Ruanna vowed that tonight she would be on her best behavior.

"Almack's assembly rooms are on King Street, off St. James Street," the earl told Ruanna as the black lacquered coach, with crested panels, transported them in that direction. Four beautiful bays were at the bits, and Suthe was on the box.

Ruanna leaned back against the velvet squabs and stole a look at the earl's lean, hard face. His eyes were focused straight ahead. He sat away from her, and only the folds of her skirt touched his thigh. Aloof, indifferent, she thought, with only one thing on his mind—training her in the proper manners of the upper orders.

"Isadora desires very much for you to learn how to go on in society," he said.

Why does he have to keep reminding me that he is here only because his cousin desires it?

"I know she does, but coming from the slums as I so recently did, it might be a torturous process for you to teach me everything I need to know. You mentioned that

203

I am a quick study, but I am not so sure."

When the earl turned to look at her, shadows from the lighted carriage lanterns danced across her face. He withdrew his gaze to look out over London. Gaslights lighted the streets, magical nimbuses of brightness, softened by the evening mist. The muted bells of St. Paul's struck the hour, the sound wafting through the air.

The earl's mind failed to be distracted. He gulped, and his heart raced across his thrumming chest. He wished desperately that he could hold her.

Then, like huge waves washing away the sand from the shore, a sudden rush of memories came to him, making bare his soul. Too painfully he remembered the hurts, the anger that he strove to keep submerged inside him. Bile rose up in his throat as he thought of the other redhead, and the thought acutely reminded him that he wanted no part of this one.

After all, she had admitted to having had a lover in India. The earl corrected himself; by her own admission, she *still* had a lover in India.

He sighed deeply, inwardly. That the woman beside him was lovely was unmistakable. If he did not know better, he could believe that she was well placed and finely bred. Looking at her now, so elegantly dressed, so demure in her behavior, it was difficult for him to believe that she was the one and same girl who had clobbered him with a homemade club, and then quickly disappeared down a back alley.

"Your gown is lovely," he said.

"Sutherland chose it for me—"

"Sutherland!" The earl's voice quickly lost its softness. "Ruanna, you are not to prose on with the hired help, and I think, tonight, we should address each other as m'lord and m'lady. A display of familiarity would not be within the bounds of propriety."

"I shall try to remember."

The earl shook his head as the carriage jockeyed for a

place in front of Almack's. A liveried footman was there to help them alight. Addressing the earl as m'lord, Lord Julian, and Ruanna as m'lady, Lady Moreton, he bowed them in, then announced their presence in a loud voice.

As they entered the enclosure, the earl offered Ruanna his arm. She noticed the dancing had stopped, and every eye was turned on them. Suddenly she was struck with fright. When the women rushed forward, like vultures closing in on their prey, the earl bent his head to hers and whispered, "You are doing just fine."

Lady Jersey gushed her welcome. "We are enormously happy that you could honor us with your presence, Lady Moreton. This naughty Lord Julian has been keeping you hidden, and we've all been simply dying with curiosity."

Yes, I can see that, Ruanna thought, as the earl made the proper introductions all round. Ruanna smiled some more, but she barely managed to retain her composure when Lady Elise swept forward, dressed in a flowing gown of deep purple. Daintily postured in her gloved hand was an elegant fan.

"Lord Julian," Lady Elise exclaimed, and dropped into a deep curtsy.

The earl bowed over her hand; then, smiling, he said, "Lady Elise, may I present Lady Ruanna Moreton."

"Why, I thought . . . er . . . the day I met you when on my way to the park, I thought they were boys you were bringing to Grosvenor House to work."

"I do work—"

When Ruanna felt the earl's long fingers tighten around her arm, she clamped her mouth shut.

"Lady Moreton and little Jim had been on a picnic, frolicking in the woods, so naturally they were dressed accordingly. I had gone to fetch them. Lady Moreton is the granddaughter of the late Countess Mary Elizabeth Waite."

Before Lady Elise could respond, dancing resumed. The earl asked to be excused and led Ruanna out onto the dance floor, leaving Lady Elise with her mouth agape.

"Just follow my lead, and you shall be all right," the earl whispered against Ruanna's ear.

Ruanna pretended to miss a step, and felt His Lordship's arm tighten around her, while his own tall frame moved rhythmically with the music.

"All eyes are turned to you, Lady Moreton. I believe you will be the belle of the ball tonight," he told her.

Ruanna's smile was genuine. Then he added, "It will please my cousin something tremendously to receive such a report."

After that Ruanna made a concerted effort to step on His Lordship's glistening highlows. She cast a demure smile up at him and stumbled again, but only slightly. "Pray, forgive me. I am trying very hard not to embarrass you, m'lord."

From the sideline, the prince regent lifted his quizzing glass to inspect the new beauty among them. Why have I not seen her before? he wondered. "I hear she lives at Grosvenor House." He sighed deeply and said, "Exquisite."

"I agree," Lord Worthington, who was standing at His Majesty's elbow, answered. "A true beauty. But the red hair! Have you not heard Lord Julian say that he would burn Grosvenor House to the ground before another redhead would abide under its roof?"

"Yes, yes, I have heard him say that very thing. But he was most likely in his cups. I wonder if he is carrying the willow—"

"Oh . . . no. I don't think so at all. His Lordship is not one to pretend. Hatred for redheads is his thing."

The prince regent smiled and let his quizzing glass drop. "Well, the other redhead deserved what she got . . . I even had a go with her. But this one, I wonder why she's at Grosvenor House. Where did she come from?"

"On-dits have it that his old cousin brought her there

206

and is so devoted to the chit that Lord Julian has had no luck in getting rid of her," Lord Worthington said.

"Then, perhaps Lord Julian will be generous and introduce us to this redhead." The prince regent ran his tongue over his plump lips. "I shall have first chance, of course."

Chapter Sixteen

An hour later, the Wendsleydale carriage was headed in the direction of Grosvenor House, the four bays up to their bits. Ruanna grabbed the strap and held on to keep from being thrown to the floor. The earl sat across from her; too stubborn, she was sure, to admit he needed a strap. The carriage lights played tricks on his brooding countenance and turned his side-whiskers a dusty gray. His blue eyes were dark with anger.

The bouncing made Ruanna's words come out in uneven spurts. "I have a list of names for prospective husbands. The prince regent—"

The earl threw his dark head back and guffawed mirthlessly. "Did he offer you third place after his wife, Caroline, and his current mistress, Lady Hertford?"

"Never mind. I did not like him anyway; he was too fat, and too forward."

That was the truth. Prinny had actually asked to call on her. And him a married man, Ruanna thought. "But Lord Worthington—"

"A rakehell, birdwitted." The earl called to Suthe to slow the horses.

Ruanna took a piece of blank parchment from her reticule. "There's more. Shall I read on. I have several names."

"None of which will do," the earl retorted.

She waited a long moment, measured her words, heaved a mournful sigh, and lifted her chin just slightly. "And I would like to know why not. You said you would find a suitable husband for me before you paid your addresses to Lady Elise. Well it seemed to me that tonight you were *already* paying your addresses—"

The earl addressed the first part of Ruanna's diatribe. "And that I intend to do. But not one gentleman there tonight, if one could call them gentlemen, would make a suitable husband. Did you not see how they were fawning over you, hanging on your every word. Gentlemen of the upper orders do not conduct themselves in such a manner."

"Lord Stewart—"

"A fortune hunter."

Ruanna drew in another deep breath. He had wanted her to be accepted into society so that his dear cousin would be happy, and when it appeared she was the belle of the ball, he had practically dragged her off the dance floor and demanded they go home . . . at once, and when they had reached the carriage, he told Suthe to spring the horses with great haste.

"Stuff!" she exclaimed. As far as she was concerned, the evening had been a success.

Even if the earl had danced with the ugly wench, Lady Elise, three times in a row.

Ruanna admitted that she was jealous, and that her actions did call for reprimand. She admitted also that her heart hurt terribly, and then she allowed wishful thinking: *Perhaps the earl is jealous, and that is why he is looking at me with such murderous fury in his eyes.*

The earl scolded vehemently, "You were informed that dancing the waltz without permission was against the rules."

"You danced three times in a row with Lady Elise. Is that not against the rules? I thought if you could break the rules, then I might, also. Did you not know that it was terribly embarrassing to me to have the man with whom I

210

had come to Almack's making a spectacle of himself, practically declaring his intentions toward Lady Elise by standing for three dances with her?''

Ruanna tossed her head to one side, looked out the carriage window, and repeated, ''In a row.''

''You will never be permitted to attend the Almack Assembly again,'' the earl said.

''Balderdash! Then there is no damage. I shall not care. I have already met the man I want to marry, so there's no need for you to concern yourself with looking for a husband for me.''

That is the whole truth. I have met the man I want to marry, and he sits across from me, as angry as a rooster caught in a hailstorm.

Aloud, Ruanna said, ''Lord Stewart did ask your permission to call tomorrow, did he not?''

''That, he did. But he did not state intentions of marrying you, and if he should have been so bold on such a short acquaintance, I would have refused permission for him to call. I told you, he is a fortune hunter. He thinks because you live at Grosvenor House that you will be well-dowered. I shall tell him the first chance that that is not the case.''

The earl did not know why he was saying those things about Lord Stewart, who was recently titled. He also had deep pockets. There was no need for him to make a marriage of convenience.

When Ruanna remained silent, the earl added, ''Do not encourage Lord Stewart—''

Ruanna was becoming angry. ''I shall most certainly do so. I do not believe he is a fortune hunter, and if he should be, I shall marry him anyway and we will be poor together.'' She paused before adding, ''I noticed the women flirting with you, outrageously, being brazen about it. Why, dancing the waltz without permission was not nearly as scandalous as that!''

Ruanna admitted to herself that the earl had seemed indifferent to their flirting. What bothered her more

211

than the ladies throwing themselves at His Lordship was how calmly he and Lady Elise conversed when they were together, with him giving her pleasant looks and her batting her eyes up at him, while half covering her face with that stupid fan.

Ruanna said, "Lord Stewart has excellent taste in clothes, and—"

"Is that all that is important to you, the way a man wears evening clothes? I thought him rather dandified."

The earl tried to ignore the smell of rose water that wafted from the redhead, and he refused to glare at her beautiful face.

But for the few freckles scattered across her nose, she has the complexion of a Dresden doll. She has a good and valiant spirit. I would like to kiss her elegant little nose.

"He smelled good, and he nibbled my ear," Ruanna said. She hoped that a half-lie would not be held against her. Lord Stewart did smell good.

The earl groaned. He could not help himself. It was more than he could bear. He felt the slow simmer of desire erupt, and an overwhelming, uncontrollable need to hold Lady Moreton welled up inside him.

But before the earl could remove himself to the banquette beside her, he heard in the distance a metallic wailing, and he felt his own carriage surge forward with great haste. Obviously Suthe had heard the same sound.

Uttering an expletive, His Lordship jerked his head around to look into the muted darkness. Gray clouds scudded across the moon, and the only light was from the gas lamps that flickered dimly. He could see an unlighted carriage, bright red with high wheels, coming up behind them, the horses' great forelegs thrusting forward as if to pull the road to them.

A cloaked figure sat on the box, and, inside the carriage, a lone man sat slumped in the corner, his high-crown beaver pulled down as if to hide his face.

The earl shouted to Suthe to give the bays the whip. Then, grabbing Ruanna, he flung her onto the floor of

212

the carriage and covered her body with his. Shouts and commands for them to stop pierced the darkness. A shot rang out.

Reaching for his pistol, the earl swore when he realized he was unarmed. Feeling the body beneath him, he knew the reason for his carelessness. His Lordship then watched in amazement a third man rear his head up from between the pursuing horses. He had been there, the earl was sure, urging the horses on, and now he scrambled back to sit on the box beside the driver.

"The devil take me," the earl said. To Suthe, he again yelled, "Give them the whip."

Even to the earl's own ears, his voice sounded hollow above the grind of wheels. He heard Suthe's loud commands, and for a short while the crested carriage outdistanced the red one. Then the carriages were even, and the man who had suddenly appeared leapt from the box onto the tongue of the earl's carriage. In a flash he was astride the lead bay, pulling back on the harness.

The man inside the red carriage, with his hat hiding his face, who, until now, had remained slumped in the corner, bounded to the ground and grabbed to open the door of the earl's carriage. In his other hand, he held a snub-nosed pistol. The earl, however, was prepared, with a diamond stickpin he'd removed from his cravat. He rammed the pin into the man's hand, while hitting him over the head with his boot, which he had removed to use as a weapon.

A screaming yelp followed, and the door remained closed against the intruder. For a short while he held on and was dragged along by the speeding carriage, and then he turned loose and fell to the street, still screeching. In the darkness, the earl had not seen the man's full face, only his chin, which was dark and sallow.

Beneath the earl, Ruanna was quiet. Not even a whimper came from the usually loquacious redhead. She was so small, so helpless, he thought, and he silently vowed that they would have to kill him to get her.

213

"Everything will be all right, Ruanna. I will not let them harm you," he murmured.

The earl realized the falseness of his words. The carriage was slowing; the man on the bay knew his business. At any moment the earl expected a bullet to whiz past his head, and he prayed that it would indeed whiz past and not into his head. But he could only pray. He swore again that he had left home unarmed.

Just then Suthe whirled his whip above his head, then with perfect aim furled it out. The leather tong wrapped around the neck of the man on the leading bay. There was a scream of anguish, and then a terrible quietness, as the man clawed with both hands to pull the tongs from around his neck.

With a yank of the whip, Suthe ripped him from the horse and flung him onto the street, which he hit with a resounding thud. Before the earl's carriage passed over him, a faint glimpse revealed a mouth with a missing tooth.

The earl let out a big victory whoop, and soon the red carriage was a dim spot in the near darkness. Uttering a prayer of thanksgiving, Lord Julian righted himself; then, reaching down, he lifted Ruanna up to sit on his lap. He felt her body trembling against his, so unlike the spitfire he was used to. She's human, and vulnerable after all, he thought. He felt his desire for her growing in a painful, delicious way. Embarrassed that she could feel the heat of his immediate growth, he placed her beside him, pulled her into his arms, and let her head rest on his shoulder, while he patted her shoulder soothingly. Momentarily he had forgiven her for dancing the waltz without permission, and he comforted her with tender words until they were home. He was thankful that she was safe.

Even so, the earl's mind was troubled. Ruanna was safe for the moment, but for how long would she be so? Obviously something had to be done, and quickly, for

214

Archibald Bennet's men were more determined than even he had thought.

By the following morning, the earl had calmed down somewhat. Letting his worry over Ruanna's safety take precedence over "her disgrace," he left the townhouse early and went to talk with Fieldings' Bow Street Runners.

So intense was His Lordship's thoughts when he left that he hardly noticed Lord Stewart already at the door, asking permission of Sutherland to see Lady Moreton. It was only when the earl returned later and found the handsome lord's tilbury still there that the earl became disturbed. He looked around and found there were two other carriages besides Lord Stewart's in front of Grosvenor House, as well as a high-perched phaeton. Highly liveried drivers waited on the boxes, and lackeys held the heads of the restive horses.

He recognized the most flamboyant of the carriages as Lady Elise's, and frowned. He could only hope that Lady Moreton would not tell about what had happened last evening at the assembly, about his anger, or about the attempted abduction afterward. Nothing was more titillating to the ladies of the ton than the on-dits they gathered in a morning of calling.

Refusing help from the footman, but greeting him with good grace, the earl alighted from the carriage and went to hand up to his driver a folded parchment on which he had written a message to his solicitor.

"Take this to George, and wait to fetch him, please," he told the driver, who happened this day to be Guard. After Suthe's bravery and quick thinking last evening, the earl had not disturbed his late sleep.

After his talk with a runner, the earl had decided that the only way to stop Ruanna from being kidnapped and taken back to India was to pay her father's gambling debts. Perhaps that would not work, but he was willing to try. He would tell George to make arrangements for Charles Moreton to be delivered to London by the next boat, if the man proved willing to come. According to Lady Throckmorton, Ruanna held hurt in her green eyes when she spoke of Charles Moreton. With the pressure of his gambling debts removed, hopefully the man would revert back to the father she had loved so much, the earl reasoned.

Inside the townhouse, the earl found Sutherland authoritatively snapping orders to footmen, instructing that refreshments for the morning callers be set in the dining room. The monstrous townhouse seemed alive and full of energy, and the butler was obviously enjoying every minute of it. With a smile on his fat face, he rushed to His Lordship, bowed from the waist, then took his high-crowned hat. "They are in the salon to the right, m'lord."

"So I see, Sutherland. Thank you."

The earl's gaze moved in the direction of the voices. Standing in the door, the earl perused the room. Ruanna sat beside Lord Stewart on a small settee. Too close, in the earl's opinion. They were almost touching.

Would the girl not listen? He had told her that Lord Stewart positively would not do for a husband. If she should marry someone unsuitable, his cousin would be more distraught than ever.

The burden lay heavily on the earl's shoulder. He looked at Lady Throckmorton, who sat with a pleased smile on her face, her cane resting peacefully by her side.

Lord Sefton, and His Grace, the duke of Beaufort, both of whom had been at Almack's the previous evening, were lounging around the room. No doubt, the earl thought, waiting their turn on the settee.

And Lady Elise was there, elegantly attired, decorously holding a small fan in front of her face. When the earl entered, she swept across the room, her prim companion no more than two steps behind.

The earl found himself pleased to see Lady Elise. After the farrago of last evening, he was more sure than ever he had made the right choice for a lifemate. He simply could not bear a wife whose beauty drew the attention that Ruanna's drew. Every man at Almack's had panted for her.

I suffered through that with one beautiful woman, the earl thought. And Lady Elise never steps beyond the bounds of propriety. . . .

Lady Elise and Miss Warren curtsied at the same time, and the earl gave a perfunctory bow, brushing one hand with his lips, and then the other.

"Lord Julian!" Lady Elise exclaimed. "We are having the most glorious of times teasing Miss Moreton for her misconduct last evening. Having never seen the like, we simply could not wait to call. Did Lady Jersey ask you to leave with your *ward?*"

The earl felt himself bristle, and he said quite sharply, "She did not. In truth, Lady Jersey and I had quite a laugh about *Lady* Moreton dancing the waltz without permission, after I explained that in India, where *Lady* Moreton was most popular in their society, there was no such rule against dancing the waltz. I apologized to Lady Jersey for my failure to explain this to Lady Moreton."

The earl shot Ruanna a sideways glance, daring her to call him a liar. Besides, that was exactly what he planned to do, apologize to the proprietresses of Almack's and take the blame upon himself.

Upon hearing the earl's explanation, a tiny gurgle of laughter bubbled up in Ruanna's throat. Waltzing in India! She wanted to tell Lord Julian that the waltz originated in Russia, and was introduced in London by Countess Lieven, the wife of the Russian ambassador.

But she was sure he knew that already. When she had come to London, all she knew of the waltz was what she had read in Byron's poem, "The Waltz."

217

But all this Ruanna kept to herself. Noting that the laces on the earl's shirt were untied, leaving the black hairs on his chest exposed, she felt her face flush with a now familiar warmth. She wanted to run to him, much as Lady Elise had done.

Instead, she smiled up at Lord Stewart.

His Grace, the duke of Beaufort, spoke. "Ah, Your Lordship." His Grace rose, lifted his quizzing glass to his eyes, and looked down his nose at his host, for his lengthy frame towered over the tall earl. He gave a little chuckle. "We thought Lady Moreton's indiscretion the most exciting thing that has happened at one of the assemblies in an age, if not ever."

"Indeed we did," chimed in Lord Sefton.

"And what did you think of it, Lord Stewart?" the earl asked as he languidly walked deeper into the room.

Lord Stewart rose from the settee and moved to shake the earl's proffered hand. "Well, since I was the one dancing with your ward, I enjoyed it immensely. She is wonderfully light on her feet, an accomplished dancer."

Cocking an eyebrow, the earl looked down at Ruanna. "Is she now? I suppose having ridden there in a swaying carriage, she was a little unsteady on her feet when she danced with me."

Lady Elise giggled, and her companion parroted her.

So my Ruanna had pretended not to know how to dance with the earl, Lady Throckmorton thought, smiling to herself. Sensing that something could go awry, the old woman bounded to her feet and tapped the floor with her cane. "I have requested Cook to prepare a repast for all of you. Shall we repair to the dining room on the second floor?"

"I am afraid I must cry off, Cousin Isadora," the earl said. "I have business to which I must attend. I have sent for my solicitor."

"You naughty boy," Lady Elise chided. "I am devastated with disappointment, for I do so enjoy your company."

218

"Ugh! Balderdash!" The words came out before Ruanna could stop them, and when the earl glared at her, she bestowed an innocent smile in his direction.

But she was glad she had spoken. At least His Lordship knew that he had not yet made a lady out of her, and that there was still a tremendous amount of work to do.

Chapter Seventeen

The earl had just finished his repast, served in the master book room by Sutherland, when George arrived. Seated behind his desk, His Lordship briefly greeted the solicitor, then reached behind him and pulled the bell rope. A servant came almost immediately to soundlessly remove the silver tray.

"'Twas good of you to answer my billet so quickly," the earl said as he walked from behind his desk to proffer a hand to his diminutive, nattily dressed solicitor.

George shook His Lordship's hand.

"Pray sit," the earl said, waving to a chair and returning to his own behind his desk.

"What's the emergency," George asked, and he listened intently as His Lordship apprised him of the incident of his carriage being accosted on the evening before.

"It is more serious than I had thought, George. I fear this Archibald Bennet means business." He sat for a moment, letting his thoughts gather. "Perhaps it would be a singularly good idea if we removed to Wilderhope no later than first light on the morrow."

He allowed a frown to crease his brow as he swore under his breath. "Dash it, that proves an impossibility. Lady Throckmorton spoke of wanting to attend the opera this evening. I don't know why I let that slip my mind.

221

But I must needs honor her wish, for, as you know, she seldom goes out."

"Did you not tell me she has made morning calls with Lady Moreton."

"Yes, of late she has. Since the young girl's arrival at Grosvenor House my cousin has seemed more animated about life, and she wants to help me teach Lady Moreton how to go on in society. That is the reason for the morning calls. I assure you Isadora does not care for them. Nor does Lady Moreton."

"The deuce! Do you suppose she lived like a heathen in India?"

"That, I can believe. Lady Moreton is inexplicably difficult to train. And she is a terrible dancer. No training at all. More than once she ruined the shine on my boots. Not that she's not intelligent, for she's well read. But she has not been properly brought up. That is plain. And, too, she absolutely refuses to abide by the rules. Why, last night she danced the waltz with Lord Stewart after my instructing her not to do so."

George smiled. "And what did you do, m'lord?"

"I demanded we leave . . . before Lady Jersey advanced on her with a strong reprimand. Of course I will explain to the proprietress that—"

"That Lady Moreton's a heathen."

"No, of course not. I will tell her that in India the waltz is an acceptable dance."

"Which it is not, as you well know. I only hope the proprietress does not know as much." From the inside pocket of his waistcoat, the solicitor removed a pad and reached for the quill on the earl's desk. "I'm ready to list my orders. What is it that you want accomplished while you are at Wilderhope?" He looked at the earl quizzically. "I assume you plan to go there after the evening at the opera. Do you think the redhead will be safe for one more evening of training?"

"I will take extra precaution, and pray, George, do not refer to her red hair. You know how I feel—"

George smiled. "Sorry, old man. I do know that you hate all redheads. Now, the list."

"First, I think it a capital idea to send someone to India in search of Charles Moreton. I'm willing to pay his gambling debts. If that can be accomplished, then perhaps Archibald Bennet will call off attempts to have Ruanna brought back to India. And, if he will come, I would like to fetch Charles Moreton to England. I know that would immensely add to Lady Moreton's happiness . . . and, in turn, please my cousin."

The solicitor leaned back in his chair. For a long moment he was silent as he looked at the earl, and then he said, "Julian, are you aware that your concern for Lady Moreton's happiness is suspect. From where I sit, you leave nothing undone that will assure her well-being . . . and her happiness."

"'Tis for my cousin."

"You stubborn jackanapes . . ." The solicitor became quiet. What is the use? he asked himself. Aloud he said, "The time element, m'lord. They could kidnap Lady Moreton a dozen times before a ship can make it to India."

"I will see that does not happen," the earl said angrily, and then, musingly, "George, you should have seen her last evening. Not a whimper that could be heard when we were being accosted. It was only when we had left the red carriage behind and I had lifted her onto my lap that I realized she was sobbing."

George's eyebrow shot up. "You lifted her onto your lap?"

"Only for a moment. Then I placed her on the seat beside me and did the best I could to comfort her by holding her and patting her. She seemed so fragile."

"I've never seen her when she seemed fragile," George retorted. Behind a smile, he added, "But holding her on your lap was civil of you."

Before the earl could think of a reply, the solicitor threw his head back and laughed. The sound filled the room. Finally, wiping tears from his eyes, he said, "What unpleasant tasks you are forced to perform, m'lord. And when you speak of her being fragile, are you speaking of the same girl who belted you between the eyes with a homemade club?"

The earl felt his face flush. "Back to the list, George. Make arrangements with Bochsa, the harpist, whom I believe is living in the Pederson household, to play for Lady Moreton's come-out, which, unfortunately, is only three weeks away."

"And what if this great harpist does not wish to play for Lady Moreton's come-out?"

"Haven't you heard of bribery, George? Offer him whatever it takes. I hear that he's short in the pockets, that he left France to escape the catchpoles, and for other reasons."

"How long do you plan to be at Wilderhope?"

"A fortnight, perhaps. I am not sure. But after the near kidnapping of last evening, I feel Wilderhope is the only safe place for Lady Moreton. I'm sure that when she is not seen in public for a length of time, Archibald Bennet's men—I am now convinced there are two—will think she has departed London for good. We will leave early, while the rest of London is asleep. I am still fuming at myself for being so careless as not to be armed when we went to Almack's. But to be honest, old boy, I was not cognizant of the real danger to Ruanna until I was forced to confront it face on."

The earl moved from behind the desk and went to sit in a chair opposite his solicitor.

George looked admiringly at his employer. His black boots glistened like Beau Brummell's after they had been frothed with champagne; he wore moleskin trousers and an impeccably tailored coat of blue superfine. On his countenance was a look of deep thought. Knowing His Lordship well, the solicitor waited, and it seemed an extraordinary long time before he broke the silence.

"At Almack's, George. You have never seen such

224

lascivious looks cast upon any woman as were heaped on Ruanna, the bandy-legged prince regent included."

George tried again to make the earl see what he was denying to himself. "Could that be the reason for this sudden departure for the country, to get your ward away from these appraising eyes? You *could* lock the lady in question inside the house and place a guard at the door to keep her suitors away."

"I will admit the thought has crossed my mind; that of taking her to the country until she has had time to become accustomed to our ways. She is so impetuous. I am afraid she will encourage an undesirable. Why, only last night she told me she had met the man she wished to marry. . . ."

George leaned forward in his chair. "The devil take me, and who was the lucky man? Did she choose from the nobility? A duke, perhaps? She would make a wonderful duchess."

"Lord Stewart, the earl of Trent. He was here this morning, making an early call," the earl said.

"Lord Stewart!" George sent a low whistle across the room. "He is a handsome buck, and quite rich, having just inherited the Stewart estates. Surely you would have no objections to such a match for your ward."

Shooting George a dark look, the earl rose from his chair and strode across the room, then turned to retrace his steps. "Yes, yes, I do have objections to Lord Stewart, though for the life of me I cannot put my finger on the exact reason. In lieu of that, I told Lady Moreton that he was a fortune hunter. I only did that to stop her from encouraging his addresses until I can investigate his character more thoroughly. Perhaps the man is too handsome, too fickle, I don't know. With his looks, I'm sure he is a womanizer." Again the earl stopped and stared pensively into the open space in the room. "Why she would express interest in him, I do not understand. After I warned her against him." He flung his hands up in an exasperated manner. "Demmet, sometimes she shows the most culpable ingratitude."

"Do you want her for yourself, m'lord?"

He had asked the questions before, and had had the same denial from the earl. He had seen the earl in love before, with the green-eyed she-devil.

The earl whirled around. "That is the most ridiculous suggestion you have made in your entire life. Lady Moreton is nothing more to me than someone my cousin deeply cares for, or should I say someone with whom my cousin is obsessed." He shook his head. "George, I do not understand Isadora."

"The old woman is in her dotage, Julian. She's lonely," George reasoned.

"Lady Moreton is not what I want in a wife. She has had this household in a turmoil from the day she darkened the doors that were so generously opened to her. If it were not for Lady Throckmorton . . ."

His Lordship stopped before he confided to George the other reason Lady Moreton was totally unacceptable to him as a wife was that she was not pure, along with her independent nature. By her own admission, she had had a lover in India. *That*, he prayed, would not become public knowledge and make her unacceptable to other gentlemen of the ton as well. He said again, "If it were not for Lady Throckmorton—"

"You would throw her out," George finished for him. "That is an untruth, m'lord, which you are telling yourself."

The earl exploded. "Demme you, you impertinent pup! You, more than anyone, know that I find the girl's presence singularly disturbing. She is far too independent, and I assure you that the only feeling I have for her is of a familial nature." After a short pause, he added, "And if I have any feeling for the Countess Charlotte, it is hatred."

George watched as the earl's blue eyes darkened, like the sea when the silt from the bottom foams up to cloud the surface. George well knew that with the earl, the past often clouded the present. "More's the pity," the solicitor said. "Hatred is so akin to love that the difference is hardly discernible. There is only a thread separating the two emotions. Will you never be rid of the hurt the first redhead inflicted upon you?"

The earl did not answer. He sighed deeply, for it was true. Every time he looked at Ruanna the same sinful nature grabbed him. He was fortunate that he recognized the feeling for Ruanna as carnal passion, the devil of his youth that had returned to ride his shoulder.

The earl went to sit again in the chair opposite his solicitor. Leaning his head back, he crossed his legs, then uncrossed them. This latest redhead was making his life unbearable; the slightest look brought him to such a state of desire that his body flamed. He wanted to kiss her the way a man kisses his mistress . . . or his wife. Her generous lips seemed to be made for just that, for kissing, and for laughter when she was happy. His dreams were filled with images of them making love.

Now, sitting there, he felt shame curl up inside him for his pleasant excursions of fantasy. *If I had never kissed her; if I'd never tasted those kisses.*

"Only the mistrust of beautiful women remains of the Countess Charlotte, George," the earl said. "With that she left me overwhelmingly endowed, and, as I told you, that is why I will offer for Lady Elise.

"And by the by, I plan to ask her to accompany us to Wilderhope. I want to acquaint her with her future home, and I believe she can be of help to Lady Moreton with the social graces suitable to the ton."

George rose to leave. "I cannot persuade myself to believe that marriage to Lady Elise is best, even though I know your desire to produce an heir. Is there anything else besides tracking down Lady Moreton's father and bribing the harpist?"

"There is one more thing," the earl said as he followed George to the door. "I would like to know more about our little pickpocket who calls himself Jim. Where did he come from? I have taken quite a liking to the little fellow, and you might inquire about a suitable school in which he can be placed, preferably one close by. I feel that he should be kept in close proximity with the family, either here or at Wilderhope. He needs the feeling of belonging, if we can possibly bring it about. I want him to know that I am responsible for his welfare, and that there is no need for him to continue stealing."

"Jim who? Does he have a last name?"

The earl smiled. "If he does, he ain't telling. And he gets quite testy when asked. But surely someone in the area where he lived will know."

"And where was that?"

"Near the docks, I'm sure. In our conversation, he has mentioned that particular area, but said nothing specific."

Frowning above a smile, the solicitor stopped to look at the earl. "You don't mind what you ask of a man, do you?"

"He is a good little boy," the earl said, sure that he was right.

Abovestairs, seven-year-old Jim Reevis lugged the silver candlestick up the stairs that led to the garret. His cache had become large and soon he would take it to the fence. Of course, he thought, that would mean he could never return to Grosvenor House.

But any day now, they will give me the big heave-ho. Me pa taught me about the upper orders.

"But I ain't dumb. It would be stupid not to be prepared."

And he would keep all the money his cache brought, he planned. Never again would he have to turn it over to his pa, who, in turn, spent in on the stuff that made him drunk and mean.

The old buzzard won't be doing that to me again. I ain't his kid no more. I'm me own man.

Stopping on the dark stairs, Jim smiled and corrected himself. "I am *my* own man."

From Lady Moreton's tutoring, he had learned to say "my" instead of "me," and "for" instead of "fer." And he hardly ever cussed anymore. At least, not much. And he could now spell his name, and write it, too. Jim, that was all. That was all anyone would ever know. He would hate it if his pa should find out where he was and come looking for him.

Jim looked around him. The grandeur was staggering. One act of kindness had led him to this . . . and to someone like Lady Moreton. He felt tears pushing at his eyes. Never before had anyone cared for him.

Disgusted with himself for being so soft, Jim swiped at the tears with his sleeve. Life is real. This is a dream, and dreams don't last, he told himself.

After resting a short while, thinking and planning, Jim plunged on up the stairs. In the garret, he deftly felt his way around in the windowless loft, until he found what he was looking for—a pillowcase hidden behind a huge trunk. With alacrity, he added the candlestick to his treasure trove. Lifting it, he mentally counted its value, and then with the quickness of lightning he crouched and froze, even held his breath, for he was sure he had heard someone coming. His heart pounded against his ribs, and he prayed that the thumping could not be heard. Never, in the whole of his life, had Jim Reevis been afraid, he thought, as he listened to the silence.

When a considerable time had passed and nothing untoward had happened, Jim decided the noise had been in his imagination. Making his swift steps as quiet as possible, he left his hiding place and soon reached the landing at the bottom of the stairs. Even though he had chosen the time when no servants would be about to squeal on him, he looked one way, then the other, glad that no one was in sight.

Chapter Eighteen

Ruanna let Lady Throckmorton choose the gown she would wear to the opera, a sheer, blue silk with an empire waist. The long skirt was adorned with two ruffles edged with Parisian lace; the sleeves were mere caps over her shoulder, and the décolletage was modestly low.

"I'm glad you chose this one, Isadora," Ruanna said. "'Tis one of my favorites."

"The color becomes you," the old woman said. For herself, she had chosen a gown of soft gray sarcenet, with a skirt trimmed in yellow roses.

Old-fashioned, some would say, she thought, but it brought back memories of days long past. She allowed her mind to wing back to a bouquet of yellow roses. But just for a moment, and then she said, "I am sure the punctual earl is awaiting us belowstairs."

When they met His Lordship belowstairs, he commented on how flattering the ladies' gowns were, and Ruanna noticed that his gaze lingered longer than necessary on her bosom, which showed only the slightest amount of pink flesh above the neckline. She was both pleased and embarrassed. Her inexperience with men did not deter her from recognizing desire in a gentleman's eyes when it was so blatantly obvious.

Desire, but not love, she thought. Her breath caught in her throat when she noted his splendid evening attire: a coat of purple velvet, dark knee breeches over white silk stockings with clocks. And, for a change, he was smiling.

When Ruanna dipped into a low curtsy, His Lordship bowed over her hand and brushed it with his lips. Then, as if the touch had burned him, he dropped her hand and turned to his cousin. "You look lovely," he told her again, going to her and giving her a quick kiss on the cheek. For a moment, he studied her, for her countenance appeared troubled.

"Thank you, Julian," she said, and then she plunged, as she always did, right into what was on her mind. "What is this about removing to Wilderhope? You know—"

"I know that you do not wish to go. I cannot remember when last you were there. But I thought this time, with the danger to Ruanna, which I apprised you of this day, you would consent to come along."

"It is not my wont to go to Wilderhope," she said. "Not as long as—"

Lady Throckmorton stopped with such abruptness that Ruanna, watching the old woman's eyes cloud with tears, could not help wondering why she refused to go to the earl's country home. And why was she so emotional about it that tears would start? Was she afraid of something?

"Well, let us not ruin our evening at the opera over what will happen tomorrow," the earl said, "but, pray, do think about Lady Moreton's safety, and she will need you while at Wilderhope. My time will be taken up with Lady Elise."

Must he keep speaking of that ugly duckling? Ruanna exploded inwardly. "Why not invite Lord Stewart?" she asked. "He could train me in the ways of society while you are getting acquainted with the future mother of the Aynsworth heir." Ruanna waited for just the slightest moment before adding, "Since I am going to marry Lord Stewart, perhaps while at Wilderhope *we* can become better acquainted."

The earl cast her a ferocious look. He spoke with resolute determination. "Lord Stewart will not be invited to come along! I am afraid grooming you for society would not be what would be on his mind, and, as I told you, he would not make you a suitable husband."

Lady Throckmorton, who had been listening with interest to the exchange, tapped her cane against the Turkish carpet and said authoritatively, "Do you not think we should depart for the theater, Lord Julian? Else the performance will be half-over before we arrive."

The earl turned and strode swiftly toward the street door where outside the carriage awaited. Still troubled, and a little angry with Ruanna, he stood aside and let a footman help the ladies, and then he bounded aboard himself, sitting beside Ruanna.

The footman put the steps up; His Lordship called to Suthe to be off, and as they traveled over the cobbled streets to the King's Theatre in the Haymarket, his eyes darted furtively about. His ears were tuned for the sound of whining wheels.

Guard, armed with a long-barreled pistol, rode on the box beside Suthe, and two footmen, equally armed, rode on the back of the crested carriage. His Lordship himself carried a small pistol concealed inside his coat.

At the theater, they were barely in the earl's box, which was in the center of the third tier in the horseshoe auditorium, when the performance began.

The earl acutely regretted that there was hardly time for Ruanna to observe the opulence of the theater, the bejeweled patrons, and the pit below where the fops and dandies made cakes of themselves, strolling about to show off the excellent cut of their clothes, and drawing attention to themselves instead of the performance. He wanted her to know everything there was to know about society, the good and the bad. Turning to look at her, he noted with pleasure that she sat as if entranced by Madame Pasta as Dorabella in *Così fan tutte*. He leaned to whisper in Ruanna's ear, "She was a sensational success

233

in Bellini's *Norma*."

When Ruanna did not answer, His Lordship wondered if the poor waif had ever observed such a performance of phenomenal range before, and then he turned his attention to what was worrying him most, her safety.

After turning this way and that, he said in a loud whisper, "Guard is at the entrance, looking for the man with a missing tooth. One footman is below in the pit, the other is behind us, scrutinizing anyone who might approach our box."

Ruanna put her finger to her lips. "Shhh," she whispered, and Lady Throckmorton brought her cane up to tap His Lordship on the knee.

After that, the earl settled down and let himself enjoy Madame Pasta's performance, and it was not until intermission that he saw a man approaching the box who resembled the character George had described meeting in Vauxhall Gardens. Although the man approaching was dressed all the crack in English attire, his skin was as dark as his black hair; his eyes, under bushy brows, were like small chips of onyx. Under different lighting, the earl could not discern whether or not it was the same man who had accosted his carriage.

The hair on the back of His Lordship's neck prickled, and he felt his body stiffen to alertness. Quickly, he put his hand inside his coat, feeling the pistol.

But then the man stopped at another box, and suddenly the earl's box was surrounded by young bucks, Lord Stewart included, all bowing and smiling at Ruanna.

The earl found this as disturbing as the Indian's presence in the theater, and his greeting to Lord Stewart was less than cordial.

Then, just before time for the performance to resume, the dark-skinned man was suddenly at the earl's box. It was clear to the earl that he had waited for Ruanna's admirers to leave.

After nodding to the earl, the stranger gave an awkward leg to Lady Throckmorton. Then, turning his attention to Ruanna, he looked straight into her eyes. "Lady Moreton, I believe. Recently from India. Am I not right?"

"And what business is that of yours?" the earl asked, and not in a kind way. In truth, he felt intense fury roil inside of him. How dare this man, or any man, pose a threat to the person who meant so much to his cousin. "You have not been properly introduced to my lady, and I invite you to leave . . . at once." His right hand edged toward the pistol; his left hand grasped Ruanna's arm, feeling the tenseness which turned to a shiver.

Lady Throckmorton, the earl noticed, held her cane at the ready.

When the man made no effort to leave, but kept looking at Ruanna, the earl waved a hand toward the footman above them, then asked of the Indian, "Who are you? What do you want?"

The dark man smiled, showing even, white teeth. He did not offer a name by way of introducing himself, and he offered no resistance when the burly footman grabbed his arm and led him away. At the end of the aisle, he stopped and turned. His gaze was intense, and his smile broadened.

A rogue, no doubt, the earl thought; but where's the man with a missing tooth?

"Can there possibly be two different factions after Lady Moreton?" he asked himself so low that the voice from the stage drowned out his words.

The next morning, long before light, Grosvenor House was at sixes and sevens. Ruanna had never seen the like. Servants were being threatened by the earl with dismissal if they so much as breathed to one person that the entourage's destination was Wilderhope. And then, after finishing with the servants, he turned to Lady Throckmorton and beseeched her to accompany them. "For Lady Moreton's sake," he said, and when the old woman

235

started sobbing into her handkerchief, he asked explosively, "Codswallop, Isadora, what is the matter with you?"

Ruanna went to Her Ladyship and put her arms around her. Lady Throckmorton's tall, thin body sagged against Ruanna. "I'm sorry, my child, but I cannot go. I have not been to Wilderhope since that woman . . ."

"What woman, Isadora? Who . . ."

"Please don't ask. I wish you did not have to go, but Lord Julian is adamant."

Ruanna asked again, "Who?" But the question only brought more tears, and more fright to the old woman's eyes. At last the earl came and gave his cousin a hug, which brought a slight smile, but not acquiescence.

"I will stay busy making ready for your come-out, Ruanna," she said, and she left and climbed the stairs; slowly, Ruanna noticed, as if suddenly ten years had been added to her age.

Within the next few minutes, another crisis arose. Lady Elise and her companion arrived at Grosvenor House in her opulent carriage, with another carriage following, loaded with so many trunks Ruanna could hardly see the two maids Lady Elise was taking to attend her.

The earl ordered a footman to rearrange the trunks to make room for Katie. He was not taking his valet, for he had one at Wilderhope. He would ride in Lady Elise's carriage, which would follow his own crested carriage carrying Ruanna and Jim.

"But m'lord, should we not ride in the lead equipage?" Lady Elise asked.

"No," was the quick answer the earl gave, and a look from her companion silenced Lady Elise.

All this Ruanna noted with interest. Earlier, the earl had explained that he could better watch out for her if he rode in the carriage behind her. "Lady Elise does not know why we are going to Wilderhope, nor should she know," he had said. As if to reassure her, he gave a small smile and added, "You will be well protected."

So while darkness still hovered over the sleeping city, the three carriages set out, leaving London and its fetid gray air behind.

Ruanna pulled in deep breaths of the fresh country air and smelled the heather and green grass. She watched the rising sun cut through the dawn, to dance on trees whose leaves glistened with the dampness of morning dew.

Wildflowers romped across the moors, as if they had been painted by an artist's brush. On the hillocks, sheep grazed, in small groups that looked like mounds of snow.

Across from Ruanna, Jim sat silently. The horses' hooves beat rhythmically against the hard-packed road, breaking the quietness.

"Why did you not want to come, Jim?" she asked. "I should think the country would appeal to a boy of your age: animals, fields of growing things . . ."

"I had things to do," he answered.

Ruanna studied the boy. She had never allayed her feelings that he was playing cat and mouse with her, but perhaps this was not the best time to broach the subject, she told herself. "You are no more unhappy than I, Jim. I did not want to come—not under these circumstances— but Lord Julian thought it best for my safety."

Earlier, she had explained about the would-be kidnappers accosting the earl's carriage, and about the man from India coming to their box at the theater. "Would you miss me, if I should be forced to return to India?" she asked.

"If the earl's so worried for your safety, then why ain't he here in the carriage with you instead of back there with that woman with a big snout?" Jim asked.

Smiling at his honesty, Ruanna leaned forward. "Shush, Jim. You must not say such things. Lady Elise is His Lordship's intended. He wants to marry her and produce an heir. Besides, the way he explained it, he can keep a better lookout, and be at better advantage if he isn't in the same carriage with me. And as you can see,

237

the man riding on the box with the driver is holding a loaded gun in his hand."

"Aye, the guard from Newgate."

"'Tis one and the same."

"I didn't think he was so stupid," Jim said, frowning.

"The guard isn't stupid."

"The earl, goofbum. He's a slowtop. How could he have a kid by that woman? The poor little thing might look like her. How could he wish that on any kid?"

Ruanna's smile advanced to laughter, though her heart did not feel the lightness indicated. "Why don't you ask him? That is, if you get a chance when Her Ladyship isn't around."

Ruanna could see the wheels whirling in the little boy's head. No doubt a plan of some sort was being formulated. Looking at him, dressed in the finest clothes, his corn silk hair combed close to his head, one would never guess that a few short weeks ago he had been bought out of Newgate.

Looking down at her own fine traveling clothes, she thought the same about herself. From Newgate to a crested carriage!

I think I had just as soon be in Newgate as to be in love with a man who can hardly bear me, she mused ruefully. She allowed herself to look back at the following carriage. *Were I a bird and could hear . . .*

Pulling her gaze from what caused her pain, Ruanna noticed that Jim's eyelids were becoming heavy. "Come sit by me, Jim," she said, "and put your head in my lap."

"Na," he protested, "I ain't no kid."

But when Ruanna told him that if he did not move to sit beside her, she would move across to sit beside him, the little boy did as she asked and was soon fast asleep, his head in her lap. She picked up one of his hands, once so dirty, now so clean. Bringing the hand to her lips, strong resistance was all that kept her from hugging him to her and telling him how she felt, how much she loved him, how much she loved Lord Julian.

238

Ruanna rubbed the little boy's cherub face with the tips of her fingers, thinking how innocent he looked. His little body felt warm against hers. Thinking that it was a comfort to feel close to another human being, her eyes filled with tears, and she wiped them away before they fell onto Jim's face. If only she could be as hard feeling as she sometimes projected to Lord Julian.

As the carriage moved with steady rhythm and the tears kept flooding her eyes, Ruanna knew that she was in a terrible spot. She could not bear to witness the earl married to Lady Elise. All hope that it would not happen was lost to her. She felt engulfed in hopelessness, like a cloud through which she could not grasp a glimmer of light. Yes, she told herself, there was a finality about his taking the woman to Wilderhope. To show her her future home, he had said.

Inside the one trunk she had brought, underneath the beautiful garments which Lady Throckmorton had purchased for her, were the boy's breeches, the dun-brown coat, and the cap that covered her red hair. Where she would go, Ruanna did not know, but she must needs go somewhere. She would abandon her plan to pretend ignorance of how to go on in society. It simply was not working. So, with her eyes opened to every opportunity, she would know when to make her escape.

The thought that she would take Jim with her entered her mind, but she knew that was a selfish wish. His Lordship would give the little tyke a chance in life. What could she offer him?

Ruanna thought about Lady Throckmorton. Why had the old woman been so determined to take her out of the East End? Why had she been so adamant about not coming to Wilderhope?

What dark secret did she hide behind those sad, faded eyes?

Once again Ruanna looked back at the carriage behind them, and pain filled her, unbearable pain, and she knew that she would do what she had to do. In the meantime, she would die before she would let the earl know the depth of her love for him.

In Lady Elise's carriage, the earl said, "Lady Elise," and then stopped.

"Yes, m'lord," Lady Elise quickly responded. She smiled coquettishly, and when the earl did not go on, she prodded, "Did you want to ask something of me? Perhaps Miss Warren could ride in the other carriage if it is of a very personal nature."

Lady Elise ignored the look from her companion. She smiled as she visualized the earl down on his knees proposing to her. In a carriage no less. Covering her blushing face with her fan, she suppressed a giddy giggle.

"No, no, it is not necessary for Miss Warren to repair to the other carriage," the earl said. "I was about to say that I hoped you like Wilderhope."

"Oh, there is no doubt that I shall love it. But of course, any place with a handsome earl such as you would be a small corner of heaven."

"When do we stop for sustenance?" Miss Warren asked. "And how long is this journey going to take?"

"It is a two-day journey, and we shall stop at a posting inn to exchange horses and spend the night. I sent a messenger ahead to make the arrangements at the Cock's Crown. And as far as noontime measure, each carriage has its own basket of food which the cook prepared."

Lady Elise gave her companion a scolding look. "Do not fret so. How could you doubt that His Lordship would make arrangements for food? And I am sure he has made our sleeping arrangements separate from *his ward* and that terrible little boy."

The earl's answer came with considerable swiftness. "Jim is not a terrible boy. He is a lad who has not been afforded the opportunity to be other than what he is."

"Of course, m'lord. And how admirable of you to be so concerned for his welfare. I just meant that surely

240

you would arrange for privacy—"

"At the posting inn, I will keep the boy with me. However, I had hoped you and Lady Moreton might become friends."

The earl stopped short of telling Her Ladyship that he thought Lady Moreton could learn the manners of society from her.

Boldly, Lady Elise placed her hand on the earl's big thigh. Surely something can warm him toward me, she thought, and was disappointed when the earl acted as if nothing had happened. Then she assured herself that it was because a gentleman never allows himself to become aroused in the company of a lady of quality.

Aroused! Even the thought was repugnant to Her Ladyship. Such bestial carrying on, she thought.

The earl, after gingerly removing the hand from his leg, opened the carriage door and leaned out.

Puzzled, Lady Elise asked, "What in the world are you doing, m'lord?"

"Listening. I thought I heard an approaching horse, single beats, not like the cacophony of sounds coming from our own horses."

"And what would that mean? Do not men travel on horses along this road?"

The earl straightened, then closed the carriage door. "Of course they do, but if we are to have company, I want to be prepared."

Chapter Nineteen

Nothing untoward happened; no horse with a suspicious rider gained on the earl's carriage. It was not until they reached the posting inn where they would spend the night that His Lordship learned the ratatat he'd heard came not from behind the three carriages, but from a horse in front of them. When the earl entered the inn, Lord Stewart stood facing him, a pleased look on his face. He was quick to speak.

"My cousin's land runs with yours in Shropshire. I thought it a capital idea to visit him at the same time you are at Wilderhope."

Blatantly, Lord Stewart's eyes were on Ruanna, the earl noticed.

"How in the devil did you know?" the earl asked.

"On-dits, m'lord. They do spread among the upper orders."

Never had Ruanna been so glad to see anyone as she was to see the handsome Lord Stewart. It was bad enough to suffer the earl's attention to Lady Elise, and to feel her heart breaking inside of her from loving him so much, but it was a matter of pride. Now *she* would have someone to talk with. She gave Stewart an appreciative smile.

The earl fixed the pair with a blue gaze. *Will the girl never learn? The way she is smiling at him, he will think she is a trollop.*

Curtsying regally before Lord Stewart, Ruanna forced a little laugh. "Will you dine with us this evening, m'lord?"

Stewart bowed over her hand. "Only if you are in accord with calling me Stewart. I could never be m'lord to one so beautiful."

Save me from throwing up, the earl prayed. He whipped around and went to speak with the proprietor of the inn. Lady Elise had requested that she and Miss Warren be excused to go to their quarters. "I want to freshen myself," Lady Elise had said.

"This way, please." The proprietor nodded his head, and the two ladies followed him up the stairs.

The earl returned to take Jim's hand. He led him to a table and ordered a tankard of ale for himself and some sweet tea for the boy. His Lordship downed his ale, and swore when he heard Ruanna's laughter trilling across the room.

Even in the dimness of candlelight, he could see her eyes twinkling like emeralds when she looked up at Stewart. He mumbled to himself, "No lady of quality acts in such a manner. I will let Archibald Bennet have her. They can take her back to India, where she will deservedly be beaten every day."

"'Tis yer own fault," Jim said, screwing up his mouth at the taste of the tea.

The earl raised a brow. "What do you mean by that?"

"Ye should be sparkin' her yerself, her so pretty and all."

The earl protested: "I am practically engaged to Lady Elise." Then he blustered, "Pretty women are all alike, Jim. Do you not know that?"

"From where I sit, a pretty gel is better'n a ugly one."

The earl knew to whom Jim was alluding, and he bristled slightly. "I hope when you choose a wife that you will take into consideration more than mere beauty, Jim. Lady Elise has redeeming qualities."

"Like what?"

"Her honesty for one thing, and she would never go beyond the pale of society in her behavior; she has kept herself pure . . . when you are older you will understand the value of the things I have just mentioned."

Jim looked at the earl, his brown eyes serious. "How'd yer know she ain't been pricked?"

The earl spewed his ale all over the table. When he had gained his composure, he scolded, "For a seven-year-old, you ask probing questions. When you are out of short coats . . . a little older, I will explain—"

"I'm older *now*," Jim said. "Me pa didn't tell me, he showed me . . . with light-skirts. Right where we slept."

The earl saw an oldness about the little boy. Reaching across the table, he ruffled his blond hair, giving him a crooked smile as he did so. He wanted to give the boy more, give him his childhood back. "You will stay with me tonight, Jim. I will tell you a bedtime story, and we'll pretend that you are three. If you like, I will rock you."

The earl found himself so choked he could not go on. He could not tell Jim that he had never been rocked by his father, or that the old earl, and his brothers as well, hated him and wished him dead. They would have roared with laughter had he asked to be told a bedtime story.

But none of that matters now, the earl thought. Love for the little thief across from him filled his heart, pushing the bitterness aside, leaving in its place a modicum of peace.

Out of the corner of his eye, the earl watched across the room Ruanna and Stewart conversing. Now sitting in two matching chairs near the proprietor's desk, they faced each other; a handsome pair, he grudgingly admitted.

Suddenly the earl felt weary. He wished he were already married to Lady Elise and settled down, an heir on his way.

"Demme," he swore, and he tore his gaze away from what was causing him pain. He felt the terrible ache return. Ruanna's traveling dress molded her ripe bosom, and the candlelight glinted off her red hair.

When the earl swore again, Jim smiled and said, "The way he keeps staring at her, all loving like, it would not surprise me a whit if she's not fallin' in love with him. M'lord, I think yer making a mistake."

The earl found himself smiling. Why did he think the little hoist was playing the wise man with him?

"I told you, she is much too pretty, and independent, and too hot tempered for my taste."

"Jest what yer needs."

"Mind your own business—"

Just then, Lady Elise and Miss Warren descended the stairs, both, the earl noticed, dressed to the nines. He went and bowed over each of their hands, then guided them into the dining room. He looked back over his shoulder to see if Ruanna and Lord Stewart were following. They were, Ruanna's arm hooked around Stewart's, while her other hand rested on Jim's shoulder.

The earl mumbled, sotto voce, "I must needs think of a way to stop his dangling after her." Frowning ferociously, he told himself that he would, at first chance, have a serious talk with Stewart, for it was plain that Lady Moreton had no notion of listening to a word he had to say when it came to choosing a husband for her.

Lady Elise's voice broke into the earl's thoughts. She was speaking to her companion. "It seems that we cannot escape eating with them. . . ."

His Lordship, after telling Jim a bedtime story, one he had made up out of his head, decided to try again to reason with Ruanna. Jim had declared himself too big to be rocked and was soon asleep in his chair. The earl picked him up and carried him to the bed, where, bending over, he kissed him on the forehead and patted his small face.

This done, the earl closed the door behind him and walked toward Ruanna's door. At supper her flagrant attention to Stewart's every word had been most disconcerting. He would try another approach, he decided, though he did not quite know what that would be. He had appealed to her sensitive nature, that of not wanting to hurt Lady Throckmorton by choosing the wrong husband. An inappropriate marriage would be devastating to his old cousin, whose nerves already seemed to be frayed to the breaking point. Her sobbing when she learned Ruanna would go to Wilderhope had been very upsetting to the earl.

Still searching his brain for what to say to Ruanna, His Lordship knocked diffidently on her door, and when Katie answered, he stammered out his request to speak with Lady Moreton. Like a boy of twelve, he thought, embarrassed.

"Yes, m'lord." Katie turned away, and just as quickly turned back and bobbed. "She ain't here."

"What do you mean, she ain't here. She's not with that unspeakable cur—" The earl stopped. He was speaking to a servant!

"I dan't know who she might be with, m'lord. She jest said she needed fresh air and was goin' to git it. She refused my company."

Disappointed, the earl thanked the maid, then made his way down the stairs and out into the night. Only a quarter moon offered light. He could not imagine a girl alone out there in the darkness. He strained his eyes and, walking on, called her name. And then he heard sobs.

On a grassy knoll, overlooking a narrow creek that ran behind the inn, Ruanna sat with her head buried into her hands. He restrained himself from running to her. She wore a green pelisse, for the night had turned quite cool. As he drew nearer, he saw that her shoulders were heaving, and all thoughts of a reprimand flew from his mind as he rushed to her side. "What is it, Ruanna?" he asked.

I've never seen the sassy redhead cry before.

The earl found himself discomfited, and at a loss for

words. He asked again, "What is it? Why are you crying?"

Then, against his better judgment, he drew her to him.

Surely, he thought, he could comfort her without his carnal nature coming to the fore.

But it did not work. The desire to make love to her attacked his loins like a raging storm, held back too long by some unseen force.

When Ruanna turned to lay her head on the earl's heaving chest, twining her arms around his neck, all His Lordship's reserve broke down and he, lifting her face to his, kissed her with such intensity as he had never felt before, not even in the salad days of his youth, or when he'd desired Countess Charlotte.

The earl's world suddenly turned into a burning inferno. Every heartbeat spoke her name, as he gently pushed her back on the grass. It smelled damp, and clean, as she did.

To keep his free hand from roaming over Ruanna's body, now pressed close to his, the earl balled it into a fist, holding it that way until his knuckles turned white. He heard a sob and a moan and knew they came from his own throat. For a long moment, he let his mind accept that he would make love to her. He would hold her and caress her until she begged for him to do what men did to women *after* they were married.

The earl vividly recalled that she'd admitted having a lover in India. So the seduction should be easy, he told himself, kissing her again. His hand refused to be a fist any longer and, instead, reached up to cup a breast, squeezing it gently, rolling the hard nipple between thumb and forefinger. He heard a moan, this time from Ruanna.

Then, she pushed him away. "I miss Papa and Mama. I was crying for them." It was a lie.

But I will never tell him the truth about the way I love him; neither will I give in to the temptation to give myself to him.

248

A cool breeze invaded the earl's paradise, and he readily admitted that he was glad Ruanna had pushed him away, and he vowed by all that was holy he would never lose control again, which meant, he told himself, that he would never kiss her again.

Pushing himself up and pulling Ruanna up to stand beside him, the earl said, "I have good news for you. Before leaving town, I instructed my solicitor to send a messenger to India with money to pay your papa's gaming debts and, if he can possibly do so, the messenger is to fetch Charles Moreton back to England."

Without hesitation, Ruanna threw her arms around the earl's neck. "Sometimes you are quite wonderful, m'lord."

The earl, laughing, gently removed her arms from around his neck. He recalled that she had reacted in the exact same way when she had seen the harp he'd bought for her. Passion had nothing to do with her show of appreciation.

In a voice filled with more emotion than he wanted to reveal, the earl said, "I am deeply sorry for my actions this night. I have no right to kiss you, but as I have told you before, you bring back cravings in me which I think are sinful in nature, and which I would like to forget. While at Wilderhope, I intend to solidify my plans to marry Lady Elise. I am sure marriage will cure me of my less than honorable actions toward you."

"And I am sure Lord Stewart will solidify his plans to marry me," Ruanna answered with aplomb. "And I will accept."

Ruanna knew that was not so. She would never marry anyone except the earl. Each day her love for him grew, along with the pain. *Therefore, I shall leave the Aynsworth household as soon as possible.*

The next day, at the earl's suggestion, Lord Stewart

rode ahead to his cousin's, and the same riding arrangement as the day before was carried out by the others.

At the end of that day, the carriage carrying Ruanna and Jim was the first to turn off the main road, which ran alongside a hillock. When a manor house, sitting in the middle of a lush green meadow, came into view, Ruanna leaned forward and exclaimed breathlessly, "Wilderhope."

The three-storied, gray stone house, with two forward wings, was bathed in the golden glow of a dying sun. Already, lighted candles inside the house made squares of the many windows.

Ruanna shaded her eyes with her hands. In the distance, rolling hills with towering trees that moved with the soft breeze furnished a backdrop for the lovely house.

When the three carriages rumbled to a stop in the circle drive, four footmen ran forward to help. Banishing restraint, Ruanna did not wait for one to open the carriage door, but opened it herself and bounded down onto the ground. Vines, deep green and exuding the smell of summer blossoms, climbed up the sides and across the front of the house, framing two huge doors that swung open to greet them.

As Ruanna walked toward the door, two squirrels, mates, she was sure, skittered down the trunk of a tall tree, then scampered across the yard and out of sight. She listened to the droning of cicadas, and to the croaking of frogs from a nearby pond. In the ensuing moments, she felt a strange feeling engulf her: the feeling that she was home.

Not in India, in the house where she had lived most of her life, did she feel that way. And yet, she knew that Wilderhope would never be her home. Alighting from the carriage behind her was the woman who would be Wilderhope's mistress.

Later, after a light repast had been served, when they

250

were reposing in the large informal withdrawing room, the warm feeling of having met her destiny once again assailed Ruanna. Looking around her, she saw books in no particular order, a litter of journals, and a scattering of chessmen on a chessboard, all testifying that the formal elegance of the Grosvenor House was lacking here. A thick, worn rug covered most of the wide-planked floor.

Ruanna stole a sideways glance at the earl, who was occupying a chair by a stone fireplace that looked as if a whole ox could be cooked in it. His Lordship helped himself to a pinch of snuff from a tiny jeweled snuffbox.

A cold, dull ache settled over Ruanna's heart when he said to Lady Elise, "Now that you have seen Wilderhope, what do you think of it?"

Lady Elise, in Ruanna's opinion, was overdressed for the country, in an elaborate gown of silk brocade. Her companion, sitting close by, was also dressed as if she were going to a ball. Ruanna wore a simple muslin dress that clung to her small frame, but nowhere did it fit tightly, or show her bosom. She had a special reason for listening intently to Lady Elise's answer to the earl's question about how Lady Elise liked Wilderhope.

"'Tis heaven," Lady Elise gushed. "I told Miss Warren while we were refreshing ourselves that I had never seen a more beautiful place than Wilderhope."

Ruanna sat forward in her chair. With difficulty, she restrained herself, for that was the biggest lie she had ever heard uttered out of a mouth. Soon after their arrival, the door to Lady Elise's room had been pushed open by the soft breeze that swept down a long hall. The same breeze carried Lady Elise's and Miss Warren's words straight to Ruanna's ears.

"I can't bear this dreadful place," Lady Elise told her companion. "I shall think of a way for us to be taken back to London."

"Oh, but you can't, m'lady," Miss Warren answered with alacrity. "Not until you are married to the earl.

251

Remember, he has not actually asked to pay his addresses. All you have to go on are his actions.''

There was a pause before Ruanna heard more, and then it was Miss Warren's voice again. "I do not know whether or not you have noticed, but His Lordship's eyes keep straying to that ward of his. And she is quite beautiful. If I were you, I would not be too hasty to depart. Mayhaps tomorrow you will feel differently.''

Trilling laughter came from Lady Elise, and then, "That redhead is near driving the earl to distraction. He is so embarrassed by her comportment. But he makes excuses for her. He told me that she had lived in that heathen country of India, and that it is very difficult for her to understand the ways of the upper orders. And what is worse, she seems indifferent to his entreaties. Why, he asked me only this morning while waiting to depart the inn if I would take Lady Moreton in hand.''

The annoying laughter again, and then Lady Elise's disgusting voice: "I would rather strangle her. She is to have her come-out in three weeks, and the earl is terribly concerned that she will embarrass his cousin. That does not in the least sound as if he is enamored with the green-eyed hen-wit, now does it?''

"I have heard on-dits that claim she is exactly like her mother, who was a terribly rebellious person.'' This was Miss Warren, Ruanna discerned. "Lady Moreton's mother paid absolutely no attention to the rules of the ton. She married a man of the trades, and then went to India to live when society cut them. Now her daughter is back, but I, for one, doubt that the upper orders will ever accept that chit.''

It had been all Ruanna could do to keep from walking right into Lady Elise's room and challenging her on what she had said about her dear Mama. Now, sitting there listening to the despicable woman gush about Wilder-hope, Ruanna was tempted to call her a liar right to her face. She looked at the earl and felt pity for him. Then anger. How could he be so blind?

Ruanna noticed that only the few hours they had been at Wilderhope had done wonders for His Lordship's countenance. Some of the hardness had gone from his face, and he seemed younger.

Unable to bear another look at Lady Elise, or for that matter, the earl, Ruanna rose from her chair and bade everyone a pleasant good night. If there was only some way she could expose the hateful woman's true nature to the earl. She wondered if she told him if he would believe her.

In her room, Ruanna decided that the earl most likely would not believe her; and, in truth, she did not know how to tell him of Lady Elise's deceitfulness without revealing her own true feelings for His Lordship.

Then, Mother Nature stepped in to give Ruanna a hand.

For the next three days it rained without letup. Soon it was evident that Lady Elise's pleasant demeanor was about to crack. She winced when the loud claps of thunder came; she cried out when the startling streaks of lightning danced across the sky, and she frowned darkly when water sluiced against the windowpanes. When the wind rattled the frames, she covered her ears with her hands.

Ruanna loved the spring storm, and she was enjoying Lady Elise's discomfort immensely.

On the fourth morning, Ruanna came down into a small dining room and found Lady Elise already seated at the table, awaiting the footman to serve her breakfast. An ugly scowl was on her plain countenance. "Good morning, Lady Elise," Ruanna said, and bobbed a curtsy.

Without acknowledging the greeting, Lady Elise glared at Ruanna and blurted out in a lofty manner, "Has not anyone ever taught you the proper way of curtsying to the nobility?"

Ruanna smiled coyly and stepped back to dip into a royal curtsy, one fit for the prince regent, she was sure. "You mean like this? Of course I know how to curtsy to the nobility. But in my opinion, one does not become noble by birth only. Being noble should be earned, and there is responsibility accompanying any title. One should be honest with one's self, and most importantly, with others."

"And what is that supposed to mean?"

Ruanna sat across the table from her adversary. "That you are attempting to trap the earl into a marriage that would make him very unhappy. You hate Wilderhope; yet, you are pretending that you love the place."

Lady Elise pushed her chair back and half rose to her feet. "Where on earth did you get such an odious idea? I must say, your manners are much worse than the earl told me."

Undaunted, Ruanna went on. "I got the odious idea, Lady Elise, from your very words. I happened to be in the hallway the first evening we arrived here, and I heard you telling your shadow, Miss Warren, that you detested Wilderhope. I also heard her warn you not to reveal your true feelings until after you are married to the earl."

"So you are on the level of a servant, listening at doors," Lady Elise accused disdainfully.

Pleased with herself, Ruanna unloaded her best shot. She was bluffing, but she suspected it to be true. "I also heard you tell Miss Warren that you had no notion of giving the earl the heir he desperately wants."

Lady Elise's mouth flew open, and she flopped back down into her chair. "Then you did have an ear to the door. *That* was said in a whisper."

Ruanna smiled. "Then you confess—"

"His Lordship will never believe you."

Meeting her gaze, Ruanna buttered a piece of hot bread, adding strawberry jam. "I do not intend to tell him. But you will. One way or the other. The earl . . ."

Just then, the topic of the ladies' discussion entered the dining room, a dark, formidable figure striding toward the table with the silent sureness of a cat. He wore buckskin riding breeches, a spencer of impeccable tailoring, and glistening black top boots. That he was angry was evident.

Ruanna wondered what she had done now. Could he have overheard her and Lady Elise talking? If so, he should be angry with his intended, Ruanna reasoned.

"Lady Moreton, Lord Stewart is awaiting your company. It seems that the two of you are to finish the game of chess you started yesterday. Or was it the day before? He has been here every day since our arrival, and he is becoming quite annoying. In truth, he is making a pest of himself."

Before Ruanna could answer, the earl turned to the footman and ordered his breakfast. The tone of his voice was less than pleasant.

Obviously the footman was not used to Lord Julian speaking in such a manner, for he hastily filled a plate and set it in front of His Lordship, almost spilling it in his lap.

Ruanna pushed her chair back and asked to be excused. She curtsied to the earl and watched his brows snap together. She knew he did not approve, but today she thought a curtsy appropriate in front of his *special* guest. Without waiting for any sort of reply, she turned and almost ran from the room, to play chess with Lord Stewart. The earl was unbearable.

Lord Stewart took Ruanna's hand and kissed it when she entered the much-used salon overlooking the meadows. She was surprised that he had come today. Yesterday, she had told him that she had used him to make Lord Julian jealous, and that it was not her way to be dishonest, or to hurt anyone.

She also told him that she enjoyed their flirtatious friendship, and if the rain should stop, and if he were still interested in nothing more from her than the friendship she could give, she would go riding with him.

Being well-versed in the ways of love for his twenty

and five years, Stewart set the record straight by telling Ruanna that he was aware that she was in love with Lord Julian. He also stated emphatically, "But I do not intend to give up my pursuit of you."

So, Ruanna thought, here he was back at Wilderhope, smiling, ready to play chess; and while they were doing so, the clouds moved over to make room for a spate of sunshine.

For the ride, Ruanna wore a riding dress of deep purple.

"You are especially pretty today, Ruanna," Lord Stewart told her. "I'm glad you didn't wear a hat. Your red hair glows under the rays of the welcome sun."

"You are most kind," she told him. She smiled, but only slightly. A sense of melancholy had seeped into her being, for she knew that she was telling Wilderhope goodbye. Through tears, she saw bluebells growing in the woods, and flowering horse chestnut trees reaching toward the clearing sky. She listened to the country sounds of a tree frog, and a bird calling to its mate. She wanted to keep the sounds with her forever.

A huge silence swallowed the two riders up, and soon Ruanna reined her horse in the direction of the manor house. At the stables, Lord Stewart helped her from her horse, and, as he did so, he brushed her cheek with his lips.

"Please," she said, pushing his hand away. There was only one man she wanted to kiss her, and he was riding with that deceitful peahen. Pain ripped Ruanna's heart. Her horse snorted and reared its head. She spoke gently to him, and even though the sun beamed warmly onto the wet earth, she shivered as if a cold wind had just separated her heart from her body, leaving nothing for her to hold on to. For sure, she thought, the clouds had left the sky and had gathered inside her body, her soul. She bade Lord Stewart a good afternoon.

"Will I see you tomorrow?" he asked.

"Of course," Ruanna answered.

Lord Stewart gave her an understanding look, and a crooked, winsome smile. "In our next game of chess, I will win."

When Ruanna turned away, she saw Jim jogging toward her, a broad grin on his little face. After handing the horse's reins to a groom, Ruanna ran to the little boy. "What has happened? Why the big grin?" she asked.

Jim reached into his pocket and pulled out the biggest, greenest, slimiest frog Ruanna had ever seen. "For Her Ladyship, the one with a big snout," he said.

"Where did you get it?"

"From the pond. This morning. The earl and me went down there. Said he wanted to talk with me."

Ruanna felt apprehensive, and she did not know why. "What did he wish to speak with you about, Jim?"

The frog gave a big croak and tried to jump, but only succeeded in elongating his body, for Jim's little hand squeezed him in the middle.

"His Lordship wants me to live at Wilderhope and go to school. He said that he 'ad located a fine day school in the village."

"Why, I think that is wonderful—"

"But I ain't going to."

"Jim, you can't possibly mean it."

"I told him I would stay only if yer gonna be 'ere, too, and he said that was impossible, that he was for sure marrying Lady Elise. I told 'im that she was lying to 'im when she says she loves the country, but I don't think he believed me."

"Jim! You didn't tell him that. How could you have known her true feelings? Did you overhear her talking to Miss Warren, as I did?"

"Na. I didn't hear 'er say it, but I just know thet she is lying." His voice dropped, and he stared at the ground. "Lady Moreton, I was brung up among liars and thieves. I know 'em like the back of my hand."

Ruanna went down onto her knees and hugged the little boy close to her heart, not knowing that not too far away, the earl raised a big hand to block the bright sunlight as he witnessed the poignant scene.

"Why are you stopping, and what are you staring at, m'lord?" Lady Elise asked. Giving her horse's rein a healthy jerk, she turned him to go back to join the earl. Her eyes followed his gaze. *That odious little boy and the earl's untrainable ward.* Aloud she said, "Very touching."

"Yes, it is. Isn't it?" the earl answered as his booted heel commanded his black stallion to run. Behind him, Lady Elise, riding hell-for-leather, screeched that he wait for her. The earl looked back in time to see the wind lift her hat, which held two purple plumes, and blow it across the green meadow. He did not stop, but urged the stallion to a greater speed. He wanted to know what was wrong with Jim, and why Lady Moreton was comforting him.

Chapter Twenty

Two evenings later, Ruanna and Lord Stewart stood in the shadow of the manor and talked, away from the earl's watchful eyes. She pulled her pelisse close to protect her from the night's chill, but knew that it could do nothing about the coldness that had invaded her heart since she had formulated her plan. The shudder was from pain, not the cold. With his hand resting on the vine-covered stone wall, Lord Stewart looked down at her, his face a mask of solemnity.

"I'm sorry," he said, "that what I felt for you never had a chance to develop beyond friendship. Your honesty with me is admirable, and last evening Lord Julian called on me at my cousin's."

"He didn't!"

"I fear so, and he let it be known that he would not permit my addresses to you." Lord Stewart waited a moment, then gave a wry smile. "But that would not have stopped me had you not already told me that ours could never be more than friendship . . . and that you were in love with Lord Julian."

"I did not want to mislead you. Her words caught in her throat. "I've never been stupid before. . . ."

Lord Stewart lifted her hand and brought it to his lips. "Sometimes one's heart rules. . . ."

"Will you help me return to London?" Ruanna asked.

"After London, where will you go? Julian and Lady Elise are bound to spend time at Grosvenor House after they are married." He paused. "Ruanna, you can't keep running away."

"Mayhaps I will go to America," she said. "I just know that I cannot witness the earl married to Lady Elise. Wherever I go, I will take my music with me. I can give harp lessons to survive."

The thought of stowing away on another ship was not to Ruanna's liking, but the old adage came to her, One does what one has to do, and she needed to find a way out of her dilemma.

"We will need a chaperone. The night's stay at an inn would compromise your reputation." Lord Stewart's face lost some of its seriousness when he added, "Unless you wish to marry me."

Ruanna was glad at last to see the handsome lord smile, and she tried to smile back at him. "What difference does it make about what the ton thinks. I don't give a fig—"

"The earl would call me out. And what a farrago that would be, for I would meet him."

"But duels are illegal," Ruanna said, knowing that what he had said was true. It would be a farrago. And gentlemen of the upper orders loved nothing more than a go at each other on the dueling field. "Katie can serve as my chaperone."

"I'm afraid that would not suffice. The fifth earl of Wendsleydale is a very difficult man to deal with where *his ward* is concerned." Lord Stewart's face lighted up. "I have a capital idea. I shall ask my cousin Alice to come along. She would love a few days in London, and she would be delighted to come to your grand ball, your come-out."

"Oh, but there won't be a grand ball. You see, Lord Stewart, I plan to leave Grosvenor House as soon as I reach London." Ruanna watched the frown on Lord Stewart's brow deepen. "What is it?"

"The earl is bound to follow—"

"I don't think so. He is too occupied with his intended bride, and besides, when he does discover I am gone from Wilderhope, he will think I caught a mail coach. He won't suspect you. That's why I'm talking with you out here in the dark."

The leave-taking from Wilderhope was planned for two days away. Long before morning, Ruanna would meet Lord Stewart and his cousin Alice on the main road. Stewart would borrow equipage.

Ruanna had not yet learned why Lady Throckmorton was so upset about her coming to Wilderhope, or why the old woman herself had not come in many years. "And I want to do that," she had told Lord Stewart, smiling when he chided her about her curiosity.

But it was more than curiosity to Ruanna. Wilderhope held a secret, and she felt that somehow it was connected to her.

Mayhaps it will explain why Lady Throckmorton fought the earl to bring me out of the East End to Grosvenor House, and why she spent her savings on a virtual stranger's wardrobe.

Albeit Lady Throckmorton was a dear friend of her grandmother's, Ruanna mused, that was not reason enough for the aging woman to point her cane at the earl and threaten to take Ruanna to Scotland if he did not permit her to come to his household.

Nor was loneliness the answer, as Ruanna had first thought. Lady Throckmorton was much too interested in the downtrodden to be that lonely.

Ruanna decided to start with Katie. Surely the maid had learned something from the household help. But Katie shook her head and said, "I ain't heerd no gossip at'al, m'lady. The maids at Wilderhope don't say nothin'. I'm ready to go home to Grosvenor House."

Then, Katie clamped her hand over her mouth to muffle her laughter. Ruanna raised a quizzical brow and asked, "Katie, what in the world—"

"The only excitement round this place was when little Jim put thet green frog under 'er Ladyship's chair. The way thet woman squealed was the talk of the 'ouse all next day."

Ruanna could not help but smile. Last evening, during one of Lady Elise's diatribes on how the beauty of Wilderhope held her enthralled, Jim's slimy, green frog, trying to escape from under the chair where Jim had placed it, tangled itself in the skirt of her gown. Another gown that was too elaborate for Wilderhope, Ruanna thought.

Screaming to the top of her lungs, Lady Elise jumped from her chair and yanked at her skirt with such force that the frog went flying out into the middle of the floor, where it sat with its glassy eyes bulging and its throat pulsating, while emitting huge croaks.

Lady Elise lunged for the frog and missed, but that did not deter her. She chased it around the room, as it hopped this way and that. Holding her skirt up and scandalously exposing her legs, she kept trying to stomp the frog, but always the frog was a hop ahead of her.

And if looks from the earl could kill, poor little Jim would have been dead, Ruanna thought. The little pickpocket was sitting near the earl's chair, with the most innocent expression on his face.

The stomping had gone on until Jim covered his pet with his body, after which Lady Elise had a splendid spell of the vapors and toppled to the floor. To Ruanna's disgust, the earl hovered over her.

"Which was what the deceitful woman wanted," Ruanna said, and Katie looked at her.

"What m'lady?"

"Nothing, Katie. I was just thinking about Lady Elise and the frog."

Another spasm of laughter shook Katie. With her skirt pulled up, she hopped about the room, stomping at an imaginary frog, and making Ruanna laugh. "Well, Jim saved his frog, and he received only a slight reprimand from the earl."

Katie became all seriousness. "Yer know, Lady Moreton, I don't like that woman. What 'is Lordship sees in 'er, I don't know."

"That is not for us to figure out," Ruanna said, discouraging further gossip. Her mind went back to the secret that Wilderhope had. If she were to leave on the morrow, time was of the essence.

"Katie," Ruanna said, "to whom would you go if you wanted to know about Wilderhope's past? Which servant has been here the longest?"

"Cook. She looks like she was on Noah's Ark, and she was borned 'ere, so the 'ead housekeeper told me."

Ruanna found Cook bending over a pan of scones, as if she were examining each one for an imperfection. The old woman was stooped, and her leathered face looked like a freshly plowed field. She wore a white apron over a black bombazine dress that rustled when she moved.

The scones smelled delicious, and Ruanna did not hesitate to take one when Cook held it out to her. "I understand you have been at Wilderhope longer than any of the servants," Ruanna said.

"Thet's right. I was borned 'ere," Cook said.

"Then mayhaps you can tell me something about Lady Throckmorton, the earl's old cousin who raised him."

"She used to come 'ere a lot, then she stopped."

"Why did she stop? Does anyone know?"

The stooped woman shook her head. "No one knows nothin', 'cept she didn't come anymore after Miss Harriette come."

So Miss Harriette is the woman Lady Throckmorton was referring to. . . .

Ruanna felt her heart racing. "Pray, who is Miss Harriette?"

Cook scooted her feet across the stone floor, carrying

the pan of scones. She did not answer until she put them in the warming oven. "No one knows nothin' 'cept her ma worked 'ere for one of the earls, and the old earl, Lord Julian's pa, brung Miss Harriette 'ere when she was too sick to work. She's in the bedchamber in thet wing, and she won't be living long, her being so sick."

Cook inclined her head southward, then went on, "On the floor with the family, not even where servants belongs. And she has her own servant to wait on her. I smelled a scandal right from the start."

Assuming Cook meant the south wing of the house, Ruanna expressed her thanks with great haste, then left immediately. After climbing the stairs, she found Miss Harriette's bedchamber at the end of a long hall. Her name was on the door, which Ruanna eased open and asked if she might enter.

A smile spread across the woman's pale, weathered face. She lay on a high bed with white silk hangings, pulled back and tied with white ribbons. Her bushy white head rested on pillows covered with the same white silk as the hangings. The old woman waved a gnarled hand—the only thing with color in the room, Ruanna thought, as she went to sit beside the bed.

"Miss Harriette, I am Ruanna Moreton, daughter of—"

"I know who you are. I heard you were here. I know also that Lady Throckmorton rescued you from the slums of London."

Ruanna noticed the woman's elocution, the cadence with which she spoke, not at all like a servant's. And her surroundings certainly did not resemble those of household help. Ruanna's eyes perused the room.

A black marble fireplace took up the wall at the opposite end of the room. A sofa, slip-covered in silk brocade, and two matching chairs that faced each other sat before the fireplace. A row of windows allowed brightness, and prongs of sunlight shimmered on the furniture, and on the white bed.

"The cook said I should come to you, that mayhaps you could tell me something about Lady Throckmorton."

The old woman lay quietly as Ruanna told her about Lady Throckmorton's refusal to come to Wilderhope, about her sobbing and saying not as long as that woman was there.

"I assume she meant you," Ruanna said. And then she asked bluntly, "Why would she feel that way about you?"

The woman smiled. "Because I am the only one left living who knows her secret."

Afraid the woman would refuse to explain, Ruanna hesitated to pry, but she knew that she must. She took the old woman's hand and, in a low voice, asked, "What is Lady Throckmorton's secret, Miss Harriette? I would not ask if I did not believe that it has something to do with me. Do you know that to be so?"

For a long moment, silence hovered over the old woman, so loud it filled the room. While holding her hand, Ruanna realized how frail she was and wondered about her age. With her being ill, Ruanna could not even guess.

In pursuing the answer to Lady Throckmorton's strange behavior, I may have come face to face with another mystery, she thought as she waited.

Although the quietness grew uncomfortably strange, Ruanna, feeling a prickle down her spine, made no attempt to break it, and finally, Miss Harriette spoke in a faltering voice. "I was lady's maid to Countess Waite. Your grandmother, child . . . except she was not your grandmother."

Ruanna rose half out of her chair. "Not my grandmother? Then who—"

The old woman fixed her gaze on Ruanna's face. "Lady Isadora Throckmorton, Countess Waite's dearest friend."

Ruanna's breath came in short spurts as she settled back in the chair. *Surely this is the way one feels with an attack of vapors.* When she spoke, she had to push the words off her tongue. "I . . . I don't take your meaning. . . ."

Miss Harriette reached for a silver bell on the table near her bed and rang it. "Let me order tea, and then I will tell you the story."

When the maid came, she propped the old woman up on pillows, and as she did so, Miss Harriette's night rail of thin muslin revealed sticklike bones with skin stretched over them. "Bring tea and a repast, Sukie," Miss Harriette said. "I need strength to talk."

Ruanna wondered about what was wrong with her, and why a servant was living her last days in such luxury. "What secret is the Aynsworth family hiding?" she asked under her breath. But she did not dare inquire of Miss Harriette, not until she learned about Lady Throckmorton.

The old woman's words had not yet sunk into Ruanna's psyche. She had to be wrong, Ruanna reasoned, Lady Throckmorton could not be her grandmother. Lady Throckmorton was a spinster.

When the tea and scones were served, Ruanna waited for Miss Harriette to continue. But the old woman ate a scone and sipped tea, while Ruanna watched her over the rim of her own teacup. "If you feel that it would be betraying a confidence . . ."

"Pshaw, it won't be betraying a confidence," Miss Harriette said at last. "'Tis time the truth was told, and I told Lady Throckmorton as much. That's why she's never returned to Wilderhope after I came. She didn't like my telling her if she got it out, it would not hurt so much."

"What hurt so much?" Ruanna asked.

Miss Harriette did not answer, and Ruanna waited.

And then the woman began again. "I was just a young girl when I was sent from here to be a lady's maid to Countess Waite. My mother had died, and the earl—I

266

think he was the third one—thought I should be exposed to a woman like Countess Waite. He had sent me to school. . . ."

The voice became weak, almost inaudible. Ruanna felt guilty, but she could not leave. She set her cup on the silver tray and took the woman's hand again, patting it.

"Countess Waite and Lady Throckmorton were like sisters and, since Lady Throckmorton lived in the household, I witnessed this close friendship," Miss Harriette said. "Then one day they said they were going to Switzerland for an extended stay, for Countess Waite's health. Even though she was a new bride, she was enceinte. I thought mayhaps she had been in the family way when she was married and this was her way of keeping it a secret."

A spell of coughing took her strength, and it was a long while before Ruanna heard her raspy voice continue.

"It was not until we were in Switzerland that I learned it was not Countess Waite who was expecting a child, but Lady Throckmorton."

The words whirled in Ruanna's head and tears blurred her vision. *Then it's true.*

"But when we returned to London, Countess Waite carried baby Mary in her arms, saying that she had given birth to the beautiful little girl while in Switzerland."

"Who was . . . who was Lady Mary's father?" *He would be my grandfather.*

"That, Lady Throckmorton will have to tell you. I doubt she will. Our greatest argument was when I told her she should tell the truth, now that Countess Waite's dead. She refused, but mayhaps since I've told you she is your grandmother, she will tell you the rest. I told her that it would be good for her soul, that it would expunge the pain."

By now the old woman's voice was so weak, Ruanna had to lean forward to hear. She knew that she had asked too much of the frail thing, but she knew also that the old woman had wanted to tell. *She believes by telling she is helping Lady Throckmorton. . . .*

Ruanna did not know if knowing had helped her. Her thoughts in a whirl, she rose to go. She bent over and kissed Miss Harriette's forehead and smelled the oldness, and her sickness. "Thank you, Miss Harriette, I will ask Lady Throckmorton to tell me the rest."

I must needs ask her about my grandfather? Who was her lover?

Tears were coming now, ever so softly; she felt them as they rolled down her cheek. At the door she turned back and asked, "How did you end up at Wilderhope, Miss Harriette?"

"When your grandmother died, Lady Throckmorton came to fetch me. I never liked living in London. I love Wilderhope." And then she repeated, "I was born here."

That did not answer Ruanna's question, but she decided to let it go and ask Lady Throckmorton when she got to London. Ruanna said good-bye.

"You will come back?"

"Of course I shall."

Ruanna painfully knew that she could not keep her word. She was leaving Wilderhope . . . and London . . . for good. Quietly, she closed the door behind her.

The rest of the day, Ruanna, her mind in a whirl, wandered about Wilderhope. She encountered the earl only once and asked him about Miss Harriette. He shook his head and said that she would have to ask Lady Throckmorton. "All I know," he said, "is that she was brought here ill and has been here ever since. I visit with her when I am at Wilderhope, but she has never told me her past. I just know she is here, and that she is to be taken care of until she dies."

As Ruanna's restlessness grew, she prepared for the journey the next day, swearing Katie to secrecy.

"If the earl should ask you, which I doubt that he will,

you must needs not tell him a thing. You will be brought back to London when he and Lady Elise return."

Katie pressed her lips together, then said, "Thet's what I'll do if His Lordship asks me."

Dinner was served as usual, with Lady Elise and Miss Warren monopolizing the conversation. As soon as possible, without appearing rude, Ruanna repaired to her own room to make ready for bed.

"How can I add to Lady Throckmorton's pain? I must needs stay for my come-out. . . . I will explain to her *why* I cannot stay."

Thoughts, thoughts tumbled through Ruanna's head. Lady Throckmorton, her grandmother, was much on her mind. She said grandmother aloud, just to hear it roll off her tongue. It seemed so unreal. All of her world seemed unreal.

Her thoughts turned from Lady Throckmorton to the earl. Why does the earl not announce their betrothal and get it over with? she wondered, giving the foot of the bed a hefty kick. Since arriving at Wilderhope only occasionally had she caught the earl's cold, blue eyes on her. His attention had been directed entirely to Lady Elise.

Peagoose, did he not say that would be so?

Even when he had ridden away from Lady Elise to where she and Jim were talking, when Jim was showing her his frog, His Lordship had knelt beside Jim, but he had averted his gaze to something over her shoulder, his eyes never engaging hers. And he seemed so cold, and so dead set against her.

Ruanna lay on the bed; tears pushed at her eyes, making her angry. She was not a crier. If she had not been so independent! If she could gush like Lady Elise, Ruanna thought.

And then she tried counting sheep. But sleep would not come, for she fancied that everywhere the world was mating, that even the owls were calling to each other of their passion and their desire. She stared at the scrolled ceiling, seeing the earl's stone-hard face in every crevice.

"Stuff," she said; then, cursing under her breath, she threw the coverlet back, bounded out of bed, and went to stand by the window. In the distance was the head of the downs where the hills looked down on the wide meadows, and on Wilderhope's manor house. She stared at the meadow, where the moon-tipped grass was gray and green in layers, shadowed by the moonlight. The beauty of it made her even more lonely, so she turned away.

But she quickly turned back to look again at something of which she had caught a fleeting glimpse.

Shading her eyes, she peered through the glass and saw the earl, dressed in black riding clothes and sitting tall in the saddle, riding his black stallion at breakneck speed, as if Satan himself were in hot pursuit.

At first, Ruanna felt an almost mercurial uplift to her spirit, and then she felt a quick and intense upsurge of tremendous pain. Why did she love him so much? It was more than she could bear, and she was glad that on the morrow she would leave Wilderhope, never to return.

And then Ruanna thought about Lady Throckmorton. *My grandmother.* Painful though it would be, she would confront the old woman about what Miss Harriette had told her. *I want to know about my lineage.*

"Codswallop, Jim, where is she? You have to tell me," the earl demanded, his voice more harsh than he intended, his heart hurting inside his pounding chest. He had woken early with the feeling that something was wrong and straightaway had found that Ruanna had left. Again!

He had searched, but she was nowhere to be found on Wilderhope. Not even Katie knew where the chit had gone.

A gaze from Jim's big brown eyes met the earl's head on, and not a word passed through the little boy's thin, compressed lips. Distraught, the earl grabbed him by the shoulders and shook him. "Do you not understand? Lady Moreton's life is in danger. You may never see her again. You must tell me. Jim, you must."

"Beat him," Lady Elise suggested, drawing back when the earl shot her a dark look.

"It appears to me that you are terribly worried about someone who is no more to you than a ward, practically a servant in your household," Miss Warren chimed in.

Lady Elise brazenly went on, "So what if she has run away to marry Lord Stewart? I'll wager a—"

Her words were silenced by an angry outburst from the earl. "No one asked you."

Wishing he could banish both women from his sight, the earl acknowledged that he had been a fool.

"Are you going to tell me, Jim?" the earl asked again, his voice more cajoling this time. "I know you know. She would not have left without telling you."

"No, I ain't gonna tell," Jim said emphatically. "I promised, and I shan't ever breach a promise to Lady Moreton, and I would never lie to yer." He looked the earl straight in the eye. "If yer get my message."

The earl studied the upturned face and saw the truth. The little pickpocket would steal, but he would not lie. "You were not lying when you told me Lady Elise hates Wilderhope, were you, Jim?"

Cutting his eyes around to look at Lady Elise, the earl was not at all surprised that her face had turned the color of yesterday's death, and that guilt rode her countenance. Her companion was fanning her, while making disparaging remarks about a certain little liar she knew.

"No, m'lord, I warn't lying. I could jest feel it in me . . . my bones. And Lady Moreton heard Lady Elise tell that other woman there"—Jim inclined his head toward Miss Warren—"that she could not abide Wilderhope, but there would be time enough to let her feelings be known *after* she was married to yer."

The earl turned to Lady Elise and said in a cold voice, "I am going after Lady Moreton. I shall have a driver and a groom accompany you and Miss Warren back to town. Katie and your servants will follow as they came."

With that, Lady Elise fainted dead away, and the earl strode past her, past the startled butler, Danby, and out to the stables.

"Suthe," he thundered, "prepare a carriage. Lady Moreton has run away *again*. When I find her this time I shall bind her, after I have turned her over my knee and soundly spanked her. And I shall beat her. . . ."

A wry grin spread across the big coachman's face. "Now that, m'lord, I should like to see."

Chapter Twenty-One

After the earl's order, it was only moments before the carriage, pulled by four fresh horses, came to a sudden stop in the circle driveway in front of the manor house. Guard was on the box beside the big driver.

As His Lordship shrugged into a coat, the door slammed behind him. Quick, long strides took him to the carriage, where he hauled himself up and gave Suthe office to be gone. "To the village first," he said.

It took considerable time for the earl to inquire in the village if anyone had seen Lady Moreton. "Perhaps dressed like a boy," he said, "but you would know her by her red hair . . . if a boy's cap was not hiding it."

After meeting only negative shakes of heads from those he asked, he went to Lord Stewart's cousin's estate to ask to speak to His Lordship.

"He's not here. He left before light," the cousin said.

And that was all the earl could learn. His departure for London was delayed considerably, all for naught. They headed for London, and the countryside passed the earl's vision in a haze, with Suthe keeping the horses up to their bits.

As the earl held on to the leather strap to steady himself in the seat, his mind held to Ruanna. He was torn, and torn again, with tormenting thoughts.

"What if she has run away to marry Lord Stewart?"

Miss Warren had asked, and the earl, thinking back on it, found the remark singularly disturbing. In truth, he admitted, it took precedence over the threat from the man from India.

He could not let the impetuous girl marry Lord Stewart. Such a marriage would be a disaster!

I am responsible for her!

She is my ward!

Lady Throckmorton will be devastated should Ruanna marry Lord Stewart!

"And if the young jackanapes has compromised her, I shall call him out," the earl murmured, forgetting that Ruanna had admitted to a lover in India; forgetting everything.

He only knew that he had to find her before she did something foolish, for he could not bear for the beautiful, the kind and caring redhead to belong to someone else.

There, I've said it. No, I didn't say it, but I admit it. Aloud, he said, "I cannot bear to have Ruanna marry someone else. What a fool I've been."

Ruanna was not like Countess Charlotte at all, the earl told himself. Lady Elise was more like the countess; they both had mean, selfish, and deceiving hearts.

The earl's lips curved into a slow smile as he settled back against the squabs. He should have known how wrong he was about Ruanna when he saw the way she cared for the little pickpocket. And who cares if her manners are not acceptable to the ton? he asked himself. The ton be damned!

His smile broadened as he recalled Ruanna's words, "I don't give a fig about the ton."

And so the arduous day passed, the earl's patience strained to the limit. Then, night with its darkness was hovering. Pulling into the third posting house for the third change of horses, His Lordship quickly alighted.

"Suthe, I shall check to see if they have come this way while you have a groom change to fresh horses. See that

274

these get a good rubdown." He inclined his head toward the sweaty horses, which were wheezing out labored breaths.

The big driver cocked an eyebrow. "You mean we be driving through the night if she ain't here?" He shook his head wearily.

"That is exactly what I mean, Suthe. Now hurry."

The earl turned, and his purposeful stride took him quickly to the door of the posting house, a lonely two-story structure, the windows square boxes of dim light. As his hand reached for the knob to open the door, he bent down to take the pistol from the top of his boot. He did not know why, except that somehow he smelled trouble.

Ruanna had thought she would feel better after she departed Wilderhope. At last, she did not have to see the earl and Lady Elise together. But she found that it was not so. Leaving had not helped one whit, for in her mind's eye, she could see the handsome earl's gaze on Lady Elise's mean countenance.

The imagery left Ruanna's heart heavy as she sat in the crowded parlor of the posting inn, Lord Stewart by her side. His cousin, Alice, had repaired to her room for the night and would have a tray sent up, she had said.

"You love the earl very much, don't you, Ruanna?" Lord Stewart asked wistfully.

"Yes, but he can't love me in return. I have red hair like the woman who married his brother. Besides, he thinks my manners are deplorable, but that is my fault, and—"

"Hey, wait a minute. None of this is your fault. You have lovely manners—"

"But I pretended to the earl that I did not know how to go on in society, and . . . and I had to leave little Jim."

Tears began to roll down her cheeks, and Ruanna swiped angrily at them.

"I find your manners charming," Lord Stewart said as he reached to take Ruanna's hand. "And I am sure Aynsworth will not allow the boy to be mistreated."

"If only I had another color of hair. Lord Julian thinks all women with red hair are alike. Am I making myself clear?" She sucked in a breath and, taking a handkerchief from her reticule, blew her nose.

Lord Stewart's eyes were not on Ruanna when he said, "Hardly, my pet, but I believe that is the second, or is the third, time you've said that. Nothing will convince me that the earl is not a jackanapes."

Ruanna turned to see what Lord Stewart was looking at. "What—"

"I don't like the way that man is looking at you. He has been staring at you for the past five minutes; I have been observing him . . . he has a tooth missing, and . . ."

Ruanna had failed to tell Lord Stewart that her life was in danger. Before she could do so, she felt a big hand clamp over her mouth, and, as she was yanked to her feet, the barrel of a pistol was pressed against her back.

Balderdash! Where's my club? Ruanna, in her haste to leave Wilderhope, had, much to her consternation, left her weapon behind.

Lord Stewart jumped from his chair, but before he could move a step toward Ruanna, a man with a swarthy complexion—the one from the theater, she noted—brought a heavy pipe to bear on the top of his head, toppling him to the floor.

Ruanna wanted to scream and couldn't. Instantly, however, her instinct for survival came to the fore, and she sank her teeth into the fleshy part of the man's hand. A stream of terrible expletives spewed from his mouth. Jerking his injured hand away, he held her pinned against him with the other. Ruanna felt too plainly the pistol barrel digging into her ribs. Beneath her fright, anger seethed. How dare Archibald Bennet . . .

"All I want is fer you to come with me," the man said. Ruanna saw blood drip from his hand she had bitten into. Sickness welled up inside of her. She heard a chilling scream which she was sure had come from her own throat. For a moment she was speechless, but only for a moment. It was not her nature to be so. When she had regained her equilibrium, she told her captor, "Archibald Bennet does not want my dead body. Besides, you will hang at Newgate if you shoot me." She twisted her head and spat at him.

Still, he held her like a vise. Shouts filled the room. "Let 'er go," the voices said, as they scrambled about, knocking chairs over and pushing closer.

Ruanna felt herself being dragged, and she knew that soon she would be outside with this awful man, and then on a ship headed for India and Archibald Bennet. But that was not to be, she soon learned. She felt a powerful presence; an impenetrable silence stilled the room. Her eyes caught a glimpse of the fifth earl of Wendsleydale's big frame standing in the doorway, his clear blue eyes like agates glistening in sunlight. "Julian," she whispered.

"Turn her loose," the earl said, and when his command was not obeyed, a shot rang out. His aim was perfect. The gun that had been pressing Ruanna's right cage sailed through the air, and she heard, with delight, a bloodcurdling scream come from her captor.

The dark-complexioned man who had been holding Lord Stewart turned and ran out the back door of the inn, as Lord Stewart, shaking his head as if to clear it, struggled to his feet.

The earl's eyes were on Ruanna. Her face had never been more beautiful. He could feel her fright, taste it, and he saw her stubborn little chin tremble. He saw her vulnerability, her need. He opened his arms, and when she ran to him, he dropped his gun and clasped her to him. Holding her gently, he whispered sweet assurances and pushed her red hair back from her face, then wiped the tears from her cheeks.

"Everything will be all right, my love," he told her, not

277

realizing he had uttered words of endearment.

Suthe appeared in the doorway, with the dark, nattily dressed man, swaddled with a rope, thrown over his shoulder. The earl smiled.

"Rocco, you will not get a guinea," the man said.

Across the room, Lord Stewart was busily tying Rocco up.

"His name is Witherspoon. I made him tell me," Suthe said. "He was trying to get away, m'lord."

"Thank you, Suthe. For that, you shall have an enormous raise in pay, which, I suspect, is long overdue with all the extra work Lady Moreton has brought to you."

The earl smiled down at Ruanna, and suddenly he knew that she was his destiny. In his arms was the woman he loved; it was meant to be. How could he have been so blindly stupid to believe that all beautiful women were like Countess Charlotte? And it mattered not that Ruanna was not pure, or that she was stubborn, haughty, and sharp tongued.

As the two prisoners were led from the room and the ahs went up from the crowd, the earl kissed Ruanna. He well knew that a gentleman does not kiss a lady of quality until he is married to her. He raised his head just long enough to commit himself to marriage, his brown face at once creased into tenderness. "I want to make you my wife. Will you marry me?"

When Ruanna did not answer, he implored, "Pray, Lady Moreton, say yes. My poor heart cannot bear another chase."

Gales of laughter went up from the crowd. Ruanna caught Lord Stewart's eye. He was laughing with the others.

Taking her arm, the earl, wishing privacy, led Ruanna from the inn, out into the dark night—without a chaperone.

"And we are not yet married," he said, laughing.

Ruanna leaned to him and whispered, "Julian, I am

278

not your Charlie."

"And I am so glad, my only love. Can you forgive me? I thought every beautiful woman was like the countess. I thought that what I felt for you was—"

"Hush," she said, laughing up at him, and he kissed her again, hungrily.

Chapter Twenty-Two

"Your love will heal his scars, child, make him whole again," Lady Throckmorton said when she learned of the earl and Lady Moreton's betrothal. She put her arms around Ruanna and held her to her flat chest. Ruanna could feel the heavy pounding of her heart and knew that her grandmother's true feelings were hidden behind each beat. She had rather hoped the old woman would blurt out the truth about being her grandmother as soon as she and the earl, with Jim and Katie, arrived back to Grosvenor House. They had returned to Wilderhope to fetch Jim and Katie and had found that Lady Elise and her companion had already left.

But Lady Throckmorton kept her silence, and her secret as well. Now, sitting in the yellow salon, Ruanna could stand it no longer. It was well and good to prose on and on about the upcoming wedding, but Ruanna wanted the old woman to tell her that she was her grandmother. Countess Waite was someone she had heard her mother speak about, but Lady Throckmorton was here; she could touch her, hug her. And she would once again have a family. Gratitude filled Ruanna's heart. She recalled that when she first came to Grosvenor House, that day she'd come from the East End, scared to death she was walking into a trap, she had hoped for nothing more than a friend.

She knows Miss Harriette told me; why does she not claim

me as her own flesh and blood?

Lady Throckmorton sat looking out over the garden. She wore a morning dress of sprigged muslin, plain and not at all becoming, in Ruanna's opinion. The black cane rested by her chair, and Ruanna expected any moment that she would grab it and start tapping, for she looked as though she might explode.

Well, the time had come, Ruanna decided; they must needs talk about what was on both their minds. "Miss Harriette told me—"

Lady Throckmorton's chin quivered perceptibly. "I knew she would. That's why I begged Lord Julian not to take you to Wilderhope."

Ruanna was instantly on her knees beside the old woman's chair. She took the blue-veined hands in hers. "But Grandmother, I'm glad she told me. I did not know Countess Waite. I know you. I love you. I'm glad. . . ."

When Lady Throckmorton pulled her gaze from the garden and looked at Ruanna, her thin face was distorted with pain, and her faded eyes seemed to have sunk even deeper into their sockets.

"I never wanted you to know; I never wanted anyone to know. Why did that mean woman—"

"No, Isadora, she is not mean. Miss Harriette is a kind woman, and she did it for you. She wants you to talk about your past. I think she knows your pain."

Ruanna vowed that she would not call her grandmother again until the old woman told her with her own words the story of her birth.

"She said once that keeping it all inside me would eat my innards," Lady Throckmorton said.

"What is *it*, Isadora? Other than that Mama was born to you and raised as Countess Waite's daughter, she told me nothing."

The news seemed to relieve Lady Throckmorton, and Ruanna feared that she would not tell her the whole of *it*, whatever *it* was. Ruanna's next words had an emphatic ring. "I want to know. Why do you not want to tell me?"

Lady Throckmorton looked away again. As she spoke it was as though she were talking to herself. Ruanna listened intently, her emotions strained, as the old woman spoke. "After Countess Waite died, Miss Harriette was the only one who knew, and not even to her could I speak of him."

"Who is him?"

"Your grandfather."

A long, terrible silence ensued. Ruanna waited. *I might as well not be here; she is not thinking of me, but of my grandfather, her lover of years ago.*

Ruanna made herself ask, "Isadora, who was my grandfather?"

"It is the way of the higher orders. One marries not for love, but for convenience, most often to join two estates. I had no wealth to bring to the marriage, and your grandfather's family needed that. I understood, though it hurt. But since we could not marry, I was happy when he married my best friend. Countess Waite was a beautiful woman, child, I was glad to share my daughter Mary with her. She was so kind . . . she let me stay—"

Ruanna's mouth fell open. She found herself squeezing Lady Throckmorton's hands, and then shaking them, almost frantically. "Are you saying that Countess Waite's husband is my grandfather, and that you—"

"Yes, Ruanna, I was enceinte when he married Countess Waite. In thinking back, I think we did it deliberately. It never happened but once, but I believe he wanted to give me a part of himself. We loved each other so much." Her voice broke then, becoming softer, almost inaudible. She brought her gaze to rest on Ruanna's face. "Do you hate me for not telling? What we did was beyond the pale of society."

"I could never hate you." Ruanna gave a little laugh. "As you know, I've never cared a fig about society's strict rules, and, in truth, the first time we met I felt we were bound together in some inexplicable way. I think you are beautiful, Isadora. Your goodness is like a beautiful star, and I am sure that Grandfather saw it, too."

Lady Throckmorton smiled wanly. "When Lord Julian told me of his coming marriage, his cold, blue eyes went all soft and warm. 'Cousin,' he said, 'she is like a million stars that, thanks to you, suddenly appeared to brighten up my dark life.'"

Lady Throckmorton shook her head and smiled. "I have never seen such happiness on Lord Julian's countenance. All because of you . . . my granddaughter. He prosed on and on. I think he secretly admires your independence, and he told me that he loved your good heart."

"I take my independence and my good heart, after you," Ruanna said. She rose to her feet and hugged the old woman. "Grandmother, I am glad you've told me your story; I'm glad you are my grandmother."

"You're not ashamed?"

"Oh, no. But society being what it is, do you want the truth known? Can I shout it from the housetop that you are my grandmother."

At last the old woman's smile turned huge. "No, but only because I do not wish questions to be asked. And because they would turn against you, as they did Mary when she married a man of the trades. It broke my heart when Charles Moreton took her to India, and with my only grandchild." She patted Ruanna's hand.

"Then I shall continue to call you Isadora." After a thoughtful moment, Ruanna added, "I doubt that I would have been so brave as to witness the man I loved entering into a marriage of convenience, which tells you that my good heart is not as good as yours. I thought I would die when it seemed Julian's wont to marry Lady Elise."

Lady Throckmorton said again, "Marriages of convenience are the way of the ton." Then, with a catch in her voice, she continued. "He did not live long. He died when he was only nine and twenty. And he never did have the male heir for the entailed estates. I always wondered if the marriage was consummated."

"And what did you do after his death?"

"I stayed on with Countess Waite and helped raise Lady Mary, until I came to help with little Julian."

"May I tell Julian?" Ruanna asked.

"Yes, he should have known long ago. I just could not bring myself to talk—"

"I know, Isadora, and we will not speak of it again . . . unless you feel inclined to do so." And then, with a little laugh, Ruanna asked, "Would you care to tell me Miss Harriette's secret?"

This coaxed a chuckle from Lady Throckmorton. "She will take that to her grave, but it is suspected that the third earl of Wendsleydale fathered her. Her mother worked at Wilderhope as the third countess's lady's maid."

"Well, Miss Harriette is being taken care of very well. She said he sent her to school."

"Yes, but he never acknowledged her as his daughter, and he could have. Society would not have condemned the third earl. 'Tis only the woman they look down upon."

Ruanna shook her head and made to leave. There were many things to be done. Little Jenny had finally returned to Grosvenor House and had taken to harp lessons like a duck taking to water; there were Jim's lessons, and the wedding was only a sentnight away. As soon as they returned to Grosvenor House, the bans had been read, and a notice sent out that instead of a come-out ball for Lady Ruanna Moreton, Her Ladyship would be marrying Lord Julian Philip Aynsworth, the fifth earl of Wendsleydale, and lord of Wilderhope in Shropshire.

Ruanna bent to kiss her grandmother's cheek. "I love you," she whispered. She left quickly, but later she remembered that there was one more question she had wanted to ask her grandmother.

* * *

The days that followed were so busy that Ruanna did not have a chance to ask Lady Throckmorton the burning question. Having heard asides about what happens on one's wedding night, she was in desperate need to talk with someone. Asides were all that she had heard, and they had not told Ruanna one truth that she could count on. And she was sure that when Lord Julian found out she had been lying about a lover in India, he would beat her.

His Lordship is expecting me to be experienced and know how to please him.

"Oh, Mama, if you had not died when I was twelve," Ruanna said to herself more than once as the days passed.

Since the earl rescued her from Archibald Bennet's henchmen, and sent them off to jail, Ruanna's mind had been in a whirl. How quickly the time had passed, the days once so long, now so short, the hours pleasant and hurried.

And when Madame Dupont had had a fit of vapors when told she was to have the wedding gown ready on such short notice, the earl had simply told her that she could, greasing her palm with many extra guineas.

Now, the wedding would be tomorrow. Ruanna could not believe it. She went to bed, but got up to stand by the window three different times, and it was not until first light was approaching that her mind finally surrendered to sleep. Waking at noontime, she rang for Katie to come attend her.

"Bring tea, please, but no tray," Ruanna told her. When Katie came, Ruanna, thinking it her last hope, immediately inquired of the maid what a woman was supposed to know on her wedding night.

"Nothin' if she's smart," Katie answered, smiling as she drew open the draperies, letting in the sunlight.

"What do you mean, nothing?" Ruanna bounded out of bed to go wash the sleep from her eyes.

"Jest what I said. No matter how many lovers yer've had, pretend that yer innocent. Most of the time the bridegroom is so foxed that the next morning he won't know if his bride was a virgin or not, and if she ain't, whether he stole 'er cherry or not."

Ruanna felt a hot flush of embarrassment creep up from her neck to cover her face. And suddenly, it was like a light exploding inside her mind: *If the earl is foxed, he will not know I have been lying to him.*

The vows were to be said at four o'clock, belowstairs in the big ballroom. There would be a grand meal afterward with dancing . . . and champagne.

A knock on the door intruded, and two footmen marched in with brass tankards of hot water, leaving Ruanna no more time to think on her problem.

The dress, shadows and light of satin, lay spread over two chairs that had been placed side by side. It had been delivered late the day before. Ruanna wondered what His Lordship would think of her dressed all in white. *He probably thinks I should wear black.*

Well, she thought, as she climbed into the tub of hot scented water that Katie had prepared, I am not going to ruin my wedding day by worrying thoughts around. She looked up at Katie, who was standing ready to rinse her red hair.

"Katie, was Countess Charlotte's wedding dress white?"

The maid bobbed her head. "Yes m'lady, it sure was." The maid giggled. "She might a'been pure when she married up with 'im, but she dan't stay that way long. But them kind just stay innocent till they trap a man of the nobility."

Ruanna laughed, a silvery, tinkling laugh that sounded happy even to her own ears. The earl could never accuse her of "trapping" him with her purity.

And she was just as sure that her boasting remark that her husband would positively never leave her bed to go to a strumpet's, was bound for failure. How could she please a man when she simply did not know how?

What a tangled mess she had made with her lies!

Chapter Twenty-Three

While Ruanna worried her fate, the earl was having his own case of wedding jitters, though of a somewhat different nature.

"If I could just change that one thing, turn back the clock and make her pure." The strangled words were muttered under his breath. So relieved had he been to hold her in his arms, and to know that she would soon be there forever, he had thought he would not give her chastity a thought. But as the wedding hour drew near, he found himself fretting the issue.

"Tonight, when I am holding her, I must not think that somewhere in India there's a man who has made love with my wife."

"What did you say, m'lord?" Adam, the valet, asked.

"Nothing of importance," the earl said, feeling his face burn with embarrassment. "Do you know if Bochsa and the boy have arrived? Has the harp been moved? Lady Moreton does not know? I told everyone she was not to know. George, my solicitor, is in charge of that part of the plans."

The valet laughed, but before he could answer the myriad of questions, the earl went on: "Lady Moreton is quite an accomplished musician, Adam. I have made arrangements with the London Philharmonic Orchestra for her to make guest appearances in the future. I have

289

just recently learned that to play with the prestigious orchestra has always been a dream of hers. And the famous harpish, Bochsa, has promised to further instruct her. He is now working with little Jeremy."

"Yes, I know," the valet said, smiling. "Earlier, I saw the harp being discreetly moved. Bochsa and the boy are with George. I'm sure things are in proper order for your wedding, m'lord, so calm yourself. I've never seen you so nervous."

The earl studied his appearance in the looking glass and straightened his high collar points for the tenth time. He laughed at himself. On-dits had it that Beau Brummell sometimes spent two hours "creasing down" his starched cravat, sometimes flinging more than a dozen away before he was satisfied.

But the Beau would not be marrying Lady Moreton.

"You know, Adam, the servants in both residences, Grosvenor House and Wilderhope, have been very vocal about their pleasure of Lady Elise's sudden departure, and Jim has not stopped smiling since it happened. Of course, he was the one who set me in the right direction with her."

As soon as he had returned to Grosvenor House, the earl had summoned his solicitor and was told, "The boy's father has a consumptive cough. He lives in filth, and is supported by a gang of hoists. I had a physician see him, but was not given much hope. It seems Mr. Reevis stays drunk as a wheelbarrow most of the time. Nonetheless, I left money with the physician to pay for more calls."

The earl asked, "Did he seem interested in his son, Jim Reevis?"

"Not a whit. Said it was good riddance when the boy left."

"Then Ruanna and I will raise the boy as our own."

"But what if he is a dedicated thief, m'lord?"

The earl laughed. "No one is a dedicated thief, George."

With the valet holding his coat, the earl slipped his

long arms into the sleeves. His mind turned from Jim to the beautiful redhead he would only minutes from now wed, the delicate beauty of her face, the beauty of her soul, her temper, her vulnerability, her haughtiness, and her independence.

She's the perfect match for me.

The earl felt his desire grow. He remembered how Ruanna had kissed him with such fervor that he had hardly been able to control himself.

Thinking back on it, the earl grimaced. She sure knows how to stir a man, he thought, frowning. And he was supposed to be pleased that she was experienced in that area.

Jealously, like a coiled snake, lay buried in His Lordship's chest, and he hated it. What did it matter . . . ?

The valet bowed. "I believe you are ready, m'lord."

"Thank you, Adam."

The earl's voice was husky with emotion. The moment was at hand! In the mirror, his reflection gazed back at him, and he was surprised at his nervousness. Like a lad of tender years and no experience, he suddenly feared that he would not measure up, would not be pleasing to his bride. Smiling at his inane thoughts, he turned away from the mirror.

Adam, as always, had seen that he was impeccably dressed; his Weston-tailored formal suit was of midnight blue velvet, his stiff, pristine white collar points were touching his black side-whiskers, and he was wearing made-to-fit boots by Hobby.

Assuring himself that his attire left nothing to be desired, the earl repaired below, to wait at the foot of the wide, curving, flower-bedecked staircase for his future wife. He lifted his eyes to the landing above. Notes from the harp soothed his nerves.

Pushing all other thoughts aside, the earl let his mind rest on the ethereal image of the beautiful redhead, when, dressed in a green dress, she had danced like a wood nymph and sung like a nightingale.

Would she never come?

Copying a picture she had seen in Ackerman's *Respository*, Lady Throckmorton pushed in place the last red curl that framed Ruanna's heart-shaped face. She piled the remainder of the fronds into a topknot on the back of Ruanna's head; the loose tendrils gently kissed her neck.

"You are beautiful," she said, stepping back to admire the wedding dress that fit Ruanna's little body perfectly. The skirt swirled around her feet like a cloud, the hem trailed behind her.

Unable to speak, Lady Throckmorton fled the room. She had to have a moment alone, a moment alone with *him*. She ran down the long hall to her own bedchamber, where she stood with her forehead resting against the mantel, staring into the empty fireplace and wiping tears from her sunken, wrinkled cheeks. For a long moment, she let herself remember another wedding day.

For that long moment Isadora Throckmorton felt sad. But only for that moment. Today, she had so much to be happy about. Lifting her indomitable chin, she smiled through her tears and called back the happier times; his face, his smile, the kiss when they had said good-bye.

As she stood there, ramrod straight, remembering, time passed without notice. Then, with only the loud silence in the room to hear her, she turned to the man whom only she could see and said, "She does not resemble you, Byron, not in looks, but she has your loving ways, your spirit, your fire, those things about you which I loved the most. Now, here, today, I have a small part of you with me. And she is marrying a diamond of the first water. I know you would be proud if you were here, other than in spirit."

The old woman stopped and listened before saying ever so softly, "I hear the harp playing. 'Tis time to go. Come, love, walk beside me."

Chapter Twenty-Four

Servants lined the hall in serried ranks. Ruanna smiled at them, and they bobbed, or bowed, depending on the gender, to her. With Lady Throckmorton walking beside her, the bride moved through the candlelit hall in luxurious folds of shimmering white satin.

On her head was a fluff of a hat, which, in a way, resembled a bonnet. The netting held diamonds that glittered like tiny twinkling stars. Around her creamy white neck lay the diamond-and-emerald necklace Lady Throckmorton had given her, a gift from her own true love of years ago. Matching earbobs hung from the lobes of Ruanna's ears.

This day, the long hall seemed forever long to Ruanna. She wanted to run to the earl and stay with him forever. She heard melodious harp notes quivering through the silence, so ineffably beautiful that her throat ached with an unexpected emotion.

The lovely music made Ruanna momentarily forget that within minutes she would be married to the man she loved. Her thoughts were on little Jeremy, of his great talent. She was glad she had not abandoned him when he could no longer pay, and she was appreciative of the earl's efforts to engage Bochsa as the boy's tutor.

And she thought of another of the earl's kindnesses, that of sending for her father. She turned to Lady

Throckmorton and asked, "Will you be angry with Papa if he returns to London?"

"Oh, no, my child. I know his coming would add greatly to your happiness, and that is all that matters to me. Let the past stay buried. I have you now, and that is enough."

Walking slowly, in tune with the music, Ruanna's thoughts moved on to little Jim, the pickpocket—how she loved him; and there was no doubt that he had peeled off the earl's hard exterior, exposing his *soft core* Lady Throckmorton had so often spoken about. The thought brought a smile.

The two ladies of quality were now near the landing, where Ruanna would descend to take her place by the earl's side. The music was louder. She stopped and listened, then whispered, "Mozart's Concerto in C Major."

She thought at first it was Bochsa at the strings, but then she knew it was Jeremy. She looked at Lady Throckmorton, smiled, then accused, "You knew."

A small, happy laugh came from the old woman. "Yes. Lord Julian's wedding present to you. He wanted it to be a surprise. And the great harpist is here."

Ruanna thought her heart would burst. "Then I will meet him." She looked down and saw the earl's upturned, side-whiskered face. He was smiling. His face was in shadow, but she could see his deeply bronzed skin and his snow white shirt glistening against it. He is so incredibly handsome, so awesomely tall, so manly in every way, she thought, as her heart hammered inside her heaving breast. She moved inexorably downward to him, her gown rustling in the sudden stillness.

Standing beside the earl was Jenny, the earl's niece, and little Jim, the pickpocket, each clutching bouquets of fresh garden flowers in their little fists. Jim wore his "penguin" clothes, and Jenny, already looking the lady of quality, wore a pink dress trimmed with delicately gathered lace.

Ruanna watched in disbelief when Jim pushed Jenny aside to establish his territorial rights next to the earl.

And then Ruanna looked away, at the great hall ablaze with lighted chandeliers, from which dripped dazzling pendants that emitted shards of light upon the upturned faces. Sparkling jewels warred with the chandeliers for brilliance. Ruanna drew a deep breath, then expelled it slowly. Spilling out from the ballroom into the great hall were the members of the ton, the comfortable bourgeois, and the aristocracy, all garbed in silks and brocades; and all their eyes were on her.

The prince regent was there, looking up at her and burning her a with studied gaze through his quizzing glass. Lord Stewart and his cousin Alice were in attendance, but Lady Elise and her companion were noticeably absent, for which Ruanna was glad.

Halfway down the stairs, as she moved regally toward her destiny, Ruanna felt her knees begin to shake. She hoped that no one would know. Carefully, she put one foot after the other onto the stairs she had once fallen down.

At the foot of the stairs, the earl waited for his bride. He thought his heart would surely burst inside of him, so filled with happiness was he. Sensing Ruanna's fright, he climbed the last few steps to take her hand and lead her to an altar of banked flowers, beside which tapers burned in gold branched candelabra, reaching far above the tall earl's head.

He held Ruanna's hand tightly, his own trembling and damp with a cold sweat. "Are you ready, darling?" he asked as he caressed her with his eyes.

"No," Ruanna answered, and when he turned and let her eyes circle the great hall, the earl's heart stilled. What was wrong? Was she disappointed that he was not her lover from India? Was she longing for that man who had delved to the depths of her passion, bringing a tender rosebud to blossom?

"Why not? Why are you not ready?" he managed to

ask, biting back his sudden anger.

"I forgot to take the flowers from Jim and Jenny. They will be so disappointed."

Quickly, she went and knelt down before the children and took the flowers they held out to her. After hugging and kissing them both, she went to stand before Lady Throckmorton, who wore a dress of the deepest blue, and she had plumes in her graying hair. When the old woman reached her long arms out to enfold Ruanna to her thrumming breast, Ruanna whispered, "Grandmother, I love you."

The old woman was crying, but her eyes shone with the happiness that Ruanna knew she felt. "Go, and be happy, my child," Lady Throckmorton said, and she smiled through her tears.

Ruanna returned to stand beside the earl, who had waited at the altar of flowers. She told him, "I am ready, m'lord."

Relief swept over the earl, and he broke into laughter as he bent to kiss the tip of Ruanna's elegant little nose. Turning to the archbishop, he quietly implored: "Pray make Lady Moreton my wife before my heart stops beating, never to start again."

The archbishop, obviously smothering his smile, began, "Dearly beloved," and silence so loud it was palpable fell over the huge crowd, broken only by music from the harp, the notes holding for long moments onto the highs, then dipping deeply into the lows, which then faded until there was no sound.

So, it was in this austere atmosphere that Lady Ruanna Moreton, her happiness knowing no bounds, became Countess Ruanna Aynsworth, the wife of Lord Julian Philip Aynsworth, the fifth earl of Wendsleydale and lord of Wilderhope in Shropshire.

There was only one untoward moment in the solemn ceremony, and gales of laughter shook the walls. When the archbishop asked Ruanna if she would love, honor, and obey this esteemed man, she replied in earnest, "Only if he will obey me."

Which His Lordship promised to do, and he sighed with great happiness, and with greater relief, when he was finally told that he could kiss his wife, which he did with great pleasure as ahs went up from the crowd.

The wedding feast was held in the huge dining room off the great hall, near the ballroom that ran the width of the house. Sideboards were laden with silver-domed dishes, haunches of beef, mutton, and pigeon pie.

Within the first hour, the bridegroom suggested to his countess more than once that they quit the blasted party and seek privacy.

His Lordship did not know that the last thing Ruanna wanted was privacy with her husband, where she would have to face the moment of truth.

"I must needs visit with Jeremy," she said. "And I would not think of leaving until I've spoken with Bochsa."

"I will take you to see him later, perhaps this coming week," the earl promised, to no avail.

"He's over there," Ruanna said, and off she went, holding to the earl's hand, pulling him along as she went to meet the great harpist.

Bochsa, in the earl's opinion, did not look like a great musician at all. He was pudgy fat, mustachioed, and balding.

Ruanna curtsied to the harpist as if he were royalty, and then stood for an interminably long time—much to the earl's consternation—discussing Sebastian Erard's harp, on which he had obtained the first English patent ever in 1792.

In a decided French accent, Bochsa said, "In 1810, he patented his double-action mechanism, a body built in two main sections, strengthened by inner ribs. . . ."

This is outside of enough, the earl thought, moving one restive foot and then the other. Beyond the windows, dusk was settling in, and the dancing had yet to begin.

It was much, much later that Katie helped Ruanna

remove her wedding gown and slip a pale green nightdress over her head. The nightdress had been especially created for Ruanna's wedding night by Madame Dupont who, Ruanna decided, had no sense of decency about her, for Ruanna's bosom practically spilled out of the tight bodice, making her feel naked. The skirt, however, was full and flowing, falling down to cover her feet.

"Well, I am glad something is covered," she said as her eyes quickly perused the room. She had never been in the earl's chambers before and found then extremely elegantly appointed—and frightening.

Mammoth was the only word to describe the poster bed, which had, above the curved headboard, navy blue hangings intricately stitched with the Aynsworth crest: two lions rampant facing a spread eagle. As Ruanna turned away, she wondered how many earls had slept in the bed, and with whom. Her eyes then engaged the rest of the room.

Deep, comfortable chairs and a Chippendale camel-back sofa of blue velvet graced the ornate fireplace.

A Shirley drop-leaf breakfast table and two chairs sat near a wide expanse of windows.

No doubt, she thought, where meals were brought to the earl when he chose to have them served in his bedchamber.

The blue velvet drapes, their fringed hems puddling on the floor, were open, exposing a moon not yet full, but which sent shadowy, silver light through the many tall windows.

The room belonged to a stranger, and Ruanna suddenly felt a stranger within. Everything, the tall bookcases, the huge dresser, the bed, was of a masculine vein, the ambience softened only by huge vases of red roses on tables of all shapes and sizes. They had been brought, she was sure, from the garden, to make the place appear to be a wedding chamber.

Ruanna shuddered; her bare feet sank into the colorful

rug as she paced the floor, from one end of the room to the other.

"You seem to be meetin' your executioner 'stead of the handsome earl," Katie said, moving to turn the bed down.

"No, don't. I do not want the bed prepared. And do not close the drapes. It would make the room too intimate. I shall do that later, Katie. Let me tell you what I want you to do. Go below, to the wine cellar, and bring three bottles of the best champagne."

"Champagne? Didn't you have enough to drink at the ball after the wedding? I thought you and the earl was goin' to dance the night away, staying down there after everyone else had long left."

Ruanna smiled. That was true. Every time the earl had mentioned that he was sure there was something more exciting awaiting them, Ruanna had begged for one more dance, fortifying him with another glass of champagne that she ordered poor Sutherland to bring.

Finally, the band packed up their instruments and left them dancing to their own music, which she made by singing as she had the night in the park. The earl dismissed Sutherland, then whispered, "That night in the park when you were wearing the green dress and singing like an angel, which I knew you were not—that is when I knew I was hopelessly in love with you."

Knowing he was only encouraging her to leave the ballroom with him, Ruanna allowed her eyes to widen when she said, "It took you a long time to admit it."

"Though I did not admit it, not even to myself, I knew the truth."

Still, they went on dancing around the empty ballroom. The earl asked her to kiss him as she had that night in the park, and she obliged, but she did kiss him as she kissed in the park. This time she kept her lips pressed tightly together, causing His Lordship to lift a brow quizzically and demand that the dancing and singing stop, and that they repair to his chambers.

So, here I am, Ruanna thought tremulously.

"Are you sure you want more champagne. I don't think . . ." The maid looked at Ruanna.

"I don't care what you think, Katie. Do as I say, and hurry."

Ruanna cast a wary glance at the door that led into the earl's dressing room. Any minute he would come to claim his marital rights, and it was then that he would discover what a liar she was.

Katie brought the champagne, and only minutes later, the earl did just what Ruanna feared he would do; he came to claim his marital rights. Ruanna looked at the twinkle in his blue eyes and knew this to be so.

Wearing a blue dressing gown that touched the floor and was held together with a gold rope with tassels, the earl kissed Ruanna and laid his hand on her partly exposed bosom. He expected a warm melting of her body against his. As passion surged through him, he swallowed and breathed deeply. He had never seen anything or anyone more beautiful than his wife, her red hair, in considerable disarray, falling down almost to her satin-smooth shoulders, her eyes shining like exquisite emeralds, her lips full and . . .

Ruanna pulled away and handed her husband another glass of champagne, saying cryptically, "We haven't drunk all our champagne."

The earl, after placing the glass of champagne down on the table, turned Ruanna to face him, in a very slow, deliberate way. "I had not planned on drinking three bottles of champagne on my wedding night."

He again pressed her body against his and, this time, felt her terror. Immediately he released her and asked angrily, "What is wrong? Are you disappointed that I am not your lover from India? Are you afraid I will disappoint you? Well, I can assure you I will—"

"Oh, it is not that, m'lord. It is just that we have the rest of our lives to do . . . oh . . . that . . . but we will only have one wedding night."

"That is true, love, and I intend to make it one to remember. For whatever reason you are trying to get me foxed, it will not work. Now kiss me as you have kissed me before, not like some prim virgin who has never known a man."

Oh, oh, it is going to be worse than I thought.

Ruanna struggled when the earl, his blue eyes ablaze, his breathing heavy, started kissing her, melting her, transporting her beyond reality.

Although trying with all her might, she could not stop the feeling that engulfed her, even her thinking.

The earl picked her up and carried her to the bed and gingerly laid her down. He then commenced trying to pull the hampering skirt up from around Ruanna's flailing legs. "Don't be nervous, darling," he said, in a voice barely above a whisper. He leaned over her.

She pushed him away. "I don't want to."

"The devil take me, Countess Aynsworth," he said, then asked again, "What is wrong? First you try to get me foxed, and now this."

Reluctant tears streamed down Ruanna cheeks, and the earl was so touched by whatever was bothering his bride that his anger suddenly left. He put his long arms around her and pulled her to him, holding her fiercely. Placing her face in the crook of his neck, he stroked her back and ran his fingers through her tangled red curls, while, mystified, he listened to her muffled sobs.

Finally, with a crooked finger under her chin, he tilted her face up so he could probe deeply into her countenance. The bedside candle flickered, making patterns of light and shade on her beautiful face. He caught his breath, then asked, "What is it, darling? Why are you so afraid? I love you. I would never harm you."

Ruanna threw both arms around the earl's neck and buried her face against his chest. "I am so ashamed. I lied to you. I don't have a lover in India, nor have I ever. I told you that because I was angry when you called me Charlie. I was so jealous, and so prideful that I lied to you. And I lied to you about not knowing how to go on in proper society so you would spend more time training me, and . . . and I know nothing of how to please a man."

The earl threw his head back and laughed. Never had he heard such wonderful news. "And you thought if you got me foxed enough that I wouldn't know of your purity?" He gave her a crooked smile and teased, "I should beat you."

Deliberately he let a long moment pass; then he sighed dramatically, and went on: "Instead of beating you, I shall teach you how to please a man." His hand cupped a breast.

"No."

The earl waited.

"You have a mistress, and you still send checks to the countess," Ruanna reminded him. These things needed to be cleared up. She had confessed her lies to him. Now he could confess to her.

A low, sensual chuckle rumbled from the earl's chest. "But that is the way with the upper orders. . . ."

His Lordship failed to contain his laughter, but when Ruanna pulled her knees up to her chin and wrapped the skirt of her nightdress around her legs, he quickly explained—because he knew in the end he would do just that. "A check is sent to Countess Charlotte because, as my brother's dowager countess, she is entitled to support from the estates. And, I promise you, darling, I shall never leave your bed for a *strumpet's*."

"Why would you not? And cross your heart." Ruanna dropped her long, dark lashes. The tips of her fingers slipped under his robe and moved across his chest to tangle in the mass of stiff hair. She felt his big body tremble.

"Because," the earl said, "I have no doubt that should I do such a dastardly thing as to visit a strumpet, you would kill me with your homemade club. Besides, I gave Lord Stewart my paramour's card."

"You haven't crossed your heart."

302

Feeling delightfully as if he were sixteen years old, the earl crossed his heart.

"You may kiss me now."

"There is more to it than just kissing. . . ."

The earl's words died in his throat as Ruanna parted her lips to take the kiss, and he stopped kissing her only long enough to slip the nightdress over her head, and to drop his own robe to the floor.

When they were naked, wrapped in each other's arms, the earl whispered, "My darling love," and then silence swallowed them up. With each kiss, he poured himself into her, finding her willing to receive his love, and glorious moments passed, and the love that had been growing from the hour they met reached a beautiful plateau.

Yet, the earl waited for her, as if waiting for a flower to open and know its full beauty. "Just love me, darling," he said in a choked voice. And Ruanna did, until at last he entered her, and shadows played on their naked bodies as they moved in perfect rhythm.

Hardly aware when she lost her innocence, Ruanna gave herself to her husband, completely, her mind, her soul, all of her; as together they climbed up . . . up . . . up, to a great plane of ecstasy, lingering there in perfect unison, each loving the other, and then, they became one. Ruanna whispered in a strangled voice, "I love you, my husband, with all my heart."

"And I love you, my darling wife," the earl answered in kind.

Satiated, he lay beside her and rested his dark head on her bosom, feeling the quick beats of her heart, which matched her breathing that had not yet stilled. Never had he been so happy, or so fulfilled. But within minutes, beyond his belief, desire again surged through the earl's veins.

Like a flooding river that could not stop its rampaging flow, he wanted to make love to his wife again.

Ruanna tangled her fingers in the earl's mass of black

hair, and she knew, absolutely knew, that no woman had ever known the happiness she, at that moment, knew in her husband's arms.

Our love will last forever, she silently vowed as her husband's body again moved above hers.

Meanwhile, on the third floor of Grosvenor House, Jim the seven-year-old pickpocket, went about setting his future straight.

"Hurry up," he said to Jenny, "do you want for us to be caught?"

"What do you mean *us* get caught? You were the one who stole all these things. Where does this candlestick go?"

Holding the nearly empty pillowcase, Jenny had been following behind Jim as he raced from room to room, putting everything back in its rightful place.

"It goes in here," he said as he darted into a dark bedchamber, lighted only by a sliver of moonlight through the uncovered windows. He looked back at Jenny. "Is 'at all?"

Jenny fixed her blue eyes on Jim reproachfully. "That is the last. Now, Jim Reevis, I want to know if you are going to stop your stealing. Or will you revert back to your old ways and become a pickpocket again?"

Jim reared his shoulders back and hooked his thumbs in the waistband of his breeches. "Aye, Jenny," he said, "you are looking at a reformed man. I shan't ever be a disappointment to the countess, or to the earl . . . or to you, you being a lady of quality and all."